continued . . .

D0645400

Tall, Dark, and Kilted

Allie Mackay

A SIGNET ECLIPSE BOOK

SIGNET ECLIPSE
Published by New American Library, a division of
Penguin Group (USA) Inc., 375 Hudson Street,
New York, New York 10014, USA
Penguin Group (Canada), 90 Eglinton Avenue East, Suite 700, Toronto,
Ontario M4P 2Y3, Canada (a division of Pearson Penguin Canada Inc.)
Penguin Books Ltd., 80 Strand, London WC2R 0RL, England
Penguin Ireland, 25 St. Stephen's Green, Dublin 2,
Ireland (a division of Penguin Books Ltd.)
Penguin Group (Australia), 250 Camberwell Road, Camberwell, Victoria 3124,
Australia (a division of Pearson Australia Group Pty. Ltd.)
Penguin Books India Pvt. Ltd., 11 Community Centre, Panchsheel Park,
New Delhi - 110 017, India
Penguin Group (NZ), 67 Apollo Drive, Rosedale, North Shore 0632,
New Zealand (a division of Pearson New Zealand Ltd.)
Penguin Books (South Africa) (Pty.) Ltd., 24 Sturdee Avenue,
Rosebank, Johannesburg 2196, South Africa

Penguin Books Ltd., Registered Offices:
80 Strand, London WC2R 0RL, England

First published by Signet Eclipse, an imprint of New American Library,
a division of Penguin Group (USA) Inc.

First Printing, November 2008
10   9   8   7   6   5   4   3   2   1

This one is for Mary Hanson.
A very special friend and lady,
she shares my great love of dogs,
does the most beautiful Christmas decorating
of anyone I know,
and has been a favorite reader
since the days of Devil in a Kilt.
She's also the loving mommy of sweet little Leo,
the role model of Leo the dachshund in this book.
You're the best, Mary!
I'm so glad we're friends.

ACKNOWLEDGMENTS

Scotland always inspires my books, and one of my greatest joys in writing is the magic of returning in my mind to the special places in Scotland that I love so much. This book is set in my own absolute favorite corner of Scotland, the wild and remote far north. Although Dunroamin is fictitious, a compilation of several privately owned Scottish castles and manor homes I've visited, its role models exist and are every bit as delightfully atmospheric. They are places where the sense of the past is vivid and much appreciated by those who dwell there.

The location I chose for Dunroamin is quite real and probably the most magical corner of Scotland that I know. Tongue in Sutherland and the tiny crofting village of Melness are places I enjoy returning to again and again, each visit enchanting me more than the last. The Kyle of Tongue is every bit as beautiful as described, and the ruins of Castle Varrich stand exactly as depicted.

Like Cilla, I've made the trek up to Castle Varrich and also scrambled into the ruin's crumbling window alcove, often spending hours perched there, watching the world go by and trying to tune in to the little shimmers of the past that I am convinced exist in such places.

Hardwick's Seagrave is also real, although I did

change the name. Readers familiar with Scotland's northeast coast south of Aberdeen may recognize Seagrave as Slains Castle, an incredibly atmospheric ruin that is indeed quite spooky and forbidding. Isolated and left alone for centuries, home to only seabirds, wind, and ghosts, I'm sure, a visit there takes you into Scotland's past in ways that a touristy cultivated historic site just can't do. Word is that Slains is to be developed into holiday flats, a fate that makes me feel blessed to have been able to see and enjoy the ruin in its original state.

Shetland is another place I love visiting, and I try to get there each time I am in Scotland. Gregor was inspired by my own experiences with great skuas in Shetland, in particular on the bird sanctuary isle of Noss. Also known as bonxies, these ferocious birds do indeed dive-bomb anything that moves across the moorland they view as their own. I've had some frightening encounters with these pterodactyl-like creatures, and despite the frights, I absolutely adore them.

Special thanks to three incredible women for their help with this book. My agent, Roberta Brown, best friend, trusted confidante, and so much more, I couldn't get by without her. She's also the only person who knows why Gudrid is so very special. Mega thanks to my amazing editor, Anne Bohner. She's supertalented and I so appreciate her help in making my stories as strong as possible. A grateful nod, as well, to Liza Schwartz. She knows why. Thank you, ladies. I couldn't do this without you.

As always, much appreciation to my handsome husband, Manfred, for his unflagging support and enthusiasm. They mean so much. Last but not least, my beloved little Jack Russell, Em. Owner of my heart and ruler of my world, he's the only soul allowed to disturb me on deadline.

"There are men and there are Highlanders. Woe be to anyone fool enough not to know the difference."

—Bran of Barra, Hebridean chieftain, appreciator of women, and Highland to the bone

Prologue

In the Twilight World of the Great Beyond

"So, you are tired of women?"

The disembodied voice boomed like a thousand angry thunderclouds. Loud and crackling, each word sent bolts of lightning sizzling through the shifting mist. Gray, swirling drifts, the fog shielded the Dark One's inner sanctum from the rest of this curious and mysterious place.

"I am weary of having to pleasure them." Sir Hardwin de Studley of Seagrave, more commonly known as Hardwick, put back his shoulders against the Dark One's wrath. "Enough is enough. Seven hundred years of nightly *bliss* would dampen any man's appetite."

Another earsplitting clap of thunder shook the cushiony mist beneath Hardwick's feet and a scorching bolt of lightning whizzed past his ear, its otherworldly heat almost singeing his hair.

"There are some who would call your curse a blessing." The Dark One's deep voice rumbled with displeasure. "Souls who would burn an eternity for a single eye blink of the revels you enjoy each night."

"Bah!" Hardwick tightened his grip on the round, studded shield he always clutched before his groin. "I would roast for two eternities for the peace of one night's unbroken sleep." Keeping his stare on the im-

mense stone temple he could just make out through
the thick, swirling fog, he willed the Dark One to
show himself.

Willed, as well, his *problem* to stop twitching in
heated anticipation of the coming night's tumble with
some as-yet-undetermined bit of eager female fluff.

He would easily stride past an endless line of naked,
writhing beauties if only doing so would grant him
eternal rest and peace.

"You have only yourself to blame, Seagrave." Puffs
of sulfurous smoke drifted out from behind the ancient,
sentrylike trees guarding the Dark One's temple. "Had
you not turned the wandering bard from your door, he
would not have cast his wizard spell on you."

Hardwick bit back a snort. "There were highborn
guests at my table that night. It was known that an
assassin guising himself as a traveling lute player had
been trailing them. I did what any self-respecting lord
of the Scottish realm would have done. I turned away
a stranger in an attempt to safeguard those within
my walls."

A gust of icy wind revealed the Dark One's opinion
of his choice.

Hardwick stood tall, refusing to acknowledge the
frigid blast. "Would *you* have handled it otherwise?"

"What I would have done scarce matters. I am not
the one who was damned to spend eternity pleasing
women without ever again enjoying my own release."
A sound almost like derisive laughter came from
within the mist-shrouded temple. " 'Tis you who were
doomed to roam the earth, satisfying a different woman
every night."

"You needn't remind me." Hardwick glared into
the mist. "I am well aware of the peculiarities of my
circumstance."

If he weren't, the permanent *annoyance* at his groin
was more than telling. Glancing down at the rigid pro-
tuberance, his mood worsened.

The Dark One gave a superior sigh. "Perhaps if you hadn't been one of Scotland's most notorious wenchers, the bard would have visited you with a less strenuous curse."

Hardwick considered throwing down his infernal shield and whipping out his sword. "Be that as it may, I would hear if you are willing to help me? I already know you have the power to do so."

"I have the means to undo the mortal magic of any medieval bard, including the wizardry of the one who cursed you. The power as to whether the counterspell works, lies with you."

"Then tell me what I must do."

"It is more what you must not do. Dare not do . . . if you wish the resolution to help you."

Hardwick took a step closer to the temple, his own temples beginning to throb with frustration when the swirling mists thickened, giving the impression that the blasted place was receding from him.

Halting, he tamped down his temper and held up a hand. The one he didn't need to hold his shield in place. "I will do—or not do—whatever is necessary to rid myself of this foul condition."

"So be it." The mists thinned, once again allowing glimpses of the Dark One's hallowed temple. "You shall be relieved of your curse and also granted the everlasting sleep you crave—if you can keep yourself from becoming aroused for a year and a day."

Hardwick almost laughed. "Think you that will be a problem? After centuries of such an affliction as I've endured? By the gray mists shielding you from me, I swear there isn't a female walking who could tempt me."

"Do not claim victory too soon, Seagrave." Another rush of icy air whipped through the inner sanctum, this time accompanied by a black, shrieking wind. Even more distressing, the tangle of exposed roots spreading out from the circle of guardian trees sud-

denly morphed into hissing dragons. As one, they
lifted scaly black heads, looking round with fiery, unblinking eyes. "Be warned. The price of your redemption is high and fraught with grave danger."

Hardwick pitched his voice as resolute as the Dark
One's. "Rid me of my *problem* and I will face any
danger."

Drawing his sword, he thrust its tip into the bil-
lowing mist rippling around his ankles. "With the
greatest respect," he said, watching the root-dragons
stare at him with eyes like glimmering coals, "I'll not
be deterred by sorcerous means or others."

On his words, the scaly beasts vanished, their great,
crouching bodies nothing more than a snarl of silent,
black-gleaming roots.

The chill air remained, but a soft rustling came from
within the temple and Hardwick could almost imagine
the Dark One nodding consent.

"As you will." His deep voice shook the trees and
sent shock waves through the fog. "But know this, you
who seek my benevolence. If you fail, the old condition will return at once, along with your curse to sat-
isfy a different woman every night. This time you will
no longer be able to roam the world and centuries at
will, choosing your bedmates as it pleases you."

The Dark One paused and the icy air grew even
colder. "One slip and you will find yourself in the
blackest, most vile level of the world-between-the-
worlds, where you'd be forever doomed to pleasure
the pathetic creatures who dwell there. Females far
different from the endless lovelies you've pleased
down through the ages."

Hardwick narrowed his eyes on the temple, then
carefully sheathed his sword. "I would ask one boon."

"Indeed?" The Dark One humphed. "Name it
quickly—before I tire of speaking with you."

"I would have the right to choose where I spend the

required proving period." Hardwick stood straighter, his jaw tight with determination. "That is all."

A place where I can live quietly and away from all temptation.

He left the words unspoken, his entire body taut with the waiting. "Well? Am I to have my boon?"

"It shall be granted." The Dark One appeared on the temple's threshold, an imposing manlike form, only discernible as a blackness deeper than the surrounding darkness. "Choose wisely—you will not be allowed a second chance."

Hardwick opened his mouth to reply, but a flash of eye-blinding lightning snatched the words. A simultaneous *boom* of thunder ripped away the trees and the temple, leaving him alone in another, less threatening corner of this mystical realm he'd drifted in and out of for so long.

Great swaths of shimmering gray-white mist slid past him now, and he knew from experience he need only find the appropriate opening, then will himself below.

Far below, to wherever on the earth plane he wished.

But first he looked beneath his shield, his heart slamming against his ribs when he saw only his plaid and wide-leathered sword belt riding low on his hips.

His *problem* was gone.

Or, better said, relaxed.

Throwing back his head, he whooped. Then he grinned broadly and lowered his shield, removing it from in front of his groin for the first time in seven hundred years.

"By all the saints!" He dashed a hand across his cheek and heaved a great sigh.

His curse was finally over.

Now he need only seek his place of refuge.

Blessedly, he knew exactly where he needed to go.

Chapter 1

Dunroamin Castle
A Registered Residential Care Home
Scotland's Far North, the Present

Someone was watching her.

Cilla Swanner dropped the pullover she'd been about to lift out of her suitcase and stood very still. Something had set the fine hairs on the back of her neck to standing and it wasn't the overall gloom seeming to fill the shadowy, dark-paneled bedchamber. Nor was it the deep silence pressing in on her from all sides, even though it wasn't much later than three in the afternoon.

She turned to a particularly suspect corner, eyes narrowing. She would've sworn she'd caught movement there. Something—her imagination insisted—that would prove to be all claws and fetid breath.

Long, flashing teeth and fiery red eyes.

Fortunately, the scariest thing she detected was a faint waft of mildew.

She almost laughed. She was bigger than the smell of damp and old furniture. And as a modern, sensible soul, she'd simply ignore how much the lavishly furnished, gothic-style room reminded her of every Dracula movie she'd ever seen.

That would be her first line of defense against weirdness.

A tactic she'd likely need, since the room would be hers for the summer.

Even so, she allowed herself a quick glance over her shoulder, half expecting the latched window shutters to slowly swing open, giving her a glimpse of the thick fog currently rolling across Dunroamin's lonely shore. Pea soup, she'd call such roiling, impenetrable fog, though the local term was *sea haar*. Either way, she just knew that if she did dare a look, more than swirling gray mist would greet her.

In her present jet-lagged state of mind, she'd likely see a seagull glide past and mistake it for a bat.

Reaching again for her pullover, she thought better of it and rolled her shoulders instead. She was not exactly a Lilliputian, and so cramming herself into an economy window seat from Newark to Glasgow had left her feeling stiff, achy, and more than a little cranky.

The endless drive north hadn't done much to defrazzle her, however breathtaking the scenery. Thank goodness she'd had competent escorts and hadn't had to brave the left-sided driving and spindle-thin roads herself. Equally good, she knew exactly how to banish her body aches and tiredness.

A long, hot shower was what she needed.

And no matter how Transylvania-like the high-ceilinged, wooden-floored room struck her, its spacious and airy bathroom looked totally twenty-first century.

Already feeling the restorative pounding of a good, steaming shower, she stripped with lightspeed. But just as she reached to unhook her bra, she noticed the framed poster of her Aunt Birdie and Uncle Mac on Dunroamin's steps.

She had a copy of it in her apartment back in Yardley, Pennsylvania. Hers was mounted in a tartan frame and had pride of place above her living room sofa. This one hung near the shuttered windows, its Old World–looking frame as dark as the room's paneling.

But at least its familiarity took away some of the room's eeriness. Thankful for that, she tossed aside her bra and went to look at the poster.

It was a Christmas card photo she'd had blown up just last year, thinking that her aunt and uncle would appreciate the way a slanting ray of winter sun high-lighted the stone armorial panel with the MacGhee coat of arms above their heads. Theirs, and the dark head of a tall, broad-shouldered man standing a few feet behind them, close to the castle's open door.

"Huh?" She blinked, certain she was now not just jet-lagged, but seeing things.

The man—who looked quite roguishly medieval—hadn't been in the poster before.

Nor was he there now, on second look.

He'd only been a shadow. A trick of light cast across the glass.

She shivered all the same. Rubbing her arms, she stepped closer to the poster. He'd looked so real. And if she was beginning to see imaginary men, handsome, kilted, or otherwise, she was in worse shape than any jet lag she'd ever before experienced.

Certain that had to be it—the mind-fuzzing effects of crossing time zones and lack of sleep—she touched a finger to the poster glass, relieved to find it smooth and cool to the touch, absolutely normal-feeling, just as it should be.

But whether the man was gone or not, something was wrong. In just the few seconds she'd needed to cross the room, the air had grown all thick and heavy. Icy, too. As if someone had set an air conditioner to subzero, deliberately flash-freezing the bedchamber.

She frowned. Unless she was mistaken, Dunroamin didn't have air conditioners.

It did, however, have strange shadows in posters.

No, not shadows.

The man was back, and this time he'd moved. Just as dark and medieval-looking as before, he now stood next to Aunt Birdie and Uncle Mac instead of behind them.

"Oh, God!" She jumped back from the poster and raised her arms across her naked breasts.

He cocked a brow at her—right through the poster glass!

Her heart began to gallop. She couldn't move. Her legs felt like rubber, and even screaming was pointless. Her throat had closed on her and her tongue felt stuck to the top of her mouth.

Disbelief and shock sweeping her, she looked on as the man, illusion, or whatever, sauntered away from her aunt and uncle to lean a shoulder against the door arch. Devilishly sexy—she couldn't help but notice—he just stood there, arms and ankles crossed as he stared back at her.

Once, he flicked a glance at something that looked like a round medieval shield propped against the wall near his feet. She thought he might reach for it, but he only looked up to glare at her.

"You aren't there." She found her voice, a pathetic croak. "I am not seeing you—"

She blinked.

Mr. Wasn't-Really-There was gone again.

Only the shadow on the glass remained.

"Oh, man." Her shower forgotten, she snatched up her bra and the rest of her airplane clothes, tossing them back on even faster than she'd taken them off. She should never have accepted Uncle Mac's welcome dram.

Not after being up nearly thirty hours.

"Miss Swanner?" A woman's voice called through the closed door, accompanied by a quick rap. "Are you awake?"

She almost flew across the room, half-tempted to answer that, yes, she was awake, but she was also having *waking hallucinations*.

Instead, she ran a hand through her hair and opened the door. "Yes?"

"I'm Honoria, Dunroamin's housekeeper. I've come to take you down to tea if you're feeling up to it?" An older woman in a heavy tweed suit and sturdy shoes peered at her, the oversized print of an unusually large badge pinned to her jacket, repeating her name.

Following her glance, the woman put back strong-looking shoulders and cleared her throat. "Some of our residents have difficulty remembering names. Others"—she looked both ways down the dimly lit corridor, tactfully lowering her voice—"don't see well."

Cilla almost choked. There wasn't anything wrong with her memory, but since a few moments ago, she had some serious doubts about her vision.

About everything.

The world she'd known and understood tipped drastically when she'd peered at that poster.

Hoping the housekeeper wouldn't notice, she stepped into the hallway, closing the door behind her. "I'd love tea," she said, meaning it. "And I'm looking forward to meeting the residents. Aunt Birdie and Uncle Mac always talked so much about them, I feel as if I know them alrea—"

"Ach, you won't be seeing any of them just yet." The housekeeper glanced at her as they moved down the plaid-carpeted corridor. "They'll be having their tea in the library. Your aunt and uncle are waiting for you in the armory."

She blinked, wondering if her hearing was going wacky as well. *"The armory?"*

Honoria paused at the top of a great oak staircase. "It's not what it sounds like, though there are still enough weapons on the walls. Your uncle uses the

room as his private study. His den, I believe you
Americans call it?"

"Oh." She felt foolish for thinking she was going
somewhere that would give her the willies.

A den she could handle, even if it did have a few
swords and shields decorating the walls.

But when Honoria opened the door, ushering her
inside, she found the armory unlike any American-
style den she'd ever seen. Full of quiet and shadows,
medieval weapons gleamed on every inch of wall
space, and two full-sized suits of standing armor
flanked a row of tall windows across from the door.

Cilla froze just inside the threshold, the willies making her stomach clench.

Her aunt and uncle were nowhere to be seen.

Her heart thumping again, she turned to the door.
"Are you sure this is where Aunt Birdie and—" She
closed her mouth, catching a glimpse of the housekeeper already rounding a curve at the far end of
the corridor.

"Ach! There you are." Her uncle's deep voice
sounded from the room's shadows. "Come away in,
lass, and have your tea with us."

Spinning around, she saw her aunt and uncle at last.
They sat in the soft lamplight of a corner table set for
tea. Aunt Birdie, with her sleek, tawny-colored hair
and large, deep blue eyes, looking so much like an
older version of Cilla's mother and herself, she started.

Uncle Mac, kilted as always, wore the bold, masculine room like a second skin.

With his larger-than-life good looks and full, curling
red beard, not to mention his horn-handled *sgian-
dubh*, the ever-present dagger peeking up from his
sock, he looked every bit the fierce Highland chieftain.

So much so, Cilla forgot herself and blurted what
she really wanted to know. "Uncle Mac—does your
castle have ghosts?"

"Ho! Not here an hour and already you're asking

what every American visitor wants to know." Slapping his hands on his thighs, he pushed to his feet, his face splitting in a broad, twinkly-eyed grin. "The only ghosts hereabouts are my ancient creaky knees. If you count both together, they're well o'er a hundred! So dinna you go all polite on me and say you haven't heard 'em cracking."

Cilla smiled. "If your knees are creaky, I would've noticed when you picked me up in Lairg and helped Malcolm load my luggage from his car to yours." She crossed the room and hugged him. "I must say, I didn't hear a thing."

"Didn't you, now?" He lifted a bushy brow. "There's some who might say that's only because young Malcolm was blethering away like a headless chicken. As he surely told you, he works at Ravenscraig Castle down Oban way."

He paused to scratch his beard. "Now *that's* a place with a ghostie or two. Not my Dunroamin. I took my first breath in these walls. If there were any bogles flitting about, sure enough and I'd know it."

Aunt Birdie sniffed. "What about the gray lady on the main stairs?" She came forward to join them, her purple-and-blue watered silk dress swirling around her like an exotic, perfume-scented cloud. "Or the little boy who sits on a stool in a corner of the kitchen?"

Her husband hooted. "The day a misty lady floats down my stairs, I'll shave off my beard." He whipped out his *sgian-dubh*, looking down as he tested its edge. A satisfied smile lit his face when a bead of red appeared on his thumb. "Och, aye, I'm all for taking off my beard when the like happens. And"—he leaned close, his tone conspiratorial—"the offer stands for any other *spook*, gray, green, or even pink, who might care to put in an appearance."

"Have a care, dear. There's always a kernel of truth to any legend." Aunt Birdie tapped his chest with a red-tipped fingernail. "Bucks County back home is

steeped in both tradition and ghosts. Here . . ." She
let her voice trail off. "Let's just say that you, as a
Highlander, should know better than to scoff at such
things."

He huffed and waved a hand.

"Tell me"—he winked at Cilla—"do you believe in
such foolery? Ghosts, tall tales, and plaid-draped,
sword-packing beasties that go bump in the night?"

"I—"

Cilla bit her lip.

From what she'd seen of Scotland so far, she
doubted Uncle Mac would like her answer.

Dunroamin made it even easier to believe in such
things.

The very blend of peat smoke, old leather, and furniture oil pervading each antique-crammed room
hinted at the possibility of another time.

Likewise the grand gilt-framed ancestral portraits
lining all the dark and must-tinged corridors.

A chill slid down Cilla's spine.

She wasn't at all keen on walking past some of those
portraits late at night when the house was quiet. More
than one of the fierce-eyed, bekilted Highlanders depicted so boldly looked more than able to belt out an
ancient war cry and leap down from his golden-
scrolled frame, sword swinging and murder on his
mind.

"If not ghosties"—Uncle Mac's voice cut the
stillness—"what say you to Selkie folk or dear old
Nessie?" He hitched up his kilt belt, his curly beard
jigging with the movement. "Nessie's big business for
some of those high-dollar tour operators down in
Inverness!"

Cilla hesitated, hardly hearing his teasing.

Her gaze kept going to one of the standing suits of
armor across the room. Try as she might, she couldn't
shake the impression that someone stared at her from
behind the narrow eye slit of the knight's silvery helm.

And the stare wasn't friendly.

She shivered, once again feeling all goosebumpy.

"Well?" Uncle Mac slung an arm around her shoulders. "Restore my faith in Americans. Tell me you know that footsteps on the stairs at night are nothing more than popping water pipes."

"Of course I know that." She spoke quickly, before she could change her mind. "I've never believed in ghosts."

She didn't add that she might soon be persuaded to think otherwise.

If she saw *him* again.

Mr. Wasn't-Really-There peeking out at her from behind poster glass.

"No, I do not believe in them," she repeated, speaking firmly and confidently.

Just in case *he* was listening.

"Good, good." Her uncle flashed a triumphant smile. "Maybe you can talk some sense into your aunt over tea. I haven't had any luck in all these years. Woman has a mind of her own."

"You won't be joining us?" Cilla looked at him, disappointed.

Uncle Mac shook his head. "Ach, lass, would that I could, but duty calls . . ."

Glancing at his watch, anticipation lit his face. Raising his arms high above his head, he twirled in a fast tricky-footed spin in the same instant a blast of lively pipe music skirled through the armory.

"Gah!" Cilla nearly jumped out of her skin.

"The Royal Scots Dragoon Guards!" Uncle Mac ended his jig with a quick little hop and flourish. " 'Paddy's Leather Breeches,' that is," he boomed, looking pleased. "One o' my favorite pipe tunes."

"It's also his cue that it's time for him to attend our residents in the library." Aunt Birdie looked up from pouring tea. "He sometimes takes naps in here," she explained, indicating a comfortable-looking tartan sofa half-hidden in the shadows near the hearth. "The pipe tune ensures he doesn't sleep through teatime. It's an afternoon ritual."

"I ne'er sleep, you!" He wriggled his brows at her. "I doze."

Cilla hid a smile. "So, what's the ritual? The pipes or tea?"

"Both!" Uncle Mac's chest swelled. "If you didn't know, in addition to pipes, there are three things Highlanders love: their home glen, a good fight, and a stirring fireside tale. Since most of our residents are far from their glens and all of them are too old to fight, they enjoy a well-told tale."

He paused, his eyes sparkling with good humor. "I try to give them one at teatime."

Laughing, he made another spirited spin—this time without the blare of "Paddy's Leather Breeches"— and then disappeared into the corridor, leaving Cilla alone with her aunt.

Her beloved Aunt Birdie, and a fusty, weapon-hung room that went even more dark and eerie without Uncle Mac and his jolly bluster.

Cilla rubbed her arms, feeling cold again.

"Come, dear. We should have warned you about your uncle's pipe alarm, but we can have a few quiet words now." Aunt Birdie waved a hand at the table. Covered with starchy-looking white linen, it glimmered with crystal and silver and held more delicacies than most people could eat in a week.

"You must be starving." Her aunt pulled out a chair for her, then took the one opposite for herself. "Dunroamin's scones will melt in your mouth. Or if you wish something more substantial, I can offer you oatcakes with hot smoked salmon and cheese."

"I'm not really that hungry." Cilla joined her, but her attention strayed to the row of windows and the thick sea haar pressing against the leaded, diamond-shaped panes.

She could almost imagine a hooded form peering in at her through the mullioned glass, but she cast aside the notion at once.

Whoever—or whatever—seemed to be watching her felt rampantly male and daring.

If it was a ghost, it wasn't the kind to drift about in the mist, shrouded and faceless.

Her ghost would snatch a sword off the armory wall, grab one of the shields hanging everywhere, and then charge out of the castle, looking for action.

He'd also have the same sexy, dark looks of the man in the poster. Just minus his rude glare.

"At least eat something." Aunt Birdie was looking at her strangely. "Cook will be offended if she happens past here and pops in to see you staring at the targes rather than enjoying her famous scones."

"Targes?" Cilla blinked. Even after several minutes the rousing pipe tune still rang in her ears.

"The shields." Aunt Birdie leaned over to set a scone on her plate. "The round, leather-covered ones decorated with Celtic interlacing and brass studs."

"Are they medieval?" Cilla ignored the scone, eyeing instead a wicked-looking targe that had a pointed spike sticking out from its center. "They look pretty scary."

Her aunt lifted a brow. "More than the swords?"

"The one over the fireplace looks like it could do as much damage as a sword."

"Likely it has." Aunt Birdie helped herself to a dainty portion of hot smoked salmon. "The targes in here are said to be of the Culloden era. Your uncle even thinks one or two might have been blooded in that sad disaster."

She set down her fork. "Don't mention Culloden to your uncle. Not if you don't want an earful. He visits the site whenever we drive down to Inverness and considers himself quite an authority on the battle."

"It was the last battle on British soil, right?" Cilla

slid another glance at the shields. "Bonnie Prince Charlie, the clans, and all that?"

"That's right." Aunt Birdie nodded. "Culloden broke the clans and proved the death knell of clan culture. The battle and its aftermath also smoothed the way for the Highland Clearances that followed. Strathnaver suffered bitterly in those times, with whole communities being put to flight, their homes torched to make way for more profitable sheep." She leaned close, lowering her voice. "People hereabouts still speak as if it all happened just yesterday."

"And Uncle Mac leads the parade." The notion made Cilla smile.

"He does." Aunt Birdie smiled, too. "He's a real crusader for the old ways. His interest in the times is one reason he's collected the targes. That's why I don't think any of them are medieval, though I suppose they could be. They certainly were around back then."

"I thought so." Cilla picked at her scone. She wasn't about to admit that the real reason the shields bothered her was because there'd been one in the poster with Mr. Wasn't-Really-There. The thing had been propped against the wall, near his feet.

And like him, it hadn't belonged there.

Which meant she was losing her mind.

Or seeing ghosts.

Needing to know which it was, she pushed back from the table and stood. "Aunt Birdie, is Uncle Mac really so sure there aren't any ghosts here?"

"Why?" Her aunt put down her salmon-topped oatcake. "Have you seen one? There are stories, you know. All these gloomy old piles have their tales."

"I know," Cilla agreed. She also knew her aunt surely believed every one she heard.

Aunt Birdie was like that.

"Out with the fairies," her mother always called her. Hearing the laughter of sprites in the tinkle of a stream or seeing *shades* in thin veils of drifting mist.

Cilla tossed back her hair and lifted her chin.

She was different.

"But what does Uncle Mac really think?" She paced a bit, her gaze repeatedly sliding to the windows. "Mom and Dad mentioned there were some problems here. Do they have anything to do with ghosts?"

"So some say. But not your uncle." Aunt Birdie dabbed a linen napkin at her mouth. "He'd laugh in the face of the devil. In fact, he thinks it's a devil causing our difficulties."

She set down the napkin and lowered her voice. "A mortal, flesh-and-blood devil out to ruin us, though we can't imagine who he is or what he has against Dunroamin."

"Oh, dear. That sounds serious." Cilla returned to the table, roguish-looking poster shadows forgotten. "Do you want to talk about it?"

"We'll discuss it later. We need to, as we're hoping you can help us with a few things. Just now, I'd much rather hear about you." Aunt Birdie patted her hand. "We were so sorry to hear about Grant."

Cilla nearly choked on her tea. "Don't be. Getting dumped by Grant A. Hughes III was the best thing that ever happened to me. I'm totally over him."

Aunt Birdie's eyes narrowed. "Are you sure? You don't sound—"

"If I sound upset, it's not because of losing Grant. It's because his new girlfriend had a hand in ruining my business." She set down her teacup. "I can't prove it, but I'm certain she torpedoed Vintage Chic."

"But you were doing so well." Aunt Birdie looked astonished.

"So well I had to sell my car to pay several months' overdue rent." Heat began inching up her throat and she slipped a finger beneath the neck opening of her top, feeling warm in the chilly room.

"You should have told us."

"I couldn't." She looked across the table at her aunt, something about her—as always—making the words spill. "Call it pride as far as you and Uncle Mac go, and, well, regarding Mom and Dad, they don't have enough as is. No way did I want them dipping into their savings to help me."

Aunt Birdie shook her head. "I'm so sorry, dear. We had no idea." She gestured with her scone at the laptop Uncle Mac had left sitting at the far end of the table. "I remember you e-mailing some while back about a local jewelry and gift shop giving you display space. You said they were very excited about your sales, that—"

"You mean the Charm Box at the Emporium, a cluster of secondhand, antique, and jewelry shops in the heart of Yardley. They cater to shoppers with eclectic tastes." Cilla tried not to sound bitter. "Paterson's Charm Box is the one who carried my broken china jewelry creations. And, yes, they were enthusiastic. Unfortunately, their daughter, Dawn, saw things differently."

"She's the one seeing Grant?"

Cilla nodded. "The last time I took in a new batch of designs, she told me my work wasn't selling and they couldn't waste the counter space on me. Even worse, I'd swear she and her family are friendly with every other antique and jewelry shop owner between Philly and Trenton. After the Patersons ousted me, no other shops would even look at my work."

"Sounds like sour grapes." Aunt Birdie stood and crossed the room to toss a few peat bricks on the fire. "Sorry, of a sudden, I'm freezing." She gave Cilla an apologetic smile as she reclaimed her seat at the table. "So, tell me. Who *is* this girl?"

"She's a force to be reckoned with, that's what." Cilla poked at her scone. It wasn't very encouraging to realize that the thought of her miniscule rival still had such power to needle her. "Born to rich and dot-ing parents, she's pampered, spoiled, and always gets her way. Or in Grant's case, her man."

Aunt Birdie reached across the table to top off her tea. "I think Grant is the loser, dear."

Cilla shrugged. "Rumor is she told him she's preg-gers. Either way, she's so tiny she barely reaches my shoulders, but she packs a mean punch. I have it on good authority that she even blackballed me with the people who run the Red Barn, a local flea market. Who knows if she did or not, but when I tried to rent space there, I was declined. Thing is"—she stirred a dollop of milk into her tea—"they had at least a half-dozen booths free, and still do."

Aunt Birdie's eyes widened. "And Grant fell for such a woman?"

"So it would seem. Either Dawn Paterson or the wealth behind her."

"But he has money of his own." Aunt Birdie frowned. "Isn't his family one of the richest on the Delaware?"

"The richest, I suspect." Cilla splayed the fingers of her left hand, her ring finger now naked of the egg-sized diamond she'd sported until so recently. "I imagine their position had something to do with turning his head in Dawn's direction. Status mat-tered to Grant."

Fool.

The deep voice came from somewhere near the row of tall windows. Loud and resonating, the single word echoed off the walls and strummed the air.

Cilla jerked. Something like a jolt of electricity tripped through her, spilling from the roots of her hair clear down to the tips of her toes.

"Did you hear that?" She flashed a look at her aunt, her pulse quickening. "That was a man's voice—"

"Shush . . ." Aunt Birdie put a finger to her lips.

"I heard him clearly," Cilla insisted, anyway. "Maybe Uncle Mac is out in the corridor? Or maybe it was another of his recordings?"

She twisted around, her gaze searching the room.

But it was empty.

No suspicious humming gave away a recorded jest.

And the dark square of the door showed only shadows. Nothing but the ever-present sea haar stared in at them from the long bank of glittering, Jacobean-era windows.

Fool. The word still filled her ears.

Aunt Birdie sat quietly sipping her tea, a faraway look in her deep blue eyes.

"There is someone here." She turned to Cilla, her gaze once more clear. "A chivalrous man who cannot stand seeing women treated poorly. I feel he'd avenge you if he could."

Cilla swallowed. "You feel him?"

"Oh yes." Her aunt tilted her head, listening. "I'd bet your uncle's beard on it."

"And he wants to avenge me?"

Cilla kept her doubt to herself. She didn't believe in gallant men, ghostly or otherwise.

Her aunt flicked a crumb off the tablecloth.

"I can only tell you the impressions I'm getting." She met Cilla's eyes, her own gaze steady. "It's mostly anger, and I'm interpreting his energy as being colored by Grant's betrayal, though I could be wrong. But come"—she jumped up and pulled Cilla to her feet— "let's join your uncle in the library. As he would say, I likely shouldn't have indulged in a second dram when you arrived!"

Moving quickly, she tugged Cilla from the room. "Tomorrow will be soon enough to think about our troubles here at Dunroamin, and whatever heartache Grant A. Hughes III has caused you."

Grant A. Hughes III.

The third, by love of all the saints. Near the windows, Hardwick stifled a snort. The man wasn't just a fool. He had a name like a pompous, limp-wristed peacock.

Certain Hughes had other, equally disagreeable faults, Hardwick stepped out of his hiding place the instant the two women exited the room.

Brushing at his plaid, he frowned at the now-empty suit of armor. Never again would he materialize inside anything even halfway as constricting.

He shuddered and flexed his fingers. Then, for good measure, he wriggled his toes, as well. A few vigorous neck rolls, first in one direction and then the other, followed by a quick set of knee bends, completed his attempts to rid himself of the kinks and knots plaguing him.

All that, and still he felt miserable.

Whoever had once worn the armor had been a small, slightly built man.

Definitely not a Highlander.

Proud to belong to that noble race himself, he should have been more wary when he'd followed the interloper from her bedchamber. His scowl deepening, he planted fisted hands on his hips and glanced around.

How typical that he'd purposely left his own shield outside, only to have the fetching creature he now knew to be Cilla Swanner not only flash her breasts at him, but to leave him no choice than to trail after her to the castle armory.

A room filled with shields—taunting reminders of the state in which he'd passed the last seven hundred years.

The dire circumstances he'd find himself in if he failed to meet the Dark One's requirements for lifting the wizard-bard's curse.

"A plague on it," he growled, scowling. "And on that long-ago lute picker. May his fingers rot and wither, or stick to his lute strings." He put back his shoulders, his own curse rolling off his tongue with enough heat to rival any fireballs the Dark One might throw at him for his insolence.

There were some things a man just shouldn't have to endure.

Dwelling beneath the same roof as his one great weakness—a damsel in distress—topped his list.

A room hung with targes proved a close second.

Glaring at them, he considered using his ghostly abilities to get rid of them. Perhaps send them hurtling into the North Sea, letting them sink into its briny depths, one shield at a time.

Or simply flicking his fingers and making them vanish. All at once, and with a fine and satisfying burst of colorful sparks.

Unfortunately, his honor wouldn't allow him such mischievous pleasures.

Mac MacGhee was a goodly sort, and in the short time he'd enjoyed the laird's unwitting hospitality, he'd grown rather fond of the man.

He also knew Mac appreciated the targes.

Still earthbound and curse-free, MacGhee hadn't spent an eternity holding one of the fool contraptions in front of his tender parts.

He just wished the man had mentioned the pending arrival of his niece.

His American niece.

He shuddered, his every shred of self-preservation clamping around him. Cilla Swanner posed a greater threat than an entire hall strung with shields.

From experience, he knew how dangerous such foreign wenches could be. Two of his closest friends had fallen for females of her ilk, even succumbing deep enough to marry them.

Blowing out a hot breath, he shoved a hand through his hair, his friends' capitulations riding him hard.

He couldn't risk any such foolery.

It'd been bad enough looking on as the maid had bared her breasts.

And what magnificent breasts! Full, well-rounded, and pink-tipped, they'd bounced as she'd crossed the room to peer at him. Seldom had he seen such creamy, succulent teats. And she'd stood so close to the poster frame that he could almost feel their silky-smooth weight in his hands.

Almost taste her chill-tightened nipples beneath his greedy, swirling tongue.

Saints, how he'd love to suckle them!

At once, he felt a stir beneath his kilt. A sudden rush of heat and twitches that heralded the start of a man's oh-so-irresistible swelling.

"Damnation," he growled, clenching his fists until the hot pulling receded.

Furious, he stared up at the room's hammer-beam ceiling. He should have vanished when the lass had stripped down to such a delectable state of undress.

Most certainly when she'd headed toward him, her startled expression leaving no doubt that she'd seen him.

But nae . . .

He'd ignored all good sense to stare right back at her like a lovestruck gawp, his old instincts rooting him in place despite the perils.

He frowned again.

The curvaceous American was a peril he hadn't expected to encounter at a remote Highland care home for the aged and infirm.

He'd hoped to spend his days being bored and uninspired.

Wholly free of temptation.

Setting his jaw, he tossed another glare at the wall of shields. Then he curled his fingers around his sword belt, preparing to transport himself up onto the battlements.

For reasons he didn't care to acknowledge, he felt a strong need for a blast of chill, bracing air.

Something told him he soon might even require a few dips in the icy sea.

Hardwick sighed. He'd chosen the refuge for his proving period unwisely.

Most unwisely indeed.

Chapter 2

"Fool."

The word followed Hardwick to the battlements, sticking as close to him as the blaring strains of Mac MacGhee's favorite pipe tune still rattled in his ears. He cupped them with his hands and pressed hard, trying in vain to rid himself of the loud, droning echo.

Not that he didn't love pipes.

He did, as did all self-respecting Highlanders.

But there were bagpipes and then *bagpipes*.

Mac MacGhee's mechanically contrived blast of Heiland skirling was an abomination.

Hardwick frowned. Never again would he make the mistake of manifesting in the laird's privy quarters just prior to teatime.

Nor would he allow himself any further moments of self-satisfaction over having chosen Dunroamin as the place of refuge for his proving period.

His decision was disastrous.

If Grant A. Hughes III was a fool for walking away from the lightsome lass, he was an even greater lackwit for putting himself in her path.

"A double-dyed *doomed* lackwit," he fumed, glaring at the mist sliding past the battlements. Thick and gray, great sheets of it swirled everywhere. He narrowed his eyes, scanning each billowy drift. It would

be just like the Dark One to lurk behind the impenetrable brew, gloating.

Twice now he'd caught what could have been a
crone's cackling laugh.

Or—saints forbid—the heinous sniggers of a whole
gaggle of them.

He shuddered, looking deeper into the fog.

But his best peering efforts turned up naught. If the
fiend or his hell hags were at Dunroamin, they were
keeping themselves well hidden. So he put them from
his mind—for now—and bowed to long habit, conjuring his shield.

A flick of his fingers and it appeared in his hand.

The shield's familiarity comforted.

He just hoped he'd never again need it for its erstwhile purpose.

Certain such a calamity was rushing his way, he
balled his fists and began to pace the wall-walk. A
cold drizzle slicked the stone flagging and darkened
the castle walls, but the rain-misted afternoon suited
him.

So much so that he didn't bother to draw his plaid
against the rising wind.

There was, after all, no need.

She more than warmed him.

With every angry footfall, her face rose before him.
She tempted and vexed him with her startled eyes of
deepest blue, the fine line of her jaw, and her creamy,
unblemished skin. The sleek fall of her thick, silky
hair taunted him, too. Honey-gold in color and just
brushing her shoulders, the gleaming strands begged
a man's touch. Just as her mouth, so full, sweetly
curved, and soft-looking, hinted at a hidden lustiness
he'd love to waken in her.

A groan rose deep in his throat and he pulled a
hand down over his chin.

He hadn't often loved a fair-haired woman. Well-
prized in his day, most proved either already taken or

were sequestered away in an unassailable tower, guarded by their fathers until the highest bidder claimed them.

How he'd love to claim this one!

He swallowed another groan, imagining the bliss of thrusting his hands into such shining skeins. He'd twine the strands around his fingers and pull her close, kissing her deeply. And if she kissed him back, he'd crush her to him, making sure she felt the thick, hard length of him brushing against her.

Just thinking about such deliciousness let him almost feel her softness pressing into him, the golden strands of her hair spilling through his fingers, delighting and bewitching him. He drew a deep breath and released it slowly.

Fair women were a prize beyond telling.

In his numberless years of carousing, most of his bedmates had sported tresses of flame or coloring as dark as his own. And of the few yellow-maned wenches he'd sampled, he'd quickly known they'd gleaned the bright shade from the local henwife.

Their *other* hair gave away the secret every time.

But he knew what the tongue waggers said about true flaxen-haired, blue-eyed maidens.

Once a man melted them, their fire burned hotter than the sun.

Need clawed at his gut. He drew a tight breath, wishing he'd ne'er heard such blether. He wasn't the man to test Cilla Swanner's passion.

Would that he could . . . in another time and place it would have been possible.

As things were, he simply stepped faster, letting his quickened pace and his fury heat his blood. His frustration also staved off the bite of the day's cold, wet wind.

Until the gusts turned, sending up spray from the foot of the cliffs to flip an edge of his plaid across his eyes.

"Damnation!" He snatched at the offending wool, yanking it down, only to discover that the maid's face still hovered before him.

Worse, he could now see even more of her!

In memory, her naked breasts bobbed right beneath his nose. Just as full, round, and plump as he remembered, and with her rosy-sweet nipples drawn deliciously tight.

"By all the powers!" He roared the curse.

Snapping his brows together, he glared at the image until the wind broke it apart.

He shoved back his hair, his mood thoroughly ruined. He didn't know how she'd done it—a long line and more centuries of women than he liked to admit had only left him disinterested, even after a particularly pleasing tumble—yet this one had somehow managed to brand herself on him.

And he hadn't even kissed her.

That could only mean trouble.

Feeling it settle around him like a dark, clinging cloud, he set his jaw and started pacing again.

If need be, he'd spend his proving time doing so.

Pacing was good.

Scowling, likewise.

Better yet, even on a fine-weather day, the battlements often stayed windswept and cold. Many a good, stout Scots lass wouldn't care to brave such a chill and blustery aerie.

With luck, an American wouldn't even attempt the climb up the narrow, winding stair.

Unfortunately, something told him Cilla Swanner might. After all, she'd crossed the room to peer at him inside the poster frame even if seeing him there clearly didn't sit well with her.

She might look as if she should be perched in a tower window, her fair hair spilling over the ledge as she pined for some noble gallant to come and carry her away on a white steed, but she had a bold and daring heart.

He was sure of it.

So he stomped on, practicing his best glares all the while.

"Ho! Here is a wonder!" A deep voice boomed behind him. "Ne'er would I have believed I'd see the day you scowl and curse o'er such a comely maid."

Hardwick whipped around so fast he nearly dropped his shield.

Bran MacNeil of Barra stood a few paces away, his huge bearlike form almost splitting with mirth. Ghostly, great-hearted, and good-humored, the Hebridean chieftain sported a bushy beard nearly as red as Mac MacGhee's, and his blue eyes crinkled with the same teasing amusement.

The gemstone in the pommel of his sword hilt shone dimly in the day's pale light and his plaid lifted in the wind, its woolen folds smelling distinctly of a heady musk-scented perfume that wasn't Bran's own.

"You great stirk!" Hardwick glowered at him. "Cease goggling at me like a ring-tailed gowk. You should know why I'm scowling."

"I can think it, aye!"

"No doubt," Hardwick agreed. "You know fine why I'm here."

He tightened his grip on his shield. A sharp bite to his tongue kept him from demanding how his longtime friend and wenching companion knew Cilla Swanner was comely.

Or, more importantly, how he knew she even existed.

"Why are you here?" Hardwick eyed him, suspicious. Though, in truth, he'd already guessed the answer. "It's a rare day that you leave Barra."

His friend cut the air with a hand. "My fair isle will keep until my return. I came to see how you're doing here in the wild and lonely north!"

"I've been passing my nights well enough until—" Hardwick caught himself.

Somewhere in the mist behind him, a wicked chortle sounded.

Hardwick's nape prickled. His blood chilled and he blanked his features, as if he'd not noticed.

Bran just kept laughing. "Until you had your head turned, eh?"

"My head hasn't been turned." Hardwick lifted his voice, hoping any lurking cacklers would hear his denial and return to their hellhole. "You're poking your nose where it doesn't belong and seeing things that aren't there."

"Say you?"

"I do."

Looking as if he was having none of that, the burly Islesman leaned back against the parapet's notched wall and crossed his ankles.

"I told you it would have been wiser to hie yourself to Barra," he said, sounding most serious. "There, you could have—"

Hardwick laughed.

He couldn't help himself.

Then he shoved a hand through his hair and spoke the truth. "Your hall is so thick with temptation you could stir the place with a spoon."

"Aye, so it is!" Bran looked more than pleased with the description. "But"—he raised a sage finger—"you have sampled the charms of all the lovelies who drop in and out of my keep. It seems to me you'd have had less trouble turning a blind eye to them than to *this* maid."

Hardwick humphed.

Much as he loved his friend, he wouldn't give him the satisfaction of an answer.

Besides, the lout's piercing stare showed that he already knew.

"She's an American." Bran spoke the word as if it were dipped in gold.

"I don't care if she comes from the moon." Hardwick glared at him. "I do not even want to *see* a fetching piece of womanhood. No' now!"

His temper rising, he strode to another section of the wall, deliberately choosing a place at least four square-toothed notches away from his friend.

"My wenching days are behind me." He cleared his throat. "I cannot return to them—even if I wished to do so."

"I wasn't speaking of wenching." Behind him, Bran made a sound as if he'd slapped his thigh. "Come you, dinna be so thrawn. Stubbornness is for soured old men!"

Hardwick slid him an annoyed look. "And you say we are no' old?"

Bran gave a great belly-shaking laugh. "Centuries old isn't what I meant, and well you know it! We are as hardy as the rutting stags on the hill."

"Speak for yourself. I am done with that kind of hardiness."

"Even so . . ." Bran stopped laughing. "There are just times I get these feelings, and this is one o' them. Think you I would leave my cozy hearth fire and a plump bed warmer for naught? I say you, that lassie—"

"Is none of my concern." Hardwick blocked his ears to whatever else his friend had to say about her.

Scowling, he braced his hands on the cold stone of the merlon and stared down at the shimmering expanse of the Kyle of Tongue far below. Even on such a chill, mist-plagued afternoon, the strait's tossing surface glimmered and shone with silvery blue light, and its wide, sandy banks glistened in every shade of gold.

Soft, gleaming tones that made him think of *her* hair.

He flinched.

The neck opening of his tunic had gone unpleasantly tight, but he refused to slip a finger beneath it. Instead he pressed his hands even harder against the damp grit of the merlon and kept his gaze pinned on the swirl of the Kyle's fast-moving current.

Such a day of strong-running seas and wind should have invigorated him.

Instead, he found his heart freezing in his chest and his gut twisting. Of his usual sharp wit and high spirits, nary a jot remained, and his mood had gone more foul than he could ever remember.

Even as a ghost—and cursed as he was—he'd never passed a day without laughing.

Now . . .

He skulked about, trying to ignore the presence of the one lass who might have really appealed to him. And, equally galling, he'd been reduced to an over-the-shoulder-glancing fool, hearing cackles in every ripple of the wind.

He frowned.

His jaw set so tight he wondered he didn't crack a tooth.

"I've done a lot of thinking about Americans." Bran appeared at his elbow. "The women, I mean. There's something about them." He paused, drawing a deep breath, as if readying himself to pronounce some great gem of wisdom. "Ach, see you, after much consideration, I'm thinking that when they come here—"

"They should turn around and take themselves right back where they came from!" Hardwick flashed a dark look at his friend. "Leastways those so brazen they'd jiggle their bared breasts under a man's nose."

"So-o-o!" Bran hopped onto a merlon with surprising ease for a man of his size. "That is the way of it! She's for seducing you!"

He pulled on his beard, an expression of feigned

puzzlement on his face. "How odd that when I saw her heading this way, she looked more upset than out to flaunt her charms."

Hardwick's entire body tensed. "What do you mean she's heading this way?"

"Just that." Bran sounded convinced. "I'd gone looking for you and nearly collided with her in one of the corridors. Poor lassie would've dashed right through me if I hadn't leapt aside fast enough. She was making for the parapet stair."

"Then you must be mistaken." Hardwick's relief knew no bounds. "She left the armory in her aunt's company. They were on their way to the library. She wouldn't be careening through the passageways."

Bran shrugged. "Be that as it may, that's where I saw her."

"You saw someone else." Hardwick willed it so. "Honoria perhaps. She's the housekeeper and by far the youngest female here excepting—"

"Ach, but you insult me!" Bran clapped a hand to his chest. "Think you a man of my wenching experience canna tell a housekeeper from an American?"

Hardwick scowled at the truth of his friend's words.

He scowled even more when the lout vanished, leaving his merlon perch empty and Hardwick alone on the wall-walk, just when the parapet door flew open and *she* burst out onto the battlements.

Not Honoria at all, but his nemesis.

And looking so delectable he was tempted to close the short space between them with two swift strides and seize her to him, clamping her face between his hands and then kissing her long, hard, and deep, until nothing mattered but the feel of her soft, red lips yielding to his own.

He wanted, needed, the bliss of her silken tongue twirling and sliding against his in hot, ancient rhythm.

The Dark One and his bargain be damned.

Instead, he simply stared at her, his frown so black he could feel it to his toes.

She stood perfectly still, poised just outside the door, her cheeks flushed pink and her breath coming hard. Hardwick's own breath snagged in his throat and he quickly jerked his shield into place. Not to hide a rise in his plaid, but to disguise his attempt to prevent one.

Furious at the need, he slid a hand behind the targe and squeezed.

Hard.

Hard, long, and tight enough to bring tears to a lesser man, but Hardwick only gritted his teeth and winced. Once, in another life, he'd have thrown back his head and laughed at his word choices.

Now they only fueled his frustration.

Long and hard was definitely what he'd love to give her. And, mercy on him, he knew she'd be wonderfully tight.

Hot, sleek, and slippery wet.

Need speared him again, a sharp and painful hunger pulsing somewhere deep inside him.

She hadn't yet noticed him, so he continued to stare at her, her appearance shattering his last hope that Bran might have erred. And, even worse, driving home how urgently he needed to rid himself of her.

Her scent alone damned him. Light, clean, and fresh as a spring breeze, it swirled around him, firing his blood and threatening to set him like granite if he didn't have such a firm grip on himself.

As it was, every other inch of him went tight with desire. His senses snapped to dangerous alert and he squeezed himself harder, struggling against her effect on him yet unable to look away.

Something had clearly upset her and—saints help him—that air of flushed, wild-eyed vulnerability drew him as strongly as her lush curves and creamy smooth skin. Her breasts, covered now in a silky-looking top of softest blue, rose and fell in agitation, and her bright golden hair whipped crazily in the gusting wind.

Cilla started forward, swiping at the tossing strands as she made straight for the walling. Notched, medieval-looking walling that surely *was* medieval.

Just as she was certain that the great bearded Highlander who'd suddenly appeared in front of her in one of the portrait-hung halls had been, well, *medieval*.

If not that, he definitely wasn't of this time.

Nor of this world.

In fact, he'd looked downright savage. In a magnificent, old-time Highland-y sort of way, that is.

Magnificent or not, she wanted nothing to do with him. Shivering, she pulled her sweater tighter against the cold air and forced her legs to carry her across the narrow stone-flagged walkway.

No easy task when they felt like rubber and her knees wouldn't stop knocking. But she kept on, placing one foot in front of the other until she reached the wall.

She needed air.

Lots and lots of cold, fresh air.

"I did not just see another ghost. I did not"—she gripped the edge of a merlon, needing the stone's solidity—"almost run through him. He did not leap out of the way when—"

"Ahhh, but he did now, didn't he?" A deep voice, well-burred and buttery rich, purred out of nowhere. "Perhaps you should leave before you run into someone who won't."

"Won't what?" She spoke before remembering no one was there.

"Won't leap out of your way, of course," the blowing mist returned.

Cilla's eyes flew wide.

Her heart slammed against her ribs.

Pea soup didn't talk!

Not in Yardley, Pennsylvania, and, she was sure, not in Scotland, either.

Not even in the remote vastness of Sutherland.

Unwilling to consider the alternative, she straightened her shoulders and—very slowly—pushed away from the wall. Three, four long-legged strides would take her safely back to the doorway and she could just pop through it, leaving Dunroamin's all-too-eerie battlements behind her.

She wasn't in the mood to deal with talking mist.

But before she could turn around, she backed into something cold, hard, and unyielding.

Something round, leather covered, and riddled with *bumps*. She could feel them pressing into the small of her back. She knew at once what they were.

The brass studs of a targe.

A medieval targe.

"Oh, no!" She spun on her heels, certain the poster ghost had come for her at last, but the man staring so fiercely at her was anything but a phantom.

Tall, dark, and kilted, he *was* clutching a shield.

He was also gorgeous, defined sensuality in a wicked, smoldering kind of way, and he had a decidedly roguish air about him. But he looked just as real and solid as anyone else. And—she swallowed as she blinked up at him—even if he did resemble Mr. Wasn't-Really-There, she doubted a ghost could make her mouth go dry.

"O-o-oh, aye," he spoke again, his honeyed voice melting her. "Did I no' warn you there'd be some who wouldn't jump aside?"

Cilla stopped melting at once.

"Who *are* you?" She regarded him warily. "Where did you come from?"

"From a place more distant than you'd believe." He ignored her first question. "And I've good advice for you," he added, taking a step closer, slowly raising his shield until it brushed the tips of her breasts. "If you're after a true taste o' Scotland, hie yourself—"

"Hie myself?" She blinked.

"Take yourself," he clarified, scowling at her. "Quit this place and journey south. Inverness, the Isle of Skye, Stirling and Perth, perhaps even down to Edinburgh. Or Glasgow. Aye"—he appeared to warm to the idea—"Glasgow is where you should be! Loch Lomond is there and—"

"I saw Loch Lomond on the drive up here." Cilla frowned right back at him. "We stopped for lunch at Luss and I've never seen so many coach tour buses crowded into such a tiny car park. Or so many people jammed into souvenir shops no bigger than a postage stamp. If that is Scotland"—she scooted around him and made a wide, sweeping gesture with her arm, taking in the rain-dampened parapet and the broad, silvery Kyle—"I'd rather be here."

He snorted. "This is the end of the world."

Cilla smiled. "Exactly."

Suddenly in her face again, he leaned close. "Be warned," he breathed, his dark gaze piercing her. "Sutherland is filled with lonely moors and dark bogs. Mountains so vast and bleak they'd eat a lass like you, bones and all, and no one would ever be the wiser."

"I *like* wild places." She tossed back her hair, defiant.

"Yet you plan to spend the summer here"—he made a broad gesture of his own—"where every soul present is at least thrice your own age? The only kind of *wild* they'll give you is complaining that their haggis is too well spiced or that your uncle tells the same fireside tales too often."

She stared at him.

His burr was getting to her again. Much as she hated to admit it, he really was six-foot-four of pure Scottish male.

She'd always had a thing for Highlanders.

Especially kilted ones.

But the absurdity of his objection and, perhaps, the exhaustion of jet lag, bubbled up inside her until she near convulsed with sidesplitting, eye-tearing laughter.

"You made one mistake." She wiped her eyes when she finally caught herself. "There does seem to be a *soul* here who isn't 'thrice my age.' "

He cocked a brow. "And who might that be?"

She smiled, triumph hers. "You."

"I am more than thrice your age." He looked at her as earnestly as if he'd commented on the blowing mist. "Truth be told, I'm seven hundred, give or take a few years."

"Indeed?" Her mouth twitched. "I suppose you'll also tell me your name is Robert Bruce?"

"Nae, but I knew the man well."

"You did?" Her smile faded.

He nodded. "My father's people were Norman Scots, as were the de Brus. Our families were friendly."

"We are speaking of King Robert the Bruce, right?" She tucked her hair behind an ear. "Medieval Scotland's greatest hero king?"

Kiltie drew himself up, seeming to grow even taller and more fierce-looking. "To my knowledge, Scotland has ne'er seen a greater ruler in any epoch," he said, almost bristling. "But, aye, he is the one I meant."

"I was afraid of that." She drew a tight breath, the effect of his burr evaporating.

An uncomfortable thought rushed her. The corridors she'd sped through after taking a wrong turn had been dark and musty with an air of disuse to them.

That, and a sense that the endless passageways with their ancient portraits and faded tartan carpet runners might hold secrets. Like barred windows and meals served through a narrow slit in the door.

Bad things best left behind thick, rubber-covered walls and good, heavy locks.

"So you've figured it out?" He sounded pleased.

"Oh yes." She spoke as calmly as she could. "I believe I have."

Not trusting herself to make eye contact and risk riling him, she stole a glance at the still-open parapet door.

It seemed miles away.

She swallowed and began inching in that direction as surreptitiously as possible. "I thought Uncle Mac and Aunt Birdie only catered to the aged. I didn't realize—"

"The MacGhees aren't aware I'm here." An iron grip to her elbow halted her escape. " 'Tis a *ghost*, I am, sweetness, no' a—"

"Ghosts can't touch people!" Cilla shot a glance to where his long, strong fingers held her arm. She could feel his strength and warmth pulsing clear up to her shoulder and down to her fingertips. "You—"

"I am what I say, and I can do much more than grab your arm." He leaned in, his gaze locking with hers. "If I were so inclined, that is."

"Oh!" Cilla jerked free of his grasp.

He stepped back and folded his arms. "Oh, indeed," he said, his eyes heating. "Be glad I am no' interested—"

"Where did your shield go?" She stared at his crossed arms. "It's gone."

"Say you?" His mouth curved with a hint of amusement. "I but set it aside so I could fold my arms. See"—he uncrossed them and held up a hand, the shield appearing at once—"here it is again."

Cilla's eyes widened. "That's impossible."

He said nothing. He simply stood holding the targe in front of him at hip level, that faint smile still playing across his lips.

The smile didn't reach his eyes, but it *did* give a vague idea of what could happen if ever he turned the power of a true, full-blooded smile on her.

He was jaw-droppingly handsome as is.

He wore a kilt and had the cutest knees she'd
ever seen.

With a killer smile, he'd be beyond dangerous.

Indeed, for all she knew, he could *be* a killer. His
intense, unblinking stare certainly wasn't friendly. Far
from it; the look he was giving her sent chills tinkling
down her spine and tied her stomach in knots.

As if he knew it, he flashed a grin that revealed two
deep dimples.

Boyish dimples, entirely too charming.

She tried not to notice. "If you're really a ghost,
why can I see you? Can everyone?"

"Everyone who is meant to, aye."

"That doesn't tell me much." She eyed him, still
skeptical.

He laughed. "Sweet lass, just because I'm a ghost
doesn't mean I have all the answers. Truth is, some
souls just see us. Most can't." He angled his head,
looking thoughtful. "If you didn't know, a ghost could
run naked through a crowd of people and chances are
only one, if any, would notice.

"And"—he glanced aside—"there are times we can
will it that everyone *does* see us. Though even then
there will be some who do not. I canna tell you why
that is so."

He looked at her, his gaze penetrating. "It just is."

"Then why hasn't Aunt Birdie seen you?" She had
him now. "She can see ghosts."

"No' when they wish to remain unseen."

"So you've been hiding from her?"

"Nae, I simply chose not to disrupt her days." He
made it sound so simple. "One of the advantages of
being a ghost is the privilege of staying out of sight
when desired."

That did it.

He was talking as if he really believed such nonsense.

Cilla tossed back her hair. "Look here, mister. If

you're trying to scare me, it won't work." Her gaze flicked to his there-one-minute, gone-the-next shield. "I've seen crazies on the streets of Philly with better tricks than disappearing shields."

"Then what say you to disappearing men?"

"What—" Her jaw slipped as he vanished right in front of her.

His *words* hung in the air.

Rich, deep, and buttery smooth, they stayed behind to taunt her. Each one slid through her like sun-warmed honey, pooling low and tantalizing even as they chilled her to the bone. Worst of all, they left her with little choice but to accept that Mr. Wasn't-Really-There genuinely wasn't.

It would seem he was exactly what he claimed to be.

A ghost.

Chapter 3

She thought he was feeble-minded.

Hardwick glowered after her, trying hard not to notice the bounce of her full, round breasts as she fled the wall-walk. He ignored, as well, the long strides of her shapely legs. Above all, he pretended not to see the swing of her luscious, well-made bottom.

The kind of bottom he could do all kinds of things to—and would—under different circumstances.

As it was, a muscle twitched in his jaw and vexation, not lust, swept him. Even so, he watched her go, his fists clenching when she darted into the stair tower.

"Damnation." He threw back his head and glared at the roiling clouds, the fast-moving sheets of mist racing across the battlements.

He could scarce breathe for ire.

In nearly a millennium of intimate encounters with the fairer sex, nary a one had ever insulted him so deeply. Most women—of the Otherworld, admittedly, but even those of her realm who'd seen him—swooned and went all weak-kneed at a mere glance from him.

If he flashed a smile, they were his.

Totally beguiled, they freely offered their charms, claiming he was braw and irresistible.

Cilla Swanner clearly felt otherwise.

Crazy, she'd called him.

Not that the word mattered. The meaning was the same and he didn't like it at all.

Unfortunately, the thought of her tearing down the stair tower's tight, winding steps sat even worse with him. He needn't exactly traverse them to know how slick they were. Worn smooth by centuries of trudging, tromping feet, the slippery hollows of the stone steps could easily send her tumbling to her death if she tripped.

And she'd looked to be in a very trip-easy mood when she'd dashed through the parapet door. An assessment underscored by the echo of her hasty, panicked descent.

Hardwick shoved a hand through his hair and scowled as he listened.

He should amuse himself elsewhere.

Dunroamin boasted at least fifty rooms. Give or take a few, to be sure. A soul could lose hours in the disused wing alone, counting the rats, bats, and roosting doves dwelling there. Great swaths of cobwebs begged examination, several chambers held dust-covered piles of candlesticks and pewter plates, clumps of moth-eaten velvet drapes, and even bolts of ancient tartan. Best of all, some of the walls hosted such a battalion of mold and mildew, the musty damp was a sure guarantee *she* wouldn't spend time there.

So there were possibilities.

Places where he could avoid her.

Too bad he'd grown accustomed to spending his days in the warmth and comfort of the castle's cozier bits.

Either way, he did need to stop mooning over the chit. Nor was it wise to make his head ache worrying about her. That road led to folly.

It was nothing to him if she fell.

If anything, he'd be spared hearing unholy cackles

on the wind. Without her around to tempt him, the
hell hags wouldn't have reason to chortle. He'd be
free of the nuisance of trying to scare her away.

Something he wasn't at all sure he could do.

Frightening women, after all, wasn't his strong suit.

So why did the clatter of her hurrying feet grate on
his last nerve?

Sure he didn't know—or want to—his scowl deepened when he blinked and realized he'd somehow materialized on the stair tower's top landing.

He hadn't meant to move from the parapet wall.

And he certainly hadn't planned to manifest again.

If she glanced back and saw him, she surely would
take a nasty plunge.

A circular patch of hard, stone-flagged floor loomed
at the bottom of the stair. He could make it out far
below if he leaned forward and looked down. Just as
he could see her bright head, her shining hair stream-
ing behind her as she sped round the spiraling steps,
racing ever downward.

Her shoe flying off her foot . . .

"Eeeee!" Cilla slipped, her right leg shooting out
from under her in the same instant her loafer sailed
into the air and went bouncing down the stairs.

In a blink, she knew she was doomed.

Her life, such as it was, flashed before her.

Then the stair tower tilted and spun and she pitched
forward into nothingness.

Down, down she fell until, with a great *whoosh*, she
slammed into something hard as stone yet as yielding
as if she'd landed smack in someone's arms.

Powerful arms holding her crushed against a big,
muscular body that felt suspiciously *kilted*.

Her eyes flew wide.

The back of her neck prickled.

"You!" She shifted in arms she couldn't see, shivers
rippling all through her.

"Aye, me." The words hushed past her ear. Soft, burred, and unmistakably annoyed. "Fool that I am."

She almost choked. She was the fool. Thinking she could run from a man who could make himself invisible. Instead she'd only tripped and plunged down the stairs, making herself look clumsy as well as unnerved by ghosts!

Phantoms.

She wriggled against his steely banded hold, but her efforts only made him tighten his arms even more. Her mouth opened and closed several times, her protest snagging in her throat at the very real feel of his rock-hard chest.

Something she should *not* be noticing!

Furious that she did, she frowned.

"You're a . . . ghost." She hoped saying the words would make him seem more ghostly, less knight in shining armor, all gleaming steel and bold, searing glances.

"Aye, that I am." He laughed, not sounding Casperish at all.

"Then . . . how can you—"

She broke off, feeling ridiculous. She was, after all, talking to thin air.

She swallowed. "Ghosts can't catch people."

"Is that so?" His scent, dark, spicy, and masculine, swirled around her, and even invisible, it was clear he'd lifted a mocking brow.

She could feel his hot gaze on her. A smoldering, intense kind of stare that made her wonder if one of his spectral powers was the ability to see through clothes. The deep rumble in his chest made it seem a distinct possibility.

Her nipples tightened on the thought and—heaven help her—great whirls of heat whipped through her, making her tingle everywhere. Something, perhaps the gold Celtic armband he wore, pressed into her side, and his scent, all clean wool and linen with a hint of sandalwood and man, persisted in doing funny things to her stomach.

Deliciously funny things she had no business feeling in the arms of a man who wasn't really there.

A man who, by his own admission, hadn't really been there for nearly seven hundred years!

She shivered again, her mouth going drier. It didn't matter that he took her breath away. Or even that he'd just saved her from certain death or, at the least, a few broken bones.

He just plain didn't exist.

Not really, anyway.

And buttery-burred, dark-eyed Highland sex god or not, that was enough to give any girl the willies.

"Put me down!" She tried to jerk free again. "Now."

A snort answered her.

Then a swish of cool, silky hair slid across her cheek and she found herself clutched even tighter to his broad, impossibly sculpted chest as she floated—no, as he carried her—down the remaining steps and set her on her feet.

"Next time I will no' use such care," he warned, stepping away so quickly the air where he'd been snapped back around her, cold and empty.

He was gone.

Whether she'd seen him disappear or not was beside the point. She felt his absence as strongly as if someone had vacuumed the air from her lungs.

He'd simply poofed himself away.

And she was losing it.

Sure of it, she stooped to snatch up her shoe and jam it back onto her foot. Then she blew a strand of hair off her face and glared up at the tight turnpike stair rising so innocently into the shadows.

The stones of the curved walls looked ancient and were dark and sooty in places where telltale iron brackets had once held smoking rush torches. A cold, damp wind whistled in through a few narrow slit windows, lending to the stair tower's eerie ambience.

Most telling of all, the worn stone steps had dips in their middle.

She stared at those grooves now, her pulse settling.

They were why she'd slipped.

She hadn't floated down the stairs in the arms of a roguish, sinfully handsome, seven-hundred-year-old Highland warrior in a kilt.

Her foot had simply slid on one of the slick, ancient steps, causing her to stumble the rest of the way down in a jet-lagged, zero-sleep-induced stupor.

There hadn't been any sexy ghost.

Not in the stair tower or up on the battlements.

Imagination wasn't her middle name for nothing. Everyone knew the mind created all sorts of havoc when people were foolish enough to run around on empty with sand grit scratching their eyes. Anyone so far past the second-wind stage was bound to experience weirdness. Who could blame her if she'd seen fluttering cobwebs and turned them into plaids? Or heard the cold whistle of wind and imagined the purr of a smooth, whisky-deepened burr.

No, a smooth, *lilting* burr not deep at all and that was calling her name.

Honoria the housekeeper.

Red-cheeked and with her great matronly bosom thrust forward like the bow of a tweed-draped ship, she came sailing around a corner just as Cilla straightened her clothes and stepped out of the stair tower.

"Ach, *mo ghaoil*, it's yourself!" The older woman hurried forward, her sturdy rubber-soled shoes silent on the plaid carpet-runner. "We were nigh after having all the staff search for you—"

"Mo gale?" Cilla blinked. The grit in her eyes stung like sandpaper.

The housekeeper waved a hand. "It means 'my

dear,' is all," she said, taking Cilla's arm and leading her in the exact opposite direction she'd meant to go. "We were quite fashed about you."

"I got lost." Cilla felt herself flush.

She shoved back her hair and tried to keep her voice light. "I couldn't find the restrooms Aunt Birdie said were near the main staircase."

She kept the rest to herself.

No way would she tell the no-nonsense-looking woman about *him*.

Nor did she care to admit that a simple search for the so-called loo had taken her into a dimly lit passage where the shadows had slid around her, blotting the way forward and backward. Or that the corridor had reeked so strongly of candle grease, old stone, and dark oak paneling that she'd feared she'd stepped into some kind of time warp.

"Right enough, that's where they are. The restrooms, as you Yanks say. They're behind the big stairs, just." Honoria made a sympathetic clucking sound. "You're not the first to lose your way looking for them."

She leaned close, dropping her voice to a conspiratorial level. "That's the trouble with these old piles, all put together in fits and starts down the centuries. If any one of the late, great builders meant to make it easy for a soul to find his way about, a hundred years later there comes his great-great-grandson adding on his own bits and pieces and spoiling the plan!"

"I like it."

"Americans always do." The housekeeper's chest puffed. "And why not? Dunroamin isn't your average country house surrounded by the prerequisite sweep of lawn and gardens. With the exception of a tearoom, seasonal tours, and a souvenir shop, we offer a little of everything."

Looking proud, she rattled off the castle's charms. "We have the oldest bits, the tower and parapets and even a dank undercroft for medieval buffs. Then there's the Jacobean wing with its tall, south-facing bays for the stone-mullioned window enthusiast. And"—she winked—"we've more than enough Victorian gothic to please the soppiest romantics."

Cilla glanced out a tall, arch-topped window they were passing, caught a glimpse of rolling moors and mist. "And you have Sutherland."

"Nae, Sutherland has us." Honoria gave her a look so serious she wouldn't have dreamed of disagreeing. "We could travel across two oceans and as many continents and still the land would touch us, calling us home."

"Dùthchas." Cilla's heart wrapped around the word. "It's the only Gaelic I know. *Dooch-hus.* Aunt Birdie taught it to me on one of her visits to Pennsylvania when I was little. She said it represents a Highlander's deep sense of oneness with his land and culture."

"No words can capture the feeling, *mo ghaoil*, but *Dùthchas* comes close, aye." The housekeeper's expression softened. "Only when you've felt that love of the land pulsing here"—she clapped a hand to her breast—"can you truly understand a Highlander's heart. Your aunt does. She wears the far north well."

Something inside Cilla twisted.

She loved Scotland, too, and had dreamed of coming here since childhood. She'd also loved Scotsmen, even founding the Mad for Plaid Club when she was sixteen. Sadly, her obsession with tartan-draped men had overridden every warning bell when Grant A. Hughes III waltzed into her life, claiming Scottish roots. When he'd arrived, kilted, to take her to a Highland Games on one of their early dates, her fate had been sealed.

Feeling heat inch up the back of her neck, she flicked a speck of lint off her sleeve.

Then she did her best not to frown.

The swell-headed lout hadn't exactly ruined her enthusiasm for Scotland. But he'd made her wary of kilt-wearing, sporran-sporting Scots*men*.

"I know Aunt Birdie loves Sutherland," she blurted, pushing Grant the weasel from her mind. "Whenever she'd visit, her eyes would light when she spoke of Uncle Mac's home. She'd gush about its wild empti-ness and what she called the vast stretches of sea, land, and sky. She said even the air was different. That it was magical, and that once you'd inhaled it, you'd be forever in its spell."

"O-o-oh, aye, that's the way of it." Honoria nodded agreement. "You'll lose your heart, too. Everyone does."

Stepping close, she fixed Cilla with a shrewd stare. "Why do you think so many English incomers are for settling here?" She put back her shoulders, clearly warming to a favorite topic. "They come north, breathe our clean air and peat smoke, fall in love with our starry nights and quiet, even the days when our mist blows sideways and suddenly—or so they say—the city fumes and crush of London or Manchester or Liverpool are something they can't bear anymore."

The words spoken, she pressed her lips tight. As if *those* incomers were an entirely different kettle of fish than Aunt Birdie.

"Too bad they often feel differently when, come winter, they discover they need thermal underwear and learn that our weekly entertainment is Quiz Night at the Village Hall or a *ceilidh* over at Old Jock's croft down by Talmine Bay." Honoria's chin lifted. "Fiddlers come from as far away as Lairg and Ulla-pool to play at Old Jock's sessions. Yet—"

"Wait." Cilla stopped before an oak-planked door studded with rusted iron. She was sure she'd passed through it earlier, certain it'd stood ajar.

Yet now it was bolted.

"I'm sure I came up here through that door." She

eyed the heavy-looking drawbar, the fine hairs on her
nape lifting again. "It was open."

"Ach, it couldn't have been." The housekeeper
shook her head. "That way leads to a house wing we
never use, save for storage." She reached to jiggle the
iron latch, proving its secured state. "The door's kept
mostly locked since a fire swept parts of that wing in
the 1930s. I'd be surprised if even your uncle could
slide back the drawbar."

"But—"

From somewhere came the sound of knuckles cracking. "Shall I—"

"Oh!" Cilla's heart stopped.

He filled her mind again. She was sure she'd heard
his voice. Almost sure she caught a whiff of sandalwood and musk on the chill, dust-moted air.

Just when she'd convinced herself she'd imagined
him!

She slid a glance over her shoulder, seeing nothing.
Naturally.

Her heart began to pound again, her hard-won
cool crumbling.

Honoria remained unruffled. "Be glad the door is
sealed," she said, pressing her point. "That's also the
wing with the ghost room."

"Ghost room?"

"So we call it now." Honoria took her arm, pulling
her down the passageway. "The room used to be a
nursery."

Cilla glanced back at the locked door.

She'd done so well putting the sexy ghost from her
mind. Yet now she could almost see him standing beside the ancient door, flexing his fingers above the
drawbar as if he meant to seize it any moment.

Pull the thing back and open the door—just to
prove that he could.

She swallowed, her pulse leaping.

"Honoria . . ." She spoke before she lost nerve. "Is the ghost room haunted by a Highland warrior who wears a big sword and carries a round, medieval shield?"

"By glory, nae! More's the pity!" The older woman tossed her a glance. "It's not a braw lad but a poor serving lass. She hails from the days of Culloden, if the tales be true."

"The mid-1700s?" A chill slid down Cilla's spine. "Uncle Mac swears there aren't any ghosts at Dunroamin," she argued, the comment causing an unexpected tightening in her chest. "I asked him."

Honoria scoffed. "That one wouldn't own to a bogle's presence if one bit him on the nose. Ask your auntie about the lass. She'll tell you the truth of it."

"Aunt Birdie saw her?"

"Och, nae, but she understands the possibilities."

The housekeeper paused to run a finger along the edge of a dark oaken table set into a wall niche. She frowned when the finger came away dust smeared.

Cilla waited, not really wanting to talk about ghosts, but curious all the same.

Honoria drew a breath. "The maid's name was Margaret MacDonald," she revealed, her voice dropping. "She was a local lass, born right here in the shadow of Ben Hope and Ben Loyal. Fair, she was, with a head of dark curls and a bright, dimpled smile. Not a day passed that she wasn't smiling or laughing. Until"—she paused, her eyes glittering in the lamplight—"she caught the laird's eye."

"He seduced her." Cilla already knew. "Then he sent her away pregnant."

"Aye, so it was," the housekeeper confirmed. "But the only place he sent her was into a hidey-hole behind the bricks of one of the chimneys."

"He walled her up?"

Honoria nodded. "Word was put about that she jumped off a cliff, heartbroken over the death of a local gallant who'd lost his life at Culloden. But she started appearing not long thereafter, and the truth came out."

Cilla swallowed. "Her body was found?"

"Aye, it was. But not till repairs were done on the chimney in the early 1900s." They'd reached the top of the main stair, and the housekeeper turned to look at her. "The laird confessed the deed on his deathbed, though he didn't have the breath to reveal where he'd put her."

"That's horrible." Cilla shuddered as they began descending the stairs. "Is she still seen?"

"Not these days, and there's little chance of her appearing again, so you needn't worry." Honoria's pace turned brisk, her tweed skirt swishing. "Your Uncle Mac was the last soul to see her."

"Uncle Mac?" Cilla couldn't believe it. "He's the greatest skeptic there is."

"He wasn't when he was three years old." Honoria stopped on the landing. "He just doesn't remember seeing her," she said, her mouth quirking. "He was ill with a fever and she sat on a chair in his room for a week, watching over him and singing to him until he recovered."

"She was worried about him and wanting to help." The idea squeezed Cilla's heart. "Not being able to have her own babe, she tried to nurture other ones."

"That's what we believe, just." Honoria peered back up the way they'd come, her gaze on the shadows at the top of the stairs. "She only ever showed herself if a child of the house fell seriously ill. Once the danger passed, she'd leave. Your uncle was the last child reared at Dunroamin. Now, with the residents all being of a certain age, we suspect she's found her peace."

"Or she's moved on to look after little ones elsewhere?" Cilla's voice hitched on the words.

Margaret MacDonald's story put a different spin on ghosts.

She sympathized with the heartbroken serving girl.

"I hope she's well. . . . Wherever she is."

"Ach, she'll be feeling better than me with my knees e'er aching from traipsing up and down these stairs." Honoria dusted her jacket sleeve, all business again. "Come now, and we'll sit you down in front of the library fire and you'll have a cup of tea to warm you."

"That'd be nice," Cilla lied, certain she'd soon need the loo again if she had to drink more tea.

What she needed was a hot shower and a bed.

But when she opened the library door a few moments later, rather than book-lined walls and tables spread for tea, it was a teetering assortment of all manner of containers that greeted her.

Plastic buckets, old pitchers and jugs, and even seed trays and empty tin cans filled the doorway, each unlikely item crammed so tightly together she couldn't see anything but darkness beyond the towering pile.

"Yikes!" She jumped when a broken-handled casserole pot rolled off its perch and tumbled forward, nearly conking her on the head before it bounced onto the carpeted floor with a dull thud. "What's all this?"

"Not the library." The housekeeper was right behind her. "That's the closet where we keep buckets and whatnot to catch the drips from the roof."

"The roof leaks?" Cilla couldn't believe it.

"Aye, it does." Honoria snatched up the casserole pot. "Only in the worst rainstorms, but then the plink-plinkety-plonks of the dripping water is so loud that a body can't hear itself think."

"Aunt Birdie and Uncle Mac didn't mention—"

"There'll be much they haven't told you about the goings-on at Dunroamin, but"—the housekeeper caught her eye—"you'll be hearing it soon enough."

"Aunt Birdie told me there are difficulties." Cilla stepped aside as the older woman thrust the casserole pot back into the chaos and shut the closet door. "Do you think someone deliberately damaged the roof?"

"Age and wear damaged the roof and naught else." Honoria started down the corridor again. "Though I can tell you that your aunt and uncle meant to have the roof repaired some while ago and would have done if business hadn't taken such a bad turn."

"Oh, dear." Cilla hurried after her, hot shower and bed forgotten. "Water drips can do all kinds of damage to an old house like this."

"Exactly." Honoria didn't break stride. "And that's just what we suspect certain bodies are hoping."

"But who would want to hurt Uncle Mac and Aunt Birdie?"

"Someone up to no good is who." The housekeeper's voice was sharp. "And one thing is sure as I'm standing here"—she stopped before a magnificent carved oak door, one hand on the latch—"it isn't ghosties what's causing the furor."

Cilla blinked. "Ghosties?"

Behind her, she thought she heard a rustle of wool. Kilted wool—she knew the sound well—coming closer, as if to listen in on their conversation.

Unfazed, the housekeeper sniffed.

"Aye, ghosties, if one was of a mind to believe such twaddle."

"I thought you believed in them."

"Ach, and I do right enough." Her tone rang with conviction. "But there are ghosties and *ghosties*, and I'll no' be buying that a gaggle of them want to scare away Dunroamin's paying residents."

Leaning close, she pinned Cilla with a stare. "I don't just work here, see you? I live and breathe this house. I know every creaking floorboard, every groan in the woodwork, each sticking window, and which shutters rattle in the night wind."

She straightened, her hand still on the door latch.

"I also know Dunroamin's ghosts. The bogles we have here, such as poor Margaret MacDonald, love Dunroamin and would never seek to frighten folk."

Cilla wasn't so sure about that, but before she could voice an opinion, the housekeeper swung open the library door and three things leapt at her, chasing Honoria and her bogles from her mind.

One, she'd never seen so much plaid.

Though the requisite mahogany bookcases lined the walls and the handsome fire surround gleamed in the expected black marble and the usual ancestral portraits held pride of place throughout the large room, a palette of tartanware covered every other inch of available space.

Heavy velvet drapes styled the windows in a sett of deep red squares and stripes. Instead of the customary Persian carpets, richly patterned plaid rugs lent warmth to the wide-planked polished floor, while tartan wallpaper peeked from between the bookshelves, gilded picture frames, and occasional molting stag heads.

Even the scattered sofas and wing chairs welcomed in various-shaded tartan dress, some offering the additional comfort of several folded plaid blankets and stout tartan-covered ottomans.

In short, the library bulged plaid.

Cilla blinked, the colorful array almost hurting her eyes.

The housekeeper, clearly immune, strode past her into the candlelit room. Looking wholly in her element, she made straight for a long, tartan-draped table near a wall of tall, mullioned windows.

Spread for tea with generous servings of oatcakes and cheeses, cakes and chocolate-dipped biscuits, and large silver platters of salmon and thin-sliced roast beef, it wasn't the tartan tablecloth that took Cilla by surprise—not after seeing the room—but the two multiarmed candelabrums illuminating the tea goods.

Real wax tapers burned in the wall sconces, as well,

and a quick glance around showed no modern lighting at all.

Today's world treads easy at Dunroamin, and our residents appreciate feeling embraced by earlier times.

Aunt Birdie's words—spoken years ago in Yardley—rushed back to Cilla now. Dunroamin really was like a living history museum; a place where those who loved old things could take refuge.

Only the dear old things she'd expected to find crowding the library, listening to Uncle Mac's afternoon tea talk by the fire, proved so scarce in number they could be counted on one hand.

And that was the second thing that surprised her upon entering the room.

The third, and most alarming, was Uncle Mac himself.

Larger than life as he was, he couldn't be missed and Cilla spotted him right away, despite the dimness of the shadowy, candlelit room.

As expected, he strode to and fro before a crackling hearth fire, his pipe in one hand and a glittering crystal dram glass in the other.

He was definitely holding court, emphasizing each booming word with a grand flourish of his smoke-trailing pipe. His reflection in the huge gilt mirror above the mantelpiece gave the illusion that two Uncle Macs paced there, kilt-swinging, red-faced, and agitated.

Cilla froze.

She lifted a hand to her breast and shook her head.

Then she blinked and knuckled her eyes, but she hadn't been mistaken.

Uncle Mac—a man who defined merriment—was furious.

And he was ranting about ghosts.

Viking ghosts.

Chapter 4

"Vikings, my eye!"

Mac MacGhee stabbed the air with his pipe. "I dinna care who says they saw a ghostly band of horn-helmeted Norsemen slinking past my peat banks—I say they saw bog mist!"

Cilla stared at him, too surprised to step out of the shadows near the door.

She did press a hand to her cheek. She needed it there to keep her jaw from dropping.

She'd never seen her uncle so upset.

That he was stood beyond question. His ruddy face glowed apple red, and he'd swelled his great barrel chest like an enraged Highland bull.

"If not bog mist"—he glared at his audience from behind a cloud of cherry-scented smoke—"then sea haar."

"Here, here." A dapper-looking gentleman with a bald pate and a trim silver mustache puffed at his own pipe and nodded enthusiastic agreement.

Uncle Mac swung toward him. "Next they'll be seeing mermaids swimming in the Kyle!"

"Jolly right." Silver Mustache shifted in an over-stuffed plaid chair and crossed his legs, revealing heavy hill-walking boots that struck an odd contrast to his neat gray suit. "Mist or moon glow, I say they also took a dram too many before they went to bed."

"Pah!" A tiny white-haired woman seared him with a stare. "I know what I saw and I'll not have either of you say me otherwise."

An equally petite woman caning her way to the well-laden tea table took her side. "Just because neither of you saw them doesn't mean they weren't there."

Reaching the table, she began helping herself to a generous serving of roast beef and boiled potatoes. "Only the other night, I heard whooping out over the moors. Shouts, they were, and in no language of this day!"

"You heard geese." Uncle Mac glowered at her.

She waved the serving fork at him. "I heard Vikings! I'd recognize their yells anywhere," she declared, jutting her chin. "I'm of Norse descent, after all."

Uncle Mac snorted.

Show me a Highlander who isn't, Cilla thought she heard him grumble beneath his breath.

The first old dear—the white-haired one—leaned forward then. "Leo saw them, too," she announced, stroking the little black-and-tan dachshund curled on her lap. "He growled at them out my window."

"Hah!" Silver Mustache slapped his thigh. "Like as not, your fool bird was sitting on the ledge."

"Leo doesn't growl at Gregor." The tiny woman sat back in her chair, looking smug. "Only you."

A flurry of coughs and titters rippled through the library.

"Enough!" Uncle Mac tossed down his whisky and sent a warning look to the other residents.

Silver Mustache and the tiny woman exchanged challenging glares.

"Becalm yourselves." Honoria stepped between them, bearing cups of tea and a plate of chocolate biscuits. "Whatever was seen, we'll soon get to the bottom of it."

It was then that Cilla saw the shield.

Round, studded, and looking suspiciously familiar, it appeared to *hover* in the shadows near one of the Jacobean window bays.

She sucked in her breath when it settled on a cushioned window seat, perfectly upright as if someone had propped it against the leaded panes.

Propped, or held it.

Her heart began to thump and she started to back out of the room, but a swirl of her aunt's exotic perfume enfolded her, announcing Aunt Birdie's arrival just as she appeared at Cilla's side.

Across the room, Silver Mustache pointed the stem of his pipe at the housekeeper. "I say it'd serve better if you passed around digestive biscuits rather than chocolate ones."

He slid a narrow-eyed look at the white-haired woman sitting near him. "I've some chewable tablets in my room if that should fail."

"I do not suffer from indigestion." The woman purposely bit into a chocolate-coated biscuit. "Though"— she dabbed at her mouth with a linen napkin—"you could easily give it to me."

"Maybe I should just slip up to my room." Cilla spoke low, her gaze on the shield.

"Oh, don't mind them." Aunt Birdie clearly didn't see the thing. "Those two always bicker."

"Even so—" Cilla jumped when the shield moved.

Only a few inches, but still . . .

It'd slid sideways, as if someone pushed it out of the way to sit down.

She swallowed.

Aunt Birdie's eyes twinkled, her attention still on the two warring residents.

Happily oblivious to anything else, she hooked an elegantly manicured hand through Cilla's arm.

"That's Colonel Achilles Darling from Bibury in Gloucestershire—the northern Cotswolds—and Violet

Manyweathers," she confided, leaning close. "The colonel joined us after his wife's death. Word is, his one great love was a Strathnaver lass from these parts. He never forgot her, or so the tale goes, so when he could, he came north to finally be near her."

"Violet Manyweathers?"

Surely the two weren't lovebirds.

"Oh, no." Aunt Birdie shook her head. "The colonel's long-lost love died years ago. She's buried nearby. Violet is local. She was born in Melness, the tiny crofting hamlet just down the road."

Cilla nodded.

It was hard to concentrate knowing *he* sat in the window seat.

She glanced down, making certain that her top wasn't clinging too tightly. It'd been bad enough to have her nipples pucker when he'd swept her with such a heated look in the stair tower.

Something told her then and there that he was a breast man, and that was definitely where he'd fixed his gaze now.

She could feel it sliding over her. Dipping into the deep-shadowed swells of her cleavage and gliding round to caress and explore every nuance of her sleek, weighty fullness. The way she grew heavier beneath his stare and the sweet, hot-pulsing thrill of knowing his gaze on her.

Much to her annoyance, it was a pleasurable sensation.

Embarrassed, she tilted her chin in the air and hoped her aunt would think the room's chill was responsible for her jutting, tightened nipples.

"Manyweathers doesn't sound like a Strathnaver name." She jumped on the chance to get her mind off of Mr. Wasn't-Really-There and his nipple-stirring stares.

She also didn't want to think of Margaret MacDonald, Dunroamin's onetime nursery ghost whose sad plight, if true, implied that ghosts could have wholly legitimate reasons for walking among the living.

If *he* had a valid reason for haunting Dunroamin, she was sure she didn't want to know it. Hoping she looked no more than mildly curious, she tapped a finger to her chin and pretended to ponder.

"Are you sure Violet's from around here?"

"Oh yes." Aunt Birdie glanced at the tiny woman. "She married an Englishman—Mr. Manyweathers of London—and, like the colonel, decided to come here when she found herself alone. She missed the far north and claims she never adjusted to London."

"And Gregor?" Cilla already knew Leo the dachshund was Dunroamin's resident mascot. "Violet's bird?"

Aunt Birdie smiled. "He's a great skua. Violet—"

"A great *what*?" Cilla's eyes widened.

Now she did have something else to think about. She'd expected a canary or a parakeet.

"Great skua," Aunt Birdie repeated. "They're large brown predatory birds also known as bonxies." Her gaze flicked to the colonel. "Violet found him abandoned with an injured wing when he was just a wee little thing. It was quite a sensation, as bonxies usually nest in the moorlands of the Northern Isles. Violet nursed him back to health. She set him free in due time, but he decided to stay."

"In her room?"

"Heavens, no." Aunt Birdie's eyes twinkled. "Gregor lives outside, though he doesn't stray far. What he does do"—she leaned close to whisper in Cilla's ear—"is make the colonel's life miserable. That's why he wears those heavy boots and a deerstalker hat."

Cilla glanced at him, just now noticing the tweedy dual-rimmed cap with the telltale side flaps on a small table beside his chair.

"The bird dive-bombs him?"

Aunt Birdie nodded. "He has, yes. That's what bonxies do. They swoop down on anyone they view as a threat. Gregor"—she waved a hand as if to lighten the bird's transgressions—"mostly just pecks at the colonel's feet whenever he dares to go outside."

Cilla laughed. She couldn't help it. "That's why the colonel and Violet don't get along?"

"One reason, yes." Aunt Birdie urged her forward. "The colonel can be difficult. He's a bit particular. But come, meet everyone for yourself."

Before Cilla let her aunt pull her out of the shadows, her gaze snapped to the window bay.

There—she was sure—sat the only soul she really wanted to meet.

Well, the only soul she'd wish to meet if he were really there.

But the shield was gone.

And if he was still sitting there—or standing, for all she knew—she couldn't see him.

Not even a dust mote stirred.

She did see the drifting mist outside. It was thinning, though, and pale evening sun now glinted off the tall, many-paned windows. But *he* was definitely gone. Instead, prisms of light slanted across the polished oaken floor and scattered tartan rugs.

Through the windows, she caught glimpses of a paved terrace hemmed by an herbaceous border and a wide sweep of velvety green lawn, the latter bounded by a dry stone wall that looked to be smothered beneath a welter of climbing roses.

Beyond the wall, rough slopes of heather and rock-strewn moors rolled steadily away toward the majestic Ben Loyal, the empty hills sparse save scattered thickets of yellow-blooming whin and broom.

Cilla shivered.

She didn't know about horn-helmeted Vikings, but

regardless of Uncle Mac's opinion, she could well imagine other kinds of ghosts choosing such a wild and lonely landscape as their favorite haunting ground.

Kilted ghosts, long disappeared from history, but still alive in the Celtic twilight.

Her heart began to thump.

She could almost see him out there.

Proud, daring, and take-her-breath-away handsome, he'd stride the hills, ever ready to blood his sword in the name of clan and glory.

He'd also know how to turn a perfectly innocent bed of heather into a scene of such hot, ravishing seduction, the lucky female he chose to devour would be left so sated and limp-limbed she wouldn't be able to walk for a week!

Oh yes, she could well see him doing that.

If he did it wearing his kilt, the lass might not ever recover.

And she'd obviously let the library's Highland flummery get to her!

"The view can grab you, I know." Aunt Cilla spoke right from her mind.

Cilla started. "I—"

She broke off when she caught a faint drift of sandalwood and musk coming from the window bay.

He was back!

For one tantalizing moment, she thought she saw him there. All hot and sensual Highland male, his dark, heated gaze almost burning her. He sat perfectly still, his gold armband and the brass studs on his shield catching the light on the ancient glass panes.

"Grab her, the curls o' my beard!" Uncle Mac joined them, and the image vanished. "She's made of sterner stuff than to stand making moon eyes at the moors. Unlike—" he flashed a look at his wife— "some people I know."

A chorus of chortles echoed around the room as a handful of elderly heads bobbed agreement.

Colonel Darling lifted his pipe. "Here, here!" he cried, a smoke wreath curling round his shining pate.

Aunt Birdie only smiled. "Moon eyes, you say?" She tilted her fair head. "If it restores your good cheer to say so, dear, I'm all for it."

Uncle Mac met her calm with belligerence. "Any chieftain worth his salt would sour on hearing about *Vikings* tramping round in his peat banks!"

"Viking ghosts," Violet corrected.

Ignoring her, Uncle Mac slung an arm around Cilla's shoulders. "Come, those of you still wanting to harp on that string! Hear what my sensible young niece from America has to say about marauding Norsemen."

"Ahhh . . ." Cilla shot another glance at the windows. A cloud must've passed over the sun because the garden and rolling moorland beyond now stood in shadow. "I'm sure there are no ghostly Vikings out there."

It was the best she could do.

She was sure there weren't any Vikings on the moors.

Unfortunately, she really could imagine *him* out there. But no one needed to know that.

"I'd think that if there were Viking ghosts about," she added, just because Uncle Mac was still watching her from under his eyebrows, "they'd rather haunt the Northern Isles or the Hebrides, don't you?"

"Aye, they would!" Her uncle's voice rang with triumph. "Shetland and Orkney is where they'd be. Sure as there's dew on morning grass!"

Rocking back on his heels, he curled his hands beneath his belt. "Folk in those isles are more Norse than Scottish, even today."

"Be that as it may"—Violet Manyweathers set down her teacup—"there were Vikings a-plenty in these parts."

Uncle Mac glared at her, tight-lipped.

"Fool woman." Colonel Darling gave her a look of

palpable annoyance. "If they were here, they aren't now."

"Say you." The tiny woman held her ground. "They go rampaging over the moors almost every night—as I've been saying for weeks."

"If there are such ghosts"—Honoria moved between them again, gliding forward to put a hand on Violet's shoulder—"do you not think they'd be at Balnakeil, on the beach, rather than Dunroamin's peat hags?"

"Balnakeil?" Cilla looked from the housekeeper to her uncle. "Peat hag? Is that a witch?"

Honoria answered her. "Balnakeil is a place, and"—she kept her hand firmly on Violet's shoulder—"a peat hag is a bog. It's where we go to cut peat from the moor."

"Oh." Cilla made a mental note to secure a Scots dictionary.

"It's where the bogles are." The old dear with the cane looked her way. "Those are ghosts," she added, turning her attention back to her roast beef and boiled potatoes.

"Humph." Uncle Mac scowled, his jaw looking more set than ever.

Taking a step toward the semicircle of bright-eyed if elderly residents, he shook a finger at the diminutive female with a walking stick propped against her chair.

"Dinna you start down that road, as well, Flora Duthie," he scolded. "Peat, plaid, and whisky is the true grit o' any Highlander, with a touch o' pipe skirl tossed in for good measure. But"—he snapped his brows together, fixing her with a scowl—"leave the Celtic whimsy to tourists and incomers soft-minded enough to buy into the like."

Flora Duthie popped a boiled potato into her mouth and scowled back at him.

"Buy into?" She aimed her fork at a succulent slice

of roast beef. "Centuries of believing in Highland magic canna be so easily erased."

"Highland magic!" Uncle Mac poured himself a second dram. "Much as we at Dunroamin strive to live in the past"—he gulped down the whisky—"this *is* the twenty-first century."

"Then what's with Balnakeil?" Cilla eyed him, some sixth sense warning her that the place was important.

Proving it, he slapped down the dram glass and began pulling on his beard.

He was clearly pretending not to have heard her.

"A Viking grave was found there." Aunt Birdie enlightened her. "Not all that long ago, either. The discovery was quite by accident, the burial site only revealed when storm winds shifted a sand dune. It was a boy's grave, but filled with all manner of Norse goods."

A chill slid down Cilla's spine.

She rubbed her arms. "So there were Vikings here?"

"Balnakeil is at Durness." Uncle Mac remained stubborn. " 'Tis miles away around the whole of Loch Eriboll and nigh to Cape Wrath!"

"And you're after saying that makes a difference?" Violet sat up straighter. On her lap, Leo barked. "The distance between here and Balnakeil Bay—or anywhere—didn't matter to the poor souls who've left Dunroamin."

She leaned back in her chair, stroking the dachshund's ears. "They knew something strange was—"

"Perhaps they left because of your pesky skua?" Colonel Darling waved his pipe at her. "That bird will be the reason, and not ghostly bands of yelling Vikings."

"Every resident who left saw them." Violet rested her case. "They told me so."

Leo barked again, clearly in agreement.

"They told me, as well." Uncle Mac swelled his

chest. "That doesn't mean they weren't seeing bog mist."

He shot a glance at Cilla. "You Yanks call it swamp gas, I'm thinking?"

She nodded, scarce hearing him.

The shield was back.

This time it was floating back and forth in front of the windows—as if someone held it at waist level or lower as he paced.

Cilla swallowed, her eyes widening.

Around her, voices rose and fell as her aunt and uncle and Dunroamin's residents argued about Viking ghosts and the likelihood—or not—of them haunting Uncle Mac's peat banks. The words soon became an indistinguishable buzz, the rush of her own pulse in her ears blotting the din.

No one else seemed to see the shield.

She couldn't take her eyes off it.

Nor could she deny that the library no longer smelled of just wood smoke and lemon polish, old books, and leather, but overwhelmingly of sandalwood and musk.

And not just a faint whiff of it clinging to the window bay.

O-o-oh, no.

Heady, rich, and darkly masculine, the scent surrounded her. Pervading the air, its spicy manliness seduced. Once again she felt strong, powerful arms closing around her. She remembered, too, the hardness of a plaid-draped, muscled chest and the grip of capable hands holding her firm.

Long, manly fingers splayed a tad too intimately across her hip.

Her face flamed. Everyone knew what they said about men with long, well-formed fingers.

She bit her lip.

Whether it meant she was going around the bend or not, the thought of the hot-eyed kiltie's *fingers* set more butterflies flittering in her belly than Grant A. Hughes III had ever given her.

Him and every other boyfriend she'd known.

She drew a tight breath. Then she willed the ghost— or whatever he was—to show himself along with his infernal shield.

But if he even was the one holding it, he remained invisible.

Temptingly close, but out of her grasp.

Then the shield vanished as quickly as it'd appeared, almost as if it'd been whisked out of thin air.

His luscious scent evaporated, too. Disappearing as if she'd imagined it.

She angled her head and tried to sniff as discreetly as possible—only to have Flora Duthie cane her way over to her, offering an orange blossom–scented, lace-edged hanky.

"Here, my dear." The woman's rheumy eyes brimmed with understanding. "It's a cold, wet summer, just," she observed, nodding sagely. "I, too, have the bug."

Cilla took the blessedly clean-looking handkerchief and mumbled thanks.

Not that she'd registered half of what the old woman had said.

In the moment she'd hobbled up to Cilla, something in the library shifted. A there one minute, gone the next *whoosh* of cold air where there should have been none, next to the fireplace.

Or simply a shivering across her soul, a sifting of time and space no one else noticed.

Then that sensation, too, was gone.

What remained was the reckless knowledge that she didn't want him to go.

Ghost, product of jet lag, victim of a plight such as Margaret MacDonald's or whatever, he excited her more than he could ever frighten her.

Not that she cared to admit anything so unwise. So she did what she could do.

She frowned.

Over by the Jacobean window bay, Bran of Barra grinned.

"Heigh-ho!" He waved Hardwick's shield above his head, his eyes dancing with merriment. "I thought you were done with this thing?"

Hardwick ignored his question. "I thought you went back to your island keep?"

"Eh?" Bran feigned astonishment. "Why should I miss all the fun here? Besides, I'm thinking you need someone to look out for you."

Hardwick snorted. "Were that so, you can be sure it wouldn't be you."

"Hah! You ought to count your blessings I deigned to come see you."

Hardwick gave his longtime friend and sometimes nemesis a pointed look.

"I came here to get away from my old life," he said, trying not to let his annoyance show.

Or that he really was glad-hearted for Bran's jovial company.

"You mean your *afterlife*." Bran made the shield vanish just long enough to raise his arms above his head and crack his knuckles. "We ghosts do have our limitations."

Hardwick glared at him, his gladness fading.

"Glower all you will." Bran lowered his arms." I say your wits have left you."

"I've only lost that which has plagued me for centuries." Hardwick brushed at his sleeve. "There's naught wrong with my wits."

Bran arched a bushy red brow.

"Say you? That's twice now you've kept yourself invisible but forgot to cloak your shield." He leapt backward when Hardwick tried to snatch it from him. "You should be more careful. The lass can see you."

"She saw you, too." Hardwick pretended to examine his knuckles, then whirled to grab his shield.

Success his, he flashed a smile. "You should learn to watch for feints. For a Hebridean chieftain, you're slow on your reflexes."

Bran laughed. "Because I am such a great chieftain indeed, I have no need of sharp reflexes." Eyes twinkling, he leaned close. "Did you no ken, Seagrave, that I'm so feared, there isn't a soul in all broad Scotland daring enough to sail to Barra to challenge me!"

"This isn't Barra."

"To be sure, it isn't." Bran's blue gaze shifted, latching on to the delectable rounds of Cilla Swanner's buttocks. "I dinna think I've e'er enjoyed such a sweetmeat in my bed. . . . Er"—he coughed, then pounded his chest with a balled fist—"in my *hall*."

"You frightened her." Hardwick took hold of his friend's bearded chin and angled his head away from the girl. "See it doesn't happen again."

"I knew that was the way the cat jumped!" Bran's face split in a grin. "But I'll no' believe I scared her, handsome lad that I am. Now, yourself—"

"What she thinks of me scarce matters." Hardwick tightened his grip on his shield. "She means even less to me, much as I'd like to see her gone."

Bran applied himself to smoothing the folds of his plaid, his lips twitching. "You've a strange way o' showing indifference."

Hardwick harrumphed.

His friend—if he was even wont to still consider him one—clapped him on the shoulder. "Dinna mind me," the lout said, smiling cheerily. "Seeing as I've yet to lose my heart, I shouldn't speak in judgment."

"Nae, you shouldn't." Hardwick turned toward the windows and assumed a casual stance, his gaze on the rolling moorland beyond the garden wall.

Across the library, gasps and disgruntled murmurs

rose at something one of the graybeards said, and Hardwick's frown returned.

He wasn't at all pleased by the things he'd heard since following *her* into the plaid-festooned room.

Dunroamin's troubles were not his own.

He shouldn't get involved.

"If you're truly wishing to see her gone," Bran spoke from beside him, "perhaps one of the raiding Norsemen will take her off your hands. They're known to favor blue-eyed, flaxen-haired wenches."

Hardwick slid him a disgusted look.

Bran shrugged. "The gel does have the look o' the North about her."

"And you have the clapper tongue of an old woman." Hardwick glared at him. "Dinna tempt me to cut it from you!"

"Ach, but you wound me." Bran laughed.

Looking anything but offended, he plucked a cup of ale out of the air and took a long swallow. "I only sought to ease your mind, since the lass clearly occupies it. If the Vikings snatched her—"

"There aren't any Vikings here."

"So you say."

"So I know." Hardwick turned his attention back on the thin mist drifting across the moors. "Think you I wouldn't have noticed them?"

"Yon graybeards think they're here." Bran dropped down onto a window seat and stretched out his legs, crossing them at the ankles. "Did you not know the folk here have been fashing about the like?"

"Nae, I didn't know." Hardwick didn't bother to keep the annoyance out of his voice. He'd been keeping an eye out for sag-breasted, knotty-fingered hell hags, not Vikings. "I haven't heard them speak of it until now. I'm a ghost, no' a mind reader."

"There does appear to be trouble afoot here. If I were you, I'd—"

"And if I were you"—Hardwick spun around to

face him—"I'd no' be getting so comfortable on that window seat. Isn't it about time you take yourself back to the lovelies whiling their time at your keep?"

Bran grinned.

Then he lifted his ale cup to his lips, sipping with deliberate leisure. "As you well know, my men and those who deign to visit my hall are more than able to see to the needs of my feminine guests."

Hardwick scowled at him.

Heat began inching up the back of his neck.

Blessedly, nary a trace of it slid across his loins. His best piece remained at ease. Unlike in days of old when the mere thought of the enticements of Bran's hall flamed his blood and sent him hastening to sift himself into the midst of his longtime friend's continuous *joy fests*.

Unfortunately, he was almost certain his newfound loss of interest in Bran's beauties had something to do with Cilla Swanner.

He risked a glance at her, but jerked his gaze away almost as quickly.

Saints above, she was kneeling on the floor!

No longer standing about frowning, she'd dropped to all fours, her well-rounded buttocks lifted in the air. Plump and delectable, they pointed right at him, bobbing temptingly as if she were offering herself to him.

And in a boldly erotic manner few red-blooded men could resist.

Ghostly or otherwise.

He clenched his hands on his shield and bit back a curse as the heat at the back of his neck flashed through him, spreading everywhere.

Including there.

Just where he didn't need it.

It took all his strength not to whip back around and goggle her, and even more to keep himself from running full rock-granite hard.

He'd known modern-day women could be brazen, but ne'er would have believed this one would resort to such a siren's trick to win his attention.

And in full view of her aunt and uncle!

Not to mention Dunroamin's guests.

"She's no' trying to tempt you." Bran's amused voice drawled from the window bay. "She's petting the wee dog. Leo's his name, I'm thinking?"

The heat sweeping Hardwick chilled at once.

His racing pulse slowed.

"I know that," he lied, glancing back at her.

She was sitting now. A vision on one of the tartan rugs, her legs crossed, as she rubbed the belly of the squirming, waggy little dog.

"Ach, to be sure you knew." Bran pushed to his feet, mirth all over him.

Hardwick stood frozen. Embarrassment flooded him as never before.

How could he have missed the wee beastie?

"I didn't see the dog right away, either," Bran said, making Hardwick wonder if, unlike him, being a ghost had made his friend a mind reader.

"But"—Bran smoothed his plaid and dusted his sleeve—"having seen your lass's . . . eh . . . better bits bouncing about like that, I'm of a mind to leave you now."

"She isn't my lass." Hardwick couldn't let that go.

She wasn't his and never could be.

Bran threw back his head and laughed. "Whate'er you say, my friend."

"I say you all speed back to Barra." It was the best the scoundrel would get out of him. "My felicitations to—"

"I'm no' heading to Barra. No' just yet, anyway."

"Then where?"

"Ach, see you . . ." Bran threw a meaningful glance across the room. "I've a sudden hankering for a big-bosomed, broad-hipped Norse lassie. Your flaxen-haired lovely is taken and"—he winked—"truth be told, she isn't plump enough for my taste. So it's Lerwick town for me."

Hardwick's brows lifted. "Shetland?"

"So I said, aye." Grinning broadly, the Hebridean cut a shapely female form in the air. "Where better to find such a delight?"

"Where else, indeed," Hardwick agreed, some annoyingly sentimental part of him wishing his friend would stay.

He glanced out the window again, not at all pleased with the day.

Something told him there truly was trouble brewing at Dunroamin, and he had a feeling he'd soon find himself in the thick of it.

Especially since *her* arrival.

If Vikings really were rampaging across Mac Mac-Ghee's peat fields at night, they might just seize the lass if they caught sight of her.

Norsemen were notorious wenchers.

And even if he'd once borne that title himself, he was also known for his chivalry.

A credo that wouldn't allow him to stand idle and watch harm come to Cilla Swanner.

Or anyone else at Dunroamin.

He'd grown fond of the lot of them.

Just as he was fond of Bran of Barra and wouldn't mind him at his back if such a need arose.

But when he turned to tell him so, the Hebridean was gone.

Only the faint warmth of his smile remained. The fast-fading echo of his laughter. Then those remnants vanished, as well, leaving Hardwick alone.

Luckily—or perhaps not—he'd also left Hardwick with a plan.

Claiming the spot Bran had vacated on the window seat, Hardwick settled his shield across his knees and started to think about it.

There was, after all, much to consider.

Not that it mattered. Bran's blather about Shetland and the upsetting discourse still going on across the library gave him little choice but to prepare.

Frowning, he snatched an ale cup of his own from the air.

He drained it in one gulp.

What he meant to do wasn't exactly how he'd planned to spend his time here.

But lying in wait for marauding Norsemen was a good deal better than moping about waiting for Cilla Swanner to tempt him again.

A good deal better, indeed.

Chapter 5

Several hours, a haggis-stuffed chicken breast, and way too many cups of tea later, Cilla stood in the middle of her room's spacious, splendidly appointed bathroom and took back everything she'd thought earlier about the lavish amenities being all twenty-first century.

The claw-foot bathtub hailed from the Dark Ages.

And the shower was criminal.

Most annoying of all, she'd stubbed her toe when she'd spent at least ten minutes stumbling about, trying to figure out how to turn on the bathroom lights.

And her toe still hurt!

She might even have broken it.

Refusing to acknowledge the pain pulsing up her leg, she gritted her teeth and clutched the edge of the fancy marble sink instead.

Soon, the hot throbbing would lessen.

She hoped.

"Geez Louise, Uncle Mac . . ." She tightened her grip on the sink and flashed a glare at the culprit, the oh-so-innocuous main power switch.

Who would've thought it'd be hidden inside an innocent-looking Victorian vanity?

Honoria, at least, could have warned her.

Certainly Aunt Birdie.

She knew American bathrooms—even ones in cheapo

apartment complexes like Cilla's own Colonial Arms in Yardley—boasted bathrooms that worked.

Especially the lights.

She frowned and allowed herself a tiny whimper.

Her toe *did* hurt.

Her scowl deepened. She'd known Scots prided themselves on being thrifty—a talent she certainly wouldn't argue with, given her own dire financial straits—but was it really necessary to have a hidden power switch to flick in order to make the light panel work?

Worse yet, to then hide that all-important lever in a place no one would ever dream to look?

It was almost too much to fathom.

And now that she had light, she couldn't get the shower to work right.

It, too, appeared to be controlled by a box.

No such thing as just turning it on and stepping into the too-tall claw-foot tub, pulling the curtain tight, and enjoying a cascade of steamy, pounding water.

Oh, no.

First you had to fiddle with a maze of buttons and switches that apparently heated and regulated a stream of water best described as a trickle or a blast, with nothing whatsoever between.

And—heaven help her—the temperature choices were only two: scalding hot or iceberg cold.

Cilla gritted her teeth and glared at the icy droplets dripping from the shower head.

She turned the knob a fraction of a hair's breadth and nearly scorched herself on the geyserlike rush of boiling water that burst forth.

"Owwww!" She leapt back, shaking her arm against the stinging heat and slamming her hip into the protruding edge of the hard marbled sink.

She glared at the shower, not at all surprised when it dwindled to nothing again. She didn't have to thrust her hand under the dribbles to know they'd be frigid.

"Sheesh." Shaking her head, she rubbed her hip. It pulsed in time with the throbbing in her toe.

If this was Scotland, she wanted nothing to do with the place.

A daily shower was a necessity, after all.

Determined to have hers, she threw down the towel she'd wrapped around herself and climbed into the slippery high-sided tub.

Surely, she'd been doing something wrong.

But the instant she touched the shower dial and it made a weird spluttering, hissing noise, she knew better than to try her luck.

It took her all of two seconds to wrench the dial back to the off position. She did briefly consider a full bath, but, once burned, thought better of it and scramble out of the tub before disaster struck.

Her mood now ruined, she yanked a towel off the pleasantly warmed towel bar—thankful for that small luxury—and opted for a cat bath at the sink.

Unfortunately, the two sink faucets proved as diabolical as the shower. While the one marked cold dutifully produced an adequate stream of clear, chilly water, a steaming torrent shot out of the other.

Before she could jump away, the hot water hit the sides of the sink and splashed back up to spray her with a shower of scalding mist.

"Aaaggghhhh!" She flung up her arms, sending the towel sailing. Her feet slid out from under her on the slick tiles.

"Oh, no-o-o!" she cried, catching a glimpse of *him* in the mirror just as she was about to slam into the edge of the tall iron tub.

"O-o-oh, aye." Strong hands seized her, hefting her in the air only to plunk her back onto her feet. But not before she'd felt the warm curve of his hands near her breasts, the tips of his fingers brushing her nipples.

She raised her own hands, splaying them across her nakedness. His sandalwood scent filled the bathroom,

swirling around her and tingeing each indrawn breath.
She shivered, unable to move. He towered over her,
his stare so heated, the air between them seemed to
catch fire.

Cilla swallowed, her heart thundering.

He let his gaze dip briefly to her breasts and lower,
that one bold perusal scorching her in a much more
dangerous way than the scalding shower.

"You!" She stared at him, every wicked, brazen
thought she'd had about him in a bed of heather
whooshing back to make her cheeks burn.

Knowing they must be glowing, she stiffened. "How
dare you appear here, in my—"

"Ach, lass. You'd be surprised at what I'd dare."
He leaned close, his deep voice soft against her ear.
"There isn't aught I—"

A weird gurgling came from the shower. High-
pitched and *screechy*, she would have mistaken it for
the titter of a sniggering old woman if she hadn't
known of the bathroom's peculiarities.

He shot a glance at the curtained bathtub, his brows
snapping together. "I dare appear where and when it
suits me. Be glad it was me here to save you . . .
again."

Cilla's eyes widened. "Are you saying there are
other . . . er . . . *ghosts* who could have?"

His big, gorgeous body tensed and his mouth com-
pressed into a tight, hard line. A muscle worked in
his jaw and he folded his arms, clearly unwilling to
answer.

Cilla bit her lip, not liking the implication. Nor
could she deny that he'd come to her aid not once,
but twice. Or that, all things considered, he was the
embodiment of her deepest, most heated fantasies,
and that if she needed rescuing she'd much rather
have him appear than whatever was putting such a
frown on his face.

Even so . . .

She raised her chin. "You could have cracked my ribs, grabbing me as you did."

"I warned you I'd no' be gentle a second time."

"You shouldn't be here at all."

His face darkened even more. "Had I known you'd be unclothed, I wouldn't be."

"People don't usually stay dressed to take a shower." She grabbed a towel, whipping it around her. "Do you?"

"I—" He turned a disdainful glance on the claw-foot tub and its wacky *boiler*. "I can think of better ways to keep clean."

Cilla curled her fingers into the towel, clutching it to her breasts. "Such as?"

He jerked his head toward the doorway into her bedroom, where a large wooden tub stood in the shadows.

A tub that hadn't been there when she'd entered the bathroom.

Lined with what appeared to be a length of fine medieval-y white linen, the tub brimmed with steaming rose-scented water she knew without testing would prove bath-oil smooth and just the right temperature.

If the tub were real.

Which, of course, it wasn't.

She frowned and decided to pretend she didn't see it.

His gaze went again to the pesky boiler contraption on the bathroom wall. "Aye, much better," he purred in that silky-deep burr. "My style of bathing is more reliable."

He stood proud, looking sure of it.

She couldn't forget that she was naked. Or that her towel didn't hide much. Something told her Scots tried to save on toweling cloth along with electricity and hot water. And the way *this Scot* slid his dark gaze over her, lingering especially on the swells of her breasts and the curve of her hips, revealed that he thoroughly approved of that thriftiness. At least regarding the size of bath towels.

Never had a man looked at her with such burning hunger in his eyes.

Or set off such a hot pulsing between her legs with nothing more than a glance.

She swallowed, sure he knew it.

The slight arcing of one brow said he did.

"Do you mind?" Her face flaming, she yanked the towel higher up her breasts. "Mister. . . ."

"Sir," he corrected, his sensual lips curving oh so slightly. "Sir Hardwin de Studley of Seagrave."

"De *what*?" Cilla's jaw slipped. She resisted the urge to poke her fingers in her ears and wriggle them.

She couldn't have heard correctly.

Either that or she'd eaten too much of the haggis filling in her chicken ecosse.

"Tell me again." She eyed him, sure it was the haggis. "Who did you say you are?"

"Sir Hardwin de Studley," he repeated, his deep burr rolling. " 'Tis a good Norman Scots name. You won't hear it much nowadays."

"I wouldn't think so."

"Friends call me Hardwick."

That's even worse! Cilla almost blurted, but before she could, he flicked a finger at the wooden tub and it disappeared, his little sleight of ghostly hand making the words lodge in her throat.

"Since you chose no' to avail yourself of it." Sounding as if that were a great shame, he leaned back against the doorjamb and settled himself, his long legs crossed at the ankles.

Cilla stared at him.

He looked much too comfortable lounging so casually in her bathroom doorway.

She couldn't let him stay that way.

Especially not when he continued his tricks, this time making a quick flipping motion with his wrist, and his shield appeared in his hand. Holding it loosely at his side, he smiled at her.

A curl-a-girl's-toes kind of smile she knew better than to let get to her.

The man was all smoke and mirrors.

Walking danger, and she wasn't even going to *think* about how his mere presence made her tingle.

His burr alone could stir a woman to climax.

She'd been hovering on the edge of one ever since his fingers had slid across her nipples. Heaven help her if those long, skilled-looking fingers ever came anywhere close to her clit.

"Look here, Sir Hard-whoever-you-are, I've already told you that your shield trick doesn't impress me." She tossed her hair behind her shoulder. "As for beaming yourself in here when I'm trying to shower, that's just rude."

"Rude?" Hardwick blinked, the heat in her eyes spearing him.

It wasn't the kind of simmer he was accustomed to stirring in women.

"I think, lass"—he pushed away from the door and drew himself to his full height—"that you have no idea what it cost me to be here."

"Then why are you?"

"No' to see you naked!" The words escaped before he could stop them.

"Oh!" Her cheeks bloomed red. "I don't believe this!" she cried, scooting past him out the bathroom door.

Hardwick scowled after her.

Good, if he'd vexed her into leaving.

Unfortunately, he hadn't meant to do it thusly. And watching her dart across the polished—slippery—floor, grab a robe off the bed, and don it in all haste didn't feel like the triumph it should.

It felt rather lousy.

Never had he seen a lass dress so swiftly. And rarely

had he felt such an urge to bite off his tongue. He'd
burned to see more of her nakedness. Ever since
glimpsing her full, round breasts the possibility had
consumed him, unwise as such yearnings were.

He pulled a hand down over his chin, furious with
himself and his plight.

"You misheard me." He spoke to her back, trying
to make it better. "I meant, seeing you unclothed is
the last thing—"

"So you're not only rude, but insulting!" She
whirled on him, her blue eyes ablaze.

"Holy heather!" He jammed his hands on his hips
and stared at her. "You still dinna—"

"I understand perfectly well." She yanked on the
ends of her robe's belt, making a knot. "And I'll ask
you again. Why did you appear in my bathroom?"

"Because I heard you scream."

Her eyes rounded. "You were listening at my door?"

Nae, I was guarding it.

The true answer hung unspoken between them. She
needn't know he was troubled by certain goings-on at
Dunroamin and meant to look into them.

Or that he hoped doing so would help him to keep
his mind off of her.

His mouth twitched on that impossibility.

The great silvery Kyle would sooner dry up and all
the noble peaks of the north slip back into the earth
before he could put her from his mind.

She'd bespelled him more thoroughly than that
wart-nosed, bent-backed bard of old could have done
in his wildest conjuring dreams.

Watching her, he almost laughed at his predicament
and would have if he didn't wish to upset her even
more. Seeing her naked had nearly undone him. Feeling her sleek warm skin, all smooth and wet beneath
his hands when he'd caught her, was a torture he
couldn't risk again.

If he'd held her a moment longer, even the Dark One's threats wouldn't have mattered.

As it was, he'd almost nipped and nuzzled her neck when he'd bent to whisper in her ear. He'd even considered slipping a hand between her legs and using one expertly circling finger to show her the kind of bliss a man could give a woman after seven hundred years of experience.

An urge that was surely responsible for causing one of the hell hags to gurgle a laugh from the shower. In the same moment, he caught a whiff of root-dragon's breath, its foulness chilling his blood.

He blinked against the lingering steam, certain the Dark One's hags and dragons wouldn't sneak so openly into this earthly realm. Yet he swore he saw sharp nails and the flash of a scaly tail.

He shuddered, turning back to Cilla when the image faded.

Even now she tempted him.

Damp, disheveled, and wearing a Dunroamin plaid robe with her name stitched across the breast in ridiculously large letters, she stirred him more than any other lass he'd ever known.

Having seen her naked was a *gift*.

And a worse burden than the curse that had plagued him for so many centuries.

"So?" She was still staring at him, her gaze intent. "Were you eavesdropping or not?"

He frowned. "I have ne'er done the like in my life. Or thereafter."

"Oh, that's right." She swept her hair behind an ear. "Let's not forget you're a ghost."

The words ripped him. "Would that I could."

She narrowed her eyes. "I'd rather hear what you were doing outside my door."

Hardwick considered how much he should tell her.

"Two lads carried coffers up here earlier and I followed them." That was certainly true enough. He just didn't mention he hadn't liked the looks of them.

Tall, red-haired, and strapping, they'd struck him as too young, too bonny, and—most damning of all— too alive.

"Coffers?" She'd come closer, her blue eyes rounding.

Hardwick blinked, the two youths forgotten.

"Aye, coffers." He glanced to where the strong-boxes stood near the shuttered windows. "They looked heavy and—"

"Those aren't coffers."

He surveyed them carefully, certain they were.

To his surprise, she laughed.

Not a mocking sort of laugh, but a light and breezy kind that slid through him with ease, warming him in ways that were more than dangerous.

"Those are packing crates full of chipped and cracked porcelain." She went to stand beside them. "Uncle Mac never throws out anything, and he said I could have them. The boys you saw are Roddie and Robbie, Honoria's nephews. Aunt Birdie mentioned they do odd jobs around the estate. They brought the crates down from the attic."

Hardwick's brows drew together. It annoyed him that she knew the lads' names. Not to mention so much about their business.

Even more irritating, although he considered himself most enlightened to the ways of her world, he'd never heard of *packing crates*.

Nor had he suspected that Mac MacGhee's fortunes had turned so poorly that he'd be forced to give his visiting niece damaged goods as a welcome gift.

The very notion made his heart sore.

"They're beauties." She'd opened the lid of one of the coffers—he refused to think of them as anything else—and withdrew a small flowered cup, lovely save the jagged crack in its side and a rather conspicuous chip at the gold-edged rim. "I've rarely seen such treasures!"

She held up the cream-colored cup for his inspection.

"Er . . . humph." Hardwick found himself at a loss for a suitable comment.

Instead, he stepped closer and examined the cup.

Decorated with pink roses surrounded by smaller flowers in purple, yellow, and blue, the design enhanced with a scattering of delicate green leaves, it would have been a treasure indeed if not so sadly marred.

Surprisingly, she didn't appear at all disheartened by the cup's flaws, which said a great deal about her character. She clearly didn't wish to offend her aunt and uncle by seeming disappointed in their gift.

Hardwick frowned. He didn't like the direction his mind was taking.

It served him better when she speared him with that fiery blue gaze.

For one thing, he now knew beyond doubt that a henwife couldn't claim a hand in the color of her honey-gold hair. That knowledge alone could have dire repercussions if he allowed himself to dwell on *how* he'd made such a discovery.

It was one thing to imagine a sweet triangle of golden curls topping her thighs, all soft and inviting.

And something else entirely to have seen those curls!

Nor had he yet recovered from the pleasant ring of her laughter. How it'd warmed him. Learning she possessed a caring heart along with her fine curves and other charms was more than he wished to know.

"Here's another." She plucked a small flowered plate from deep inside the coffer's strawlike filling. "Who would have thought Uncle Mac's attic would hold such gems?"

"No' I, to be sure." Hardwick tightened his grip on his shield.

Then, because her delight in the pathetic wares apparently overrode her objections to him, he peered dutifully at the plate when she held it in his direction.

Covered with pink and deep-red roses, again with a few artfully placed green leaves and gold trim, this piece, too, had seen better days. A jagged crack zigzagged across its center, marring its onetime perfection.

She didn't seem to see the defect.

Far from it; she beamed at the dish, her excitement clearly mounting when she turned it over and studied its underside.

"English." She ran a finger along the crack, pausing over a line of squiggly black lettering. "Early 1900s, I'm guessing."

Hardwick's gut clenched.

She sounded overjoyed that the plate was not only damaged but, considering her time, quite old.

"Uncle Mac isn't the only one in the family who loves old things," she mused, her eyes misty. "This"—she hugged the cracked dish to her breast—"is just what I needed."

"Nae, it isn't. No' at all." Hardwick couldn't help the denial. Every chivalrous bone in him railed against seeing her so soppy-headed o'er such shameful offerings.

Equally painful was imagining Mac MacGhee's reaction.

A proud man, the laird surely knew his niece deserved better.

Unable to stop himself now that he'd spoken, Hardwick indicated the two coffers with a flick of his hand. "More's the pity your uncle couldn't give you something finer as a welcome gift," he said, hoping his voice held more sympathy than disapproval. "A maid like yourself ought be welcomed with ropes of shining pearls and glittering gemstones, no' cracked and chipped bits of cast-off cups and—"

She laughed.

A beautiful golden sound, rich and honey-edged, but damning in its portent.

Somehow—and he didn't know where—he'd erred.

Just as embarrassing, he'd blethered on like a love-sick calf.

Ropes of pearls and glittering gemstones, indeed!

If Bran had heard him utter the like, he'd be the laughing stock of ghostdom and beyond.

He frowned, already willing himself elsewhere.

Perhaps Mac MacGhee's armory, where he could claim a chair and let scores of targes glower down at him, each one reminding him of his plight and how he'd best hold his tongue—and his lust—around the laird's fetching niece.

Or maybe he'd sift himself out to MacGhee's peat banks and watch for Viking ghosts.

That, after all, had been his original plan before he'd spotted the two redheaded giants, Roddie and Robbie, lugging the *coffers* abovestairs.

Coffers that had somehow managed to make him look the fool again.

He bristled.

It was a mistake he wouldn't make a second time.

"Broken china is my passion." Her words came to him as if from afar.

He watched her return the plate to the coffer, now seeing her and her chipped treasures through the mist beginning to whirl around him.

She didn't notice as the grayness swirled faster, almost cloaking him.

He could have—should have—simply vanished. Leaving in the mist took longer. But despite his embarrassment, he wanted to savor those last lingering moments to admire how her hair, so glossy and bright, spilled across her face as she bent over her prizes.

His heart squeezed, and he damned his curse.

How he'd love to see those fair tresses spread across

her pillow, twine his fingers in the silken strands as he settled himself above her, kissing her. . . .

Then trailing an openmouthed blaze of fire down her naked skin to dip a questing tongue into the slick, sweet heat he knew waited between her thighs.

Hardwick groaned, knowing she'd no longer hear him.

He clenched his fists and drew a tight, uneven breath, willing the mist to spin faster. Once, something hot, dry, and clawlike snatched at his ankle, but he jerked free, keeping his gaze on her.

"The broken china is my work," she said then, still rummaging in the coffer's straw. "I make jewelry from antique porcelain." She picked up a crescent-shaped shard of rich blues, appearing to admire it. "Necklaces, earrings, bracelets, rings, you name it. I even do some wall art, mirrors and stained glass pieces and such. That's why Uncle Mac gave the boxes to me. Not as a welcome gift."

Cilla made a sweeping gesture, taking in the paneled bedroom with its clutter of Victorian gothic furnishings. "I didn't need a welcome present from Uncle Mac. Being here is gift enough," she added, not mentioning how she'd dreamt of coming to Scotland all her life.

How she hoped her time at Dunroamin would fill the emptiness inside her. And not the void left by Grant A. Hughes III. Since Hardwick's arrival in her life, she could hardly even picture Grant's face. But she hadn't designed a thing—not even a beaded hairpin—in weeks.

And that frightened her.

Her creative well was dry.

"Oh yes." She swallowed against the tightness in her throat. "Being here is exactly what I needed."

Humph.

The snort sounded muffled, almost more like the

wind soughing past the window shutters than Hardwick's buttery rich burr.

"In return"—she tucked the bit of Delft china back into the crate—"I've agreed to teach Dunroamin's residents how to make broken china jewelry. Aunt Birdie and Uncle Mac hope that if they have something creative to keep them busy, they won't think so much about the Viking ghosts—"

She broke off and clapped a hand over her mouth.

Heat flamed her face.

Who was she to make light of old folks thinking they saw Viking ghosts running across the moors at night when *she* was standing in the middle of her bedroom having a conversation with one?

When she erupted in a blaze of orgasmic tingles each time he appeared?

"Oh, man." Her entire body went cold and hot at the same time.

What she needed to do was tell him to stop *materializing* everywhere she went. If that was what his sudden appearances out of thin air were called.

She didn't want to be haunted.

And if she was imagining him, she wanted to stop that, too.

It couldn't be good for her.

But when she turned around to tell him so, he was gone.

Her jaw started to slip but she didn't let it. Instead, she put on her best I-am-in-charge look and made a careful circuit of the room, turning on mock Victorian oil lamps as she went. One by one, they cast little pools of softly glowing light, but not near enough to chase the shadows from every empty space and corner.

She paused near the hearth, glad for its cheery birch-and-peat fire.

Much better to continue her survey of the room from here, standing in the warmth and light of the fire, than to keep stalking about with her every footstep echoing off the polished wood floor to unnerve her.

Each *tap-tappity-tap* gave her the willies, making her think someone was sneaking along behind her.

Frowning, she considered just going to bed and pulling the covers over her head.

But her bed—great, dark-wooded four-poster that it was, complete with heavy, embroidered hangings—seemed to hunch in wait for her. As did the other, equally clunky furnishings, each piece appearing to hold its breath in the silence, watching to see what she'd do.

She shivered and rubbed her arms.

"I am not on the set of a bad horror film." She spoke the words slowly, distinctly. "There's nothing any more odd about the shadows in this room than the ones in my apartment back in Yardley."

The room was just a little heavy on the gothic.

It was simply Dunroamin.

Her echoing footsteps had been just that—footsteps. The few creaks and groans breaking the stillness were only the sounds of ancient woodwork settling down for the night. All old houses made such noises.

And all antique dresser mirrors had ghosts in them.

"Gaaaah!" She jumped.

The ghostly woman leapt closer to the mirror glass and gaped at her. Pale, wild-eyed, and with a tangled mane of hair, the specter shook her head and began withdrawing into the mirror's depths. Each retreating step took her deeper into the shadows until she stopped cold, frozen in place, the very moment Cilla backed into an enormous overstuffed chair.

"Oh, for heaven's sake!" She threw her hands up, laughing out loud when the *ghost* did the same.

Regrettably, the image also revealed how shell-shocked she looked.

What she needed was fresh air.

She gave herself a little shake to settle her nerves and then marched across the room and opened the nearest window. She unlatched the shutters, deliberately ignoring the weird screech of the rusty hinges.

Such things wouldn't bother her again.

She had the backbone to stand above them.

For the moment, she'd simply enjoy the view. And there really was a lot to relish. If one appreciated fine mist and drizzle, a touch of brisk, chill air, all of which she certainly did.

Clutching the edges of the window, she breathed deep.

Never had she seen a place of such haunting beauty, though *haunting* wasn't the best word choice at the moment. Even so, it suited. She took another long breath, air scented with the rich earthiness of peat, a tinge of rain and damp, ageless stone. Her cares began to roll off her shoulders.

She'd always understood why Aunt Birdie had fallen for a Highlander.

Now, finally, she saw why her aunt had also lost her heart to Scotland's far north. Wild, empty, and soul-piercingly beautiful, the vista before her was so spectacular it almost hurt to gaze upon.

But she did, letting her troubles melt away as she stared down at the liquid glass surface of the Kyle, silver-blue and gleaming. She leaned out the window to better watch the moon rise above what looked to be a ruined tower perched on the edge of one of the cliffs on the far side of the inlet. Rising like two fingers held up in the victory sign, the ruin appeared to have a window arch in one of its remaining walls.

How old it must be!

Certainly older than Dunroamin.

She shivered. This time with excitement. Who would have thought her room would look out upon an ancient castle ruin? There could be no mistaking that it was a crumbled tower. Even at this late hour, the sky

shimmered with a luminosity that let her see everything.

She saw not just the lines of the distant ruin, but
also the great mass of Ben Loyal, bluish-purple in the
night's clear, limpid light, and—if she squinted—the
one-track thread of a road, impossibly narrow and
mist-sheened, that curved around the long sea loch
that was the Kyle of Tongue. She could even see—if
she craned her neck—a sliver of the rolling moorlands
where Uncle Mac cut his peat.

Fine peat, the best in the north. Or so he claimed.

Looking that way now, she blinked, then gasped,
her eyes widening.

The *devil* filled her vision.

Huge, red, and wickedly horned, his leering face
hovered in the air just outside the window.

"Eeeeee!" She grabbed the shutters and yanked
them into place.

The window wouldn't budge.

"Come on!" She pulled, but nothing happened.
"Shut, will you?"

When she broke a fingernail, she got mad.

She glared at her torn nail. The back of her neck
caught fire. "Enough," she seethed, her smarting cuti-
cle pushing her over the edge.

Could it be her Kiltie? Would he reappear so
quickly, disguised as the devil to scare her?

She knew in her heart he wouldn't.

The red devil face had to be someone else.

Something else.

Maybe even Satan himself. Whatever it was, she
wouldn't show any fear. No matter that her knees
were knocking, she wouldn't be from anywhere close
to Philadelphia if she didn't know how to look brave.

But in the instant it took her to throw open the
shutters to prove it, the hovering devil had vanished.

And without leaving so much as a pitchfork or a
puff of brimstone in his wake.

"Whew . . ." She let out a shaky breath.

Then she curled her fingers around the cold, wet iron of the shutter latches, her gaze once again on the tower ruin across the Kyle. Wrapped round with a veil of thin, whirling mist, its stones called her.

But not near as much as *he* did.

And that scared her more than floating devil faces. Much more.

Chapter 6

Early the next day, Cilla stood at the entrance to Dunroamin's breakfast room—actually a conservatory overlooking the paved terrace and garden lawn—and decided bright morning sunshine went a long way in dispelling the castle's air of gothic gloom.

Easier to find than the library, she'd only needed to follow the delicious aroma of bacon and the clatter of dishes and cutlery to find the airy, glass-walled room.

And, of course, the raised tone of Colonel Darling's clipped English voice.

She'd heard him the minute she neared the bottom of the main stairs. Now, as she hurried to join her aunt at a small corner table, his bellowing proved even louder.

She turned a questioning look on her aunt. "What's with—"

"It's a morning ritual." Aunt Birdie appeared unconcerned. "After all these years, I can't imagine breakfast without their sparring. It keeps things lively."

Cilla leaned forward to peer around a potted coffee bean tree at the elderly combatants. She wasn't sure such bickering should count as liveliness, especially not so early in the day. But she kept the thought to herself.

More important, Hardwick didn't seem present.

Not kilted. Not invisible. Nor in his latest—and ridiculous—red devil getup.

She frowned, feeling a twinge of guilt for suspecting him again. But after hours spent tossing and turning, and especially in the bright light of morning, the notion of the devil at Dunroamin struck her as absurd.

Ghosts she could handle.

She already knew one was here.

And much as she felt herself attracted to him, however crazy that might be, it was obvious he wanted her gone. He'd already said so, and his insulting comment about not wanting to see her naked only underscored his feelings.

So maybe he had made himself look like the devil? It was a safe enough bet that most women would run for the hills after seeing such a thing.

If so, it was his tough luck that she wasn't every woman.

But still . . .

She worried her lower lip and glanced around, expecting to see him. But she couldn't sense him anywhere in the sunny room. Filled with light and a touch of Aunt Birdie's bohemian charm, with its crowding of exotic greenery, crisp blue table linens, and windowed walls of sparkling glass, the conservatory felt totally ghostless.

Just to be sure, she glanced at an oak sideboard near the door. Massive and stacked with china, pitchers of juice, and colorful serving bowls of muesli, the dresser cast the room's only shadows.

Satisfied that those wedges of darkness held nothing more than a standing rack of weekly papers, she returned her attention to her breakfast.

Her first full Scottish breakfast, as a tartan-edged hand-printed card declared in large, bold letters. She'd heard about the heartiness of such feasts. The meal was a treat she meant to enjoy without worrying about *him*.

Or the arguing residents.

Determined to put them all from her mind, she picked up the menu and read the selection.

Fresh fruit salad or fruit slices.
Any style eggs, bacon and sausage, black
    pudding and haggis, smoked haddock or
    salmon.
Fried tattie scones, soda farls—*whatever they
    were*—mushrooms, baked beans, and toast,
    white or dark.
Muesli, yogurt, and porridge.
Tea or coffee.
Juices.

Cilla's mouth watered. Her stomach made an embarrassing noise. Fried potato scones sounded like her idea of heaven, though she might pass on the black pudding. Everyone knew it was really blood sausage. Still, she was hungry enough to have a bit of everything. Maybe even one of the mysterious-sounding soda farls.

But first she needed caffeine.

She was so not a morning person.

Knowing it, Aunt Birdie indicated the teapot. The silver bangles on her arm tinkled as she tapped the pot's handle. "You can have coffee if you prefer."

Cilla shook her head.

She'd *love* coffee, but the tea was on the table. Readily accessible caffeine was the best caffeine.

"Where's Uncle Mac?" She poured a cup of the tea. "Is he sleeping late?"

"Your uncle?" Aunt Birdie nearly choked on a piece of smoked haddock. "He was up and away before the sun. It's him that they're all fussing about this morning."

"Uncle Mac?"

Aunt Birdie nodded, her gaze flicking to the agitated colonel.

"Bollocks!" Seated at the head of a large antique pine table, he waved a speared sausage. "He'll not find anything but bog cotton and muck on his wellies! You didn't hear *him* saying he was going off to look for Vikings, did you?"

Across the table from him, Violet Manyweathers sniffed. "Of course he didn't say the like. He doesn't want to alarm us unduly."

"You've gone full dotty." The colonel popped the sausage into his mouth and chewed angrily.

"The laird never goes out so early," Flora Duthie chimed, tucking a napkin into her collar. "Not before his breakfast. We all know that."

As unobtrusively as she could, Cilla parted the glossy dark green leaves of the coffee bean tree and sneaked a look at the other table.

The only one occupied besides hers and Aunt Birdie's.

"Mac MacGhee's business is just that—his business." Colonel Darling forked another sausage. "He won't appreciate a gaggle of old biddies speculating on how he chooses to fill his morning."

Flora ignored the insult. "The Vikings were especially active last night," she said, adding a pinch of salt to her porridge. "Like as not he saw them, too, and hoped to catch any that might still be floating about."

"Might still be floatin' aboot!" Red-faced, the colonel mimicked the tiny woman's burr. "The only thing floating about this place is that insufferable boxtie."

He yanked his tweed cap more snugly onto his head and shot an angry look at Violet. "That abominable bird of yours is the real spook. Mark my words."

Her expression infinitely calm, Violet spooned a helping of haggis onto her plate. "Gregor is a bonxie, not a boxtie. And"—she returned the serving spoon to the dish of haggis—"who the spook around here is, is a matter of opinion."

Flora tittered.

Colonel Darling reached for his tea, nearly dropping the cup when Leo shot out from under the table and leapt up to snatch the napkin off his lap.

"Damnation!" He half rose from his chair, shaking a fist at the retreating dachshund. "Long-backed little bugger! I'll get my hands on him one of these days!" he roared, dropping back onto his seat. "Him, and that wretched boxtie."

"Great skua, affectionately known as a bonxie." Honoria waltzed into the room, bearing a platter heaped with crispy bacon, black pudding, and steaming scrambled eggs.

"*Affectionately!*" The colonel glared at her.

Looking pleased to have corrected him, the house- keeper plunked her tray onto a large oak buffet near his table. "You'll not be touching either creature or you'll have to contend with me."

"Bah!" He grabbed a piece of toast and started smearing it with butter. "Bring me another napkin or you'll have *me* to deal with."

"I'm trembling in my shoes." The housekeeper's lips twitched as she did as he bid, even spreading the napkin on his lap for him.

"Harrumph." He nodded gruff thanks and returned to his toast.

Cilla released her grip on the coffee bean tree leaves and turned back to the table. Through the win- dows she caught a swift movement out on the lawn, near the sundial. Her heart leapt, then dipped when she spotted two rabbits playing chase in the grass.

She'd thought it'd been *him*.

Her Kiltie.

Despite his antics—if he was indeed behind the red devil face—some crazy-mad part of her wanted to see him again.

But nothing moved on the emerald green lawn ex- cept sun shadows, the rabbits, and a sparrow that seemed intent on pecking at something on the stone face of the sundial.

"Honoria!"

Cilla started. The colonel's bark brought her back inside the conservatory.

"Cook forgot to serve Flora's porridge in her wooden bowl." He held up the silver porringer as evidence. "Porridge cools too quickly in this contraption, fancy as it is."

Cilla watched as the housekeeper took the silver bowl without a twitch of irritation.

Holding the porridge before her, she started for the door. "I'll fetch another serving and make sure we use Flora's special bowl."

The colonel nodded, clearly appeased.

Flora gave him a twittery smile.

"See?" Aunt Birdie reached across the table to nudge Cilla's arm. "The bickering between them is pure stuff and nonsense. They're all actually quite fond of each other. I suspect that's a reason they've stayed with us when others have left."

"Did the others really leave because of Viking ghosts?"

Aunt Birdie shrugged.

"That's what they said, yes." She lowered her voice. "See, my dear, with the exception of those like your uncle and Achilles—that's Colonel Darling—many people hereabouts still believe in the old folklore and traditions."

"I know they do." Cilla smoothed her napkin into place. "I remember you saying so when you'd visit Yardley."

"It's still true." Aunt Birdie brushed at her skirt. "Seers and second sight, healing rituals and sacred places are all things that are still widely accepted. And"—she glanced out at the sun-bright morning— "not just in gathering twilight or on long winter nights."

"Then you'd think the notion of ghosts wouldn't bother them." Cilla slid another look at the sundial. The rabbits and the little sparrow were gone. "Why—"

"Because along with the harmless and good, like believing a branch of rowan tacked above the byre door will safeguard the health of the animals within, there are other, darker beliefs, as well."

"Such as?"

Aunt Birdie looked at her, her face as sincere and earnest as ever. "Omens and taboos that can be quite frightening. The evil eye and the powers of goodwives whose magic is anything but."

"Even today?" Cilla had trouble believing it. "People really worry about those things?"

"Don't forget you're in Scotland, dear." Aunt Birdie topped off her teacup. "And Sutherland, remote and rugged as it is, is Highland Scotland at its best and its worst, depending on your viewpoint."

Visions of the red devil face rose in Cilla's mind and she opened her mouth to say so, but closed it as quickly. Aunt Birdie and Uncle Mac had enough on their plates without her adding hovering devils to the brew.

She cleared her throat, pushing the image aside. "So the residents who left really were afraid of Viking ghosts?"

"Indeed they were, sadly." A tiny crease appeared between Aunt Birdie's brows. "One woman confided she feared the Norsemen were harbingers of doom. That they'd come to get her in her sleep. Sort of like the tales down south of those huge phantom dogs said to slink about the moors at night. To see one of the great black beasts meant certain death."

Cilla shivered. "I'm sorry. I wish—"

"Things will improve. Our stalwarts are still here and soon others will join us. I am sure of it." Aunt Birdie flashed a smile and reached for a basket of what looked to be very large and thick scones.

"Have a soda farl." She jiggled the basket. "Cook really has a way with them. And"—she cast a look at the colonel and his buttered toast—"they're much better than toast. Like the English, the Scots never seem able to serve anything but cold toast."

"What about you?" Cilla took one of the soda farls. "Do you think there are Viking ghosts?"

"Me?" Aunt Birdie set down the basket, her arm bangles jingling again. "You know I believe in ghosts. I'm sure there are plenty Viking ones all up and down Scotland's coasts. But I've yet to sense any here."

"And the chivalrous ghost you said was angry at Grant for ditching me?" Cilla's heart skittered on the words. "Is he still here?"

She had to ask.

Even though she knew the question put two bright spots of red on her cheeks.

"A ghost angry at Grant?" Aunt Birdie didn't seem to remember.

"That's what you said." Cilla wished she'd never mentioned him. She could still feel his hot gaze raking her. His fingers brushing her nipples, and his soft, warm breath tickling her neck when he'd leaned close that once.

She shifted on the chair, crossing her legs before such thoughts brought on another attack of the tingles.

"Ahhh, it's coming back to me." Aunt Birdie tilted her head, peering into nowhere. "He was quite dashing if I recall correctly. At least"—her lips curved in a soft smile—"his *energy* was bold, even rakish. That's all I caught, regrettably. A fleeting impression, no more."

"And now?"

Aunt Birdie's brow creased again. "Now . . ." She closed her eyes, concentrating. "I cannot sense him at all."

"He's gone?"

"He's not here at the moment, no." Her aunt's eyes popped open, clear and focused again. "That doesn't mean he won't return. Many ghosts come and go at Dunroamin, even if your uncle scoffs at the notion. I'm not the only one who notices them. My theory is that they feel at ease here, perhaps because we keep things as they were."

She picked up her teacup and took a sip, watching Cilla over the rim. "To our residents—and us—Dunroamin is a refuge from the stresses of modern life. Why should that change in the afterlife? Why wouldn't such souls seek a slower-paced, edge-of-the-world haven if they appreciated such places in their earthly lives?"

Cilla bit her lip.

Something told her that Kiltie had very different reasons for popping by Dunroamin.

Reasons she suspected might be dangerous to know.

As was the kilted ghost himself, she was sure!

"Aunt Birdie . . ." She drew a breath to change the subject. "What did the colonel mean about bog cotton and muck on Uncle Mac's boots? Where is he, anyway?"

Her aunt's mouth twitched. "He's just there where the colonel so aptly described. Out in the middle of his peat cuttings, but not to look for ghosts. He's helping Honoria's nephews load a lorry with peat."

"Loading peat?" Cilla's eyes widened. "Isn't that backbreaking work?"

"It is." Aunt Birdie's brow crease returned. "Although this is the first year we haven't had a score of helpers, young Robbie and Roddie are perfectly capable of doing the work on their own. But you know your uncle. . . ."

Cilla set down her fork. "He is rather stubborn."

"That isn't the half of it." Aunt Birdie glanced over to the residents' table, where voices were rising again.

"It'd be easier to soften stone by boiling it than to get him to see reason sometimes."

"But why does he need a whole lorry of peat? As close as his moorland is—"

"That bloody bird has a wingspread of five feet!"

Cilla jumped, Colonel Darling's outburst about Gregor cutting her off.

Someone—Violet?—tsk-tsked. "If you'd be nice to him—"

"Nice, you say? To a dive-bombing pterodactyl?" The colonel flushed red. "I once heard of a chap who lost the tip of his nose to one of your beloved boxties!"

When he quieted, Cilla turned back to her aunt. "I meant, with Uncle Mac's moorland so close by, can't he just have Robbie and Roddie bring up the peat as needed?"

"We do that with the peat we burn at Dunroamin." Aunt Birdie sipped her tea, immune to the ruckus at the other table. "It's the distillery peat that needs a lorry."

"Distillery peat?"

"That's right." Aunt Birdie looked at her, a touch of pride in her deep blue eyes. "Dunroamin has superior peat, or so your uncle believes. If you didn't know, it's peat smoke that distinguishes Highland whisky. Distilleries use it to dry their barley. All peat has its own distinctive reek, depending on area. That's what determines a whisky's ultimate flavor. Our Dunroamin peat is prized for the rich, earthy-sweet tang of its smoke and—"

"So Uncle Mac's gone into the distillery business?" Cilla tried to remember.

"No, the *peat* business." Aunt Birdie refilled their teacups. "He's been trying to sell our peat to a few of the area's smaller distilleries. Simmer Dim and Northern Mist are just two that have shown interest. Now, with their initial orders coming in and"—she set down the teapot, frowning—"the local young men who'd agreed to help refusing to set foot on our moors, we're in danger of losing this avenue of supplemental income, as well."

"Don't tell me the locals are afraid of Viking ghosts, too?" Cilla stared at her aunt. Shades of Dawn Paterson and her parents whirled across her mind. "Or is there another reason Uncle Mac's helpers left him in the lurch?"

"That's the million-dollar question, my dear." Aunt Birdie sighed. "Sutherland has never been an easy place to make a living. Your uncle suspects someone bribed the young men, luring them away with promises of better-paying jobs elsewhere."

Cilla frowned.

That she could believe.

"So it isn't about ghosts?"

"I'd say it's a little bit of both." Aunt Birdie squinted in the bright sun slanting in through the windows. "People hereabouts *are* superstitious. Word spreads quicker than a brushfire. If you sneezed, I can guarantee you everyone in Tongue would know it before you had a chance to reach for a tissue."

"That sounds like Yardley." Cilla couldn't keep the bitterness out of her voice. "Before I drove home from the Charm Box, everyone along the Eastern seaboard knew I couldn't sell my jewelry."

"It's a far cry from Yardley." Aunt Birdie was her serene self again. "Who could blame the local lads if they were lured away by better-paying jobs? Many have young families to support. If they backed out because they fear something evil haunts our peat banks, well, that's understandable, too."

"Because this is the wilds of northern Scotland," Cilla borrowed her aunt's earlier words, "and Viking ghosts really might be putting in an appearance."

Aunt Birdie took a sip of tea. "Exactly."

"I still think it's lousy." Cilla sat up straighter. She

knew all about how it felt to watch one's livelihood crumble away to nothing.

She swept a hand over her hair, frowning. "It really is rotten, Aunt Birdie. I know you need the money. Honoria told me about the roof and how Uncle Mac—"

"Uncle Mac will do just fine." Aunt Birdie's smile said she believed it. "I've never known a more resourceful man. Even if all our residents leave and no one buys our peat, he'll think of something to keep Dunroamin going."

"I know, but . . ." Cilla felt her heart squeeze.

The thought of Aunt Birdie and Uncle Mac losing Dunroamin was unfathomable.

Worse, with Aunt Birdie's sometimes dippy ways and Uncle Mac's penchant for living in the past, she doubted they'd last long living anywhere *but* at Dunroamin.

"Ach! Don't look so glum." Sounding almost as Scottish as Uncle Mac, Aunt Birdie leaned forward. "With the help of Robbie and Roddie, your uncle will get his first load of peat off to Simmer Dim and Northern Mist, Viking ghosties or no. And he has a lot more plans for further—"

"You sound like you really believe in them."

"Viking ghosts?"

Cilla nodded.

"I do." Aunt Birdie's eyes twinkled. "I just haven't sensed any here, as I've told you. But"—her voice dropped to a conspiratorial whisper—"I have sensed them at the ruins of Castle Varrich. You might have seen the ruined tower from your window?"

"The ruin across the Kyle, perched on a cliff edge?" Cilla's interest perked. "I saw it last night. Is it said to be haunted by Vikings?"

"Not that I've ever heard, but I'm certain I sensed a Norsewoman there once." Aunt Birdie's tone turned wistful. "I was there very late one night, well after midnight—you know summer nights here never get truly dark—and I saw her for just an instant. She was standing with her back to me, her long blond braid hanging well below her hips, as she gazed out to sea. Even though I couldn't see her face, I knew it'd be tracked with tears."

Aunt Birdie glanced aside for a moment, her own eyes suspiciously bright. "I knew here"—she touched a hand to her heart—"that she was pining for a lover who'd gone to sea and would never return."

"And then she was gone." Cilla guessed.

"If she'd even been there. Your uncle said she was just moon glow reflecting on the stones." Aunt Birdie looked back at her, blinking. "I believe otherwise. I even sensed her name. *Gudrid*. If she was there, I like to think my sympathy was a comfort to her."

"So Castle Varrich was Viking?" Cilla could see the ruined tower's crumbling, V-shaped walls in her mind. "I thought it looked medieval."

"The ruins are medieval." Aunt Birdie dabbed at her eyes with a napkin. "The castle belonged to Clan Mackay and dates back to the fourteenth century. But local tradition claims a Norse stronghold stood on the site long before the Mackays set the first foundation stone."

Cilla shivered. "I'd like to see it."

"And you should." Aunt Birdie looked determined. "If you don't mind riding in a lorry, Robbie and Roddie can drop you off in Tongue later today. They'll pass through the village with our peat and can leave you at the Ben Loyal Hotel. The path up to the ruin starts near there, just beside the bank."

Cilla's heart gave a little flip. "Can I walk back?"

"You could." Aunt Birdie considered. "But that would mean walking clear through Tongue, not that it's more than a blip in the road, then you'd pass some sheep fields before heading back across the Kyle causeway. Once on our side again, you'd turn right at the cemetery and then face an even longer trek back here."

"That sounds like quite a hike."

Aunt Birdie tapped her chin with a long, red-lacquered fingernail. "Yes," she decided, "it's much too far. I'll drive over to the Ben Loyal myself and wait for you in their Bistro Bar or restaurant, An Garbh."

"An Garbh?" Cilla lifted a brow.

"It's Gaelic for 'hilly place.' The restaurant has huge picture windows with views of Ben Loyal and Ben Hope and even your castle ruin. And if the scenery isn't enough, they play classical music as you dine." Aunt Birdie sat back, looking pleased. "Maybe we'll grab dinner there. They have the most divine menu."

"Well . . ."

"You'd love their hand-cut chips." Aunt Birdie pulled out the big guns. "They really are the best."

Cilla swallowed.

She could feel her mouth watering. The corners of her lips twitched upward. From nowhere, *his* sandal-wood scent swirled around her, flooding her senses. Excitement started beating inside her. The day, as her aunt painted it, did sound like a lovely and enjoyable outing.

And it would be—whether Kiltie chose to show himself or not.

After all, who could resist a cliff-top castle ruin?

Especially when followed by the promise of delicious hand-cut French fries?

As a lover of atmospheric old places and a dedicated, card-carrying potato zealot, she couldn't think of a better way to spend the afternoon.

She also loved classical music.

Still . . .

"Will I find my way up to the ruin and back okay?" That was her only consideration. "The cliff looked pretty steep and wooded from my window."

"The path is well marked—no worries." Aunt Birdie dismissed her concern. "It isn't all that steep. I haven't been up there in a while, but I don't recall it being too difficult a climb."

"If you're sure . . ." Cilla didn't want to admit she wasn't in the best shape.

She bit her lip.

If only she was one of those lucky women who lost their appetite when things went wrong.

Unfortunately, getting ditched by Grant and then seeing her business crumble had increased her passion for food and decreased her desire to exercise.

"Of course I'm sure." Aunt Birdie smiled in satisfaction. "Besides, the fresh air will do you good and—"

"Eeeeee!" A woman's high-pitched cry rose from somewhere else in the castle, accompanied by a loud, clattering crash and a dog's wild barking.

Cilla's heart slammed against her ribs. She whirled toward the door, her ears ringing.

Aunt Birdie leapt to her feet. Her teacup shattered on the tile floor.

"Aaaaaaaiiiiii!" The woman screamed again.

This time a low, heavy-sounding *thud* cut off her screech.

"That was Behag, the cook!" Aunt Birdie sprinted from the conservatory.

"Wait!" Cilla hurried around the table, her feet slipping in the spilled tea.

Colonel Darling and Violet Manyweathers were already out the door. They chased after Aunt Birdie, the three of them streaking down the corridor with incredible speed. Flora Duthie hobbled in their wake, the tap-tapping of her cane loud in the vaulted passage now that the echoes of the ruckus were fading.

Only Leo kept up the din.

His frantic yapping filled the corridor, the shrill

barks cresting the ear-piercing level only achieved by the smallest of dogs.

Far ahead of Cilla, her aunt and the old dears disappeared around a curve in the passageway, leaving her to pull up the rear.

Heart in her throat, she ran ever faster until she barreled around a corner and nearly slammed into the colonel's gray-suited back.

Fisted hands on his hips, he blocked the arched entry into the kitchen. "I've said for years that she dips into Mac's spirit cabinet!" he scolded, sounding righteous. "Now we have the proof!"

"Proof schmoof." That came from Honoria. "She was making *your* breakfast is what she was doing. Everyone else eats scrambled eggs. You order yours soft-cooked and not a jot over or under six minutes!"

The colonel's back stiffened. "Harridan."

"Oh, stop, both of you!" Aunt Birdie pushed past him, her usual calm flown.

Colonel Darling moved then, and Cilla caught a glimpse of the housekeeper past his square-set shoulders. Kneeling, Honoria pressed a cloth to the forehead of a huge blond-haired woman, her entire apron-clad bulk lying prone on the kitchen's stone-flagged floor.

Smashed crockery and a spreading puddle of steaming porridge lay beside her. A great wooden stirring spoon, Flora's silver porringer, and an upturned basket of freshly baked soda farls added to the chaos.

A few yards away, Leo ran in circles in front of the long work counter, his gaze repeatedly darting to the window above the large copper sink.

"Goodness me!" Aunt Birdie's voice rose. "What happened here?"

"Did she have a . . . is she . . . ?" Cilla clamped her mouth shut, realizing too late that the words *heart attack* and *dead* were best left unspoken in a place like Dunroamin.

"Nae, she isn't deid." Flora tottered forward to poke the cook with her cane. "But this *is* the work of the Vikings, sure as I'm standing here! Behag Finney is one of them"—she touched the tip of her cane to the cook's flaxen hair—"so they've come to collect her. She just fainted before they could spirit her away."

"This has nothing to do with Vikings." Honoria dipped her cloth into a basin, then, after wringing it out, slapped it once more onto the cook's forehead.

" 'Twas the devil, it was," she insisted, splaying her fingers to better press the cooling rag against Behag's pale skin.

"The devil?" Cilla's stomach dropped.

Surely Hardwick wouldn't stoop to frightening helpless old women? Overweight, middle-aged cooks in faded blue dresses and flour-stained aprons?

But Honoria was nodding, her face grim.

"I saw him myself." She flashed a look at the colonel, as if expecting him to deny it. "Bright red, horned, and big as the day, he was. Looking in through the window just there"—she flung out an arm to indicate the sink—"when I came in here to fetch Flora's wooden bowl."

"Humph!" Colonel Darling snorted.

Aunt Birdie wrung her hands.

Cilla stared at them all, wondering.

What a pity she didn't have any answers.

Chapter 7

Several hours later, Cilla paused about halfway up the steep and overgrown path to Castle Varrich. She'd never dreamed a supposed hiking trail would be barely wide enough for her feet. She eyed the ever rising track and considered turning around. Great was the temptation to return to the cozy, oh-so-level public rooms of the lovely Ben Loyal Hotel.

She could call Aunt Birdie and go back to Dunroamin. Sort through the packing crates of Uncle Mac's broken china, organize her tools, and wait for *him* to make another appearance. On the thought he loomed before her mind's eye, his big, strong hands hooked around his kilt belt and looking ready and eager to sate any woman's hottest dreams.

Cilla's breath caught and her heart began a slow, hard thumping.

A shiver slid through her and, God help her, but her breasts went tight and her nipples puckered, almost aching to feel his touch again. Worse, his rich, whisky-smooth voice played across her memory, the deep, lilting tones strumming vulnerable places and, she was sure, dampening her panties!

She pressed a hand to her mouth and willed away the sweet warmth beginning to pulse deep in her belly.

Then she choked back a bitter laugh.

How typical that she'd hoped to spend the afternoon not thinking about her sexy Highland ghost, yet she couldn't get him out of her mind.

She should be angry at him, not fantasizing about how good he'd be in bed.

She bit down on her lip, her breath slowly returning to normal.

And with it came reason.

If her suspicions were true, he'd used a silly devil disguise to try and scare her and then did the same thing to the poor innocent cook. She didn't want to believe he'd do such a thing, but she *had* seen his conjuring skills. Any ghost who could appear so real and also make a solid-looking medieval shield pop in and out of thin air could surely whip up a devil face, too.

After all, hadn't he flicked his fingers and created a wooden, water-filled bathing tub in the middle of her bedroom?

So yes, it was possible.

She did have reason to suspect him.

Yet here she was—away from his ghostly reach—and just thinking about him made her heart do flip-flops.

He'd caught her twice when she could have done serious bodily injury to herself, and he'd looked at her with so much smoldering heat she'd almost swear her skin was still sizzling from his gaze.

She was also sure she'd felt a tremor ripple through him when he'd held her so briefly. Almost as if he, too, recognized an irresistible pull between them and struggled against acknowledging it.

Even so, he'd made it clear he wanted her gone. And however she turned it, the result was the same.

She wanted him.

No man had ever affected her so intensely.

A man who was a ghost!

Cilla shoved back her hair. Her breath hitched again, this time in frustration. Feeling the back of her neck blaze, she glared at the trail rising in front of her. She had no business struggling up slippery, weed-infested footpaths. What she needed to be doing was making an appointment with a shrink.

Instead, she did her best to put *him* from her mind. Then she bent down to plunge a finger beneath the top of her sock, fishing around until she located the tiny, impossible-to-identify beetlelike creature who'd just decided to get on intimate terms with her ankle.

Pleased to have ended the association before it could get too serious, she gently placed the bug on one of the giant bracken fronds clogging the path. Then she allowed herself a shudder.

A shudder and—she just couldn't help it—another frown.

Aunt Birdie had lied out her ears.

The only thing easy about getting up to the ruined tower was finding the prominent wooden FOOTPATH TO CASTLE VARRICH signpost next to the Tongue bank.

After that, it'd been a nightmarish trek that had her huffing and puffing and growing hotter with each step along the almost vertical path. Only suffering the hots for *him* was worse. Her lungs burned, a nasty stitch jabbed her side, and the back of her shirt stuck to her skin. That last despite the shade of the dark, thick-growing trees and the earthy-damp chill of the woodsy air.

Not that she should be surprised.

Of course, the ancient Mackay castle builders or the Norsemen before them wouldn't have built a defensive stronghold in an easily accessible place. She'd seen the height of the tower's jutting headland from her window.

She should have known it wouldn't be easy.

Or that piece-of-pie to her was a whole 'nother animal to Aunt Birdie.

After all, her aunt had once spent six weeks back-packing through the wilds of Indonesia. Alone, save

for the company of an equally adventurous girlfriend
and—gasp!—her friend's nine-year-old daughter.

With the exception of a few close encounters with
leeches while skinny-dipping in a pond in a bamboo
wood on Bali and contracting food poisoning after
dining with locals somewhere in the rain forest of Su-
lawesi, Aunt Birdie called the adventure a delight.

Cilla rolled her eyes.

Then she swiped her forehead with her shirtsleeve.

She had to be tougher.

But finding a bug in her sock wasn't funny. In fact,
it'd been the last straw. She could ignore ghost-
induced tingles and heart flips. Even wicked thoughts
like wondering if he was naked beneath his kilt.

Bugs were something else entirely.

She bit her lip, contemplating her options. The footpath had shrunk to a muddy thread barely discernible
beneath a sea of clinging, waist-high bracken. She suspected the beetle thing had innumerable friends and
relatives lurking there, each one eager to make her
acquaintance the instant she plunged onward.

She grimaced.

A cool pint in the Ben Loyal's Bistro Bar was
sounding better by the moment.

But she really did want to see the tower ruin.

Besides, stomping up a mountain might just purge
her of wicked, not-good-for-her-mind wanderings! So
she braced her hands on her thighs and breathed deep
and slow until she was no longer quite so winded.

She straightened, her mood lifting when she caught
a glimpse of the tower through the trees. Still high
above her, its stones beckoned, using lichen and age
to lure her on.

"You're hopeless," she muttered, disgusted by the
ease with which old stones won out over a pint of real
ale in a pub that reeked of charm and coziness.

Quickly, before she could think too deeply on Mr.

Beetle and his pals, she tossed back her hair and struck off through the bracken.

Barbed deer fencing soon blocked the way, but a tricky scramble up and over a rickety ladderlike stile brought her to a low hand-railed causeway across a bog and—lo—not far from the end of the wood-planked walk, the footpath rose in straight line to the ruin.

Unfortunately, the last stretch of the way looked to be the steepest.

She took a deep breath and stepped onto the path. Her feet slid a few times on the mud, and once a scatter of pebbles almost sent her plunging down the grassy slope into the Kyle. But then she was at the top, picking her way over a small heap of tumbled masonry to reach a jagged opening in the tower wall.

Whether a door or just a gap caused by falling rubble, she clambered through it into the ruin's interior.

Little more than a dim, earthy-smelling enclosure, surprisingly small and circular, Castle Varrich's roofless walls embraced her. Shadows shifted, then wrapped around her like a cloak, soft and beguiling. A slanting ray of sun picked out a drift of old leaves beneath the half-ruinous remains of a window embrasure.

Halfway up the wall, the gaping niche held a sense of poignancy as if the onetime window remembered sharing its views with long-ago souls, and missed them.

Cilla's heart thumped.

She could easily imagine Aunt Birdie's Viking maid standing in the arched alcove. Or sitting on the embrasure's stone bench, its hard contours softened by fur rugs and colorful pillows instead of blurred by smears of mold and dirt, the flotsam of ages.

She took a few steps deeper into the tower, her pulse quickening.

Each muddied, moss-grown stone shimmered with

the past. If only they could speak. Tell tales of all they'd seen and heard down the centuries.

Cilla shivered.

Aunt Birdie once said that every blade of grass in Scotland had a story clinging to it, each stone and clump of heather its own mythic bit of legend and lore.

Now she believed it.

This was the stuff of dreams.

Scotland as she'd always imagined it.

To experience this kind of *history live*, she could handle a bug or two in her sock. Even tromping up a path that was so steep she could have bitten into the ground before her.

None of that mattered anymore.

Not now.

She peered about, her shoulders relaxing and her tense, overexerted thigh muscles beginning to loosen. For the first time since passing the footpath sign, she smiled.

No, she grinned.

She was inside a genuine, honest-to-goodness castle ruin. And the thrill of it was almost more than she could bear.

Carefully, with all the awe and reverence she knew she'd feel at such a moment, she placed her hands on the chill, damp stones. Ancient stones, most worn smooth by countless raindrops, some cracked and broken by constant exposure to icy northern wind.

She pressed her palms against them, letting her fingers explore the cold, uneven surface. She tried to breathe in their essence, almost expecting—no, hoping—to feel a slight pulse or vibration.

Nothing happened.

But she did hear sheep bleating somewhere in the distance.

A soft sigh followed by a slight rustling.

She blinked. A chill sped down her spine and the fine hairs on the back of her neck lifted.

Such a rustling noise could have been Gudrid. Aunt Birdie's Norse maid stepping into the window embrasure. More likely, it'd have been the soughing of the wind through the ivy spilling down one side of the ruin.

Even so, in the hopes of increasing her chances of glimpsing the maid—if indeed she'd made the noises— she studied the stretch of wall rising up to the crumbling window alcove.

There *were* enough footholds to get her up there.

If she didn't slip.

She glanced at the hard-packed earthen floor. Stones and fallen bits of rubble were everywhere. Not to mention what she was sure must be stinging nettle growing around the wall edges. Whatever goo and whatnot hid beneath the piles of old, dead leaves.

Falling wouldn't be pretty.

And a spill in the other direction, out the window, would be even worse. She'd tumble straight down the grassy slope, roll over the cliff edge, and land right smack in the Kyle.

Where she'd promptly drown, if she was still alive when her body hit the water.

She took a step closer to the wall, her mind working furiously.

Climbing up was way too dangerous. But the window was where the tower's hall would have been. She could see the line of joist holes for the hall's wooden floor. If she could climb that far, she could swing herself into the embrasure.

She hesitated.

Now that she was close, the alcove looked even higher than before. Peering up at it, she inhaled deeply. The she willed herself to be brave. After all, she was Aunt Birdie's niece.

She had courage in her blood.

But still . . .

She frowned. A rock protruded near the base of the

wall, so she stuck out her foot, nudging the stone to see if it wiggled.

It didn't.

She eyed the rock, considering.

Then she heard the rustling noise again and made her decision.

Heart thumping, she shimmied up the wall and scrambled into the alcove before fear could change her mind. Her goal reached, she pushed to her feet. Then she braced her hands on either side of the recess and felt her heart drop.

The window was much higher than she'd calculated, but she'd been right about one thing.

Falling *out* would be worse than falling back in.

It was a long way down to the Kyle.

Long, rocky, and steep didn't begin to describe it.

It was that bad.

Trying to pretend her knees weren't trembling, she cast a look at the cracked stone bench against one side of the alcove. There should have been a second, opposite-facing seat, but that one had apparently done what she was determined not to do. At some point in time, it'd fallen out the window.

Broken bits of it dotted the ground at the base of the tower.

She shuddered and—having decided the remaining bench wasn't going anywhere for a while—she eased herself onto its cold stone seat.

Maybe she'd stay there forever.

There were worse fates.

And it seemed a better option than thinking about how she was going to get back down.

You could have spared yourself this. . . .

No odd fluttery rustle, but the purring voice of her old nemesis, Dawn Paterson, seemed to brush past her ear.

Cilla swallowed. She could almost see her rival before her. How she'd preened in the front room of her parents' Charm Box Antique and Jewelry Shoppe. Haughty and snide, she'd sneered the words that squelched Cilla's livelihood.

You always did act without thinking. A shame you didn't consider how poorly your wares were selling before bothering to make more. . . .

Cilla closed her eyes and blocked her ears.

She didn't need to be reminded that Vintage Chic had gone down the tubes. Or that she was presently stuck on an ice-cold medieval bench that might crumble beneath her any minute.

Just because it looked solid enough didn't mean it was.

Hardwick looked and felt solid, but he was still a spook.

Cilla leaned back against the wall, trying to squelch the wish that he wasn't. To that end, she snapped open her eyes and lifted her chin, giving her jaw just enough thrust to make her feel bold.

And she did . . . until two things happened at once.

The weird rustling returned with a vengeance, this time sounding like the flapping of big, leathery wings.

And then *he* was there, too!

Once again disguised as the devil, he hovered in midair, leering down at her from just above the top of the roofless tower.

"Waaaaa!" She leapt to her feet.

He swooped lower, his horned visage bobbing crazily against the broken ridge of the tower's rim.

His eyes glittered, black as coals.

With eye-blurring speed, he popped over the rim, dropping a few feet into the tower before *whooshing* back up again.

"It won't work!" She shook a fist at him. "I know it's you and you can't scare me away. Not kilted, not red-deviled, and not even if you show up as a werewolf!"

The words made her feel good.

Brave.

But her foot slipped on the edge of the window recess and she slammed onto her knees, nearly toppling over the side to the rock-strewn floor.

"Arrrgggh!" She grabbed the bench, holding tight.

"Have a care, lass." His soft voice sounded low, deeply seductive.

More surprising, it came from beneath her, while his red devil face soared ever upward, finally swinging back and forth high above the tower.

"I dinna think I can catch you a third time." He spoke again, his burr sliding around her like a caress. "No' here, anyway."

"Then we're even." Cilla braced herself against his honeyed words, kept her gaze on his devil disguise. "I don't want to be caught by you anywhere. Your ventriloquist skills don't impress me."

"My what?"

"The word isn't important." She tightened her grip on the bench, her pulse skittering. "It means the ability to make your voice sound as if it's coming from somewhere else. Any two-bit magician can—"

Auk-auk-auk!

A set of powerful pinions rose from behind the devil's curving red horns. Cinnamon-brown with a narrow band of white, the wings beat furiously as the entire ferocious-looking bird came into view.

The devil *mask* dropped several feet, only held aloft by a red cord clutched in the bird's talons.

Cilla gasped.

Beneath her, near the tower doorway, stood Hardwick, eyes narrowed and jaw fiercely set. A breeze tossed long, silky black hair around his powerful, plaid-draped shoulders as he stared up at her, his shield clutched in his hands.

His gaze held hers, dark and intent. "So that's what you meant by red-deviled."

"I—" Cilla flushed. She started to deny it, but just

then the rustling came again, now recognizable as the bird's rapid wingbeats.

Auk, auk, he screeched, keen eyes watching them as he made several high-speed swoops around the tower. Then he soared upward, the devil mask trailing after him like a surreal red-painted kite.

Clearly enjoying himself, he looped back to dive at them, his wings almost completely closed. Coming fast, he sped over the tower rim with barely an inch to spare. He shot up again, this time twirling and spinning in a series of aerial acrobatics before once again sailing around the tower. He released the mask on his fifth pass.

Overlarge and unwieldy, the thing fell like a stone, landing with a loud *thwack* near Hardwick's feet.

Another *auk* and the bird beat away over the Kyle.

He bent to pick up the mask and carefully propped it against a heap of nettle-covered stones.

Cilla cleared her throat. "It's a mask."

He shot an annoyed look at her. "Aye, so it is."

He touched a finger to one of the glistening horns, examining its curve. A muscle ticked in his jaw and his eyes held an unreadable expression.

It could have been anger.

Watching him, Cilla knotted her hands against the stone bench and pushed to her feet. She could feel hot color blooming on her cheeks. Her heart began a slow, shame-driven thumping. Ghost or not, she'd wronged this man. Every inch of him screamed that he knew it.

Knew she'd suspected him of guising himself as the devil to frighten her.

Her gaze again slid to the mask. Hideous with its black glitter eyes and leering smile, it reminded her of the getups worn at Carnival in New Orleans and Rio.

I'm sorry. The apology stuck in her throat.

She owed him one, for sure.

Big time.

But he'd stepped into the shaft of light slanting into the tower and he looked so rock-hard solid and gorgeous standing there that she just knew if she opened her mouth she'd babble something she'd regret.

Something like *oh, my, oh, my.*

She moistened her lips, knew she was blushing.

He set down his shield and folded his arms. "I've been called many things in my time, but ne'er red-deviled."

"I—" Cilla glanced briefly out the window arch. The bird was now a black speck above the moors on the other side of the Kyle. "I wouldn't have called you that either if—"

"Nor—until this day—has anyone e'er suggested I might enjoy sprouting fur and growing fangs." He sounded highly insulted.

"As for my kilt—"

"Oh, please!" Cilla tossed back her hair. She didn't want to hear about his kilt.

Not when, just a short while ago, she'd wondered about what she'd see if she peeked beneath it.

"What was I supposed to think?" She indicated the mask with a flick of her hand. "I open the shutters to see that *thing* sailing toward me. Behag Finney—or whatever the cook's name is—fainted from fright after it appeared at the kitchen window. Then I come up here to . . . to get away for an afternoon, and there it is again, popping up out of nowhere."

"And you thought it was me."

"Of course I thought it was you!"

He remained unmoved. "I see."

"No, you don't." Cilla glared at him. "But you should. It's uncanny the way you're here, there, and everywhere."

"That, sweetness, is what ghosts do." He said that as if she should know it. "After seven hundred years, it's become a habit."

"Exactly, and that's just what I meant. You're a

ghost. Since meeting you"—she waved a hand, struggling to find the right words—"I have to believe *anything* is possible."

"Even flying red devils and werewolves?"

Cilla swallowed. "Even them."

"Then, lass, I must correct you," he stated, an odd note of regret in his voice. "There are some things that are *not* possible."

Cilla started to argue the point—if *he* was possible, then anything should be—but he was suddenly directly beneath her, having crossed the tower without her having even seen him take one step.

"That's another thing ghosts do, isn't it?" She pointed out the obvious. "Move across a room in the blink of an eye."

He shrugged. "Being a ghost does have some advantages. Moving quickly is one of the little things that amuses. It helps break the tedium of our daily . . . lives."

"You call it a life?" The words slipped out before she could stop them.

He blinked. Then he ran a hand over his head and his chest as if assuring himself that he was really there.

Heat seared the back of Cilla's neck, embarrassment scalding her as he held his arms out to his sides and wriggled his fingers. He examined first one hand and then the other, before looking back up at her.

"Aye, I call it a life." His mouth quirked. "Such as it is. I am here. That is enough."

"But how did you get here? You haunt Dunroamin." Her brow knit. "I thought ghosts were bound to a particular place. Did you follow me here?"

He clapped a hand to his chest and pretended to reel backward. "So many questions," he jested, his dark eyes twinkling. "Why don't we get you down from there and I'll answer them for you?"

Cilla blinked. She'd completely forgotten she was still stuck in the window recess. Even more startling, that one quick glimpse at his humor did funny things to her knees.

The man . . . no, the *ghost* . . . could smile!

But the smile disappeared when he spread his arms again and stepped closer to the wall.

He peered up at her, his expression earnest. "I told you, I may not be able to catch you here. But I should be able to *cushion* a fall if you slip. You need to turn around and climb down using the same footholds you used to get up there."

Cilla's heart dropped.

She couldn't remember where a single one of the footholds were. Nor could she see them from this angle. Looking down, she measured the distance between her and the tower floor and frowned.

For once, she'd hoped—no, expected—him to help her.

It really was a long way down.

Her knees began to tremble. "Why can't you catch me again? You did before."

"Because this is not Dunroamin." He said that as if it explained everything.

"I don't understand."

"It cost me much energy to come here." A line etched into his brow on the admission. "Without my full strength, I cannot be certain I can catch you. I'll no' risk that. It's safer if you climb down."

So she did, dropping first to her knees and then scooting round so she could scramble down before any other thought could enter her mind except that his outspread arms would at least soften the worst of a possible fall.

Safely at the bottom, she dusted her hands to give her heart time to stop galloping. Then she took a deep breath and braced herself against *other* dangers.

The most notable being his proximity.

"So why did you follow me here?" She tilted her head, aware of his exotic sandalwood scent, heady in

the closeness of the ruin. "Since you lose strength outside Dunroamin?"

To her surprise, he laughed.

But it was a humorless laugh, empty of the delicious
tinge of bemusement that had lit his eyes when he'd
pretended to stagger beneath her questions.

"Ach, lass." He put his hands on his hips and
glanced up at the sky above the roofless tower. "I didn't
follow you here. I was here well before you arrived."

"But why? If you haunt Dunroamin—"

"I do not *haunt* Dunroamin." Pride made Hardwick
clarify. "If you would know the truth of it, ghosts have
better things to do with their time than haunt people
or places. I stay at Dunroamin because"—he paused,
searching for the best words—"it suits me to do so."

And I came here to get away from you.

"Why?"

"Why what?" He blinked. His mind was elsewhere.

Indeed, he'd scarce heard her. She'd bent to pick
up the devil mask and in doing so, presented him with
a tantalizing view of her shapely backside.

"Why what I asked you before." She made it sound
like he was a lackwit. "Why are you at Dunroamin
and here? You don't have a Highland name, so I don't
think you're attached to Uncle Mac's family and—"

"My mother was a Shaw." He tried to tear his gaze
from her bobbing buttocks and couldn't. "Clan Macin-
tosh and Highland to the bone."

"That still doesn't explain your business here."

"You do not want anything to do with the reason
I'm here."

"Color me curious." She straightened then, the
devil face clutched in her hands, but the damage was
done. And the way she gripped the mask, holding it
fast against her, pushed up her full breasts so that they
swelled against the clingy blue top she wore.

Hardwick swore beneath his breath. He could even
make out the contours of her nipples. Chill-tightened

and thrusting, they were as visible as if she once again stood damp and naked before him.

Damp. Naked.

The two words whipped through him, blotting reason.

His blood flamed and heat swept low, gripping his vitals and squeezing tight. So exquisitely tight that he reached for her, setting his hands on her shoulders and holding her still, lest she move again and cause her beautiful breasts to jiggle. Or worse, present him with another delectable glimpse of her plump little bottom.

Remind him of the sweet triangle of lush golden curls topping her thighs.

"Curiosity, lass, is no' always a good thing." He shook his head slowly. "No' a good thing at all."

Her chin shot upward. "Even so—"

"Nae, lass." He couldn't give in to her. "Trust me and leave it be."

"Trust you?" Her eyes flashed blue. "When you won't even answer the simplest questions?"

Hardwick raked a hand through his hair. In that moment, a crack widened in the wall of the ruin and where a moment before crumbled mortar had filled the narrow space between stones, several sets of fiery red eyes peered out at him.

He jerked, releasing Cilla just as a thin, papery hand reached out of the crack to crook a finger at him.

Oblivious to the jeering hags in the wall behind her, she stared at him, too. His heart racing, he ignored the crones and looked down at her, willing himself to see not her large blue eyes peering up at him so defiantly, but Bran of Barra's ugly bearded face.

The Hebridean varlet owed him a favor or two, so he doubted the lout would mind.

He took it further, imagining his friend rocking back on his heels, then slapping his thigh in mirth. Roaring with the irony that for once, he—Hardwick, the rogue of all rogues—couldn't just toss a lass o'er his shoulder, carry her off to bed, and air her skirts just because it pleased him.

Not that he'd treat this one thusly.

This lass begged a slow and thorough ravishing, hell hags or no.

He swallowed hard and reached for her again. But his strength was ebbing and he couldn't grip her shoulders. Leastways, not as firmly as he'd hoped to do.

He *did* groan.

The exact groan men make just before they lower their heads to kiss a woman.

Cilla's breath caught, her agitation forgotten. Her heart split. He was only testy because she was provoking him. And she was doing that because he made her nervous. Because ever since she'd spotted him limned in that ray of sunlight, she'd *wanted* to kiss him.

And now it was going to happen!

She was sure of it.

Despite every shrill warning bell in her head, she leaned up onto her toes and lifted her face to make it easier for him.

She even puckered her lips.

Pulse racing, she waited for his lips to close over hers, first brushing gently, then with increasing insistence until he crushed her against him and devoured her mouth in a rough, bruising kiss.

The kind Grant A. Hughes III had only given her in her dreams.

Pleasure she wasn't going to enjoy now, either, because just when he leaned in so close she could feel his warm breath on her cheek, he released her again so quickly she dropped the devil mask.

Whipping about, he strode across the tower and snatched up his discarded shield. When he turned back to face her, he held the thing in front of him as if he expected her to run him through with a broadsword.

He did not look like a man who'd been about to kiss her buggy socks off.

He looked furious.

And he couldn't even seem to meet her eyes, his gaze repeatedly darting past her to a spot on the crumbling, moss-grown wall.

Mortification swept Cilla. Heat jabbed into the backs of her eyes, making her humiliation complete.

Even Grant the rat fink hadn't made her cry.

Scowling, he finally stepped up to her and reached to brush her cheek with his thumb.

"This, sweetness"—he glanced at his hand, the wetness glistening there—"is the reason you should not have come to Dunroamin."

Cilla kept her chin raised and glared at him.

The blaze in his own eye could have lit a bonfire. "It's also the reason I came here, to Castle Varrich, today. I'll no' make such a mistake again."

Unable to bear having him see her embarrassment a moment longer, Cilla stooped to snatch up the devil mask. This time when she straightened, he was gone.

"Damn!" She swiped a hand over her cheek.

Then she tossed back her hair and started for the doorway. Beyond the jagged opening, she could see clouds building out over the Kyle. Soon it would rain. Already, she could smell the chill moisture in the air.

That and a lingering whiff of sandalwood.

Just enough to pinch her heart.

But as she hefted the devil mask against her hip to scramble out of the ruin, she knew two things she hadn't known before she'd entered it.

Firstly—the mask was *not* the devil face she'd seen outside her window. She glanced at the name label sewn into the inside of the mask, sure of it. However the devil face came to be in the possession of a giant bird, it wasn't sinister.

She'd seen the real thing.

This was simply a mask that had once been the property of one Erlend Eggertson.

She shuddered, not about to contemplate the implications when she had a long trek through dark and creepy woods awaiting her.

Instead, she considered her second and most important revelation. She'd almost been kissed by a medieval Highland ghost.

And she'd wanted that kiss badly.

So badly, in fact, that she meant to do everything in her power to find out why it'd gone wrong.

Then, if for once her luck would change, she just might be able to make things right.

At the very least, she meant to try.

Chapter 8

"It had to have been Gregor." Aunt Birdie nodded for emphasis. "The big question is, where in the world did he get such a thing? A red devil mask here"—she gripped the edge of the small round table and leaned forward—"in the middle of nowhere."

"I'm sure I can't imagine where he got it." Cilla popped a mini pretzel into her mouth.

Compliments of the Ben Loyal Hotel's Bistro Bar, where they sat in a quiet corner, the tiny salted tidbits were addictive. Already, she'd nibbled her way through one rather full bowl. And this second portion—served with equal generosity—would soon be gone, too.

Especially since each bite she took helped take the edge off her worry about where *her* devil face had come from. The obvious answer—*hell*—was a road she didn't want to go down. Not in her own mind and certainly not in a discussion with Aunt Birdie. She rather doubted her aunt's ghost-friendly outlook would extend to the fiend of all fiends.

Frowning, she shoved aside the bowl of pretzels.

Too much salt wasn't good for you.

Neither was dwelling on things that would only add flames—perhaps literally—to the already scary situation at Dunroamin. She also needed to stop fretting over almost-kisses that hadn't and never would happen.

She shifted on her chair, even now feeling his strong, warm hands settle on her shoulders. She remembered, too, how her senses had leapt into overdrive, her entire body igniting as he'd stepped so close and looked down at her with such hot, scorching heat in his eyes.

How sure she'd been he was about to lower his head and kiss her.

And not just *a kiss*, but the deep, plundering kind that burned into a woman's soul and left her melting all over a man. Breathless, needy, and begging for more, sure the world will stop spinning if he didn't slake her craving.

With a gusty sigh, she crossed her legs, squeezing them together just a tad more than she'd usually do.

No, a lot more.

She frowned.

She really needed to forget the man.

Er . . . the ghost.

Sitting up straighter, she cleared her throat. "You really think the bird was Violet Manyweather's great skua? The bonxie, or whatever they're called?"

"Bonxie, that's right." Aunt Birdie sounded fond of him. "He's quite clever. Though he usually only snatches things from Colonel Darling. Small items like a pen or reading glasses, and once, his favorite pipe."

Cilla's eyes widened. "Was it lit?"

"The pipe?" The smile twitching her aunt's lips said it was.

"And with the colonel's own custom blend, too," she elaborated. "A fine-smelling mix of vanilla and rum. Achilles was livid."

"From a gentleman's pipe to a devil mask." Cilla shook her head, glad to get her mind on something else. "I still can't believe we managed to get the thing into your car, big as it is."

Aunt Birdie laughed and glanced at the two broken fingernails on her right hand. "We may have wedged it in, my dear, but I'm not so sure we'll ever get it out again. In any event, its horns are ruined."

"Maybe Erlend Eggertson will be so happy to get his mask back, he won't care that we bent the horns."

Aunt Birdie took a few of the mini pretzels and sat back. "I don't think there is such a man in these parts. Unless he's a recent incomer, and even then—"

"You'd have heard of him."

"Let's just say that if I hadn't, you can bet one of the residents would have. A shame—"

A burst of muted female laughter issuing through the wall behind the bar cut her off. Excited and girly sounding, the giggles came from the hotel's An Garbh restaurant.

When the noise died down, Aunt Birdie continued, "A shame the An Garbh is so full tonight. You'd have enjoyed dinner there, and I could have asked the proprietors if they know of the Eggertsons. But they looked to have their hands full with"—she paused as another shriek of laughter erupted—"their coach-tour guests."

"Coach-tour guests." Cilla smiled at her. "They struck me more like a pack of rabid hyenas."

Aunt Birdie's mouth quirked again. "You saw them?"

"I peeked in there when I first arrived. I thought you might be here already." Cilla allowed herself one last mini pretzel. A reward for getting her mind off a certain sexy ghost and how good she knew he'd kiss. "I think they're a group of college girls or something."

"They're definitely not the usual visitors we see in Tongue. Hill walkers, stac climbers, and the like. And they aren't girls. They're Australian *women*, though some might be fresh out of college." Aunt Birdie took a sip of soda water and lowered her voice. "According to Claire, who works the shoppie at the petrol station, they're fans of Wee Hughie MacSporran—"

Whoosh . . . crack! A standing bar menu flew off a nearby table. Small but sturdy-looking, it smacked into a chair leg before spinning away across the red-carpeted floor.

Both women swiveled toward the sound, but no one else was in the pub. Even the friendly young barkeep had left his post and wasn't anywhere to be seen.

Aunt Birdie's eyes narrowed, but then she gave a light shrug and took another sip of her soda water.

Cilla glanced at the fallen menu board, wondering. She sniffed the air, certain she'd caught a tantalizing trace of sandalwood swirling at her from that direction. She looked around, her pulse leaping. The windows to the street stood open, but she couldn't detect a breeze. Nothing at all that would send the menu sailing off its table.

Or cause his delicious scent to waft beneath her nose, teasing and tempting her.

Unless . . .

Her heart skittered.

Foolish, wild hope swept her.

Getting up, she retrieved the menu and returned it to the table. More to check on the drift of sandalwood than from a sudden urge to tidy the hotel's pub. Little good the ploy did her.

If the scent had been there, it wasn't anymore.

She tamped down her disappointment. Then she reclaimed her seat, careful not to look at the bowl of mini pretzels. The blasted things seemed to be calling her again, and she was *not* going to weaken.

Not for mini pretzels.

And—if she knew what was good for her—especially not for imagined whiffs of sandalwood.

Dark, smoldering glances and a deep Scots burr so beautiful on the ears that the man ought to walk around wearing a warning sign around his neck:

CAUTION! PLUG YOUR EARS OR LOSE YOUR HEART.

Moistening her lips, she blotted his honey-rich voice from her mind. She also closed her nose to his unbelievably rousing scent, if it'd even been there. She'd outgrown the Mad for Plaid club of her teen years. Now she was made of sterner stuff and she wasn't falling for a Highland ghost!

Especially one she imagined ate one woman for breakfast, two for lunch, and a full dozen for dinner!

Her brows snapped together and her cheeks flamed. Without doubt, he'd be a master at *that* kind of eating, making a woman feel that she was a feast to be savored. Cilla inhaled sharply, annoyed by the jab of resentment that pricked her on knowing he hadn't even wanted to kiss her.

She squirmed on her chair again, certain her thoughts must be branded on her forehead.

Hoping they weren't, she gave Aunt Birdie her full attention. "Who is Wee Hughie MacSporran?" she asked, grasping for a safe topic.

"We-ll . . ." Her aunt drew out the word. "He calls himself the Highland Storyweaver. In short, he's an entrepreneur."

A sound that could have been a snort came from the back of the pub.

Cilla's breath caught and she shot a glance that way, namely toward the table with the flying menu board, but nothing stirred.

Her aunt flicked at a pretzel crumb. If she'd noticed, she gave no indication.

But Cilla knew. Hot little flickers of awareness flashed down her spine, and her belly went all soft and fluttery. Worse, her nipples tightened and pushed against her top, almost as if they had a mind of their own and were straining for another of his oh-so-rousing finger brushes. Furious about her body's reaction to him—to a mere snort, for heaven's sake!—she risked another quick glance at the corner table.

It looked quiet as ever.

Not that the corner's stillness mattered. Even if he was doing that ghost-power trick he'd told her about and keeping himself invisible, she'd bet the farm he was near.

And she wasn't about to let him see how much he affected her.

She cleared her throat. "So Wee Hughie's a businessman?"

"Oh yes. But it's himself that he markets." Aunt Birdie's brows drew together. "He's written a book or two. His own family history, a bit of Scottish root-searching, and the like. He also lectures and he's—"

A bluidy windbag!

A gust of chill air blasted in through the windows as if to prove it. The pub door flew open and slammed shut with a loud bang.

"Oh, dear." Aunt Birdie placed a hand to her breast. She glanced first at the door, then the windows. "It would seem a storm is brewing."

Indeed, my lady.

Aunt Birdie's face went suspiciously noncommittal.

Cilla's heart pounded wildly. Her nipples almost hurt. Now she *knew* he was here. A snort and two comments—all delivered in that buttery-rich burr— was more than enough proof.

His tone and the nature of his comments revealed he didn't like the Scottish author, the entrepreneur, as Aunt Birdie called the man.

Cilla wanted to know why.

With luck, talking about the author would keep her grounded if Hardwick's sexy voice rolled past her ears again. It didn't matter what he said, not even that he sounded really annoyed. It was the *way* he said things, his Scottish accent, that curled her toes and sent a flash flood of heat tingling across her tender parts.

"So-o-o"—she tried to keep her own voice level— "why does Wee Hughie have a busload of Aussies trailing after him?"

"Did you not see the placard outside, next to the

hotel door?" Aunt Birdie looked surprised. "It has HIRE A HIGHLANDER scrawled in blue across the top. I can't believe you missed it."

"If I'd seen the name Wee Hughie I would've noticed. And HIRE A HIGHLANDER would've stopped me in my tracks." Cilla curled her fingers around her pint of Stella Artois lager, squeezing lightly.

She needed focus.

Aunt Birdie didn't need to know that her mind had been so occupied on her tramp down the hill that she'd marched straight past the hotel. She'd only discovered her mistake when the little whitewashed croft houses she'd been passing grew sparser, the fields between larger, and the sheep in the fields more plentiful.

She'd been walking blind.

Worrying about the devil at her window that hadn't been a mask and fretting about Hardwick.

Especially Hardwick.

Thinking about him still, she looked at her aunt. "What does a poster have to do with Wee Hughie's groupies? I don't see the connection."

Aunt Birdie laughed. "Think again, dear. The poster shows why they're with him. Wee Hughie MacSporran runs Heritage Tours. Guiding, some call it. Anyone can sign on, and he then escorts them around the Highlands, regaling them with tales along the way."

"Oh." Cilla nodded, not really caring.

She was too busy concentrating on willing her nipples to de-pucker.

She couldn't prove it, but she'd swear *he* was staring right at them. Maybe even using ghostly magic to make her imagine slick, hot tongue swirls circling first one, then the other nipple.

That's what it felt like, anyway.

She frowned and reached for a pretzel, determined to ignore the sensation.

"Wee Hughie's done an Australian book tour or

two," her aunt was saying. "These women are fans. Apparently, they sign on for a Highland tour with him every summer."

Cilla blinked. "What?"

Aunt Birdie made a gesture. "You'll soon meet Wee Hughie yourself. He's scheduled to speak in Dunroamin's library next weekend."

Another gust of icy wind swept in through the windows, this time lifting a small stack of coasters off the bar and sending them cartwheeling through the air.

The barkeep returned then, pushing in through a door behind the bar. He carried their order on a tray, jacket potatoes with cheese and baked beans. Coming straight to their table, he plunked down the plates with an apologetic smile. Then he scurried, unasked, to refresh their drinks, his young face flushed from hurrying.

"Sorry you had to wait." Quick as lightning, he turned away, scooping up the scattered coasters on his hasty retreat to the bar. "There's an *event* in the An Garbh this e'en," he tossed over his shoulder before disappearing through the door he'd used to enter the pub. "Keeping us right busy they are, just!"

"Goodness." Aunt Birdie looked after him, then put down her glass of soda water and went to the bar. A few books and a little pile of flyers were displayed there. Taking one of each, she returned to the table. "Here. These will give you an idea of who Wee Hughie is."

Cilla set down the fork she'd been about to plunge into her baked potato and picked up the book. The title, *Royal Roots*, jumped out at her. Several inches tall, the words blazed across the top of the book in bright gold letters. A subtitle, *A Highlander's Guide to Discovering Illustrious Forebears*, followed in smaller lettering. The rest of the cover showed a tall, rather corpulent Highlander posing in front of the famous Bannockburn statue of Robert the Bruce.

The flyer announced a series of "Meet Your Ancestors" tea-and-talk events to be held at the Bettyhill Museum, the Loch Croispol Bookshop and Restaurant in Balnakeil, and—no surprise—Dunroamin Castle Residential Care Home.

Humph.

The snort came so close to Cilla's ear she would've sworn *he* was leaning over her shoulder. But before she could glance around, the main pub door opened and closed again, this time falling shut with a quiet click.

An almost imperceptible little snick that sounded oddly final.

Cilla frowned. The book and the flyer felt suddenly cold beneath her fingers.

She set them down, not missing that the chill wind had stopped gusting through the window. The whole feel of the air shifted and changed. That last humph and the closing of the door clinched it. If Hardwick had been there, perhaps watching her from the menu table, he'd now left.

Which had a silver lining—she could finally bring up the subject she'd been dying to discuss.

And Wee Hughie MacSporran seemed a perfect way to ease into it.

"What's a 'Meet Your Ancestors' tea?" She pitched her voice casually. "Does Wee Hughie introduce a parade of ghostly forebears during his presentations?"

Aunt Birdie almost choked on a bit of baked potato. "Oh!" She dabbed at her mouth with a napkin. "That would be interesting, my dear. The man claims direct descent from Robert Bruce and just about every other notable in Scottish history. It'd be quite a roll call of luminaries if he summoned them all to his lectures."

"So what does he do?" Cilla hoped her aunt didn't see her nervousness.

"He tells tales about them." Aunt Birdie waved an

airy hand. "He'll surely regale us with anecdotes from his famed ancestors and then do a question-and-answer round. Supposedly, he can spin a yarn about your own family history if you challenge him with a Scottish surname."

Cilla looked down, toying with her food. "Maybe he'll know something about the Eggertsons?"

"Could be." Aunt Birdie took a bite of baked beans. "He's rumored to have extensive knowledge of the clans, so he might well know of other names."

"I wonder if he would know anything about a place called Seagrave or"— Cilla drew a breath, then rushed on—"a medieval family named de Studley?"

"You could certainly ask him." Aunt Birdie smiled, her deep blue eyes crinkling at the corners. "Seagrave rings a faint bell. I believe it's a ruin on the east coast, south of Aberdeen. Rather like the touristy Dunnottar, but left wild, totally untouched except by time."

"What about the de Studleys?"

Aunt Birdie shook her head. "I can't say that I've heard of them, my dear. Sorry."

. . . Can't say that I've heard of them.

The words hit Hardwick like a kick in the shins.

He winced and stepped deeper into the shadows near the door. To be sure, Birdie MacGhee had never heard of his family. He'd left no issue, and those who'd remained and could have, though not directly cursed, met their own untimely ends until the line was no more.

Even Seagrave, mighty holding that it'd been, had suffered. Other families came and went, tearing down towers or adding wings until, ultimately, they, too, disappeared into the mists of time.

Leaving Seagrave to crumble into the sea, stone by stone, until the curse ran its course. A sorry state and the very reason he had no business standing here, deliberately letting *her* think he'd gone.

Souls who insisted on peeking beneath rocks were bound to discover things they didn't want to see.

Or hear.

Yet he couldn't leave.

She drew him like a lodestone. And try as he might, he couldn't blank his mind to the image of her tilting her head back for his kiss, her face going all soft and dreamy and her lips just beginning to part. A brief glimpse of the tip of her tongue to tantalize and enflame him.

He clenched his hands, squeezing them tight when she shifted on her chair, causing her jacket to gape slightly, allowing him a splendid view of her full, round breasts and hardened, thrusting nipples.

A sweet temptation he had no business ogling, not that he could tear his gaze away. Nor did it help that she was looking right at him, her eyes earnest and her brows drawn together. Almost as if she saw him despite the cloaking shield he'd willed around himself.

There were, he knew, some souls who could see ghosts always, regardless of a ghost's honest attempts at remaining unseen.

Or, he strongly suspected, times when the pull between two souls was so powerful that the veils separating time and place just ceased to exist.

Sure that was the way of it, his heart started a slow, hard beating. A rush of warmth swept him, filling him with a deep longing that had nothing to do with her nipples, much as he burned to get his hands and mouth on them.

He frowned, almost willing himself wholly visible until her gaze shifted past him to the windows and the direction of Castle Varrich. She stared out at the ruin, but her mind was clearly turned inward.

Hardwick's body tensed and he narrowed his eyes on her, waiting. Seven hundred years of womanizing let him know that she was about to make some important pronouncement.

"Aunt Birdie . . ." She returned her attention to

her aunt, her tone proving him right. "There was another reason I wanted us to eat here before going
back to Dunroamin. I need to talk to you alone."

Hardwick's ears perked.

Chivalry forgotten, he sidled nearer.

"About Grant?" One of Birdie MacGhee's brows
arched ever so slightly. "You know you have my
sympathies."

"It isn't Grant." A pink tinge stained Cilla's cheeks.
"I really am over him. Truth is, looking back, I can't
imagine what I ever saw in him."

A jolt of triumph shot through Hardwick.

He edged closer. So near that her clean, fresh scent
swirled up to tempt him. Nae, to bewitch him, because
for one crazy-mad moment he forgot he was a ghost!
His lips started to curve in a slow, seductive smile.
The kind designed to melt a woman's knees and make
her all hot and achy inside. But then he remembered
his *situation* and frowned instead.

As if she knew her power over him and meant to
plague him even more, she leaned forward and her
shoulder brushed lightly against him.

He froze, not daring to move as the warmth of her
touch spiraled through him. Not just warm but golden
and prickly, it spread like honey fire, flaming his blood.
A fierce longing gripped him, and for two pins he
would've grabbed her, yanking her to her feet and
into his arms. He'd steal her breath with hot, furious
kisses and free her breasts, letting his hands slide over
them, kneading and plumping.

But then a shadow fell across the room, the brief
darkening reminding him of the futility of such desires.

Even so, he reached to touch a finger to her cheek,
savoring its silky-smooth softness, knowing she'd think
it was the wind.

She blinked in response, her breath catching
audibly.

"Grant was jerk," she said then, speaking to her aunt but looking right at him. "He wasn't even a good kisser. Actually, he was a bad one."

Hardwick's heart soared.

All ears now, he flicked his wrist and conjured a three-legged stool to sit on, plunking it down a good—safe—two tables away from hers.

He dropped onto it, waiting.

"Well?" Her aunt was looking at her, too. "What did you want to talk about?"

"Ghosts." She cleared her throat. "I want to talk about ghosts."

Her aunt didn't bat an eye. "A-ha!" She smiled. "So you ran into Gudrid the Viking maid up at the ruin? I rather hoped she'd show herself to you."

Hardwick sat forward, eager for her reply.

"No-o-o, I didn't see her." She sounded distracted. "What I really wanted to know was"—she paused, her fork poised over her baked beans—"if Uncle Mac had been a ghost when you met him, would you still have fallen in love with him?"

"What—?" Her aunt's eyes widened.

"Don't make me repeat it, please." She set down her fork, tucked a strand of hair behind her ear. "I feel silly enough already. Just imagine Uncle Mac had been a ghost. Not a Casper-like ghost, but real-seeming. Like"—she bit her lip, clearly searching for words—"a flesh-and-blood man. A really gorgeous and sexy man, too."

Hardwick grinned.

She was talking about him. He knew it as sure as Bran of Barra's beard was red.

Her aunt angled her head, studying her through narrowed eyes. "A ghost? Your Uncle Mac?"

"Yes." She nodded. "What would you have done?"

"Well . . ." Birdie MacGhee gazed out the window, appearing to consider. Then her face brightened.

Turning back to her niece, she slapped the table with her hand, silver armbands jingling. "I'd have jumped his bones, my dear," she laughed. "No pun intended."

"Aunt Birdie!" Cilla felt her face flame. "I was serious."

"So am I." Aunt Birdie sat back in her chair, nursing her soda water. "I was much younger than you when I met your uncle. And *very* romantic." She winked. "I'm quite sure I would have fallen for him, yes."

"Despite the impossibility of it?" Cilla remained skeptical.

"The *impossibility* of it—the romance—would have spurred me on." A dreamy look entered Aunt Birdie's eyes. "Remember, I'm the one your mother says is 'out with the fairies.' I would have hoped to find a spell or whatnot to make things work out for us."

"I think you mean that."

"I do."

Looking wholly in her element, Aunt Birdie lifted an arm and examined the bangles on her wrist. "I'll prove it to you," she said, fingering one of them. "Once, well before I met Mac, I stayed in a lovely castle hotel near Edinburgh. Dalhousie Castle, now a luxurious tourist resort, yet preserved as one of the finest thirteenth-century strongholds you'll find in all broad Scotland."

Cilla felt a flutter in her belly, knew her aunt had more to tell. "What happened?"

"Ah, well—" Aunt Birdie laughed, sat straighter in her chair. "I was given the hotel's de Ramseia suite in the oldest part of the castle, a wonderfully re-created medieval bedchamber deep in the castle's vaulted basement."

"You saw a ghost there?" Cilla pounced on the possibility.

Aunt Birdie's gaze went past her. "Let's just say

that Dalhousie's five-hundred-year-old well was in my room. And"—she looked back at Cilla—"it gave me certain ideas."

"Like what?"

Aunt Birdie studied her arm bangles again. "The well," she began, speaking slowly, "was in a corner of the room. For safety's sake, it'd been fitted with a clear glass covering and an iron grill, but little spotlights shone into the shaft. You could look right down into it, clear to the bottom, where the water winked back up at you."

"You loved it." Cilla knew her aunt.

"More than that, it fascinated me." Aunt Birdie's voice went soft, distant. "Highlighted as the well was, combined with the room's period furnishings, made it more than easy to lie awake at night and imagine a dashing warrior knight climbing up out of the shaft to ravish me!"

Cilla smiled. "But one didn't."

"Sadly, no." Aunt Birdie shook her head. "But"— she winked—"had such a gallant appeared, ghostly or otherwise, you can bet I would have considered his appearance a gift of the cosmos and taken full advantage!"

"You know . . . I think I believe you."

"You better." Aunt Birdie reached across the table and squeezed her hand. "Despite your uncle's blustering, there are things in this world that just can't be explained. That doesn't mean for an instant that they aren't real. And remember"—her eyes started twinkling again—"this is—"

"Scotland," Cilla finished for her, "a magical land where such things just might happen."

"And do."

"Oh, Aunt Birdie, I—" a sudden burst of wind shook the nearby windows, splattering rain against the glass and through the opening, onto the edge of their table.

"Goodness me!" Aunt Birdie leapt to her feet and carried her chair around to Cilla's side. "We'd best finish up and be on our way," she added, reaching for her plate. "I hadn't realized the weather was turning so quickly."

"I saw storm clouds earlier but forgot about them." Cilla spoke a half-truth.

He'd taken her mind off all else.

And now, with the increasing wind moaning around the eaves of the pub and rain pelting the walls, the magic moment had passed.

She'd have to wait for another opportunity to tell Aunt Birdie about her sexy ghost.

Her aunt might be receptive, but her mind was no longer on some romantic castle hotel and its medieval well. Now she was thinking about the long drive back to Dunroamin in the rainy dark and on slick, wet roads.

Slick, wet roads made more hazardous by sheets of drifting mist.

"I can't believe it's so dark out there." Cilla glanced at the windows. Light from the hotel shone out into the road, but otherwise the world had turned a deep, thundery gray. "I thought—"

"It will pass." Aunt Birdie sounded confident. "As soon as the storm blows over, the night sky will be as shining bright as always this time of year."

"Should we wait then? Maybe—"

A movement outside the window caught Cilla's eye and she snapped her mouth shut, blinked several times. She might be wrong—the sword and his shield were missing—but unless her eyes were fooling her, *he* stood outlined against the overcast night.

Seemingly oblivious to the rain and whirling mist, he leaned against the wall near the hotel entrance, his arms folded and his feet crossed at the ankles.

He was clearly waiting for someone.

And she had a good idea who.

Her breath snagged and her heart started racing. Then she nearly jumped out of her skin when Aunt Birdie placed a hand on her shoulder. She hadn't even noticed her getting up.

"I think it's time." Her aunt smiled down at her.

Cilla's jaw almost slipped. But then she realized her aunt only meant the drive home. "Out with the fairies" or not, Aunt Birdie wasn't a mind reader.

"Well?" Aunt Birdie stepped back, hitched the strap of her bag onto her shoulder. "Are you ready?"

"Yes." Cilla pushed to her feet before her knees could start knocking.

She *was* ready.

Aunt Birdie was right. Scotland was a magical place.

And some of that magic was about to happen to her.

She could just feel it.

Chapter 9

"You're slipping again, my friend."

Bran of Barra stood on the strip of pavement outside the Ben Loyal Hotel and winked broadly at Hardwick. Then he whipped out his sword and, with a bit of a flourish, jabbed at the empty space where Hardwick's own sword—and his shield—should have been.

"You've once again manifested without your best pieces." He sheathed his blade and planted balled fists on his hips. "The lassie's addled your wits!"

Hardwick frowned at him. "My best pieces are here, right enough."

All of them, he added. Naturally, to himself.

For Bran's benefit, he held up his hands and wriggled his fingers. Instantly, his trusty shield and brand appeared. "They are here if I need them."

He refrained from commenting on his wits. They did seem to be in a questionable state of late. Leaning back against the wall, he vanquished his sword and shield. Then he assumed the most casual stance he could muster.

He also damned his luck that he'd sifted himself out of the pub only to reappear in nearly the very same spot and instant that his Hebridean friend chose to manifest his great hunkering self.

The collision of their foreheads had been formidable.

Most annoying of all, the impact hadn't seemed to faze the bearded lout at all.

His own head was splitting.

So much so that if the knave didn't stop grinning at him, he'd be sore pressed to challenge him to a bit of swordplay on the edge of the nearest cliff edge. A plunge down a five-hundred-foot rock face and into the cold, dark sea would dampen even a wild Isleman's humor.

Instead, he left his blade safely out of reach and tried another, equally effective tactic.

He smiled.

"So-o-o, Bran." He spoke as if they were sitting in Seagrave's massive great hall, enjoying fine ale and finer women. "How is it you lost interest in Norse wenches so quickly? I didn't expect you back from Shetland for a good while. Or"—he deepened his smile—"did the bonny northern maids snub their pretty noses at you?"

Bran stepped back, legs apart and shoulders squared. "There wasn't an hour I was away when I didn't have a willing lass perched on each knee, make no doubt about it."

"Then why are you here?"

"You ask! The whole bleeding Lerwick town was astir." Bran paused, tossed a flap of his plaid over his shoulder against the cold wind coming down off the hills. "I'd ne'er seen the like. Even the womenfolk were as up in arms and for carrying on as the men."

He shook his head, pulled on his bushy red beard. "You'd think the world was coming to an end."

"Indeed?"

"Did I no' just say so?" Bran's chin jutted.

Hardwick folded his arms.

Glancing aside, he pretended interest in the mist-bank blotting the scatter of houses at the far end of the road. From somewhere closer by came the sharp tang of wood smoke, welcome on the chill, damp air. He took a deep, deliberately audible breath, waiting.

He knew better than to rush a Hebridean bent on sharing a juicy bit of blether.

"Heigh-ho!" Bran's face loomed in front of him, mere inches away. "Quit doing as if you're counting raindrops. I know you're keen to hear what's set all Shetland on its ear!"

"And I know you'll tell me whether I wish to hear it or not."

"Is that so?"

Hardwick tried to keep his lips from twitching.

Bran needed less than an eye blink to detect the hidden smile, his own face splitting in a grin. "You great lump!" he roared, clapping Hardwick on the shoulder. "All these hundred years, and still you get the better of me!"

"I'd say the score is about even, my friend." Hardwick reached up to give Bran's hand a hardy squeeze. He wasn't about to admit it, but he'd missed the lout.

Stepping back, he resumed his leaning-against-the-wall pose. "Now tell me what drove you from some sweet Norsewoman's breast?"

"A raid!" Outrage swelled Bran's voice. "The whole of Lerwick town is out for vengeance."

Hardwick's brows lifted. He could scarce believe it.

But Bran's bobbing head said that it was so.

"A raid?" Hardwick looked at his friend. "You're certain?"

"Sure as I'm standing here."

"Was there rape and pillage?"

Such was, after all, the old way of raiding.

"Nary a drop of blood was shed." Bran huffed. "Nor was a single war cry given. It wasn't that kind of raiding."

"What, then?"

"They took things." Bran lowered his voice, glanced

over his shoulder. "National treasures, Seagrave. All that's most dear to a Shetlander's heart."

"The women?" Hardwick could think of nothing else.

"Nae, you great muckle sumph!" Bran laughed. " 'Twas far worse than that. They raided the Galley Shed, for the love o' Thor!"

Hardwick blinked. "The what?"

"Just what I said. The Galley Shed." Bran hooked his hands in his belt and rocked back on his heels. "Dinna tell me you've forgotten the place. It's the great warehouse—*a shed*—where the good men of Lerwick build their Viking longboat each year. They—"

"Vikings?" Hardwick's brows arched.

"Up-Helly-Aa *guizers*!" Bran's voice boomed. "Braw, proud men taking care to uphold their Norse heritage by burning a galley at their fire festival each winter. Now their exhibition hall's been looted!"

"The boat was stolen?"

"Nae, but I'll vow they only left it because it was too big to carry away." Bran scowled. "The weasels took nigh all else they could get their hands on. Word is, if the town can't recover their losses, next year's Up-Helly-Aa will have to be cancelled."

Bran slapped his thigh, his eyes blazing. "You see why the Lerwick lassies had more on their mind than warming my bed! Blood calls when a Viking's wronged."

Hardwick rubbed his chin. Finally he understood.

Up-Helly-Aa *was* Shetland.

The festival, with its blazing procession of costumed *guizers* and the burning of their dragon ship, went back more than twelve hundred years. He and Bran had even attended a few such wild and raucous celebrations together, in their earth lives and thereafter.

What he didn't understand was why Bran returned to Tongue rather than staying on to help the locals find the perpetrators of such a crime against tradition.

Eyeing him now, the truth hit Hardwick like an upturned pail of icy water. A muscle in his jaw jerked and he pushed away from the wall, needing to move.

"You said the thieves took national treasures from the Up-Helly-Aa exhibit." He started pacing, his kilt swinging about his knees. "I'd hear what was taken."

"About time you asked!" Bran's face brightened.

"Then tell me."

"The list is long." Bran played for time, pausing to snort at the HIRE A HIGHLANDER placard displayed beside the hotel door. "The journey from Shetland is tedious. I may need to refresh myself before—"

"You sifted yourself here the same as I did." Hardwick stopped pacing to glare at him. "It takes less than a wink. But here"—he snapped his fingers and produced a cup of heather ale, offering it to the Hebridean—"let no man say I'd deny a friend his comforts."

Bran snatched the ale, quaffing it in one quick swig. "Ahhh . . ." He tossed aside the cup, laughing when it vanished before it hit the ground. "Now where was I?"

"The Galley Shed." Hardwick folded his arms.

"Aye, right enough." Bran drew his sleeve over his mouth. "Makes my blood boil, it does. The blackguards made off with the Guizer Jarl's entire Viking chieftain array and a good score of the other *guizers*' costumes. Horned and pointed helmets, mailed shirts, and woolen cloaks. Even a few fantasy disguises. Not to mention the swords, axes, and spears gone missing!"

Hardwick narrowed his eyes. "That's why you came back, isn't it?"

Bran's face turned a faint pink. He glanced down, shuffled his big feet on the wet pavement. "I did the same as you would have, and we both know it."

Hardwick started to agree but his throat had gone thick. He frowned. Of late, he'd been plagued by more than his share of such heart-pinching moments, and he wasn't sure what to do about them.

Especially when they were inspired by Bran of Barra.

So he simply gripped the varlet's heavily muscled arm and squeezed. There'd be time enough later to ponder just what *she* was doing to him. For now, he cleared his throat and leveled his most earnest look at his friend.

"If you're thinking what I am—that the *Viking ghosties* at Dunroamin are men using Up-Helly-Aa costumes to disguise themselves—we'll have to do something about it, and soon." He glanced at the hotel windows. Soft yellow light fell out onto the road. Golden and glowing like Cilla's hair. "I'll no' have the folks at Dunroamin set upon by a band of thieves."

Or worse.

He kept that thought to himself, but his gut clenched and his mouth went dry at the possibilities. Already he'd seen how brazen the hell hags were behaving, cackling in the mist of shower steam and peering out at him through cracks in Castle Varrich's ruined walling. He was sure he'd seen a root-dragon or two, as well.

He knew he'd smelled one.

If aught happened to Cilla and he couldn't protect her, he'd never forgive himself.

"We'll get to the bottom of it!" Bran boomed the words with gusto. "When we find the dredges, we'll hang them by their toes!"

"Must you yell when you're standing so close?" Hardwick rubbed his right ear.

Bran hooted. "That comes from living in the Hebrides. All those howling gales leave a soul no choice but to talk o'er them."

Hardwick couldn't argue with that.

He did need to get rid of his friend. Soon Cilla and her aunt would leave the hotel, and he'd rather be alone to greet them. Especially in light of Bran's tidings.

But the knave was leaning forward, fire in his eye. "Do you think *he* had a hand in any of this?"

"Who?" Hardwick blinked.

"Him yonder!" Bran's sword appeared in his hand and he thrust its point at the placard by the door. "I ne'er did like that preening peacock."

"Nor do I." Hardwick glanced at the poster. "But it's his belly winding that makes my head sore. I don't think he has aught to do with Mac's troubles."

"He's here." Bran remained stubborn.

"He's here to give talks." Hardwick ignored his friend's indignation. "Take another look at his placard. He's calling himself the Highland Storyweaver these days. And he's hauling adoring female admirers the length and breadth of the land. Do you truly think he'd ruin such a soft living by hieing himself up to Lerwick to steal Viking guises?"

Bran's expression soured.

He kicked a pebble in the road. "I'll still be keeping an eye on the rascal."

"You'd do better to go rally your friends." Hardwick warmed to the idea. "We might need them," he added, hoping such a showing wouldn't be necessary. "I'll see to MacSporran."

Bran waggled his brows. "And here I thought you'd been seeing to *her*."

"Who?" Hardwick feigned indifference.

"Hah!" Bran sent an exaggerated eye roll in the direction of the hotel's lit windows. "I saw you in there, lounging at a corner table and making moony eyes at the lass. Saw you true as my name's MacNeil!"

"I wasn't making eyes at her." Hardwick gave his friend a cross look. "A red devil mask turned up at Dunroamin and also Castle Varrich when you were away. I thought it in the best interest of all to see what the ladies had to say about the matter."

Bran barked a laugh.

Hardwick didn't care.

The half-truth was all the bushy-bearded Hebridean was getting out of him. It was no one's business but his own that he'd gone to Castle Varrich to get away from the lure of Cilla Swanner. The proud, upthrusting swells of her full, lush breasts with their pert pink nipples, or the impossibly rousing way her close-fitting hose drew a man's attention to the plump ripeness of her well-curved buttocks.

He scowled and swept a hand through his hair.

It was even less anyone else's concern that he'd followed her to the hotel pub because her scent reminded him of bright spring days, sun-washed and smelling of new grass and budding flowers. Or, saints preserve him, because he found the deep blue of her eyes irresistible.

"Best interest, eh?" Bran wasn't going to let it go.

"You err, my friend." Hardwick met the scoundrel's eye. "I had good reason for being in the pub. My efforts were well rewarded."

"Whate'er you say." Bran winked. "Far be it from me to argue with a man in love."

Hardwick ignored the taunt. "*Lounging* at that corner table enabled me to learn the name of the devil mask's owner. If I heard rightly"— he paused for effect—"the man is one Erlend Eggertson."

That won Bran's attention.

"By thunder!" His eyes rounded. "That's a Shetland name if e'er I heard one!"

"So I'm thinking." Hardwick waited as an old man walking a dog hastened past. "Now you see why I've asked you to gather your men. If Erlend Eggertson's devil mask was burgled from the Galley Shed, it can only mean—"

"War!" Bran raised a balled fist, looking more than pleased at the prospect. "By the powers, I'm away to Barra! The scuttling fools will learn the price of trying to cozen an Islesman. Or"—he threw a meaningful glance at the pub windows—"those we hold dear!"

Agreement flamed in Hardwick's heart. But before he could say so, his friend whipped out his blade and gave a bloodcurdling yell. Thumping his broad chest with one hand and using the other to slash the air with his steel, he vanished in a swirl of plaid and Gaelic curses.

In the same moment, the hotel door swung open.

A bright wedge of golden light spilled out into the rain-misted night. Cilla and her aunt stepped outside. Hardwick drew a deep breath. Then—making certain his blade and shield were indeed invisible—he squared his shoulders and strode forth from the shadows.

"Ladies." He bowed low. "A word, if you will . . ."

"Oh!" Cilla slammed into her aunt's back. Her jaw dropped, but she snapped it shut at once. Heat rushed through her, blazing hottest on her cheeks. She had the oddest sensation of the pavement dipping beneath her feet. She'd expected him to vanish again before she left the pub.

Yet there he stood, gorgeous as ever and looking even more corporeal than before.

He'd changed his appearance, leaving off his medieval trappings. Though still kilted, *this* kilt looked worn and a bit ragged around the edges. A khaki shirt, equally old-seeming, was unbuttoned just enough to reveal a tantalizing glimpse of his powerfully muscled chest. A dusting of black hairs glistened there, the sight of them doing funny things to her belly. Heavy work boots and thick, downturned socks completed the picture, as did the faint and irresistible scent of sandalwood still clinging to him, despite his modern-day garb.

Cilla swallowed, her heart beating wildly.

She slid a glance at her aunt, not daring to speak.

But if Aunt Birdie was surprised, she'd recovered

beautifully. Indeed, she was looking at him as if he were a long-lost friend just returned from a journey.

"Of course!" She flashed her brightest smile at him. "What can we do for you?"

All the charm of the Gael went into his own smile. "I am Seagrave. Sir— . . . er . . . Hardwick de—"

"Studley." Aunt Birdie didn't bat an eye.

She *did* toss a knowing look at Cilla.

"I've heard you were about," she added, cool as a cucumber. "It's a great pleasure to meet you."

Cilla looked from one to the other. It was clear her aunt recognized Hardwick. She obviously remembered Cilla mentioning his name in the pub. Likely, she'd *even* seen him, which would explain her repeated glances to the menu board corner.

A corner where Cilla was sure he'd sat listening to much of their conversation.

Her cheeks flamed. Aunt Birdie then also knew he was a ghost and not just any ghost, but the one that had caused her to ask how her aunt would have reacted if Uncle Mac had been a sexy, melt-your-bones ghost when they'd met.

The way Aunt Birdie was beaming at him proved it.

His own smile was devastating. "Word is," he said, his deep Scots burr smooth and rich, "that you've been having difficulties at Dunroamin. That you've reason to believe prowlers are roaming your peat fields of a night. I'm here to offer my services."

His services.

Cilla almost choked.

The heat in her cheeks intensified until she was sure she must be glowing like a Chinese firecracker. The place between her legs clenched, fiery tingles running rampant. She smoothed a hand down the front of her jacket, pretended to right a nonexistent crease in the perfectly sitting wool.

Aunt Birdie didn't appear to have any issues with his word choices.

"Your services?" Her aunt spoke without the slightest hesitation.

Hardwick nodded. "I've heard that your husband lacks men to cut his peat." He glanced in the direction of Dunroamin. "Sadly, I canna be of help with the peat. I've come here to"—he cleared his throat—"recover from a longtime malady, and am no' able to do much physical labor. But I can spend my nights walking your moors."

"Like a security guard?" Cilla looked at him, her heart thumping.

He blinked. "I would guard your uncle's peat hags, aye."

For the first time, Aunt Birdie looked uncomfortable. "I can't say Mac would agree. Times are difficult and we"—she fingered the fringed edge of her royal blue wrapper—"no longer have the—"

"Uncle Mac will come around." Cilla put a hand on her aunt's arm, certain her objection had more to do with worrying what Uncle Mac would say if he discovered Hardwick is a ghost than not having the funds to *hire* him.

"I have friends of Norse blood, my lady." Hardwick's voice rang deep, reassuring. "Even in the worst days of yore, many were simple farmers. Good men plied the seas as honest traders, dealing with merchants along the Baltic coasts and supplying much-needed goods to Viking settlers in distant Iceland and Greenland."

He paused, waiting until Aunt Birdie stopped fidgeting with her wrapper fringe.

"So you see"—he spoke with conviction—"it doesn't set well with me to learn there are souls who would guise themselves as my friends' more notorious forebears for the purpose of frightening others."

Aunt Birdie's head came up. "You've heard of our Viking ghosts?"

"I have."

"Running into them could be unpleasant." She glanced at Cilla. "Mac doesn't believe they're ghosts. They could be dangerous."

Hardwick barked a laugh. His eyes glittered in the light from the hotel entry. "I promise you, ladies, I also do not believe they are ghosts. And whoe'er they are and whate'er they're about, it will be dangerous for *them* when our paths cross."

Aunt Birdie considered. "Even so, we still—"

He cut her off with a raised hand. "Having done with them would be my pleasure. It's a matter of honor. And for that, I couldn't accept recompense. No Highlander worthy of the name would do so."

"Well . . ." Aunt Birdie stood straighter. "If you put it that way, perhaps—"

"I do." He took Aunt Birdie's hand, bringing it to his lips.

When he straightened, he turned to Cilla. For a moment, she thought she'd caught a hint of his sword belt slung low around his hips. The long, sheathed blade looking so right against his thigh, the brass studs of his shield flashing in the light from a passing car.

Her heart began to hammer.

She moistened her lips. Whether in medieval trappings or, as now, gorgeous in a sexy modern-day kilt, he simply took her breath. Especially when his eyes narrowed, seeming to heat and smolder as he kept his gaze fixed on her.

"It could be"—he turned back to her aunt—"that a friend or two might join me on my nightly patrols. They, too, are Highlanders. Islesmen I've known for . . . years."

An almost imperceptible smile twitched his lips. "Good fighting men and sharp-eyed, they'd eat your Viking ghosts for breakfast and spit out the bones."

Aunt Birdie beamed.

"Then it's settled, barring Mac's objection." Her gaze flicked across the road to her car. "I'd offer you

a lift to the castle now. I'd like you to speak to him.
But there's not an inch of spare room in my car."

She hesitated, as if weighing her words. "Cilla
climbed up to Castle Varrich's ruin this afternoon and
she brought back a red—"

"Devil mask, I know—"

"But how . . ." Aunt Birdie blinked. Then her face
cleared as quickly. "I should have known—"

"Of course, you should have." Cilla put a hand on
her aunt's arm, improvising. "You're the one always
going on about how well the gossip mill works in
Highland Scotland."

She brushed a raindrop off her sleeve. Hopefully
she'd spared Hardwick an awkward moment if he
hadn't yet realized her aunt knew just who—and
what—he was.

"I wouldn't be surprised if everyone above the
Highland Line knows about the mask by now." She
made a little hand flip to emphasize her point.

"You're right, of course." Aunt Birdie caught on.
"Even the stones are said to have ears here, every
clump of heather a pair of watching eyes. And"—she
smiled at Hardwick—"each burn a wagging tongue."

"Word has spread, aye." He nodded wisely. "I
have an idea who the mask's owner might be, or at
least where to find him. And I've an equally good
notion about the origins of your Viking ghosts.
Unfortunately"—he glanced at the lowering clouds—
"standing here in the drizzle isn't the time and
place—"

"You'll speak with Mac?" Aunt Birdie didn't make
a second offer of a lift.

"That's my intention." His eyes went dark, almost
fierce. "I'll visit him at the soonest."

Stepping back, he sketched another bow. *"Ladies."*
Then he turned and walked away. The silence of
his heavy, steel-shod boots on the pavement gave the
only indication he wasn't a true flesh-and-blood man.

"How did you know?" Cilla spun to face her aunt the instant the night mist swallowed him. "He looked just as real as we do and—"

"My dear"—Aunt Birdie flipped the edge of her wrapper over her shoulder—"I've known he was about since well before you arrived. I just didn't know who he was or his purpose until now."

Cilla blinked. "His purpose?"

"Why, it's all about you, of course." Aunt Birdie spoke as if that made perfect sense.

"And Uncle Mac and his peat fields?" Cilla hurried after her aunt when she started for the car. "The men-dressing-up-as-ghosts or whatever. What about all that?"

"That'll be part of it, too." Aunt Birdie opened the car door—people in Tongue didn't lock their vehicles—and slid behind the wheel.

She waited until Cilla dropped into the passenger seat and fastened her seat belt. "It's this man's karma to meet you. Perhaps to help us, too." Her voice took on a sage note. "I'm quite sure."

"But how do you know he's the ghost you've been sensing at Dunroamin?" Cilla worried her lip. "Maybe you've picked up on Margaret MacDonald? The nursery spirit Honoria told me about? She sounded very protective."

"Margaret hasn't been at Dunroamin for years." Aunt Birdie made a dismissive gesture. "I'd feel her if she were. She left Dunroamin when your uncle passed out of his boyhood."

"But . . ."

"No buts, dear. You told me yourself who this man is. How significant he's become to you." Aunt Birdie backed out of the parking space, her eyes now on the road. "Have you forgotten you mentioned his name and estate in the pub?"

Cilla looked out the car window. Curling wisps of smoke rose from the chimney of a roadside cottage.

Then they passed a cluster of sheep huddling near a dry stone wall. The whole lot of the shaggy woollies lifted their heads to stare at her.

Deep, penetrating stares, as if they knew how easily he'd scattered her wits.

Then the long causeway back across the Kyle loomed before them. But she took scarce note of how gray and white-capped the usually sparkling blue water had gone.

"Aunt Birdie"—she glanced at her aunt—"we only *talked* about him. When you bumped into him as we left the hotel, he could have been anyone. Or, as I suspect, did you see him in the pub?"

The slow curve of Aunt Birdie's lips was answer enough.

"I knew it!" Cilla eyes rounded. "You *did* see him!"

"And you didn't?" Aunt Birdie shot her an amused glance. "He was at a back table in the Bistro Bar nearly the whole time we were there. My dear, I do believe he's quite enamored of you. He looked ready to eat you up with a spoon."

Ready to eat her.

The image of his dark head between her thighs flashed across Cilla's mind. Her belly clenched and a flood of tingly heat swept low. She fisted her hands in her lap, ignoring the sensations.

"He's quite handsome, isn't he?" Her aunt chattered on. "Can you imagine being kissed by such a man?"

Cilla could. That was the problem.

She felt her face heating. "Why didn't you tell me you could see him?"

"I was hoping you'd mention him first." Aunt Birdie reached to flip on the CD player. A lively pipe tune filled the car's interior. "Not that it matters now. Your young man has solved that particular hurdle for us."

"And the other hurdles?" Cilla lifted her voice

above Uncle Mac's favorite pipe tune, "Paddy's Leather Breeches."

A short melody, the screaming pipes faded away quickly. But they started up again at once, the blaring tones even louder the second time.

Cilla's ears began to throb.

Aunt Birdie looked oblivious.

Even when the tune ended and started up a third time, once more louder than before.

"That's your uncle's doing." Aunt Birdie brimmed with amusement. "The CD plays that same little tune over and over again. But—"

"You don't mind because you know how much Uncle Mac loves it."

"That's right. Seeing how his face lights when he hears that tune makes the listening worthwhile." Aunt Birdie swung into Dunroamin's long drive. "You see, my dear, when someone matters, when you love them more than life itself, living and breathing to see them happy, you look past things that others might find irritating."

"Or impossible." Cilla now knew why her aunt switched on the pipe music.

"That, too." Aunt Birdie slid a meaningful glance her way. "Where there's love there's always—good heavens!"

She slammed on the brakes.

Her eyes rounded. "What's Violet doing on a creepie in the middle of the garden?"

"A creepie?" Cilla's breath caught, shades of her window devil—the real one—flashing across her mind.

Aunt Birdie flicked a finger toward the lawn. "The low, three-legged stool Violet is sitting on."

"Oh." Relieved, Cilla leaned forward, peering through the mist until she spotted the tiny woman.

Just as Aunt Birdie said, Violet Manyweathers appeared to perch on an unusually low stool. Great swaths of fog swirled around her and she sat hunched over, her stooped back and all the mist giving her the look of a crone out of some ancient Celtic saga.

Cilla thought of one from a series of Scottish medieval romance novels she'd once read. A fearsome old
bat called Devorgilla or something.

She shivered.

"What's she doing?" She could feel her brow
crimping.

"I don't know, but she isn't alone." Aunt Birdie's
gaze went past Violet to the clutch of residents gathered
on the paved terrace outside Dunroamin's glass-walled
conservatory. "Everyone but your uncle appears to be
out in the rain with her."

Cilla glanced at the terrace. Gently illuminated by
several mock gas lanterns, it was easy to make out the
cluster of anxious-faced onlookers.

Aunt Birdie was right.

Uncle Mac wasn't there.

But before Cilla could puzzle why, Léo shot into
view. Barking wildly, the dachshund streaked across
the lawn, making straight for Violet. Reaching her,
he ran circles around her, his short legs pumping at
great speed.

Cilla's eyes flew wide.

Aunt Birdie stared. "What the—"

"It's *him*!" Colonel Darling's voice pierced the
chaos. "That bloody boxtie!"

Hurrying toward the car, he held his walking stick
high in the air, waving it over his head as he ran. He
used his other hand to hold his protective deerstalker
hat clamped tight on his notably bald pate. His face,
ruddy on the best of days, had taken on a purple hue.

"Oh, dear." Aunt Birdie tossed Cilla a here-comes-
trouble look, then leapt from the car.

Cilla did the same.

"Achilles." Aunt Birdie reached to grasp the colonel's tweed-jacketed arms when he skidded to a halt in
front of them. "What in the world is going on here?"

"I just told you!" He kept his cane whirling round
his head. "It's that damned bird."

"Gregor?" Aunt Birdie used her softest voice.

"Is there any other?" The colonel scowled and shook free of her grip.

Huffing, he brushed at his sleeves. "The abominable creature showed up on a library window ledge just as we were settling in for tea."

He sounded scandalized.

Aunt Birdie kept her cool. "Gregor often perches on windows."

"With red cord snagged all round his damty legs?" Colonel Darling's brows snapped together. "A shame the cord wasn't wrapped round his neck, I say!"

Aunt Birdie and Cilla exchanged looks.

"A red cord?" Aunt Birdie looked to where Violet still sat on her stool, her back bent near double. "Is that what she's doing? Untangling a cord?"

The colonel's face turned a deeper shade of purple. "Fool woman announced she had to *save* him. If she didn't, the bird might hurt himself. Can you imagine?" He leaned close, his silver mustache quivering. "Off she went into the rain and wind, the whole bleeding household trailing after her! I ask you, have you ever heard such nonsense? We'd be better off without that vile—"

Auk, auk!

Gregor's cry cut him off. Then the bird appeared, waddling away from Violet's stool with the awkward rolling steps used by so many great birds of prey on land.

Cilla recognized him at once. He was the big bird from Castle Varrich.

His cry, too, was unmistakable. As was the cheeky way he held his brown-feathered head.

But the mentioned red cord was nowhere to be seen.

The bonxie's legs were free.

As if testing that freedom, Gregor took another few tottering steps and then turned around to fix Violet with a piercing stare. His white-patched wings shot upward in a victorious V-shaped greeting.

Auk, auk, he screeched again.

Violet laughed delightedly. Pushing slowly to her feet, she clapped her hands.

On the terrace, a great cheer arose.

Achilles Darling huffed.

When the bird took flight, winging away toward the moors, the colonel lowered his walking stick and released his grip on his deerstalker hat.

Then his gaze fell on the interior of Aunt Birdie's car.

His eyes bulged, comprehension swift. "That's the devil face Cook saw!" He yanked open the backseat door, peering inside. "And this"—he grabbed a long red cord dangling from one side of the mask—"is the same cording that was tangled round Gregor's legs!"

"That would seem the way of it." Aunt Birdie gave him her sunniest smile. "A riddle solved, yes."

"Humph!" He stepped back, dusting his hands. "I knew that bird caused the uproar!"

"Perhaps it's a good thing that he did." Cilla kept her thoughts on *her* devil face to herself. "If he hadn't found the mask, we'd never have known it *was* a mask. Behag Finney might have had nightmares for the rest of her life."

Colonel Darling snorted. "If you asked me, I'd wager he didn't find the mask. I say he stole it!"

"Wherever he got it"—Aunt Birdie started pulling the mask from her car—"Mac needs to hear about it." She glanced over her shoulder at the colonel. "Do you know where he is?"

"I do." The colonel's chest swelled with importance. "He's in the armory with a kilted young Highlander who looks like he walked off the set of *Brigadoon*."

Cilla's heart slammed against her ribs. "He's here already!"

Aunt Birdie's face wreathed in a smile. "So he's a man of his word."

"Eh?" The colonel gave them both a narrowed-eyed look, but held his tongue.

Of course, Cilla wouldn't have cared what he said.

She had other things on her mind. Delightfully reassuring things like her aunt's vow that where there's love, nothing is impossible.

Cilla couldn't have agreed more.

She also meant to prove it.

Chapter 10

A trace of sandalwood greeted Cilla the instant Aunt
Birdie threw open Dunroamin's front door. A trill of
excitement made her heart jump as they hurried into
the castle's vast mausoleum-like entry. Behind them,
Leo's excited, high-pitched yips still resounded from
the garden.

Glancing back, Cilla saw the little dog dash across
the lawn, racing for the terrace. Violet Manyweathers
followed at a slower pace. Colonel Darling trudged
along behind her, the three-legged creepie tucked beneath his arm.

Amazingly, Violet sported his deerstalker hat.

"Would you look at that?" Cilla grabbed her aunt's
elbow, pulling her back to the door. "He gave Violet
his hat."

Aunt Birdie laughed. "I told you he's all bluster."
She shifted the devil mask on her hip. "He'll be wor-
ried Violet will catch a cold if she gets her head wet.
Between us, I think he's a bit soft on her."

Cilla smiled and reached to turn up her jacket collar. Violet Manyweathers wasn't the only one in danger of getting drenched. Colder and increasing in
strength, the wind slung icy splinters of rain against
the castle and across the stone of the outside steps.

A wet gust swept past them into the entry, lifting
the edges of the tapestries and making a few of the

standing suits of armor rattle in their wall niches. Aunt Birdie shoved at the heavy oaken door with her hip and Cilla rushed to help her, pushing with both hands. They strained against the wind until the door slammed shut with a bang.

"Wow, those have to be gale-force winds." Cilla swept a hand through her hair, pushing it out of her eyes.

Then she frowned.

An aquatic chorus filled the air.

And it wasn't the rain lashing at the windows. The great din came from the dark passage leading away from the entry and deeper into the castle.

Drips, plinks, plonks, and—most alarming of all—the distant gush of running water.

"The roof leaks!" She flashed a horrified look at her aunt. "I didn't realize it was so bad."

Aunt Birdie glanced at the rain-streaked windows. "Only on such nights. As you can see"—she jerked her head at a plastic bucket near the silvered feet of one of the standing knights—"we're quite prepared."

A door on the other side of the entry flew open and Honoria sailed in, her arms lined with what looked to be dented and rusting milk pails.

"We've used up our supply of drip catchers." She didn't break stride as she hurried past. "I fetched these from the old byre. They should keep us dry!"

Then she was gone, her tweedy bulk nipping around a corner as quickly as she'd appeared. The ancient milking pails clinked in her wake.

Looking not at all put out, Aunt Birdie hitched the red devil mask against her hip again and started down the dimly lit passage.

The one that echoed with the loudest drip serenade.

"Aunt Birdie!" Cilla hastened after her, dodging trickles and weaving her way around the assorted buckets, pails, and cook pots lining the plaid-carpeted passage. "You can't live like this!"

Her aunt stopped at once.

Turning around, she waited for Cilla to catch up with her.

"My dear, have you forgotten what I told you in the car?" She bent to adjust the placement of a large glass casserole dish so it better caught drips.

Straightening, she tucked her hair behind her ear. "Just as I love your uncle, so do I love his home. This"—she indicated the drip containers—"will all pass when the time is right for it to do so. Until then, if need be, I'll sit on the floor and catch the water in my hands."

"You would, wouldn't you?"

The look on Aunt Birdie's face was answer enough.

It was also enough to put a hot, swelling lump in Cilla's throat.

How wonderful to love so fiercely.

She swallowed hard, in the same moment catching another waft of sandalwood. Her breath caught and her heart did a little flip. She hadn't realized how deep into the passage they'd gone. The door to Uncle Mac's armory loomed right ahead of them.

And something told her that once she crossed the threshold, there'd be no going back.

Her Dunroamin waited within, and once she embraced it she had a feeling she'd be as ready as Aunt Birdie to listen to overloud pipe tunes and catch water drips in her hands.

There was only one way to find out.

So she took a deep breath and glanced at her aunt, reassured to see the older woman's encouraging nod.

Then—before she could change her mind—she put her hand on the door latch.

Her heart started pounding.

The door swung open with incredible ease.

"Ach, laddie!" Uncle Mac's mirth-filled voice boomed from across the weapon-hung room. "You're a man after my own heart! A pity it is you've just now found your way here."

Cilla and her aunt exchanged swift glances.

Aunt Birdie hid a smile.

Cilla stared at her uncle and her ghost, amazed by their apparent ease with each other. Both kilted and looking like two Celtic chieftains of old, they stood near the tatty tartan sofa placed halfway between the hearth and the room's row of tall, mullioned windows.

A flash of lightning silvered the leaded panes, lining their silhouettes against the rainy night. Cilla blinked, her pulse leaping.

Again, she imagined the sword at Hardwick's hip. The notion that he wore—and likely knew how to wield—such a proud and ancient weapon weakened her knees.

Every wildly romantic, sword-swinging Highland-y film she'd ever seen flashed through her mind. She could see Hardwick in such a role, especially in the heated love scenes that often followed, with the hero riding off into the hills, his lady sitting astride behind him, arms wrapped tight around his powerful body, and her long, unbound hair flying as they streaked across the heather.

She drew a tight breath, her heart thundering.

Unaware they'd been disturbed, her uncle and Hardwick clinked dram glasses, sharing a manly moment. They didn't look around until—almost on its own—the door jerked from Cilla's grasp and fell shut with a loud click.

Hardwick's gaze snapped to hers. The air between them ignited, rippling and crackling as if ablaze. The power of it scorched her. His mouth curved in another of his slow, heart-melting smiles. As if he, too, felt the sizzling pull between them. Then his eyes went dark with a heated, simmering look that curled her toes.

Aunt Birdie nudged her with an elbow. "That's it," she whispered. "The look I told you about."

"Ho!" Her uncle swung toward them. "It's about time you two returned."

"We ran into someone." Cilla's gaze stayed on Hardwick. Looking anywhere else was impossible. Even in the room's deep shadows, he dazzled her. "And he—"

She broke off, her chest tightening with almost painful awareness. The sight of his long, strong fingers holding his dram glass reminded her of the feel of his hands on her bare skin when she'd slipped in the bathroom.

He'd not just touched her; he'd seen her naked.

And the wicked glint in his eye suggested he knew exactly what she was thinking.

Fair was fair, after all. She knew enough about Scotland to know that—as a true Highlander—he was equally naked beneath his kilt.

The thought electrified her.

She moistened her lips, her heart galloping. Desire pulsed through her, heated and tingly. Worse than that, an almost irresistible urge to march across the room and lift his kilt swept her.

No, the wish consumed her.

Could there be any thought more rousing?

Doubting it, she cleared her throat, forcing her attention on her uncle. "We met someone," she repeated, not sure what Hardwick had told him. "We lost track—"

"We'd hoped to have dinner at the Ben Loyal's An Garbh restaurant, but they were full up." Aunt Birdie came to her rescue. "If we'd dined there as planned, we would've been much later."

"I know that fine." Uncle Mac hooked his thumbs in his kilt belt. "And I know all about how you met my young friend here." He rocked back on his heels, looking delighted. "Thanks to him—a Highland Shaw of the good Clan Chattan—I also know about Gregor's mask. It's been a grand e'en!"

He flashed a grin at Hardwick. "You'll ne'er believe who we just talked to!"

"Oh?" Aunt Birdie lifted a brow, slid a knowing glance at Cilla. "You might be surprised at what I believe."

Cilla stepped on her toe.

Hardwick—clearly the other half of her uncle's exuberant *we*—came forward to take the red devil mask from Aunt Birdie's arms.

Leaning close to Cilla, he dropped his gaze to her foot, pitching his voice for her ears alone. "He doesn't know. No' that."

Cilla's face warmed. She knew exactly what he meant.

His ghostdom.

She removed her foot from her aunt's at once. "I—"

"Dinna tell me you aren't curious?" Uncle Mac was staring at them, his bearded chin jutting at a stubborn angle.

"Of course we're interested." Aunt Birdie went to sit on the sofa. "Who did you call?"

"Erlend Eggertson!"

Cilla had to smile at the triumph on her uncle's face.

"Erlend Eggertson?" She put a deliberate note of wonder in her voice. "That's amazing."

"Isn't it, just!" Uncle Mac's chest swelled.

He slid a glance at Hardwick. "There aren't many souls what can hide when two Highlanders put their heads together."

"How did you find him?" Cilla really wanted to know. "Aunt Birdie said there aren't any Eggertsons around here."

"And there aren't!" Uncle Mac folded his arms, looking smug. "That didn't stop us from tracking him down."

"The man's in Lerwick. He's a *guizer*." Hardwick

propped the mask against the wall. "I had a feeling we'd—"

"A geezer?" Cilla's eyes rounded.

"No, *guizer*." Aunt Birdie settled herself on the sofa. "There's a Guizer Jarl, the leader, and then"— she pulled a plaid cushion onto her lap—"his squad of attending *guizers*. There can be hundreds of them. I've seen their parades on BBC. They dress up as Vikings in celebration of Up-Helly-Aa, an ancient Norse fire festival."

She paused when a great crack of thunder shook the windows. "It's quite a thrilling spectacle." She continued when the rumbles faded. "They carry blazing torches through the streets and then burn a mock galley."

"And now they've been burgled!" Uncle Mac roared the words. "The Galley Shed—a sort of Up-Helly-Aa museum and warehouse combined—was raided some weeks ago. According to Eggertson, the thieves took scores of Viking costumes."

"Viking guises, weaponry, and"—Hardwick leaned back against a table and crossed his arms—"Eggertson's red devil garb."

"Including the mask." Cilla was beginning to understand.

Hardwick nodded.

Uncle Mac flashed a wicked grin. "Little good it did them. We're on to them now!"

Cilla considered. "If Eggertson is a *guizer*, and they dress like Vikings, what's he doing with a red devil costume?"

"They don't all parade as Vikings." Uncle Mac picked up an iron poker and started jabbing at the peats in the hearth. "Some of the men wear fantasy getups."

"But . . ." Aunt Birdie didn't sound satisfied. "How did you know to look for Eggertson in Shetland?"

"Tchach . . ." Uncle Mac set aside the poker and

dusted his hands. "Besides Eggertson being a Norse name"—he winked at Hardwick—"some might say providence is finally beginning to smile on us!"

Hardwick felt himself smiling, too.

He'd stopped believing in the benefices of providence many long years ago. But it made him feel good to see Mac MacGhee bursting with pride and confidence. And if he could play any small role in catching whoever was sneaking about the moors at night guised as Vikings, and doing the saints knew what kind of foolery, that was no small thing.

Mac was looking at him, his face alight. "Tell them."

Hardwick cleared his throat. "A friend recently returned from Lerwick. He mentioned the raid on the Galley Shed." He spoke the truth as he'd told it to Mac earlier, only leaving out that his friend happened to be a ghost. "In light of your troubles, I suspected a connection."

Birdie MacGhee raised her brows. "Are you suggesting someone brought the Viking costumes here? That our nightly peat-field prowlers are using them?"

"Of course that's what he's saying!" Mac tossed down his malt, then dragged the back of his hand across his beard. "That'll be the way of it. I knew there weren't any real Viking ghosts spooking across my moors!"

"I don't know. . . ." His wife kneaded the cushion on her lap. "There *is* something going on. Don't you agree, Cilla?"

She looked across the room at Cilla.

"Eh, lass?" Her uncle eyed her, too.

Cilla hesitated, the devil face from her window flashing across her mind. She started to bite her tongue, then blurted, "I'm not sure Gregor's devil mask was the only devil spooking around here. I . . . I saw such a face, too. Outside my bedroom window,

and"—she took a breath, hating to say it—"I'm posi-
tive it was real."

"Pah!" Mac scowled at her. "What's going on here
has nothing to do with ghosties and devils. No' real
ones, anyway. That I know!"

"I know what I saw." Cilla folded her arms, too
deep into it to say otherwise. "It wasn't Gregor's
mask."

Her uncle swung to Hardwick. "There's no such
thing as bogles, right? Red devil faces hovering outside a lassie's window?"

On the sofa, Aunt Birdie glanced quickly aside.

Cilla looked at Hardwick, waiting.

He hesitated only a moment. "I can't say as I've
encountered any ghosts hereabouts."

That, at least, was true.

Excepting himself and Bran.

"And you won't be. I guarantee it!" Mac stood tall
in a most lairdly manner. "But—as we now know—
you might run across a pack o' scoundrels *dressing up*
as Viking ghosts!"

"Be that as it may"—Hardwick felt a need to de-
fend Cilla, more disturbed than he cared to admit
about her mention of a *real* red devil face—"there are
things in these hills no living and breathing man
should e'er encounter."

"Ho!" Mac slapped him on the back. "You've been
breathing in too much peat smoke, laddie! As for my
niece, her imagination is as inflated as her aunt's!
There's nothing spooking about here but those costumed loonies out on my moors."

"But why would anyone bother?" Cilla voiced the
question that had been plaguing Hardwick for days.
"It doesn't make sense."

"Maybe they want to steal my peat!" Mac aimed a
fierce glare at the windows. "There's nothing else out
there but heather, bracken, and stones!"

"What about our sheep?" His wife spoke quietly from the sofa. "Even if Dunroamin peat is superior, our business ventures with the Simmer Dim and Northern Mist distilleries are only now crystallizing. To date, our sheep turn a greater profit."

"And what do you think Robbie and Roddie do every morn when they feed the woolly buggers for us?" Mac started pacing, his kilt swinging. "They count 'em, that's what! Our Viking ghosties haven't yet lifted a single one."

"They could yet." Birdie persisted.

"It's the peat, I tell you!" He threw her an outraged look. "But they won't be getting it now."

He slung an arm around Hardwick's shoulders. "Not only will the moors now be guarded at night, Hardwick here has friends who might pop by to patrol with him." He drew a great breath, then roared the last words. "Brawny lads with beards and kilts!"

Birdie MacGhee and her niece shared a knowing glance.

A telling one.

Heat shot up the back of Hardwick's neck. Apparently, Birdie knew of his *condition* after all. But before he could worry about that unsettling bit of knowledge, Mac gave him a bone-crunching squeeze.

"Beards and kilts, did you hear?" He waggled his brows at the ladies. "There's not a fake Viking ghost alive brave enough to withstand a Highland charge! Before they can shout 'Up-Helly-Aa,' we'll have 'em by their danglers. And that's not all the good news!"

Taking his arm from Hardwick's shoulder, he stamped across the room to a darkened corner. Bending, he snatched up a rusty milk pail. He returned clutching it before him.

Hardwick bit back a groan.

He knew what was coming.

Cilla looked on with interest, which only made it worse.

Proving Hardwick's dread, Mac waved the pail before his wife's nose. Water sloshed over the sides and onto the room's threadbare tartan carpet. Some also splashed onto Birdie's knees, but to her credit she said nothing, only peered up at him curiously.

Mac plunked down the brimming milk pail and jammed his hands on his hips. "Thanks to our new friend here"—he flashed a glance at Hardwick—"and the fine quality of our own Dunroamin peat, our days of roof leaks and drip buckets may soon come to an end!"

"What?" Cilla and her aunt spoke together. "A new roof?"

"Sure as today and tomorrow are long!" Mac's beard jigged with pleasure. "Hardwick offered a suggestion that should bring us at least enough funds for a roof. If all goes well, we might even be able to tackle the unused wing."

"Ooooh." Again the ladies cried out in unison.

Birdie MacGhee's eyes began to glisten.

And he was sure Cilla's lower lip was starting to quiver!

Mac hooted a great, belly-shaking laugh.

Hardwick struggled against the urge to throttle him. And to keep from cutting off his own flapping tongue to keep it from getting him into such a pickle again.

Not that he begrudged Mac the money.

If indeed it came.

Truth was, if he had access to his own former riches, he'd gladly give Mac every last coin.

It was the *way* he was revealing the plan.

Oblivious to the harm he was about to cause, Mac rocked back on his heels, savoring the moment.

"Did he suggest other distilleries?" Cilla sounded hopeful. "Does he have contacts for you?"

"Aye, he does. Thousands of them!" Mac looked near to bursting. "Thousands of American women to buy Dunroamin peat!"

Cilla's eyes widened. "Thousands of American women?"

Uncle Mac bobbed his head enthusiastically. "He says they swoon for anything Scottish, including our peat."

"I'm sure." Cilla folded her arms. "I like peat, too. And don't you, Aunt—"

"Let's hear what Mac has to say, dear." Birdie spoke over her.

Then she reached for her niece's hand and squeezed. "Go on, Mac." She nodded to him, one voice of reason in the cold, shadowy room.

"He's met all these women, see you?" Mac blundered on. "He says they bemoan not being able to smell peat smoke when they go home. So-o-o, he had the idea that we might export Dunroamin peat to America!"

"To his thousands of American women friends." Cilla spoke low.

"To any American who'll buy it!" Mac grinned. "But it was the women that gave him the idea. They're the most passionate. They loved—"

"I'm sure they did." Cilla glanced at the door and started edging that way.

Hardwick scowled.

Respect and honor kept him from correcting Mac's interpretation of his peat-for-Americans suggestion. Nor did he wish to dampen the man's well-deserved pleasure in revealing the idea to his wife.

Dunroamin needed hope.

And he needed to get Cilla alone.

So he did a bit of lightning-quick sifting, putting himself between her and the door before Mac and Birdie noticed he'd moved.

Cilla did.

She froze where she was, her back ramrod straight.

Hardwick swore beneath his breath. She looked like she'd swallowed a broomstick. And he never would have believed she could compress such full, sensuous lips into such a hard, tight line.

But she had, and seeing it killed him.

Again.

Lass. It isn't what you think. He willed her to hear him.

She arched one brow, indicating she had.

Hardwick started to relax. But then her back went even more rigid, and although she couldn't *sift*, she'd somehow managed to shoot past him and reach the door.

Ignoring him now, she grabbed the latch and pulled.

Hardwick swore.

He threw a quick glance across the room. Mac stood with his back to him and was still blethering on about Americans and their great love of peat fires.

But Birdie was watching him.

To his surprise, she winked. Then she made a little flipping gesture with her fingers.

She mouthed the word *Go*.

Hardwick understood at once.

He whipped back around, but he was too late. The armory door stood ajar. Cilla was gone, the echo of her retreating footsteps all that remained.

For one ridiculous moment, he considered following her as a man would do. Purposely following her through Dunroamin's winding passages and then up the various stairs she needed to traverse to get to her room.

He could keep a discreet distance. Then, upon reaching her bedchamber, he could knock politely at her door. He could state his purpose and request admission. If he were a man, he could do all those things.

But he was a ghost, after all.

And being a ghost did have a few advantages.

So he glanced back at Birdie one last time, giving her an appreciative nod.

Then he sifted himself out of the armory and directly to the one place he knew Cilla would be so startled to see him, he'd have at least a few minutes to speak to her before she ordered him to go.

In a blink, he was there.

The only problem was, now that he'd materialized in her bed, he knew he'd want to be there again.

And under very different circumstances.

Heaven help him.

Chapter 11

Thousands of American women.

Cilla couldn't blot the words from her mind. They whirled in her head, growing louder until she could hardly think. No matter how fast she hurried through Dunroamin's dim and dripping corridors, she couldn't outrun them.

They kept pace.

Jeering each time she almost knocked over a drip container or stubbed her toe on the incredibly hard stone of the ancient castle's tight-winding stairs.

Making it worse, the women weren't the only ones. Two Scots chased her, too.

More appropriately said, two Scotsmen.

American-born Grant A. Hughes III, so proud of his supposed Scottish ancestry even if he likely couldn't trace it farther back than the New York tartan shop where he'd acquired his custom kilt.

And historian-cum-author-cum-tour guide Wee Hughie MacSporran, also known as the Highland Story-weaver. If his enthusiastic pack of Australian groupies was any indication, he was an even greater skirt-chaser than Grant.

Cilla shuddered.

She'd had enough of such men.

Who would have thought she'd have to add a *ghost* to their tartaned, womanizing ranks?

Furious that it was so, she paused to press her side. It burned and ached with a stitch she really didn't need. Keeping a hand to her ribs, she mounted a few more steps. Then she stopped again, this time on a little landing with two doors opening off it.

Leaning against the wall, she frowned.

She shouldn't care that she had to lump Hardwick in the same pot as Grant and his scribbling, tour-guiding Scottish counterpart.

She *did* care that she'd made a fool of herself.

Ghost or not, Hardwick surely knew why she'd dashed out of Uncle Mac's armory. Women didn't run from men they didn't care about.

Everyone knew that.

It was a universal truth. One that made her face burn and her hands curl into fists.

She blew out a breath, trying to pretend she didn't feel like a white-hot vise had clamped around her chest, stealing her air. After Grant, she'd sworn to stand above such things. To never again fall so hard for a man who wielded such power over her heart.

Trouble was, she hadn't realized she'd done just that until her uncle had oh-so-unwittingly revealed Hardwick's womanizing ways.

Oh, she'd known she was interested. How could she not know when she need only catch a hint of his deliciously exotic scent to have tingles sizzling all through her? And if he turned that slow, seductive smile on her, she really lost it. As for his deep, husky burr and the dark, heated looks he gave her . . .

She didn't finish the thought.

The clench she felt between her legs each time he said *anything* didn't bear admitting.

It was just too plain humiliating.

She really did care about him. Big time. And hearing about his legions of women—Americans, no less— had been a blow behind the knees.

A *revealing* blow.

And there was only one thing to do about it.

She should turn around, march right back down-
stairs, waltz into the armory, and plunk herself onto
the sofa as if nothing had happened.

Then she'd lift her chin or examine her fingernails
and casually announce that she ate too many mini
pretzels at the Ben Loyal's Bistro Bar. Everyone
would believe her if she claimed the salt had made
her stomach queasy. No one would lift a brow if they
thought a roiling tummy had sent her flying from
the room.

"Yeah, Swanner, you need to go back down there.
Save your face if you can't salvage your heart." She
spoke to the door across the landing. Age-darkened
and indifferent-seeming, she had the strangest feeling
that the closed door was staring at her.

She blinked, her blood chilling.

The door might not be looking at her. But it *was*
opening.

Creaking open in the way of all squeaky-hinged
doors in centuries-old castles: slowly and with just
enough weirdness to turn her legs to lead, freezing her
to the spot.

She swallowed.

Her planned diva-on-the-sofa scene dispersed like a
burst soap bubble.

Chills swept her, and the fine hairs on her nape
lifted. Until the door completed its slow, ear-grating
arc to reveal a small, oak-paneled chamber.

Dark and low-ceilinged, the room appeared empty
except for a dressing table and washstand. A dust
cover protected something that might have been a
chair. If a bed had ever graced the room, it was gone
now. But the room *did* have two windows opposite
the door.

Twin and narrow oblongs that looked out onto the
Kyle, over which the moon now hung, its bright cres-
cent just sailing out from behind a cloud. She could

make out the black outline of Castle Varrich, too. High on its cliff, the ruin's crumbling window arch was bathed in silver and shadow.

She took a step closer, her gaze going through the open doorway to the windows, where she half expected to see the devil face sweep into view. A thin rain fell, the droplets glistening on the ancient, rippled glass. Somewhere thunder rumbled, but what really caught her attention was that some of the lower panes were missing, allowing cold, damp wind to pour into the room.

Wind that—she was sure—had caused the door to swing open.

She gave herself a shake, releasing the breath she'd been holding. That was twice tonight that she'd made a fool of herself. Lucky for her, no one had witnessed this second beyond-silly little episode.

No one, that is, except the strange woman in the dark little room.

Cilla started, her legs going all rubbery again.

Tall, blond, and stately, the woman could have been Aunt Birdie, except she was still in the armory. Even in younger years, Aunt Birdie had never worn her hair in a single, hip-length braid. She favored French twists or a fashionably knotted silken head scarf.

And although Aunt Birdie possessed a certain grace and style, she walked like everyone else. She didn't *glide* across rooms as if her feet didn't touch the floor.

Nor was it her habit to run around in ankle-length woolen gowns of deep red-purple, the seams edged in finest embroidery, the sleeves long and tight. A shawl of brilliant blue draped the woman's shoulders, and a wide, colorfully patterned belt cinched her waist, but if she wore any other adornments, Cilla couldn't see them.

The woman now stood at the windows, her back to the door.

Cilla blinked. Then she knuckled her eyes.

It didn't help.

The ghost—for she could only be one—was still there. In the wink it'd taken Cilla to rub her eyes, the apparition had splayed a beringed hand against the rain-streaked window glass.

Sea-Strider.

The word—a name?—seemed to drift around the woman. As real as if she'd whispered it in Cilla's ear, the word held all the anguish of a woman who'd loved and lost.

Forgetting the fright the woman's sudden appearance had given her, her heart squeezed at the pain drenching the tiny, dark-paneled room.

Very slowly, the woman turned her head and stared at her, her eyes beseeching. For a long moment she held Cilla's gaze, her lips moving silently before she looked back out the rain-splattered window. Her gaze, Cilla just knew, was fixed on the ruin of Castle Varrich.

She *had* to be Aunt Birdie's Gudrid. Though what she was doing at Dunroamin, Cilla couldn't begin to imagine.

She shivered. Remembering her aunt's musings about the ghost, she imagined a big, burly man standing near the woman. She could see him clearly. Unnoticed in a corner, he stared at the woman with great, sad eyes. Bearded and fair as she, he wore a plain, pointed helm with a nose guard and a long mailed tunic. In one hand, he held a huge nine-foot spear, and in the other, he clutched a large round shield, colorfully painted a rich dark blue and decorated with an interlaced pattern of white, red, and green lines. Seeming to glow despite the shadows, the shield looked nearly double the size of Hardwick's.

On thinking of *him*, both images faded.

But not without leaving her with the distinct impression they'd had something important to tell her. Regrettably, she hadn't been able to hear the woman's voice and the man hadn't even glanced her way, having eyes only for the woman.

Cilla pressed a hand to her breast, wishing she'd understood their message. As it was, she could only guess their names, Gudrid and Sea-Strider, before the little room's door inched shut again, blocking its secrets from view.

"Holy guacamole." Cilla rubbed her arms, chills all over her. She felt a strong urge to go back to the armory and real people, including Hardwick.

To her he was real.

She needed to settle things with him, one way or the other.

But the poor lighting in the stair tower struck her as even more dim than before. Deep shadows danced everywhere, and the night wind sounded ominous. Almost a wail, it whistled past the medieval arrow slits cut so deep into the walls. No way was she going down those stairs, into the darkness.

Her room was much closer.

She shivered again, her decision made.

For now, Hardwick would just have to think what he wanted of her flight from the armory.

Tomorrow would be soon enough to deal with him.

First she needed a sound night's sleep. Maybe she'd even take a hot bath. She'd found that using the bathtub made it much easier to regulate the water temperature than risking a go at the dodgy shower.

Then bed and a good book to get her mind off the ghost woman and her Sea-Strider, and she'd be fine.

Feeling better—but still a bit shaken—she resisted sliding another glance at the dark little room's door, now closed tight and silent.

Instead she dashed up the remaining steps, then down the long corridor to her room. This passage didn't seem to have any drip buckets to run an obstacle course around. Or she'd just not seen them. A distinct possibility, as the old-fashioned wall sconces her uncle loved so much appeared to throw off less light than usual.

The passage was positively gloomy.

Except for the thin band of light showing beneath her closed door.

For a beat, chills whipped through her again. But they vanished quickly. The light had to be thanks to Honoria doing turn-down service. With the night's rainstorm, her room would've been really dark otherwise.

And she'd already pulled in her stubbed-toe quota for the entire summer.

Light was good.

So she vowed to remember to thank the house-keeper for her thoughtfulness, and opened the door.

Closing it, she took three steps into the room and froze.

Her jaw slipped.

There'd been a reason chills swept her upon seeing light beneath her door. Her first reaction had been spot-on, and the bar of light had nothing to do with Honoria.

It was *his* doing.

Hardwick's.

"What are you doing here?" She stared at him, heart in her throat.

"I'm waiting for you, as you can see." He spoke from her bed.

Bold as brass, he lounged against the pillows mounded against the headboard. He was staring right at her, his gaze hot and angry. Equally distressing, he'd drawn up one leg and although he'd clasped his hands around his knee, clearly arranging his kilt to try and hide certain *things*, she could still see them!

An errant kilt fold with a mind of its own had slipped, revealing him in all his impressive glory.

She blinked, her eyes going wide. Even *relaxed*, he was formidable. Heat whipped through her and she could only stare, certain she'd never seen such a magnificent man. He made at least three of Grant, possibly even four.

When he *twitched* and started to swell, growing even longer, the hot tingles whirring between her legs increased to such a fever pitch she almost climaxed.

"Oh, my . . ." She sucked in a breath, but the air wouldn't go down her throat. It lodged there, almost choking her even as a ragged little moan pushed past to break from her lips.

She *was* going to shatter. Reaching for a chair back, she held fast, her knees turning to water and her panties starting to dampen.

"O-o-oh!" She still couldn't breathe right. He twitched again, the long, thick length of him no longer hanging at ease between his powerful thighs but throbbing visibly and lengthening beneath her gaze.

"Hellfire and damnation!" Leaping off the bed, he brushed furiously at his kilt, swatting its folds into place. "I didn't come here for *that*."

Heat flared in Cilla's cheeks. "I didn't say—"

"Ah, but your eyes did." He folded his arms, looking at her. "Such is the hazard of wearing a kilt."

Cilla lifted her chin. "I know that." She hoped her voice didn't sound as shaky to him as it did to her. "What I don't know is why you're here."

He arched a brow. "I think you already know. We need to talk."

She swallowed, her pulse still racing. "Oh?"

"Aye, . . . *oh*." He scowled at her, his dark eyes glinting in the dimly lit room. "You shouldn't have run out of the armory. I told you it wasn't what you thought."

"What wasn't what I thought?" Cilla brushed at her sleeve.

He saw right through her. "The thousands of American women. Your uncle misspoke what I'd told him."

"I left the armory because I wasn't feeling well."

She went for a white lie, her pulse finally slowing. "I ate too many mini pretzels at the Ben Loy—"

"Nae, that's no' the reason." He shook his head, his gaze locked onto hers. "Just as I made it up here faster than you, so do I know you're speaking untruths. And, nae, I canna read your mind."

He flashed a devilish smile. "Centuries of experience allowed me to spot a lie the moment one is born. Most ghosts have the same ability unless they were dull-witted in life. Then they remain dim in their afterlife."

"In the same way a skirt-chaser remains woman-hungry?" Cilla shot him a smile of her own. "I mean, in their afterlife, of course."

"Bloody hell!" He shoved a hand through his hair. "If I am hungry for any woman, it's you! As I believe you just observed." His burr deepened on the words, his eyes taking on a dangerous light. "But since that canna be, I wanted to ensure that you dinna think poorly of me."

"Why would I do that?" Cilla's her heart started to hammer again. "You've kept me from banging myself up more than once now and"—she glanced aside, not wanting him to see the effect he had on her—"you stood up for me against Uncle Mac when he laughed about the devil face I saw."

She looked back at him, pitched her voice challenging. "I really did see something weird. The face *did* look real. And . . . and I don't know why I'm telling you this, but I just saw two other ghosts. They were a Viking couple in a dark little room off one of the stair landings!"

Holding his gaze, she jutted her chin, expecting him to laugh at her.

But he surprised her by closing the distance between them in several long strides and wrapping his arms around her, pulling her close against him.

"Sweet lass." He drew her head to his chest, "I

ken better than you that such things abound. I'm no' surprised real Viking ghosts would make an appearance here, no' with all that's going on out on Mac's peat fields. They'll likely be upset by the furor, perhaps distressed to look on as unsavory souls impersonate them.

"As for the devil face you saw . . ." He tightened his arms around her, splaying his big hands over her hips, his grip firm and, she couldn't deny, soothing.

"Such creatures as the face in your window are another reason I'm here, lass." He pulled back to look down at her, his expression letting her know he was serious. "The fiend was surely looking for me, no' you. There's no reason for you to fear, and I doubt you'll see the like again. Indeed, I'll make certain of it."

"But—"

"No buts." He pulled her close again, nuzzled his cheek against her hair. "I ken why they're here and can take measures to keep them at bay."

"The devil?" Cilla's chest went hot and tight, as if a giant hand had swooped down out of nowhere to squeeze the breath from her. "I didn't want to believe it. I can handle ghosts. They—"

She broke off, mortification sweeping her.

But Hardwick only laughed, the sound as rich and warming as his honeyed burr. "Dinna feel bad, sweeting, I'm no' offended. And I'll no' be having you worry o'er things you shouldn't even know about."

Releasing her as quickly as he'd seized her, he went to the hearth and stood there, resting one arm casually on the mantel. "As for the rest"—his voice deepened again—"my other reason for being here, I'll have you know that I am no' a skirt-chaser."

"I didn't say . . ." Cilla felt her face flame again. "Oh, all right," she corrected, swiping a hand through her hair. "I did think so. But how could I not?"

"Indeed." He smiled.

And it was another one of his curl-all-through-a-girl

smiles that made her forget about red devil faces, Viking ghosts, and just about everything else except the warmth pulsing inside her.

The kind of warmth that didn't have anything to do with her reaction to that one wildly erotic glimpse beneath his kilt and everything to do with the slow, steady thumping of her heart and the way the look in his eyes made her mouth go dry.

She swallowed, knowing in that instant that she was falling in love with him.

"If you'd hear the truth of it," he said, something in his expression telling her he knew, "I did tell your uncle that I knew thousands of American women who would show interest in his peat. And, aye, I've met those women. Though I'm quite sure they never noticed me. I just happened to be where they were. So, of course, I heard them speaking."

"I see." Cilla blinked at him, hoping he couldn't hear the racing of her pulse. "Where did you meet them, then?"

"I have friends, see you? Ghostdom can get lonely, and so we visit each other. Some of my . . . er . . . oldest companions enjoy frequenting Ravenscraig Castle near Oban. Its laird is friendly toward us and so we often meet there."

"And the Americans?"

"They visit, too." His gaze on her didn't waver. "The Ravenscraig laird married an American. They run a place called One Cairn Village on the castle grounds. Every summer, Americans gather there in great numbers to research their—"

"Roots," Cilla finished for him, the mundane subject helping her gather her wits. "You mean genealogy nuts. There are lots of Americans like that, but the ones of Scottish descent are the most dedicated."

He shrugged. "Whate'er they are, they come in droves. And when they're here, they blether on about everything they love about Scotland. The castles and our mist and hills to our pipes and, aye, our peat smoke."

Pushing away from the hearth, he started pacing. "Many of the visiting Americans mentioned Irish peat, claiming they procured it using the Internet, something I've heard of but wouldn't want to try and explain. The peat selling sounded like a venture that might benefit your uncle. Dunroamin's peat *is* of particular quality."

"Uncle Mac certainly thinks so." Cilla was beginning to understand. "Obviously, he liked the idea."

"And well he should. I suspect he'll do fine with such an undertaking." He paused, a shadow crossing his face. "At the least, it's worth a try. It would be a shame if he lost Duroamin. I know he holds his home dear."

"And your home? Seagrave?" Cilla didn't care for his tone, the way his eyes had clouded. "You never speak—"

He made a dismissive gesture. "Seagrave is no more."

"But Aunt Birdie said—"

"I heard what she told you." He went to stand by the windows. "The walls of my home still stand, it is true. And she guessed the location rightly. The ruins are on Scotland's northeast coast, south of the fine city of Aberdeen. Since my time, and much closer by, a small fishing village thrives not far from Seagrave's cliffs."

Cilla started to follow him, then decided better of it and remained where she was. "Have you been back?"

"To Seagrave?" He rested a hand against the arch of one of the windows and looked out into the rain. "I glimpsed the fishing village from a distance once. It looked a fair place. But the shell that remains of Seagrave is no' the home I knew. I've no desire to return."

Cilla frowned. "When were you last there? Maybe now—"

"Leave be, lass." He whirled and went back to the hearth, where he stood staring at the fire. "Since my time new wings were added, great monstrous things. Walls that had stood for centuries have been refaced and are no longer recognizable. Leastways, no' to me."

He shoved a hand through his hair, remembering the day Bran alerted him to the damage. "When I learned of it, my stomach churned for months. It was a bad time."

"I can see why you don't want to return." Cilla was at his side then, touching the sweep of his plaid with light, tentative fingers.

He tensed, that one gentle touch rocking his world. It'd been too long, perhaps never, that a woman had touched him in kindness.

Lust, aye.

He'd had more than his fill of uninhibited, base urges. All thrashing limbs and panted cries, the crazed, searing heat that can consume a man until his release douses the flames and he's left more empty and yearning than ever before. He looked at Cilla, knowing she'd never leave him drained except in the sweetest of ways.

"I'm sorry I asked." She slipped her hand beneath the swath of tartan, her fingers seeking, so welcome and warm against his chest. "Uncle Mac seems to really like you," she whispered, sounding so pleased. "And you seem happy here, so why don't you just stay at Dunroamin?"

"Because . . ."

Hardwick shut his eyes and drew a sharp breath. He'd love to stay at Dunroamin. Especially with her at his side, were such a miracle possible, but he couldn't stay *anywhere* on this earthly plane.

Only at Dunroamin, and so long as his testing time allowed.

A time he'd cut short if he could, knowing what the Dark One could do if he wearied of plaguing Hardwick with mere hell hags and root-dragons. More than once he'd strode into the Dark One's inner sanctum, seeking a word with him, only to catch glimpses of beautiful naked women bound by their own hair to the temple's mist-shielded guardian trees.

Living, breathing women like Cilla, seized from this world at the Dark One's whim and then, when the Dark One tired of them, given to the root-dragons for their own mauling pleasure.

Or equally horrifying, they'd find themselves tossed into the pit with the hell hags until the passing centuries turned them, too, into withered, flat-breasted crones.

It *did* happen.

And he'd dive into that pit himself before he'd allow Cilla to land in its seething, sulfurous brine.

Shaking himself, he flung her hand from his chest and sprang backward, away from her touch. "I canna stay at Dunroamin," he almost snarled, his voice more harsh than he would have wished. "No' a day longer than allowed."

She blinked, staring at him like he'd grown horns.

He could've laughed at the irony.

Instead, he swiped an arm over his brow, not surprised to find it damp. His heart was about to burst from his chest, so fiercely was it pounding with dread.

"Why did you do that?" She stepped close, frowning.

The kind of frown—he knew—that wouldn't go away unless she received the absolute truth for an answer.

He groaned, stepping back again, this time putting a good two stride lengths between them.

She folded her arms. "Well?"

He blew out a breath. "I wanted, no, I *had* to get away from your touch."

"My touch?" Her eyes widened.

He nodded.

She pinned him with a look, clearly not satisfied with a simple head bob. "Why? I know you want me."

He almost choked.

He did wince. Wanting her didn't begin to describe it.

"Did you ne'er wonder why I always wear my kilt?" He knew the words sounded pointless, but he just couldn't come right out with the truth.

Her eyes narrowed, just as he'd known they would. "I don't see what that has to do with it."

"Och, it has everything to do with it." He ran a hand through his hair, searching for the right words. "See you, there are things a man notices more swiftly if he's wearing the kilt." He looked at her, waiting for comprehension to flicker across her face.

Nothing happened.

She only peered at him, her face an innocent blank.

"Ach, lass." This time he rammed both hands through his hair.

He'd have to be blunt.

He cleared his throat. "A kilt allows for an easy *swing*," he said, rushing the words. "That freedom means a man notices unwanted stirrings almost before they happen."

Her eyes rounded. "You're talking about *those* kinds of stirrings, aren't you?"

He nodded.

Her face bloomed pink. "You're saying—"

"I'm telling you there's a reason I almost kissed you twice and didn't." Going back to her, he gripped her arms. "I told you, I broke away from your touch a moment ago because I *had* to, no' because I wished to."

He risked a quick kiss to her brow. "You cause

stirrings in me that I've ne'er felt for any woman. And, aye, I mean *those* stirrings. But there are other feelings, too. Deep ones that I have no right to—"

"O-o-oh!" She jerked free and flung her arms around his neck. "You should have told me," she cried, peering up at him with bright, shining eyes.

She smiled, hope all over her. "It doesn't matter that you're a ghost," she said, clearly not understanding. "You're as real and solid as any man. You can touch me and I—"

"Nae." He shook his head. "We cannot touch."

Her smile faded. "But—"

"It is no' that simple." He reached up and circled her wrists, removing her arms from his neck. "If my ghostly status were the only difficulty, we could. I have seen one or two such relationships prosper. But our situation is different. Our meeting came too late."

Her chin shot up. "If meeting you as a ghost isn't too late, how can anything else be?"

"You would be surprised how easily."

"So surprise me."

"My life, such as it is, is no longer my own." He waited a beat, hating what came next. "I bargained it away to the Dark One in exchange for eternal peace."

"Eternal peace?" She stared at him. "Isn't that what you found when you . . . er . . . became a ghost?"

"Nae." He shook his head slowly. "I haven't known a moment's peace since the day. Leastways, no' until I came to Dunroamin."

She bit her lip. "If you bargained away your life, how can you still be here?"

"Because," he began, "the Dark One doesn't grant bids without stipulations."

"And yours was not to touch a woman?"

"Something very like that, aye."

Her eyes narrowed. "I see."

"Nae, you dinna." He grasped her chin when she

started to glance away. "You're thinking of Mac and his thousands of Americans again."

She flushed. "They do come to mind."

"Grant A. Hughes III comes to *my* mind, and I'd love to cross blades with the man and leave him with a few cuts and bruises to teach him ne'er to treat a woman so shabbily again."

She puffed a hair off her forehead. "You're changing the subject."

"Nae, I'm leading into it."

"Oh?" Her eyes were starting to glitter.

Damning himself for being the cause, he steeled himself against how much he wanted her. Then he reached for her, pulling her into his arms.

"I am no' that man, Cilla. Nor any other who might have hurt you." He spoke gently, laying bare his heart. "But I *did* have my share of women in my time. I lived no differently than other men of my position. Being unmarried, I saw no harm in enjoying myself."

She stiffened but made no move to pull away, so he continued.

"My hall was a merry place and visitors came to Seagrave from far and wide." He paused, bile beginning to rise at what was coming. "At times, great nobles and their entourages called, often staying for weeks. It was during the stay of such highborn guests that my troubles began."

"What did they do?"

"They didn't do aught." He could see them still. How they'd lined his high table, wine chalices raised in good cheer. "They were fine men."

"If they were good, what happened?"

"They had bitter foes." He tightened his arms around her, remembering. "A wandering lute player had been trailing them for days when they arrived at Seagrave. We'd had it on good authority that this man was a paid assassin. When, a few days into their stay, such a man appeared at my gates, I turned him away."

"What else could you have done?" She pulled back to look at him.

"I could have welcomed him to my hearthside, offering a warm pallet and hearty viands for as long as he wished to stay. Such was the custom." He released her and moved to the windows, needing air. "I violated the ancient code of hospitality. Unfortunately, I unwittingly did so to a man who was not only a genuine minstrel but a powerful wizard."

"He cursed you." She spoke at his elbow.

"He did." He turned to face her. "It was to get relief from his curse that sent me to the Dark One."

"And he sent you here?" A glimmer of hope lit her eyes.

"Nae," he said, dashing that hope. "I chose Dunroamin on my own. It seemed the best place for me to spend my proving period."

She blinked. "Your what?"

"My testing time." He drew a long breath. "The Dark One agreed to grant me an end to the minstrel's curse and the eternal peace I desired only if I could spend a year and a day without becoming aroused by a woman."

"I see." And this time she clearly did. "You thought Dunroamin would be free of such distractions."

"That was the way of it, aye."

"Then I arrived."

"Aye, and what an entrance you made." He smiled, unable to stop himself. "I would not have missed you, lass. No' for anything."

She wet her lips. "So what happens if you . . . if we—"

"If I let my feelings for you run full course?"

"That, too, but I meant what if you fight it?" She stood straighter then, her chin lifting. "We have a saying in my world that two heads are better than one.

Maybe two hearts are more powerful than one wizard?"

Hardwick looked at her, his own heart swelling.

She hadn't yet asked what his curse *was*. But her willingness to stand by him did something to him that he'd never thought would happen.

He was falling in love.

And the longer he looked at her, seeing so much hope and confidence lighting her eyes, the easier it became for him to hope, too.

Two hearts where before there'd only been one.

He did like the notion.

Better yet, it just might make a difference.

Chapter 12

Cilla knew the minute she'd won.

A great *whoosh* of relief swept over her. She drew a deep breath, trying to stay calm. She could so easily toss back her hair and pump a fist in the air. Maybe whoop with triumph or try her luck at one of Uncle Mac's whirling, fast-footed jigs.

Hardwick was hers.

He stood watching her, his dark eyes smoldering with a heat that confirmed it. If she didn't want to push her luck, she'd march over to him, grab his plaid, and pull his head down to hers, kissing his kilt right off him.

She'd do a lot more, too.

Maybe seize his face with both hands, holding tight and gentling her lips back and forth over his until he couldn't take it anymore and yanked her hard against him, demanding deeper and hotter kisses. She'd tease him with her tongue, making him crazy as he swept his hands up and down her body, revealing that he needed intimate contact with each and every inch of her.

She shivered, wondering what he'd do if she maneuvered him onto a chair and then yanked up his kilt so she could swing one leg over him and then settle uninhibitedly onto his naked lap, riding his rock-hard thighs and, hopefully soon, something even more granitelike.

At the least, she was sure that the next time he made an attempt to kiss her, he'd follow through. And with much more than just deep, soul-searing kisses, full of tongue, breath, and silky-hot sighs.

But first they needed to do something about his minstrel gone bad and whatever curse the bard had cast over him. She couldn't, absolutely wasn't going to let that go. Not so long as her name was Swanner and she had fine, strong Philadelphia, Pennsylvania, blood coursing through her veins.

In fact, she already had some ideas about how they could break his curse. So she rubbed her hands together confidently, sure she'd be able to convince him.

He'd taken up his usual stance at the hearth, legs crossed at the ankles and one arm hooked oh-so-casually on the mantel. His gaze intent on her, his rock-solid, exquisitely male body glowed in the firelight, and the black silk of his hair glistened like a raven's wing, the sheer masculine beauty of him almost overwhelming her.

There was just something about a man in a kilt. A smile from such a man, and a girl's knees turned to water. If he then *kissed* a woman, she was a goner.

Totally lost.

Cilla swallowed, a giddy sense of *being lost* and just plain, pure female want welling inside her until she could hardly draw a breath.

Unfortunately, he didn't appear to share her excitement. Something twisted inside her and her heart skittered. There had to be a way to make him believe that together they could meet any challenge. She bit her lip, considering. She'd seen the quick burst of hope that had flared in his eyes when she'd shared her two-hearts analogy.

He *was* interested in the possibilities.

He just didn't trust in them.

"I don't blame you for being skeptical." She opted for bluntness. "If I were in your shoes, I would be, too. But I can assure you that"—she placed a hand over her heart—"I know something of curses. These are different times than yours. People are more open. They share information about all kinds of things. Including how to break a—"

"My curse doesn't need to be broken."

"I've read about such things." She spoke right over him, warming to the topic. "There are books on everything from the evil eye and spells to the effects of negative energy. Just as curses are known to exist, so are there ways to block or lift them. White candles and sea salt come to mind. There are even people who, for a fee, will come and—"

She snapped her mouth shut, staring at him. "What did you say?"

He arched a brow. "Just now?"

"Of course just now." She put her hands on her hips. "You said your curse doesn't need breaking. How can that be?"

"Because"—he spoke softly—"my curse already has been broken."

"What?" She frowned. "I don't understand."

He tensed visibly. "The Dark One lifted the curse before I came here. Now I have, shall we say, other difficulties to contend with, as I've explained."

"You mean about having to stay *uninterested* in women for a year and a day?"

"That is the way of it, aye." He left the hearth to stand at the windows. As before, he braced a hand on the carved stone of the window arch and appeared to avoid her gaze.

"It seems a strange stipulation." Cilla persisted. "Maybe you should tell me what the original curse was."

His brows snapped together.

Even though he stood half-turned away from her, she could tell.

She took a few steps toward him, ready to prod even though the stiff set of his shoulders and the dark look on his face warned her to leave him in peace.

"Trust me, you dinna want to hear about the curse." His voice sounded final. "The tale isn't fit for your ears."

She bristled. "I think I'd like to decide that."

He shot an annoyed glance at her.

She folded her arms. "If you won't speak of it, maybe I should? Let's take this *testing time*, for instance. Why was such an illogical penance chosen? There must have been a reason."

His jaw tightened. He still wasn't looking at her.

In case he did, she pretended to inspect a loose thread on her sleeve. "Did you know," she began, plucking at the thread, "that in my country, we say that where there's smoke, there's fire."

"And I say that those who jab sticks into wasps' nests get stung."

"Be that as it may"—she kept examining the thread—"I am not a wasp."

"Then be satisfied to know that my penance wasn't wholly unjust." He turned to face her. "Truth be told, it was more than fitting. The minstrel's curse demanded that the Dark One require me to spend my proving time as he did."

Cilla frowned. "So the curse had something to do with women?"

She wouldn't have believed it, but he blushed.

The heat of it branded his cheeks and blazed up and down the back of his neck. The truth, for she deserved nothing less, sat like a clump of granite in his gut. Equally annoying, his head was beginning to ache and his mouth had gone so dry that he doubted he could form the words, even though he was now quite ready to do so.

"Well?" She'd moved closer.

He bit back a groan. "Aye, the curse had to do with women." He stilled, already seeing the edges of his world curl and blacken. "Topping his outrage that I'd shut my door in his venerable face, the bard-wizard envied my supposed renown with the fairer sex."

Cilla's eyes widened. "So you were a ladies' man."

"Aye, and so I was, though no more than any other man of my station." He laughed, but the sound was bitter. "The bard saw it otherwise and, once riled, took punishment on me in a way he knew would forever ruin my pleasure in women."

Her eyes grew rounder. "He ruined your ability to . . . ah . . . you know, *enjoy* yourself?"

"Nae, he did just the opposite." Hardwick's heart almost stopped on the words. "He cursed me to be in a permanently aroused state, damning me to pleasure a different female every night for all eternity."

"What—"

He raised a hand, silencing her when she tried to speak. "The dalliances weren't a pleasure, sweetness. Leastways"—he spoke true—"no' after the first fifty years or so. Thereafter, what should have been bliss turned into a living, or un-living, nightmare."

"I see." Her back went straight again, her shoulders squared and forbidding.

"You must." He left the windows to stride forward and grip her by the arms. "My weariness of the task is why I asked the Dark One to relieve me of the curse. And, it must be said, his required payment is why I am now unable to touch or kiss you as I would so love to do."

She glanced aside. "I thought you were weary of women."

"I believed I was." Hardwick tightened his hold on her. "Until the day I decided to relieve my boredom by sifting myself about Dunroamin, and you happened to enter a room I'd just arrived in."

"You hid in the poster." A smile tugged at her lips. "I thought you were a symptom of my jet lag."

"And I thought I'd wakened from a seven-hundred-year sleep." He slid his arms around her, pulling her close. "You took my breath and still do."

She pulled back to look at him. "Even after so many other women?"

His voice deepened. "Especially after them."

"But . . ." She glanced aside, her lower lip caught between her teeth.

"You canna doubt me." He reached for her chin, turning her back to face him. "I am speaking true to you."

"Oh, I believe you." She met his gaze, her eyes clear and shining. "It's just a great deal to consider. Your status as a ghost and now—"

"You've accepted my ghostdom."

"I . . . well . . . of course, I have." Her brow creased. "I've told you often enough."

"Then accept me as a man." He looked at her deeply, willing her to do so.

She closed her eyes. When she opened them, Hardwick knew he had a chance. Hope flashed through him, and he shoved a hand through his hair, scarce able to believe it. Half-afraid he might say something that would change her acceptance, her willingness to trust him. Then, before the world tilted and tipped him off its edge, he sent a prayer to whate'er saints or gods or whatnot might aid him.

He couldn't bear to lose her, didn't want to slip back into the empty dark he now knew he'd dwelt in for so many uncountable years.

His jaw clenching on the possibility, he drew a tight breath, bracing himself to continue. For him, at least, there was no going back. Not now, and even if he could ne'er truly make her his. He could pleasure her in other ways. After all, he'd already seen how responsive she was to passion. His, though much restrained, and, for truth, her own.

For the rest, the sweet warmth that had filled him when he'd spoken of his home and she'd touched a caring hand to his chest, trying to comfort him . . .

Such bliss was more than enough for him.

He only hoped she'd feel the same.

"See you, lass"—he considered his words, seeking ones that would explain rather than unsettle her— "although I did enjoy the women I *encountered* in the early days of my cursed state, I canna recall the name or face of a single one of them."

Her face bloomed pink, but she didn't glance aside. The rapid beat of her pulse at her throat showed her struggle against her emotions. And seeing it made him wince. If only he could just bend his head to hers and kiss her until the doubt and worry left her and he, too, could forget his oh-so-sordid-sounding past.

Instead he simply reached out and smoothed the back of his knuckles down her cheek, hoping to soothe her.

Then he cleared his throat. "Hear me well, lass. Of the ladies who've crossed my path in the centuries between then and now"—he paused, watching her— "let it be known that they are naught but a great blur."

She blinked. "A blur?"

He nodded. "I can think of no other way to describe them. Now, since meeting you, my time with them is as if it ne'er happened. They are no' even a faint beat in my memory."

"And me?" Her eyes started glistening, and there was a catch in her voice. "Where do I fit in with all those others? How would you descr—"

"You?" He looked at her, his heart bursting. "You are the sweet, golden light I didn't know I was missing.

The honeyed warmth I doubt I e'er knew existed, even in my earth life. You may no' be the first woman I've drawn into my arms, but you are the only one I've given my heart."

"O-o-oh . . ." She slid her arms around his neck, leaning—no, *melting*—into him. "Hardwick—"

"The women before you are of no importance." He spoke over her, his heart thundering. "What matters is that you are the one I would love to see as my last, with no one coming after you. If"—he had to tell her—"we are e'er able to find a way to undo my pact with the Dark One."

She pulled back, her eyes rounding again. "What do you mean your pact with the Dark One?"

"Exactly that." The truth lanced him.

He'd been dreading this all night.

He sighed, knowing he had no choice but to tell her. "Once a year and a day rolls around and I have remained *un*aroused, I will be granted the eternal sleep I requested."

She paled. "You mean a different kind of ghostdom than you're living now?"

"It will be no ghostdom or afterlife at all." He tried not to shudder. "There are many layers to the Otherworld, see you? I asked the Dark One to send me into a deep, black sleep from which there is no waking. He agreed."

He looked at her, wishing that with all his ghostly powers he could turn back time and undo his request.

"But that's horrible." Her brows snapped together and her face clouded. She fisted her hands against his shoulders and he caught the tremors rippling through her.

"Such was my own desire, sweetness." The admission just made it worse. "I only wanted relief at the time. A way out of a curse I could bear no more. Would that I had known I'd meet you . . ."

Her frown was formidable.

Almost frightening.

But just when he reached to smooth her brow, her face brightened.

She moistened her lips. "Am I correct in understanding that this forever sleep will claim you if you get through the proving period without becoming aroused?"

"Aye, that is the way of it."

"O-o-oh, but I have it!" She did a fast little spin, her smile sunnier than he'd ever seen. "I know what we need to do to save you!"

"I canna be saved, lass." He folded his arms. "The Dark One is all powerful and always holds a soul to his bids."

"But that's excellent." She beamed. "We want him to keep his word."

"Och, he does that, to be sure."

"Then we're home free! Don't you see?" Her voice rose with feeling. "We only need to get you *aroused*, and the pact with him is null and void. He can't whisk you off into some deep, dark oblivion."

"Ach, lass, forgive me." He winced inside, hating that he had to dash her hope. "I did no' explain the testing period well enough."

Her face fell. "You mean there's more?" She stared at him, her eyes bright.

He couldn't lie. "The most damning part, aye."

"Then tell me so I know."

"If I allow myself to become aroused, in the fullest sense, mind"—he spoke quickly—"the proving period will end immediately."

Her eyes narrowed. "But that isn't all of it."

"Nae, it isn't." He reached for her arms, lowering them from his neck. "Should the like happen, the minstrel's curse will return at once. Only this time I will not have the freedom to roam the world at will and choose my own *partners* for each night's required bedding. The Dark One would whisk me into the coldest corner of hell, leaving me to pleasure the hags who dwell there."

"And if we refuse to accept that?"

He blinked, not sure he'd heard her.

She laid a hand on his arm, her grip firm. "We can just go on as we are, can't we?"

Hardwick almost choked. To be sure, he wanted what she suggested. The notion rode him day and night. But he'd ne'er been a man to build his castles of clouds. Truth was, he doubted he could *go on* this way much longer.

He was more than close to overstepping himself.

But her touch and determination made it impossible to naysay her. As did his own burning desire to make such a foolhardy, shaky-footed proposition work.

He started to scowl at the improbability of it, but slung an arm around her instead, pulling her close. "Aye, sweet, we can continue as we are."

For the now, he added in silence.

A good while later, in the smallest hours of the night, Hardwick stood just inside the bolted door to Dunroamin's unused wing and tried his best not to sneeze. Damp and musty, the chill, seldom-seen rooms reeked of dust, old leather, and moldy books. With surety, there were a few other things he couldn't identify.

Molting stags' heads, ancient stuffed birds, and faint traces of candle wax were reasonable guesses.

Blessedly, he couldn't detect the slightest tinge of dragon breath. Nor did he catch any subtle wafts of sulfur or the unpleasantly sharp-sweet odor of hell hag. Not that he was presently in the state of mind likely to attract his heinous watchers.

Even so, he frowned.

His brow furrowed even more when a small four-footed something scuttled out of a shadowed corner and darted across the uneven wood-planked floor.

Tiny legs pumping, the wee creature disappeared into the unsavory-smelling blackness beneath a torn and tattered armchair.

As if, like him, the mouse wanted nothing to do with dark and dust-coated places, he reappeared in a wink. He took a few cautious steps forward and then sat up on his haunches, fixing Hardwick with a curious stare.

The wee beastie didn't appear frightened of him, as some creatures were wont to do. Far from it, the mouse angled his head jauntily.

His cheeky perusal made Hardwick's heart clutch.

Any other time, he would have smiled.

As things were, he flicked his fingers to conjure a fine morsel of cheese. This he threw to the teeny, bright-eyed mouse. Snatching it, the beastie scampered behind a cracked gilt mirror propped against a wall.

Feeling an odd tightness in his chest, Hardwick placed his hands on his hips and looked around. He took care not to breathe too deeply. While not quite malodorous, the air held enough piquancy to twitch a sensitive nose.

And—as he'd only now just learned—it would seem his nose was quite discerning.

His heart, too, saints preserve him.

He swallowed a sigh.

Now wasn't the hour to dwell on such revelations. He was here for a reason, and an important one. So he moved deeper into the dingy passageway, taking care to peer into each open door and shadowed niche. Dark, dreary, and filled with indistinguishable clutter, these less-frequented rooms and deliberately hidden corners beckoned with treasures.

In particular, the room he knew to be filled with bolts of ancient tartan. He'd seen the room once and meant to find it again now.

His pulse leapt at the prospect.

He quickened his step, his mien purposeful.

He needed the tartan.

To that end, he nipped into the dimness of a promising room only to walk straight into the pointed corner of a dark oak table.

"Owww!" He rubbed his hip, scowling.

He made matters worse by backing away from the table and nearly tripping over a great, untidy pile of moth-eaten velvet window draping.

When a great swath of hanging cobwebs brushed across his face, clinging, he almost sifted himself out of the cramped and cluttered rooms.

There was only so much that a man—corporeal or otherwise—should be made to endure.

But the lure of the plaid bolts was greater.

A piece of *true* tartan, deftly applied, would protect him far better than any strip of plaid crafted in his usual finger-snapping way.

Sure of it, he threw open the door to yet another of the dark little rooms. He spotted the tartan at once. The colorful cloth was everywhere. Great teetering piles in such profusion, his heart near jumped from his chest. In one corner, the stacked bolts even reached the ceiling.

The room was empty otherwise, though a spill of ivy grew in through a crack in one of the grime-coated windows. The spreading green had claimed much of the far wall and some of the bolts stored there.

Even so, there was more than enough cloth to suit his purpose.

Relief—and hope—pumping through him, he stood on the threshold and surveyed his choices. Ancient and covered with a thick layer of dust, the tartan patterns were difficult to distinguish.

Not that the sett mattered.

What did was the tartan's strength.

He needed one whose weave hadn't been weakened by damp and centuries. Or worse, its proud threads assailed by moths and beetles. A single strip was all he required. But whatever he chose, the cloth had to hold securely, not giving at all once he'd fastened it into place.

His life—or *un*life—depended on it.

And though he had little cause in his ghostdom to raise his sword in battle, his warring instincts were still finely honed. He hadn't gone through life on the winning end of a blade without having first used his head, always making the land and circumstances work in his favor.

So he eyed the bolt stacks carefully, considering.

It took him all of two beats to know what must be done.

Rubbing his hands together, he strode directly to the largest pile of tartan and thrust his arms deep into the center of the dusty bolts. He closed his fingers around the one that felt right, pulling the bolt swiftly from the pile.

He'd chosen well.

Not a mote of dust marred the ancient MacDonald tartan. A fine hunting weave of muted greens and blues, shot through with white, red, and black stripes, he recognized the sett as belonging to the MacDonalds of the Isles, longtime friends and allies.

He smiled, ran appreciative hands over the smooth, well-aged wool.

The MacDonald connection was surely a good portent.

Better yet, the bolt smelled fresh and clean.

Its position in the middle of the pile had allowed the tartan to defy the ravages of time, leaving its precious wool almost as pristine as the day some long-forgotten soul had added the bolt to the stack.

Hardwick set the bolt aside and flexed his fingers, readying himself for what he must do. He felt a twinge of regret. It pained him that now, after centuries of lying untouched, he should be the one to mar such a noble tartan.

Fortunately, he was certain the MacDonalds wouldn't mind.

As with his good friend Bran of Barra, more than one of the braw MacDonalds stood in his debt.

So he closed his eyes and drew a deep, preparatory breath. Then he reached for the bolt and began unrolling it with care, measuring just enough to suit his needs. Another deep breath and a few more finger flexes, and he was ready.

Gripping the tartan, he drew it taut and ripped off a suitable length.

Before guilt could besiege him, he dug his fingers into the cloth, holding it fast as he willed away the rest of his garb. Once naked, he wrapped the tartan around his hips. He wound the cloth band ever tighter, slipping it between his legs and using the plaid to secure his best parts until he was certain even the slightest twitch would prove impossible.

Satisfied at last, he knotted the tartan, well pleased with his handiwork.

He shoved a hand through his hair, excitement beginning to quicken his blood. Deliberately, he envisioned the sweet golden triangle topping Cilla's thighs. He imagined his hand cupping her heat and finding her slick, moist, and warm.

Soft, slippery, and eager for his caress, she'd surely also welcome his tongue. If not, he knew ways to persuade her to allow him the pleasure.

At the thought, heat flashed through him, his loins tightening as fierce need fired his blood.

But he didn't twitch.

The plaid wrapping worked well.

Tight, stifling, and a lust damper if e'er there was one, the binding enabled him to swiftly switch his thoughts from plundering his lady's heat with his tongue to things as uninspiring as polishing the mail of his hauberk or watching several of the kitchen laddies at Seagrave empty and then scrub the sides of the stronghold's cesspit.

Hardwick's smile returned. His delight was boundless.

Uncomfortable as it was, the binding would allow him many freedoms.

Truth be told, he'd ne'er had a better idea.

He looked down, feeling his grin to his toes.

For good measure, he retied the binding's knot, making the fit just a bit tighter.

"By Thor's hammer!" A familiar voice boomed behind him. "What in a god's name are you doing?"

"Bran!" Hardwick's good humor vanished at once. Mortification swept him.

He spun around to face his friend, summoning his kilt even as he wheeled about. "What are you doing here?" He slapped at the familiar woolen pleats, brushing the folds in place and righting his sporran. "You—"

"I'm no' after the kind of foolery you're up to, that's for sure!" The Hebridean stared at him, gog-eyed. "I know fine that some modern women run about wearing wee bits o' cloth that barely cover their bottoms, but I haven't yet seen a man donning such a style!"

Hardwick glared at him. "It isn't a *style*, you great buffoon. It's something I'm hoping to use to get around the Dark One's stipulation that I daren't—"

"Run hard." Blunt as always, Bran rocked back on his heels.

Then he laughed, wiping the mirth from his cheeks. "Och, then—more like you'll wither!"

"As e'er, you're a man of few words, my friend." Hardwick folded his arms. "Be glad you haven't such a need."

"I ne'er turned a bard-wizard from my door." Bran

drew his brows together, eyeing Hardwick's kilt as if he could still see the tartan binding hidden beneath it. "Be that as it may, I'll own that—were I in your position—I might consider such measures. Even if I'll vow for all time that a Highlander's man piece wasn't made to be constricted!"

"Humph." Hardwick refused further comment.

He knew too well how much a Highlander appreciated a free and unrestricted *swing*.

But the twinkle in the Hebridean chieftain's eye was warning enough that he'd take the subject to embarrassing heights if allowed to do so.

Hoping to avoid such a debacle, Hardwick steered him in another direction.

"I'd hear why you're here? I thought you'd gone back to Barra to gather your lads?"

"And so I did!" The lout flashed a grin.

"But?" Hardwick waited.

Bran looked down, shuffling his big feet on the dusty floorboards. "Ach, it was so. My friends were in the midst of some serious merrymaking when I arrived." He glanced up again, his foot shuffling at an end. "It will take a while for their heads to clear sufficiently for them to sift up here and join us. So—"

"You sifted yourself here ahead of them?" Hardwick couldn't keep the skepticism out of his voice. "Since when do you—the greatest fest giver in the Hebrides—walk away from a night of bawdy revelry?"

A stain of pink bloomed on Bran's cheeks.

"Perhaps I'm growing old?" Looking anything but, the burly Islesman whacked Hardwick on the shoulder. "Seven hundred years wears on a soul."

Hardwick humphed again, not buying his friend's excuse. He arched a brow to show it.

Bran jutted his chin. "Mayhap I was worried about you?"

"Worried about me?"

"Aye, so I was." Bran's tone took on an edge of

belligerence. "The saints forgive you for no' believing me. We *are* friends, you know."

This time it was Hardwick who looked down at his feet.

Or he would have if he hadn't caught himself fast enough. What he couldn't prevent was the way his chest tightened on his friend's admission.

As he'd already noted, since meeting Cilla, he'd grown way too soft-hearted.

So he summoned his most indifferent mien and pretended to adjust his plaid's gem-studded shoulder brooch. "I've no need of someone to look o'er me."

"Say you!" Bran grinned. "But no matter," he added as quickly. "Truth is, I also returned because the feasting in my hall bored me. I thought I'd do a bit of scouting on Mac's moorland. Maybe see if I saw any signs of his Viking *ghosties* before my lads arrive."

Hardwick cocked a brow. "Did you see them?"

Bran stroked his beard. "If I had, you can be sure I'd still be busy with them." He made a few grand flourishes with his hand, as if wielding an imaginary sword. " 'Tis overlong since I've bloodied my fists, no' to mention swing my blade in earnest!"

"So after you didn't meet up with Mac's Norsemen, you came here to tell me?"

" 'Sakes, no!" Bran swelled his chest. "I would have returned directly to Barra if that was all of it. You wouldn't have seen me again until I came back with my men."

"Then why are you here?"

"Because I found something."

"Indeed?"

"Aye, and have you a good look at it!" Bran held out a hand, wriggling his fingers to produce a shovel-like tool, its pointy head shiny and flat-bladed. "There's more where this came from. A whole cache of the things, tucked in a wicker basket hidden in a fold of peat."

Hardwick frowned, reaching for it. "A whole cache?"

Bran bobbed his head. "I counted a good dozen, maybe more."

"In Mac's peat fields?"

"Aye, so I said, just." Bran nodded again, his expression earnest. "The basket was deliberately hidden. I'd bet my beard on it."

Hardwick turned the tool over in his hands. Tiny words were inscribed on the steel of its triangular-shaped blade: MARSHALLTOWN COMPANY.

A word that made little sense, but for the cold prickles it brought to the back of his neck.

He curled his fingers around the tool's wooden handle and looked at Bran. "Have you e'er heard of such a workman's mark as this?"

Bran shook his head. "No' that I can recall, though the thing does look familiar."

Hardwick nodded sagely.

He, too, had seen such a tool before. It was just a matter of time until he remembered.

And when he did, he was sure, the *Marshalltown Company* and their tools would lead them a step closer to solving Mac's problems.

He felt it in his bones.

Just as he knew that whoe'er had hid the basket out on the moors would soon have hell to pay.

He'd see to it personally.

With a wee bit of help from his friends.

Chapter 13

OFFICIAL KILT INSPECTOR.

Emblazoned in bright red satin across the front of an Australian woman's royal blue jacket, the words jumped at Cilla each time she looked out at the expectant faces staring back at her from the small audience of her first Dunroamin-held broken-china jewelry-making class.

A fan of Wee Hughie MacSporran, the woman—Elizabeth, according to the name stitched in large, equally scarlet letters on the back of her jacket—clearly wasn't interested in the little piles of colorful broken china lining the worktable set up in Dunroamin's vaulted basement.

The woman's gaze kept sliding elsewhere.

Namely to the stairs, where Hardwick stood on the bottom step, his arms folded as he leaned against the wall, watching the proceedings.

Light from a mock medieval torch streamed down from higher up in the stair tower, illuminating him in all his kilted magnificence. Soft and flickering, the fake torchlight drew attention to the sheen of his silky black hair and the width of his powerful shoulders. His cute knees and attractive, manly calves also caught the eye.

His hallmark sandalwood scent wafted on the air.

Above all, the light spilled across his kilt. Cilla tried not to notice.

Aussie Elizabeth looked nowhere else.

An annoyance Cilla really didn't need, especially since she hadn't seen Hardwick for over a week. A sleepless seven nights wondering if he'd appear out of the darkness, towering above her bed and ready to ravish her. Nights of tossing and turning and wishing he would.

Knowing he'd spent the time prowling Uncle Mac's peat fields didn't help, either. Sure, she knew he was more than able to make short work of whoever was slinking about the moors, pretending to be Viking ghosts. But she knew, too, that there were other things *spooking* about Dunroamin.

And those things frightened her.

He'd meant to reassure her when he'd sided with her about the devil face. His rallying had touched her deeply. But knowing that he didn't doubt the existence of such nightmare creatures was unsettling.

The devil face hadn't made a return sweep past her bedroom window, but she feared what would happen if Hardwick encountered the fiend in the small hours on the moors.

She shuddered, trying to disguise her shiver by fiddling with her broken-china tools. She shuffled them about on the worktable, doing her best to look busy.

As if she weren't worried about devils and hell hags. Much better to appear cool and calm, as if just breathing his scent wasn't making her all hot and weak-kneed.

Which, of course, it was.

No man should smell so delicious.

That he'd returned now was just her luck. This was a time when her composure was crucial and—damn it all—she'd chosen to give her workshop in Dunroamin's basement. Used regularly as a workstation, the

vaulted undercroft was the most brightly lit area of
the castle.

The high-powered spotlights trained on her worktable also shone brightly on her, surely picking out the
dark circles and puffiness beneath her eyes. Not to
mention the little roll of *pudge* at her tummy that
made it just a tad difficult to fasten the button at the
top of her pants zipper.

She'd clearly eaten too much shortbread since arriving in Scotland.

Aussie Elizabeth appeared to have eaten nothing at
all since leaving Sydney.

Cilla frowned.

If Ms. Official Kilt Inspector didn't soon stop ogling
Hardwick—or cease wetting her wine-red lips—she'd
find herself reimbursed for the cost of the evening's
creative workshop.

Tempted to give the woman a refund immediately,
Cilla tightened her fingers around the mosaic nippers
in her hand and began her talk. "I've always loved
old things. Treasures bursting with character and history, but perhaps in need of a bit of whimsy and imagination on your part if, like me, you'd enjoy bringing
them back to life."

Aussie Elizabeth yawned.

In the front row, Colonel Darling puffed on his
pipe.

Hardwick's stare narrowed on her. She could feel it
without looking at him. It was one of those slow,
heavy-lidded stares that roamed her body, rousing her
physically and leaving behind a sizzling trail of heat
that made it almost impossible to stand still.

Flustered, she put down the nippers and picked up
a box of especially lovely bits of porcelain. She angled
it so that her audience could see the tiny pieces, hoping they'd keep their attention on the broken china
and not notice how her cheeks were surely flaming.

Hardwick was trying to tell her something with his

hot, dampen-her-panties stare, and she had a good idea what it was. She might not have ever experienced the wild, dizzying kind of raw, untamed sex that supposedly shook hills and made the world stop spinning, but she'd read enough romance novels and seen enough films to recognize Hardwick's message.

Something had happened.

Some difference that—dear God—meant he was going to make love to her.

She knew it instinctively, and the thought electrified her. She slid a glance his way and immediately wished she hadn't, because as soon as their eyes met, he lowered his gaze to move slowly down and then up her thighs, finally settling *just there*, where she'd swear she could feel the stirring touch of expertly stroking fingers.

"Oh!" She disguised her gasp as a cough.

His gaze went even darker and one corner of his mouth lifted in a smile. "O-o-oh, aye," he mouthed the words, his gaze still focused on the vee of her thighs.

I want you, Cilla lass.

She jumped. The words hushed past her ear, deep, rich, and smooth, and pitched so that no one else could hear them. She hoped, too, that no one could guess that his ghostly *finger magic* was shooting beyond the mere rousing stage.

No longer just stroking, his hot stare now made her feel as if those skilled fingers were slipping beneath the edge of her panties to *really* toy with her. Imagined or not, however he was doing it, he *was* making her wet.

Hot, damp, and tingly.

She swallowed and tried to discreetly press her thighs together.

Noticing her discomfort, he arched a knowing brow. His barely there smile went positively wicked.

Cilla recognized its portent, and her knees nearly buckled.

Giving herself a shake, she wrenched her gaze from

him and purposely looked down at the box of broken
china in her hands. Each piece gleamed in the stark
lighting. Most were irregularly shaped and showed antique patterns of floral design, the colors soft and
muted.

She tightened her grip on the box, willing the blaze
between her legs to recede by focusing on the porcelain. Bolder shards appeared of American origin. Vi-
brant reds, blues, and yellows marked them as having
started their career as much-sought-after Fiestaware.
While other, more fragile pieces proved edged with
finest gold.

Violet Manyweathers leaned forward, her gaze on
the box. "You're after helping us to make jewelry with
these wee bits of china?"

"Pah!" Colonel Darling shot her a derisive glance.
"Of course she is! Why do you think we're sitting
here? Though"—he waved the stem end of his pipe
at the worktable—"unlike the rest of you, I'm only
here to observe."

Violet dismissed him with a quick flip of her age-
spotted hand.

"Speak for yourself," she quipped, her gaze on a
bloodred square of the dinnerware. "I might be for
having a new pendant."

"And you can." Relieved to get her mind on something else, Cilla made a mental note to be sure Violet
received the bit of red Fiestaware. "I'll help you with
every step."

Violet sat back, looking pleased.

The colonel stuck his pipe in his mouth and returned to puffing.

Cilla cleared her throat. "Before we begin, you must
understand one thing. These bits and pieces of cracked
china are much more than that. They are broken
beauties." She glanced around, her heart warming to
a beloved theme. "Small shards of onetime cups and
saucers, dessert plates, and anything else that was once

well-loved and, through no fault of its own, became damaged."

A matronly woman raised a hand in the back row. "How did you become interested in making such jewelry?"

"Long before I actually started." Cilla looked her way, remembering Aunt Birdie introducing her as the owner of Tongue's hair salon. "When I was about six or seven, I had a beautiful tea set. It was tiny, the pieces more doll-sized than for a child. Although my mother gave it to me, the set once belonged to my great-grandmother."

She trailed a fingertip across the china pieces. "The tea set was a lovely antique bisque shade decorated with pink and mauve roses and rosebuds. And, if I recall correctly, there were also little swirls of delicate green leaves. Very much like this . . ."

Looking down, she sorted through the box of china bits until she found a similar piece. She held it up for the audience's examination.

A round of appreciative oohs and aahs rewarded her efforts.

"You must've been a good child." Flora Duthie's twittering voice rose from the first row. "I never allowed my girls to play with anything so fragile."

"Oh, my mother didn't, either." Cilla smiled, remembering. "The tea set was for *looking*, not playing. It was kept behind the glass doors of a curio cabinet, and"—she paused, trying to catch everyone's eye— "I found the pull of the miniature cups and saucers quite irresistible."

I find you irresistible.

His words hushed past her ear again. Deep, burred, and so honey-rich smooth she almost forgot to breathe. Heat consumed her anew and she set down the box of china pieces. She didn't dare look at him. She was quite sure he knew what his sexy Highland voice did to her.

What he didn't know was how desperately she wanted to do the same to him.

But it'd been a while since she'd heard of anyone swooning over an American accent.

If ever.

She bit her lip, his tingle-stirring burr still spooling through her. Heaven forbid if he started his slow, heated, body-roaming stare magic again.

Half wishing he would, she took a deep breath. "One day when my mother was out, I climbed onto a chair and tried to take the tea set from its shelf. I slipped, grabbing hold of the curio cabinet's glass shelf as I fell."

"Ach, dearie me!" A bespectacled woman in the second row gasped loudly.

Colonel Darling twisted around to glare at her. He also muttered something about interruptions, clearly excluding himself.

"Needless to say"—Cilla hoped her voice only sounded breathless to her—"I pulled down the entire curio cabinet. It landed on top of me, leaving scars I bear to this day. But most importantly, the mishap shattered my tea set."

A chorus of *ooohs* answered her.

She rested a hand on the worktable. "I was bereft. Trying everything, I begged my mother to let me fix it. But she wouldn't allow me to glue back the broken pieces, claiming the tea set was ruined."

"But you saw it differently." The Tongue hair salon owner spoke up again. "You told her you wanted to make jewelry out of the smashed porcelain?"

Cilla laughed. "Not quite, but almost. I was just a child, remember. But the experience did impress me, giving me my later passion for taking something that's been broken and turning it into something beautiful again."

On the words, a swirl of sandalwood slid around her, almost a caress. Tender this time, but equally potent. As if he knew she'd thought of him as she'd said the words.

She did mean to *un*break him, make him whole again.

In the audience, Aussie Elizabeth stirred in her chair. Her red lips went pouty and her gaze—still on Hardwick—turned come-get-me seductive.

Cilla frowned at her.

The Aussie shifted again, wittingly or unwittingly revealing that she'd neglected to wear panties beneath her short, hip-hugging skirt. Cilla nearly dropped the broken-china link bracelet she'd just picked up, intending to pass it around as an example of her style.

Ms. Official Kilt Inspector's *style* was bare.

Cilla's jaw slipped. Her fingers tightened on the bracelet until its lobster claw clasp pinched her thumb.

Aussie Elizabeth stopped shifting. But she'd settled in such a way as to keep her charms exposed.

"Here's a seat if you're joining us." She patted the empty chair beside her, her gaze on a spot just behind Cilla's shoulder.

Hardwick!

Cilla's breath caught. He stood right behind her. His sexy sandalwood scent swept around her, bold and possessive. She swallowed hard, her heart racing as another, less welcome emotion jabbed green-tinged needles into her most vulnerable places.

Standing where he was, his view of Aussie Elizabeth's wiles was surely as good as her own. Perhaps even better, as, being a man, he wouldn't look away as she had.

A thought that sent bolts of white-hot fury whipping through her.

Setting down the pretty little sterling silver and broken-china link bracelet, she sucked in a hot breath. She also hoped the word *jealous* wasn't stamped in bright, flaming letters across her forehead.

Something told her it was.

"There's a name for such women, but I'll no' speak it in your presence." Hardwick stepped closer to her, his deep voice low.

He did fix the brazen wench with a carefully neutral stare, her display leaving him cold. "I thank you, lady," he offered, inclining his head. "But like the colonel here"—he glanced at the man—"I am only here to observe. Miss Swanner and her porcelain pieces, mind."

The tart's legs snapped shut. "And I am here to make a Celtic brooch for the Highland Storyweaver." She sat up straighter, assuming a proprietary air. "Something Robert the Bruce-ish is what I have in mind. Wee Hughie is his grandson, eighteen generations removed."

"Indeed?" Hardwick arched a brow.

The chit wasn't worth the breath it would take to tell her that in his seven hundred years of ghosting, he'd encountered enough supposed Robert the Bruce descendents to populate all of Scotland and then some.

Instead, he slid a sidelong look at Cilla, not liking the dark circles beneath her eyes. The slight puffiness that betold she hadn't been sleeping well.

"You look tired, lass." He regretted his honesty the instant the words left his tongue.

He'd meant to rouse her further by whispering some choice bit of seductive wickedness in her ear. Perhaps suggest that after he'd finished tantalizing her with his fingers, he'd use his tongue to give her release. That's why he'd left the stairwell and approached her.

To let her know he meant to make love to her this night. Leastways, as far as his present situation allowed.

Now he'd broken one of the first rules of wooing.

He'd commented on how ragged she looked.

He frowned, wishing he could kick himself.

"Lass"—he tried to make it better—"that's no' what I meant to say."

"I'm fine, thank you. Not tired at all." She snatched up her box of broken china and summoned the two red-haired youths he now knew to be Honoria's nephews. "If you'll excuse me, I'll get on with my workshop."

"You're also the loveliest sight to grace my eyes since"—he leaned close, ignoring her ire—"the last time I looked upon you."

Her mouth tightened and her gaze flicked to the trollop.

So that was it. She was jealous.

Hardwick almost whooped for joy.

"She canna hold a candle to you." He folded his arms, feeling smug. "Later, when we are alone, I shall prove it to you. As I've been trying to do the while, as I am sure you know."

To his delight, she blushed.

Looking sweetly flustered, she half turned away from him to pluck a small, deep red square from her box of treasures. Then, clearly taking great pains to conceal how much he'd ruffled her, she handed the little piece of china to Violet Manyweathers, who accepted it with glee.

When she returned to the worktable, her cheeks still glowed with anticipation and—he was certain, for he could see it—her pulse beat excitedly in the hollow of her throat.

She couldn't wait to be alone with him.

Her eagerness shone like a beacon.

Then she ruined it by flashing a bright smile on the two brawny lads, Robbie and Roddie.

Hardwick frowned.

She handed the taller of the two lads her box of broken china. "Robbie, if you'll pass this around so everyone can select a special piece, and you, Roddie"—she gave the other youth a tray piled high with the tools she called *mosaic nippers*—"if you'll hand out these, as well, we can get started."

As if on cue, Honoria and Behag Finney the cook stepped out of the shadows on the far side of the vaulted chamber. Coming forward, they held small tables he'd heard referred to as *folding work trays* clutched beneath their arms.

Nodding to them, his lady quickly returned her attention to the audience. She held up her own nipper and an uneven piece of porcelain.

"Most of the broken china pieces I use for my Vintage Chic collections are cut into squares, ovals, hearts, and rectangles." She set down the bit of porcelain and her nipper. "Even so, some of my most prized offerings have been made from irregular shapes. I'd suggest holding your piece in your hand while closing your eyes and then letting the china tell you in its own way how best to cut it."

Almost everyone except Colonel Darling nodded appreciatively.

Aussie Elizabeth rolled her eyes.

And at the back of the room, Birdie MacGhee was clearly using her wifely influence to keep Mac from slapping his thigh and hooting loudly.

Hardwick, too, could have easily guffawed.

He'd lived too long and too hard to waste time listening to cracked and broken bits of porcelain.

He did look on as, contrary to his word, Colonel Darling fished not one but two pieces from the proffered box. Choosing first a small bit of what Cilla termed *chintz*, a delicate-looking floral pattern in yellows, pinks, and greens; his second choice proved equally fine, this piece boasting hand-painted deep purple flowers and green leaves.

The colonel's puffed chest and the telling glances he bestowed on both Violet and Flora left little doubt as to whom he had in mind as recipients for his labors.

As if pretending not to notice—or, at the least, to have forgotten his avowals not to get actively involved in jewelry making—Cilla continued on. She moved about the rows of class attendees, the slight jiggling of her full breasts and the tempting sway of her hips making it difficult for Hardwick to think of much else.

Until she stopped beside wee Violet Manyweathers's folding work tray. The old woman's hands shook, making it difficult for her to cut her square of deep red Fiestaware into the oval shape she wished for a pendant.

Again and again, Cilla encouraged her, finally leaning down to cover the woman's trembling fingers with her own strong ones so that, together, they managed to clip and cut the square into Violet's oval.

Hardwick moved closer, watching silently and not even realizing he'd drawn so near to them until a loud yelp shattered the spell.

Eyeing him accusingly, Dunroamin's little mascot dachshund, Leo, peered up at him from where he'd been curled at Violet's feet.

"Sorry, laddie." Hardwick reached down to pat the dog's head.

But much as he regretted stepping on Leo's tail, his mind was elsewhere.

Instead of Dunroamin's well-lit vaulted undercroft, he saw Seagrave's great hall. Rather than Cilla and Violet Manyweathers, his long-ago intended and his mother loomed before him. Recalled from the hazy mists of time, the two souls from his past filled his vision, one much loved and cherished, the other inspiring only shudders and distaste.

As if it were only yesterday, he looked on as the beautiful Lady Dolina appeared behind his mother's chair and then leaned down to snatch the spoon from his mother's bent and trembling fingers.

"She should be locked in a tower! Kept away from the hall, where a nurse can hand feed and coddle her." Lady Dolina slapped the spoon onto the high table, well out of his aging mother's reach. "It offends my gentle eyes to watch her food dribble down her chin!"

"And you offend me." Hardwick took the beauty by the elbow, pulling her from the dais and, ultimately, out of his hall.

It was the last he'd seen of her, not that he'd minded. What he did mind was her intrusion now.

She'd robbed him of the pleasure of watching Cilla bend down to help Violet Manyweathers cut her square of red dinnerware. Prepared as he was—he'd pulled his tartan binding especially tight—he'd been enjoying how her well-rounded buttocks bobbed with her every move.

He didn't need to examine the tightness in his chest.

Born of an entirely different emotion; one Bran would surely call *love*, neither his lustful urgings nor the swellings of his heart mattered at the moment.

His mother and Lady Dolina were gone.

And they'd taken Cilla and Violet with them.

Hardwick frowned, blinking.

He knuckled his eyes, but nothing changed. The vaulted undercroft was empty. Only the vacated seats and his lady's worktable remained.

Furious that he'd spent much more time than he'd thought peering into his own past, he took a piece of brilliant blue Fiestaware from the box of broken china. He turned the shard over in his hand, his heart thumping harder the longer he peered at it.

It was the same blue as Cilla's eyes.

"Where were you?"

He whirled around at her voice. The shard of blue flew from his fingers. "I . . . hell and botheration, I—" He reached down, swiping the little piece of dinnerware off the undercroft's stone-flagged floor.

"Well?" She stepped out of the shadows, the neat stacks of folding work trays lined against the wall behind her, indicating what she'd been doing.

"I was thinking." He set the shard on the table. "Thinking of you, and so deeply that I didn't realize you'd ended your—"

"I didn't mean now." Her gaze slid to the chair where the trollop had sat. "I meant all this week?"

His brow furrowed. "I was patrolling your uncle's peat fields. I thought you knew." It was the best answer he could give her, unwilling as he was to reveal that he'd spent the time drilling himself on the moors.

Using every passing moment to dwell on his desire for her in order to test the strength of his tartan binding, only returning once he'd assured himself he could pleasure her without suffering his own arousal.

He looked at her now, not missing the bright color staining her cheeks. Nor did he fail to note that she was avoiding his eyes. When she once more flashed a glance at the trollop's seat, he knew why.

"By Odin!" Disbelief swept him. "Dinna tell me you think I—"

Her eyes flashed. "Everyone knows men go wild over smooth women like Elizabeth."

"Smooth women?" He stared at her, at first uncomprehending.

When he did, his jaw nearly hit the floor.

He took a deep breath, releasing it quickly. "It wouldn't have mattered to me if she'd shaved her head, as well, do you hear?"

Picking up the blue shard again, he wrapped his fingers around it, squeezing hard. "She could have thrown off her clothes and pranced about naked, for all I care. I would still no' have seen her. No' in the way you mean."

Cilla bit her lip, wanting to believe him. But just that moment her waistband was biting viciously into her recently acquired belly roll.

She flipped back her hair, met his gaze full on. "She has a flat stomach."

The words sounded petty even to her.

Unable to retract them, she started to frown when— to her amazement—Hardwick jammed his fists on his hips and, throwing back his head, began to laugh.

His dark eyes alight, he grinned at her. "I can see you've ne'er known a Highlander if you think we lust after stick women!"

Cilla tried to appear unaffected. "I'm sure I don't know what a Highlander lusts after."

"Then, my sweet"—he stepped closer, his thumb rubbing slow circles over the piece of blue Fiestaware in his hand—"perhaps it is time you learned."

She glanced aside, painfully aware of the bright overhead lights shining down on them. They'd highlight the puffiness beneath her eyes and her mussed hair. Having attempted to look calm, cool, and collected, she'd adopted Aunt Birdie's signature french twist.

Only on her, it hadn't worked.

The pins had slipped and the elegant do was now nearly undone.

"My ex was of Highland stock." It was a lame excuse, but bought her time. "At least he claimed to—"

"Sweeting, if he'd been a true Highlander, you would have known it." His voice deepened, his burr sliding through her like sun-warmed honey. "As a good friend of mine is wont to say, 'There are men and there are Highlanders. Woe be to anyone fool enough not to know the difference.' "

"I can tell the difference." She looked back at him, her heart clutching. "It's a big one."

"Aye, so I've been told." He flashed a wolfish smile.

Cilla's eyes widened.

He laughed.

Heat consumed her, his nearness and the look on his face rousing her even more than the ghostly magic of his hot stares and roving fingers. Her heart began hammering, and her mouth went dry.

"Then tell me again how you can seem so real," she blurted, nerves making her grasp for a safer subject.

"Because I will it so and"—he paused, his voice

turning earnest—"because I've had seven hundred years' practice."

Unable to argue with that, Cilla glanced to where Leo slept curled beneath the worktable. "And him?" She waited until he, too, looked down at the little dog. "Why isn't he afraid of you? I've always heard dogs ran from ghosts."

"And do you always believe what you hear, Cilla lass?"

"I—"

"Dogs are no different than people, sweet." His smile returned, his eyes twinkling. "In spirit or in life, they are the same souls. Dinna tell me you've ne'er noticed that dogs can tell when someone likes them or no'."

He cast another quick glance at the sleeping Leo. "They also ken a good soul from a bad one. That knowledge doesn't change just because the soul they see might be *others*."

Cilla blinked. "Others as in a ghost?"

He nodded.

Under the table, Leo stretched and started snoring.

Hardwick stepped closer, something in his eyes warming her to the roots of her own soul. Never had a man touched her so deeply both inside and out. She couldn't imagine what would happen when he *really* touched her, something she knew was going to happen very soon.

She moistened her lips. "Are you trying to tell me you're a good man?"

He shook his head slowly, his eyes going dark. "I'll leave that for you to decide. What I wish to do is show you how good *you* are."

She blinked. "Me?"

He leaned close to nuzzle her neck, letting his lips brush across her skin. "You and no other, aye," he declared, nipping her ear.

"O-o-oh . . ." Cilla's heart began a slow, hard thumping.

He lifted the shard of blue Fiestaware he still held and appeared to examine it. "Did you know, for starters, that your eyes are the same brilliant blue as this? Or"—he put down the bit of blue dinnerware and picked up a cream china piece with a delicate gold edge—"that your hair glistens with the same golden sheen as the rim of this porcelain?"

He looked at her for a long moment, his gaze burning her soul. "A man could lose himself in such eyes as yours." He put down the fragile bit of gold-rimmed china and reached for her hair, twining a strand through his fingers. "In my day, kings would have gone to their knees for a maid with such silken tresses of gold. This day, this e'en, I am telling you that I have dreamt of touching your hair."

He let the strands spill across his hand. "I have dreamt of much, Cilla."

She bit her lip, unable to speak.

His words were making her melt.

As for his eyes, it almost hurt to look into them, so intense was his stare. No man had ever looked at her with such naked hunger.

"Eh . . ." She stumbled over her tongue, the wild hammering of her heart making it impossible to think. "No one ever said—"

"More's the pity." He turned back to the table, taking a sliver cut from Violet's red dinnerware. "And more is my pleasure in showing you. Behold the rich color of your lips," he added, holding the tiny shard to the light before returning it to the table. "Sweet lips that beg kissing, Cilla."

The world tilted. "A Highlander's kiss?"

His smile went devilish. *"My kiss."*

Before she could blink, he pulled her into his arms and slanted his mouth over hers in a hot, demanding kiss. Her blood sizzled and the room spun. A whirlwind of desire whipped through her and she clung to him, pressing close as he deepened the kiss and they lost themselves in a swirl of lips, tongue, and soft, heated breath.

"O-o-oh," she gasped, pulling in air even as he claimed another bold, soul-slaking kiss.

He wrapped his arms around her, dragging her even closer. He let his hands glide low until he splayed his fingers across her hips, holding her tight against him as he kissed her again and again.

"Now, Cilla"—he pulled back to grin at her—"now you've almost been kissed by a Highlander."

She blinked. *"Almost?"*

He slid a hand into her hair, plucking out the remaining pins and tossing them onto the floor. "Aye, almost," he purred, winking. "There's another kind of kiss we specialize in, see you."

Cilla almost choked. "What do you mean?"

"I think you know." He smiled.

He lowered his gaze, and she knew indeed.

"Oh, no . . ." Heat scalded her cheeks. "You can't mean—"

"Och, but I do." He reached for her blouse, already unbuttoning. "I always keep my word, Cilla lass. I'm about to show you how good you are."

She gulped.

He folded his arms, looking supremely satisfied. " 'Tis time you learned what it's like to be pleasured by a man who lives to please you."

Chapter 14

"Wait."

Cilla reached up and grabbed Hardwick's wrists just as he neared the last few buttons of her top. Already, her breasts felt tight and heavy, her nipples puckered and achy, needing his touch. She bit her lip, holding back a moan. She wanted this, everything, but still . . .

"The light"—she glanced at the overhead spotlights—"is too much."

"Och, nae, sweeting." He grinned. "There canna be enough light. I would see you clearly." His gaze dipped to her half-opened blouse, his eyes glittering darkly. "All of you that I can feast my eyes on."

"But—"

He pressed two fingers against her lips, silencing her. "*But* is a word I dinna acknowledge."

"It has its purpose." She aimed another glance at the spotlights.

They really were bright.

Almost blinding.

So much so they'd surely pick out each and every one of her faults. The little belly roll that suddenly felt quite big and obvious, maybe even a bit jiggly.

She frowned. "The lights bother me."

His smile faded. "Why do I think you mean that?"

"Because I do." She glanced aside. She could feel her face reddening. "You heard my talk tonight; the

part about the glass curio cabinet that fell on me when
I was little."

He was on her in a wink, seizing her chin and forcing her to look at him.

"For truth, lass!" His brows snapped together. "Dinna
tell me you're fashing yourself o'er childhood scars?"

"It isn't that. . . ." She hedged.

The curio cabinet scars were tiny and barely visible.
A magnifying glass would be needed to find them.
What she'd meant was how she'd reached for something she'd wanted so badly, only to have it come
tumbling down on top of her.

Now she wanted Hardwick that desperately.

And she didn't want to risk anything that might
send him running from her.

Stepping closer, he brushed his lips across her brow.
"I'll kiss every one of the wee scars until you forget
them."

"The scars don't bother me."

He arched a brow. "What then?"

"It's, well . . . everything."

She lifted her chin, not about to tell him how Grant
used to harp at her about her yo-yo'ing weight. Or
that he'd badgered her to be like Aussie Elizabeth.

A request she'd flat-out refused.

"You're forgetting one thing." He folded his arms,
his smile going wicked again. "I've already seen you
naked. And"—his voice deepened, the rich, silky-
smooth tones spilling into her—"unless I've lost my
skill, you've already felt my hands on you. I saw how
much you enjoyed it. You know I'm not talking about
the other times I've touched you."

He paused, lowering his gaze so that, again, she felt
what could only be described as his hand between her
legs. A long, strong finger gliding oh, so intimately
along her cleft, teasing and tantalizing her.

When the finger dipped into her, she jumped. Liquid fire streaked through her, taking her breath.

"Wait till it *is* my finger, Cilla lass." He circled his thumbs over the swell of her breasts as he spoke, rubbing her nipples through the lace of her bra. "When it's my tongue, your world will shatter."

Cilla almost climaxed on his words. She wanted his hands on her, playing and toying with her, driving her wild. And she *burned* for him to touch his tongue to her, to kiss and lick her there.

But she couldn't forget her belly roll.

"Would you like a sample tongue swirl?" He leaned close, whispering the words against her ear. "That, too, is within my ghostly powers, though I'd rather really tongue you."

"Yes!" The word burst free before she could stop it. "I mean no. Not . . . yet. It's the lights. They—"

He drew back, looking at her. "The lights are of no import."

"But—"

"No buts. Though"—he turned a gaze of his own on the blaring spotlights—"I'll own your modern lights are lacking in grace. Were this Seagrave, and in my day, I'd ravish you by candlelight. As is . . ."

He grinned and snapped his fingers.

At once, the awful overhead lighting vanished and a warm golden glow surrounded them. Soft and flickering, it spooled everywhere, broken in places by deep shadow that felt equally inviting.

Cilla blinked.

She looked around, her jaw slipping when she saw that the scattering of Uncle Mac's mock medieval torchlights in the stairwell now burned for real. As did the iron-bracketed wall sconces lighting the vaulted undercroft.

Wall sconces that—she knew—hadn't been there a moment before.

Yet her worktable and broken china tools remained. And, she noted with relief, little Leo still slept where he'd curled up on the undercroft floor. The only difference was that a sweet-smelling layer of herbed rushes now covered the stone flagging, and Leo—bless Hardwick for his thoughtfulness—reposed on a soft and warm-looking bed of plaid.

Cilla swung back to Hardwick. "How did you do that?"

He shrugged, trying without much success to look modest. "I told you I've had centuries of practice. Truth is, I could have conjured a much more splendiferous setting, but I am selfish this night."

"Selfish?"

"Aye, sure as rain, I am." His eyes glinted with mischief. "I'm saving my strength to please you."

"Oh." Her heart skittered.

Her knees started going soft again and she drew a great, shuddery breath. It was all she could do not to fling her arms around him and beg him to kiss her again. What she *really* wanted was for him to kiss her down there.

She caught her lower lip between her teeth, the idea electrifying her. She'd never experienced anything so deliciously intimate.

Her entire body started trembling, heat streaking through her from head to toe.

"Och, aye, lass." He stretched his arms above his head, cracking his knuckles. "I dinna want to expend a jot more of my powers than need be. No' "—he lowered his arms, winking—"till I've finished with you."

"I wouldn't call that being selfish."

"Nae?" He leaned close, his mouth just grazing the edge of her ear. "Then maybe you're no' considering how much pleasure I'll have in the doing. Can you no' imagine how I've ached to kiss every sweet inch of you? To see you spread naked before me and then use my tongue to sate myself on you? Licking, laving, and tasting you until you writhe and scream out your pleasure, begging me to stop?"

The words spoken, he swirled the tip of his tongue across the curve of her ear, the caress sending shivers rippling all through her.

"So dinna tell me nae, sweetness." He nipped the side of her neck. " 'Tis too late by far."

Stepping back, he reached for her blouse again, but before he set his fingers to the remaining buttons, he slid a meaningful glance toward the far wall, where she'd stacked the folding work trays earlier.

The wall was empty now.

Until he narrowed his eyes and a tall standing candelabrum appeared. Resplendent, a good dozen fine wax tapers burned brightly in the candelabrum's curved and swirling arms. A further flip of one finger and a beautiful low-slung *bed* joined the candle stand.

Richly carved of what looked to be gleaming, high-polished oak, the lovely chaise-cum-bed beckoned with a lush covering of royal blue velvet.

Cilla's heart slammed against her ribs. She knew exactly what he intended to do to her on that bed. He'd just told her, for heaven's sake, and she burned for every wild and earthy thing he'd promised.

She took a deep breath, unable to take her eyes off the blue bed.

A whole battalion of butterflies took flight in her belly.

"Lass." His fingers were warm against her breasts, even slipping inside her bra to rub and squeeze her nipples. "I see the bed pleases you."

She nodded, too overcome to speak.

Again, she was hovering near climax. And she was still fully clothed! From nowhere, she remembered the saying about Highlanders being different from other men. Now she knew how true the saying was.

But it wasn't complete.

Highlanders weren't just different; they were better.

"The bed is . . . beautiful," she said then, needing to say something before a very telling moan escaped her.

Looking pleased, Hardwick grinned and set to undoing the last of her buttons. "The blue"—he tossed a glance at the little bed's luxurious trappings—"is for your eyes. The rest, of course, is for your pleasure."

"And yours?" Her breath hitched as he slid her top down her shoulders and made quick work of her bra, tossing both aside before she even realized he'd removed them. "What about your pleasure?"

"Ach, but I've told you. *You* are my pleasure." His eyes darkened as he looked at her nakedness, his heated stare making her nipples tighten and her breasts swell and ache with need. "It is enough."

He reached for her, his hands palming and kneading the fullness of her breasts, his thumbs circling and teasing her hard-puckered nipples. Shivers of exquisite pleasure spiraled through her, a thousand times greater than the rousing *heated stare* caresses he'd already given her.

His touch, for real, undid her.

"Oh, Hardwick . . ." She leaned back, causing her breasts to lift, offering herself to him. "I want to touch you, too. . . ."

"You enchant me." He leaned down, flicked his tongue across first one, then the other nipple. "I need naught else."

But when he swept her up against his rock-hard chest and strode for the low blue-cushioned bed, she knew that *she* needed more.

She wanted to please him, too.

Unfortunately—or not, depending—he was already lowering her onto the chaise bed, his fingers deftly working the clasp of her belt.

Try as she might, the feel of him undoing and then peeling off her pants—her panties!—robbed her of all cohesive thought.

She wanted, *ached*, to be naked with him.

Her mind blanked to all but the touch of his warm, strong fingers as he pulled off her clothes, tossing aside each piece to fall onto the rush-strewn floor. The flickering torchlight slid over her, casting her body in soft light and shadow. And even she had to admit the effect was flattering, like nothing of this world's harsh and glaring light.

Even her slightly too-rounded tummy looked more feminine than fat.

But before she could think too much about it, he knelt to ease her thighs apart, opening her for his caress.

Those special Highland kisses he'd warned her about.

Her mouth went dry and her heart stopped beating. It was time.

"Precious lass," he hushed the word against her belly, his breath soft and warm. A light, teasing wind across her intimate curls, a barely there sensation so earth-shaking in its intensity, she would have sworn trapped lightning sizzled between her legs.

"O-o-ooh!" Her eyes flew wide and her hips bucked.

Hardwick chuckled, a deep, low rumble, pure male and brimming satisfaction.

He looked up at her. "I've no' yet gotten started."

"But—"

"No buts, I've told you." He returned his attention to her belly, nuzzling, nipping, and licking her skin. "Relax, sweet, and let me love you."

His hands slid up and down her hips, then moved lower to stroke along her inner thighs, urging them wider. "Now, sweet, open to me. Spread your legs so that I can see and kiss all of you."

"O-o-ooh . . ." His words were pushing her over the edge. Almost there, she did as he'd asked and let her knees fall wide, giving him the access he craved.

Hardwick looked down at her. For one crazy-mad moment, he almost reached to rip off his tartan binding and sink himself deep inside her, taking her as he knew he daren't. It'd be heaven if, for one forbidden heartbeat, he could glory in her tight, silken heat. Revel in the sweetness of her legs wrapped around him as he slid in and out of her.

Instead he drew a great shuddering breath and prayed the binding would hold.

Then he spread her legs even wider and, with an almost feral groan, he lowered his head and began licking the satiny insides of her thighs. He glided his tongue over her, the torture—and bliss—almost too intense to bear.

She writhed and trembled in response. "O-o-oh, man . . ." She dug her fingers into his shoulders, holding tight. "I can't stand it. . . . Don't stop!"

"Och, I shan't."

Not for another seven hundred years, if he had his druthers.

Instead, he thrust his hands beneath her buttocks, squeezing and kneading them as he slid openmouthed kisses along her silky skin. His heart thundered and his entire body throbbed at her pleasure.

And he hadn't yet even neared her sweet female heat.

He paused, his grip on her bottom tightening as he braced himself to nibble and lick his way closer. Already the scent of her hot, musky arousal rose between them, tingeing the air and absolutely intoxicating him.

Opening his eyes, he looked right at her, treating himself to the beauty of her glistening golden curls. The soft and slippery temptation of her sleek, wet need and the way she quivered beneath his stare.

He swallowed hard, his own need straining against the tightly wound tartan.

He swore, disguising it as a groan.

Almost hating himself for the need, he blotted his mind. With all his strength, willing himself not to see the lush golden triangle only a breath away from his eager tongue. Instead, he imagined the pile of bricks and stones generations after him had used to deface his beloved home.

Closing his eyes to give the image more power, he lowered his head and licked, using pure male honing instinct to run the tip of his tongue first up, then down the damp and fragrant center of her.

"Ah-h-h!" Her legs stiffened and she near shot off the little bed. *"Hardwick!"*

His name on her tongue nearly broke him.

His eyes snapped open. The sight of her splayed wide—and so close before him—took his breath, leaving only a blazing fire that scalded his lungs and left him wondering why he didn't burn to a crisp.

Then she rocked her hips, the movement bringing her nakedness higher so that her soft wetness brushed his chin and the wild tangle of her damp, musk-scented curls tickled the tip of his nose.

"Living saints!" He jerked his head back, his restraint almost shattered.

Desire exploding, he yanked his hands from beneath her, fisting them against the chaise bed's rich blue cushioning. Needing her desperately, he opened his mouth over her, drawing hard, sucking fiercely on the whole of her until only his need to breathe made him tear himself away.

"Oh. My. God." She looked right at him, glaze-eyed and panting. Her soft, well-curved body glowed in the candlelight, her wide-spread legs thrashing as she sought to open herself more fully.

He groaned. Again and again, he licked her, only stopping to give her most sensitive spot the quick little circling swirls he knew she needed. Or to give himself the pleasure of dipping his tongue inside her, probing her deepest heat and letting himself drown in the hot, stirring wetness of her.

She trembled from head to toe, shivering with pleasure.

He shook with the taste of her. Her clean, tangy scent flooded his senses, making him burn. He daren't risk the like again. As it was, his every muscle strained with the effort of squelching his arousal.

"Please." She twined her fingers in his hair, clutching him to her.

Somewhere, something ripped—he heard the tearing cloth—but he no longer cared. The taste and scent of her on his tongue made him wild. So he growled, something he couldn't recall ever having done, then set to pleasing her one kiss, lick, and tongue swirl at time.

He released his fierce grip on the bed cushioning to run his hands over her breasts, plumping and squeezing, using his fingers to roll and toy with her swollen nipples. He, too, felt swollen. But he also felt the strength of the plaid wrapping holding him back, some small part of him realizing that it'd been the blue bed covering that he'd torn.

His binding, painful as it was, held firm.

His lady was unraveling.

She needed release.

So he slid his hands beneath her again, cupping her bottom and lifting her hips. "Spread your legs wider, lass." He locked gazes with her, wanting her to see him pleasure her. "As wide as you can and keep them that way. Look on as I lick you."

"Oh, God . . ." She bit her lip, but nodded.

"See me touch my tongue to your most sensitive place." And he did, not taking his eyes off hers as he lowered his head and licked the tiny, pulsing bud he knew would send her sliding into ecstasy.

Again and again he circled his tongue across her special place, every few swirls easing back just a breath to lick down the length of her. He let his tongue glide and probe, then return again to flick at her little lust-spending nub.

And with each honeyed whirl, he envisioned another stranger's brick or stone marring the face of his home.

One brick, one heated tongue swirl, as he imagined the defilers taking the brick from the pile. A new stone, another slow, lascivious lick down his lady's cleft, tasting and relishing.

Beads of sweat began dotting his forehead, so great was the strain, but he couldn't stop if his life—or *un*life—depended on it.

Truth was, he'd devour her till the end of time if he only could.

But before he'd gone through even half his imagined piles of bricks and stones, she arched her back and tossed her head, crying out her release.

"Agggghhhh . . ." She jerked and then fell back against the little chaise bed, gasping. "Hardwick . . ."

Seagrave . . .

A second voice called for him, too. High-pitched, female, and cacklelike, it came from the deep shadows near the undercroft's stairwell.

Beneath the table, Leo snarled.

Hardwick's blood chilled.

Not wanting to, but unable to do otherwise, he looked down at the little dog. Not surprisingly, the dachshund's hackles were raised and his brown gaze was fixed in the exact direction Hardwick had suspected it would be.

Leo knew.

And, saints help him, so did he.

His gut clenching, Hardwick swiveled his head toward the stairs. But they were no longer there. And the woman—the hell hag—who'd called to him wasn't alone.

She stood front and center in a great gaping hole where the softly lit stairwell should have risen to Dunroamin's kitchens. Uncountable look-alike crones crowded behind her, the lot of them jostling and shoving to peer and jeer at him.

"Seagrave . . ." The first hag lifted gnarled hands to rip open her cowled black robes, the withered flesh beneath curdling Hardwick's innards. "We're waiting for you. . . ."

Another stepped forward. Baring her thin, pendulous breasts, she lifted them in offering. "It's been so long since we've had a man," she trilled, her lips curling in a horrid, gap-toothed smile.

Then the vision was gone.

The warning.

Leo's growls subsided, turning slowly back into snores.

And Cilla's hand was inching beneath his kilt, her questing fingers curling round his thighs and gliding provocatively higher.

So high, she almost reached the bottom edge of his tartan binding.

"Nae!" He jerked back, leaping off the little blue bed. "Dinna touch me. No' now!"

He'd ne'er dreamed the creatures would come so close. That they'd manifested so fully in the same room as Cilla—even if she hadn't seen them— frightened him more than anything ever had, in both his earth life and the long centuries of his ghostdom.

"But why?" She looked at him, her eyes luminous in the candle flame.

Her breasts were still flushed with passion, her nipples hard and thrusting.

The scent of her arousal hung heavy in the air, headier than wine.

Confusion and hurt flashed across her face and, seeing it, Hardwick flinched. He dropped back down onto the little bed and drew her into his arms, cradling her as best he could without letting himself truly *feel* her pressed against him.

A next-to-impossible feat, but not near as difficult as what he must do.

"It has naught to do with you, sweetness." He cupped her chin, risking a soft kiss.

He prayed she'd believe him.

"What we did—what I did—was wondrous beyond telling." He sat back, smoothed a hand down over her hair. "Were the world different or were my life, if we can call it such, other than it is, I would spend every waking hour making love to you."

She frowned at him. "But?"

"But"—this time he let the word go—"we should ne'er have gone so far. I should have known better. There are dangers greater than I thought and I canna allow them to seep into Dunroamin more than they already have."

"If you think I'm afraid, you're wrong." She slung a leg over his lap, scrambling onto his kilted thighs.

She wriggled on top of him, all hot, slippery woman. For one heart-stopping moment, he'd have sworn she lowered herself onto him. Slick, burning heat, tight and wet throbbed around him, the glory of it almost blinding. But then he felt her wetness glide across his naked thighs and he knew he'd been mistaken, his desire for her letting him imagine.

Much as he'd let her imagine his hand pleasuring her earlier.

Almost hating himself because it couldn't be otherwise, he gritted his teeth, thinking again of bricks and stone. "It doesn't matter how brave you are, Cilla," he said, the words breaking his heart. "It was wrong of me to do this."

"No-o-o!" She shook her head, looking frantic. "*Because* we've come this far, I refuse to let you go. Not now, not tomorrow, not ever."

"Ach, lass." He caught her arms when she tried to sling them around his neck. "I've told you of the curse. If you believe in me and"—he lifted her off his lap—"after what we just experienced, we both know that you do!"

He stood, needing distance. "That being so, you must also believe in the *spell* I'm under. I would no' mention such matters if I did no' respect them."

"We can fight them together." She pushed to her feet, coming after him. "I can—"

"I am no' a piece of your broken china, sweetness." He shoved a hand through his hair, almost wishing that he was. "You canna put me together again with a bit of your glue and molten silver."

She frowned at that, her eyes brightening.

"And if I'd like to try?"

"There is nothing you can do, Cilla." His heart twisting that it was so, he began moving around the undercroft, flicking his fingers at the conjured bits of his world until they vanished one by one.

He left the candelabrum and the little blue bed till last.

And then they, too, were gone.

His lady's modern spotlights glared brightly down onto her worktable. And little Leo once again slept curled on the naked stone flags of the floor.

Hardwick sighed, feeling all the weight of his centuries bearing down on him.

"I must go, lass."

"Go?" Her eyes rounded.

The way she said the word ripped him.

He took a great breath, knowing one of them needed to remain calm. "There is one chance that might help us. It's a slim one, but I see no choice but to risk it."

"By leaving?"

"Nae." He shook his head slowly. "By pleading the Dark One's mercy."

Blanching, she clapped a hand to her cheek. "You're going *there*? To hell?"

This time Hardwick nodded. "To the Dark One's corner of it, aye."

He'd go there, demand entry, and state his piece.

No matter the consequences.

"So you are not tired of women?"

The Dark One's voice ripped through the whirling

gray mist of the Great Beyond. Though yet within the walls of his massive stone temple, he spoke with authority and power, his every word deep as rumbling thunder and edged with the crackling sizzle of loosed lightning bolts.

Hardwick strode into the swirling gray, breaching the first rule of the Dark One's inner sanctum by arriving at his own behest. As if personally affronted, the ever-present fog shimmied and thickened around him. Undaunted, he pressed on, his only concession being the hand he let hover close to the hilt of his long sword.

He could feel the Dark One's displeasure at his boldness.

But he kept his hand where it was.

He did stop a respectable distance from the ring of thick-growing guardian trees surrounding the temple. Blessedly, there weren't any naked beauties tied to them, bound by their hair and ropes of shimmering, unbreakable mist.

"I wait, Seagrave." The Dark One's voice cracked like a whip. "Are you weary of women or not?"

"I am a Highlander. We ne'er tire of women." Hardwick spoke at last, even though the trees and the mist kept much of the temple from view. " 'Twas the curse and its *requirements* that plagued me."

Silence followed.

He imagined the Dark One raising a thin black eyebrow.

"Have you not found the peace you sought in your quiet Dunroamin, sequestered haven in the fair hills of Scotland's far north?" The disembodied voice rose, booming loud enough to echo to infinity. "I see you do not carry your shield. Is it not enough to be rid of such a burden as you've suffered these centuries?"

"My shield is here if I need it." Hardwick flicked his fingers and the shield appeared in his hand. "As for my burden"—he stood tall, willing to give thanks where it was due—"I am grateful it is done and by with."

"But?"

Hardwick blinked, not trusting his ears.

For a beat, the Dark One sounded so much like Cilla that he almost laughed out loud.

Even more surprising, he thought he caught a soft chuckle coming from inside the temple.

But if he had, the Dark One's next words ruined the image. "Then what of the peace, Seagrave? Did you find your heart's desire at Dunroamin?"

Hardwick's ears sharpened. "My what?"

Again he heard the soft noise that might have passed for laughter.

"Why, your desired solitude and boredom, of course." A rustling of robes and a gust of icy wind indicated the Dark One had moved nearer. "Your days must be most empty and tedious there in the great wilds of Sutherland. . . ."

"They are anything but—as well you know!" Hardwick's temper broke. "I have seen your minions scurrying about, watching me. I did no' come here to dance around the fire with you. I've come for two boons and I'm no' leaving until you grant them!"

"Two boons?"

The Dark One's voice thundered through the inner sanctum, followed almost immediately by a loud noise reminiscent of Mac slapping his knee.

Around the sentrylike trees, the maze of exposed roots swiftly shifted into a troop of crouching, hissing dragons. Pushing up on their scaly, long-clawed feet, they swung black-glittering heads in Hardwick's direction. Their angry red eyes and slashing tails left no doubt that they didn't take kindly to boon seekers.

"Have done!" The Dark One showed himself briefly, his tall, imposing form appearing silhouetted in the open temple doorway as he flung a berobed arm at the root-dragons. "Sleep until you are summoned!"

At once, the beasts vanished, leaving a tangle of harmless-looking roots in their wake.

"So, Seagrave!" The Dark One's voice came again from within his sheltering temple.

The still-lit arch of his doorway loomed empty.

"What boons would you have now. . . . After the generosity I showed you before?"

"I am a different man than when I last stood before you." Hardwick folded his arms, unwilling to bend. "As such, I have different *needs*."

"Needs important enough to bring you here?"

Hardwick swallowed, prepared to give his all. "Needs important enough for me to offer everything you required of me now, before the end of my testing period."

He could almost see the Dark One's brow arching again.

He wasn't prepared for the long stretch of silence.

A quiet peppered with a noise that sounded very much like a man scratching his beard.

Almost as if he were mulling.

Hardwick frowned.

Good things weren't known to come when the Dark One mulled.

"Tell me, Seagrave, do these *boons* have aught to do with the maid?"

"You know that they do."

The Dark One reappeared on the threshold, a silent wind whipping his robes. "There is naught I do not know."

Hardwick felt the back of his neck flame. With surety, the Dark One's hags had extolled on all they'd witnessed in Dunroamin's vaulted undercroft.

"Do not forget I was once a man." The Dark One's words proved the hags had spoken.

The heat on Hardwick's nape whipped round to flush his face, as well.

"We were all once men and still are. . . . In whate'er

form allowed us," he snapped, curling one hand around his sword hilt and tightening the fingers of the other on the handgrip of his shield. "What I want from you is one night to lie with Cilla, to truly take her as befitting two who love. And"—he kept his gaze on the black silhouette in the doorway—"I want your word to leave Dunroamin in peace. I'll no' have your hoary hags manifesting there again."

"Indeed?" The Dark One appeared to study his knuckles. "You forget that you are not in a position to make such demands. But"—he lowered his hand and a gust of chill wind rushed through the trees—"be that as it may, I'll speak with the ladies."

"*Ladies?*" Hardwick nearly choked.

The Dark One sent him a reproving stare.

Hardwick felt it to his bones.

"They were but a bit overeager." The Dark One took their side. "They, too, once knew love and have missed it."

"And my boons?"

"Done."

"What?" Hardwick's eyes flew wide.

Relief washed over him, and triumph, hot and sweet, nearly buckled his knees.

Until the Dark One raised a quelling hand. "Done, that is, after you've mastered one last proving."

"A last proving?" Hardwick's heart plummeted. "Is it no' enough that I'm offering you my soul? Now, well before the year and a day you required?"

He wasn't sure, but he'd swear the Dark One shrugged.

" 'Tis a grave matter, Seagrave." His deep voice filled the inner sanctum. "You ask me to grant you a night of bliss with your lady and"—there came that soft chuckle again—"then deny *my* ladies their pleasure. Yet it can all be arranged if you are willing."

Hardwick crossed his arms. "Name your price."

"Your lady's soul."

"What?!" Hardwick stared into the mist, not at all surprised that it'd suddenly thickened again, blotting the Dark One and his temple from view.

"You heard me, Seagrave." The voice came from within the temple walls again. "One night of pleasure, Dunroamin left in its Brigadoonish innocence, and—the price—Cilla Swanner's soul."

"Nae!" Hardwick roared the denial.

Then he was falling, twirling and tumbling through a deep black tunnel that seemed bottomless. Down and down he spiraled, cold winds tearing at his kilt and whipping his hair.

And as the darkness rushed to claim him, one word slid round his heart, giving him comfort.

Cilla.

Chapter 15

Several evenings later, Cilla perched on the edge of a plaid-covered sofa in a back corner of Dunroamin's heavily tartanized library. Flickering candles glowed everywhere, the only lighting Uncle Mac allowed in the room. Standing candelabras, wall sconces, and table candles; each one offered an eye-catching, golden pool of light for her to focus her attention on.

Something she appreciated, as she was trying hard to look anywhere but at the tall, teddy-bearish man lecturing at a podium near the library's black marble fireplace.

Wee Hughie MacSporran—*the Highland Storyweaver*—was everything she hadn't expected.

She leaned into Hardwick, sitting beside her. "I thought he was a renowned ladies' man."

Hardwick shrugged. "Whate'er he has, I do no' see it. Or"—he cocked a thoughtful brow—"perhaps he is skilled at giving Highland kisses?"

Cilla's face flamed. "Somehow I doubt that."

No one could be better than Hardwick at *those* kisses. He'd made her positively addicted to them. Not that he'd given her any in days, much to her regret. Thinking about them now, the sweet, hot glide of his tongue and all those incredible little swirls across a certain sensitive spot, sent a flood tide of blazing tingles whipping right down there.

She crossed her legs and squirmed in her chair, certain everyone present could see where her mind was.

Embarrassed, she made a point of looking back to the front of the library, studying the evening's speaker. Her tingles cooled at once.

Although at least six-foot-four, Wee Hughie appeared well-pudged rather than muscled. Even his scholarly high forehead and thinning auburn hair couldn't keep his round, apple-red cheeks from giving him a jolly, clownish air. If only he wouldn't puff and strut like a preening peacock.

"Time is of little importance in the Highlands," he was saying, his burr smoothly buttered, almost a touch too rich. The words rolled, as if he'd said them again and again. "Our hills are a magical place of picturesque beauty, languorous and seductive."

He paused, casting a look at the little cluster of Australian women who made up his entourage and had claimed front-row seats.

"Scotland, the whole world knows, is a place where you can believe the distant past happened only yesterday, and the faraway and long ago is not lost at all but waiting to be discovered by those with eyes to see."

He looked about, baiting his audience. "Do *you* have such eyes?"

A round of quiet nods from Dunroamin's residents answered him, while his Aussies, all sporting Official Kilt Inspector jackets, oohed and aahed agreement.

Beside Cilla, Hardwick snorted.

She slid a glance at him. "You really don't like him, do you?"

"I do not like windbags." He folded his arms. "Such fools annoy me more than a pebble in my shoe."

He glanced toward the windows, appearing to eye the approaching rain clouds. But not before Cilla caught a twitch at the corner of his mouth.

"I saw that!" She nudged him, relieved to see the

recent harsh lines in his face soften, if only for a moment. "You think he's funny?"

He ignored her, his face once again hard-set and almost expressionless. Much as it'd been ever since he'd returned from his mysterious visit to the Dark One and announced he'd met with failure.

She frowned and reached for his hand, twining their fingers before he could pull away. "You really should have stayed in bed." She leaned close, dropping her voice. "Uncle Mac said you could have the room as long you needed. He thinks you're ill from walking his moors at night, believes you took a chill. He doesn't know that it's—"

"The Dark One's warning taste of what awaits me when my time runs out?" Now he did look at her, his dark eyes glinting in the candlelight. His voice held a tinge of bitterness. "And I've no' been using Mac's kindly proffered quarters to sleep. I've been out on the moors with my lads every e'en. We're still looking for the Viking ghosties."

"Maybe there aren't any."

"Ach, there's something about, for sure." He waited as Honoria bustled past, offering scones and shortbread. "Whoe'er they are, they've just been lying low. But we're on to them. As for me"—he dutifully took a piece of shortbread when the housekeeper passed by a second time—"the queasiness or whate'er it is the Dark One inflicted on me will pass. It takes more than a spell of dizziness to slow down a Highlander."

His gaze flicked to a tartan-covered wing chair not far from where they sat. "I wouldn't have missed tonight's performance for all the haggis in Scotland."

To her delight, he winked. For one brief moment, his face lightened and he looked just as devilishly roguish as before his disappointing visit to the Dark One. Certainly as toe-curlingly handsome, not that now was the time to let her mind wander in that direction.

So she smoothed her skirt and, for the sake of her aunt and uncle, attempted to feign interest in the evening's entertainment.

His kilt swishing smartly, Wee Hughie paced in front of the fireplace, his chest swelled and his shoulders proud. "I've the blood of a thousand kings in my veins," he boasted, pausing for an effective moment. "My lineage dates back over two thousand years. From the legendary Celtic High King, Conn of the Hundred Battles, dating back to third-century Ireland and the days of the Sidhe, the famed Tuatha De Danann, to"—he cleared his throat meaningfully—"our great warrior king, Robert the Bruce, and many more."

Picking up his book, *Royal Roots*, he raised the tome high, holding it round for all to see. "Now, with the help of my book or my freelance researching services, you, too, can uncover the truth of your own ancestral story. Perhaps you will find the likes of great kings and nobles. As I've done for countless satisfied clients, I can take you step-by-step through the process, showing you—"

A wild skirl of pipes ripped through the library, the Celtic blast shaking the walls and rattling teacups.

"Aaaaagh!" Wee Hughie lurched backward, arms wheeling as the pipe tune—"Paddy's Leather Breeches"—blared up again, even louder than before.

"Blazing heather!" Honoria jumped, dropping the tray of scones and shortbread.

Colonel Darling waved his pipe in the air. "It's that bloody pterodactyl! Mark my words!"

"Pterodactyl schmocktyl! That's my tune!" Uncle Mac laughed, grinning ear to ear.

Next to Cilla, Hardwick pretended not to notice the clamor.

And in the tartan-covered wing chair nearby, a big, burly Highlander with a shock of red hair and a great bushy beard slapped his kilted thigh and nearly convulsed with laughter.

Looking their way, he grinned and winked broadly. Then, as the tune skirled on, getting louder by the minute, he started tapping his foot. Still grinning, he lifted his hands to mimic the motions of a piper's lively fingers.

Cilla stared at him. Her jaw slipped.

Heart pounding, she whipped around to face Hardwick. He had the good grace to look a touch guilty.

"I know him!" She grabbed his arm, squeezing. "He's the ghost . . . er . . . the *man* who appeared so suddenly before me in the corridor when I first arrived!"

As if to confirm it, the bushy-bearded ghost stopped his fancy handwork and foot tapping to jump to his feet and cut her a jaunty bow.

"Bran of Barra, my lady." He touched two fingers to his temple in salute. "The MacNeil of MacNeil, no less."

"Cilla Swanner." Cilla replied without thinking. "Of Yardley, Pennsylvania."

"Another fair American!" He winked, looking most pleased with his observation. He flashed a bold glance at Hardwick. "Can it get any better, my friend? Nae"—he slapped his thigh again—"I say it canna!"

Cilla blinked, not understanding their exchange.

She did look back and forth between the two, vaguely aware of Uncle Mac and Colonel Darling dashing about the library, peeking under chairs and behind curtains as they searched for the source of the music.

At last she remembered something that had been niggling at her. She nudged Hardwick. "Uncle Mac only has the armory rigged with that tune. It's timed to start at the end of his afternoon naps, remember?"

She raised her voice above the screaming pipes.

"What's playing is the pipe CD Aunt Birdie keeps in her car."

"Or not." Hardwick's gaze slid to his friend.

Sitting again, the burly Highlander had his legs stretched out comfortably on the wing chair's ottoman, and his arms crossed over his plaid-draped girth.

"What do you mean 'or not'?" Cilla tugged on Hardwick's arm.

He flicked a speck of lint off his kilt. Then he slid a telling glance at Wee Hughie.

"It could be that Bran wished to enliven the evening." He couldn't quite keep his lips from twitching. "His humor has been known to run away with him."

"And yours?" She poked him. "Don't tell me you didn't have a hand in it."

"Ach, well . . ." He didn't try to deny it. "Bran and the lads have been working hard out on the moors. They deserved a bit o' levity."

Her eyes rounded. "They?"

He winked. "You don't really think that's your aunt's pipe CD playing so robustly, or do you?"

"More ghosts?" Cilla glanced about, seeing none.

"Ach, you willna be seeing them." He slid an arm around her, pulling her close. "Some of the lads are a bit shy about showing themselves, but there's a mean piper or two amongst them. Bran and I gave them the evening off from Mac's peat fields to do a spot of playing here."

"To ruin Wee Hughie's presentation?" Cilla's own lips quirked.

"His Kilt Inspectors will make it up to him." He pulled her closer, dropped a kiss to her temple. "I'll have the lads wind down in a beat. It's about time they head back out on patrol, anyway. The scent of men guising themselves as Vikings has been heavy on the air of late. Could be we're closing in on the dastards."

Twisting round, he jerked a nod at the heavy red

plaid drapes pulled across the library's corner windows.

"Paddy's Leather Breeches" faded at once.

And although Cilla hadn't seen them, she felt a cold air current sweep by as they departed.

"They're gone?" She snuggled against Hardwick, amazed as always by his warmth and rock-hard solidity.

"Aye, they're away now." He was watching Wee Hughie again, studying the man with narrowed eyes. "Bran and I are the only ghosts left standing, so to speak."

Cilla bit back a sigh.

She couldn't put a finger on it, but although his moods had been dark as thunder—so to speak—since returning from the Dark One, he'd never seemed less ghostly.

Heaven help her when the time came to say goodbye.

Not wanting to think about how their farewell would split her, she took a deep breath and steeled herself. Then she sat up straighter and followed Hardwick's gaze, hoping Wee Hughie's lecture would take her mind off of how swiftly the summer was passing.

Unfortunately, in following Hardwick's gaze, her own snagged on a shadow in the corner behind the library's black marble fireplace

Or, more aptly, two shadows.

Over there was Gudrid, the tall and stately blond Viking ghost whose long, thick braid and rich, deep red-purple and blue clothing Cilla instantly recognized. She stood with the fair-haired giant of a helmeted Norse warrior she knew went by the name of Sea-Strider.

Cilla's eyes flew wide. Her pulse kicked into overdrive and the roar of her blood in her ears almost drowned out Wee Hughie's droning voice.

The pair stared right at her, and she knew instinctively that no one else saw them. She flashed a glance at Hardwick and, sure enough, he didn't seem to notice them.

Looking back at the couple, Cilla knew they had a very good reason for being here. She just wished she could figure it out this time.

But it wasn't easy.

Sea-Strider stood unmoving as ever, a good pace behind his blond-braided woman. Though not exactly frowning, his face was etched in hard, solemn lines. And as he scanned the ranks of those sitting about Dunroamin's candlelit library, he held fast to his large painted shield and nine-foot spear.

Cilla's chest tightened, the breath she'd been about to exhale lodging in her throat. She fisted her hands in her lap, willing the ghosts to reveal their message. But Gudrid's lips weren't moving this time, though her eyes still looked sad and beseeching.

Sea-Strider seemed to have turned his attention on Wee Hughie, his unblinking stare steady and intense.

"My repertoire of Scottish tales is rich and vast," the Highland Storyweaver was saying, lifting his voice to fill the library. "Having enjoyed a sampling of them, perhaps you have a special theme you'd like me to expound on? A query about a clan ancestor?"

He looked around again, one brow arching in expectation.

When no one spoke, he lifted a hand to his mouth and coughed behind it. "If there are no questions, I'll end the evening by apologizing for having to postpone my talk. It was kind of the laird"—he gave Uncle Mac a nod—"not to complain that I couldn't hold the tea talk a few weeks ago as originally planned."

"Tell them why." One of his Aussies leaned forward, gushing. "Maybe they don't know . . ."

The expressions on the faces of the two Norse ghosts sharpened.

They drifted nearer.

"I assumed they did know." Wee Hughie's back straightened. "All the newspapers in northern Scotland carried the news."

"Harrumph!" Uncle Mac swelled his chest. "I know everything that goes on in these hills."

Wee Hughie took the bait. "Then you'll have heard that on the evening I was to speak here, I was called to Balnakeil to accept"—he produced a shiny mason's trowel—"this Marshalltown Archaeology trowel in honor of the attention several of my talks brought to the Viking burial at Balnakeil Bay."

Stepping closer to the audience, he held out the trowel for their inspection. He took care to display the pointy, flat-bladed tool so that everyone could see HIGHLAND STORYWEAVER etched on the steel.

Hardwick sat forward, his gaze on the trowel.

He shot a glance at his friend, Bran. But the jovial Highlander didn't notice. His attention, too, appeared riveted on Wee Hughie.

Oblivious to their scrutiny, Wee Hughie droned on. "The tourist numbers at Balnakeil have increased more than threefold since I've educated the public to the wealth of Viking burials and ruins along our northern coasts."

He paused, his voice taking on a boastful tone. "Indeed, I'll soon be journeying to Shetland to inspect a Viking-related find there. The site is on St. Ninian's Isle. It's a lovely place, perched on a grassy cliff at the far end of a white-sanded tombolo, but it's also a site overlooked by many."

"Eh? And you're for changing all that?" Uncle Mac glowered at him from beneath down-drawn brows. "There's some that appreciate left-alone places, just!"

Wee Hughie reddened.

"The people of Shetland have asked me to help them attract visitors." He looked round, as if expecting applause. "The site was first discovered in the 1950s. It will be a privilege to alert the public to—"

"What's a *Viking-related* find?" The question leapt off Cilla's tongue before she realized she'd formed it.

Across the room, the blond-braided woman and her Sea-Strider nodded significantly.

Then they joined hands, smiling. Their expressions lighter, they held Cilla's gaze, looking as if a great burden had been lifted from their shoulders.

In a wink, they vanished.

Chills swept down Cilla's spine. She blinked and moistened her lips, certain now that the Viking pair were so-called messenger ghosts. The kind that appear again and again until someone understands what's burdening them and their unfinished earthly business is resolved.

At the front of the library, Wee Hughie drew a breath for his answer. "A Viking-related find," he explained, setting down his trowel, "is an archaeological site that isn't necessarily of Viking origin but that has been influenced by them in some way."

"Such as?" Cilla sat forward, compelled to probe. In her mind she could still see the Norse pair watching her, their smiles and nods encouraging her. "I'd like an example."

Wee Hughie rolled his shoulders, eager to oblige. "The Balnakeil burial, a youth's grave, is a clear-cut Viking archaeological site. It dates back to the ninth or tenth century, when the Norse frequently raided our coasts. The grave goods found with the lad were typical Viking wares."

He took a glass of water off the table, draining it. "The St. Ninian's site in Shetland is different," he continued, wiping his mouth with the back of his hand. "The ruins there are of an early Celtic church and, as such, are worthy of any visitor's time. What makes St. Ninian's unique is the spectacular hoard of Pictish treasure that was discovered beneath a stone slab in the chapel grounds."

"Buried treasure?" Cilla's eyes widened. She could almost see Gudrid and Sea-Strider beaming.

Beside her, Hardwick swore.

He shot a terse look at Bran, and made a jerky gesture with his clenched fist.

"Aye, you could say buried treasure." Wee Hughie basked in the attention. "St. Ninian's gave up one of the most fabulous stashes of Celtic silver ever to be found in the British Isles. A boy found the hoard, uncovering a wooden box brimming with silver bowls and brooches, sword hilts and trappings, pins, spoons, and innumerable objects yet to be identified, all more dear than a king's ransom."

"And the Vikings?" Cilla didn't turn her head, but knew without looking that Hardwick was scowling. "What did they have to do with it?"

"Everything." Wee Hughie preened. "Without them, the treasure would never have lain hidden for hundreds of years."

Cilla darted a glance to where the Viking pair had stood, her heart thumping.

She looked back at Wee Hughie. "How so?"

"It's like this. . . ." He raised a learned finger. "The hoard is believed to have been buried in the mid–ninth century, a time when Viking raids were particularly ferocious. Many scholars support the theory that when Viking sails were spotted on the horizon, the treasure was buried to avoid detection."

Cilla nodded, sure she was on to something.

Hardwick was still grumbling. Angry Gaelic words that sounded like curses.

"There are"—Wee Hughie accepted a fresh glass of water from Honoria—"other possibilities, including that the Vikings themselves might have buried the hoard, hoping to keep looted goods safe from other raiders."

Cilla let out a breath. "So that's why you called it a Viking-related site."

"Exactly." Wee Hughie nodded. "Such sites abound in Scotland. The possibility of happening across such a treasure, hidden by peat or sand dunes for centuries, is what makes archaeology so exciting."

It was then that Cilla noticed Hardwick and Bran were gone.

Shooting to her feet, she glanced round, Vikings and Wee Hughie forgotten. Hardwick had warned that the Dark One might claim him any moment. If he'd been zapped away now, while she'd been talking about buried treasure to a man who called himself the Highland Storyweaver, she'd never forgive herself.

"He went that way, dear." Flora Duthie indicated the open library door.

Cilla started at the tiny woman's words, ashamed she'd almost plowed right into her.

Unfazed, Flora caned her way nearer, a plate holding two large jam-and-cream-filled scones clutched in her free hand. "I saw him go past when I fetched my tea scones."

"Thank you." Cilla turned toward the door.

Flora thrust out her cane, blocking her path. "Have a care, child," she tsked, shaking her head. "He looked mighty angry, he did."

"I can handle him." Cilla smiled reassurance as the old woman lowered her cane. "It's not me he's mad at."

Ignoring her aunt and uncle's flashed glances, she pushed her way through the milling Kilt Inspectors, who were now gathering around their hero's book table, fawning and squealing.

They could have their red-cheeked raconteur.

She had to find Hardwick.

She paused outside the library door, peering both ways down the long and dim corridor. Retreating footsteps, rapid and masculine, gave a clue from the shadows to her left. But by the time she raced down the passageway, Hardwick was nowhere to be seen.

Pulse racing, she let herself out the castle's massive

front door and hurried down the steps to the graveled drive and gardens. Her gaze darting everywhere, she sprinted across the wet lawn, making for the moorland and the dark edge of Uncle Mac's peat fields.

She'd covered only a few yards before Hardwick stepped out from behind a thicket of dripping rhododendrons to grab her arm, stopping her in motion.

"Whoa, lassie." He pulled her roughly against his chest, his strong arms snapping around her like an iron vise. His big hands clamped onto her hips, his fingers gripping firmly into her buttocks. "You're no' going anywhere."

Cilla sucked in a breath, the feel of her breasts crushed against his hard-muscled chest and, heaven help her, the press of his not-to-be-ignored *bulge* against her stomach almost making her dizzy.

"I thought the Dark One had taken you." She clung to him, slinging her arms around his neck and thrusting her fingers into his hair, holding tight. "The Viking pair, the ghosts I saw, were there, in the library, and when you disappeared I thought maybe they'd come to warn me that your time here was over."

His brows shot upward. "The Viking pair? Why didn't you tell me?"

"I just did." She choked on the words, twisting her fingers deeper into his hair. "I knew they were there for a reason, and when I saw you couldn't see them I feared it had something to do with you. Now, after hearing Wee Hughie—"

"Enough." His mouth swooped down on hers, hard and silencing. He tightened his grip on her buttocks and swept one hand up her back and around to her front, cupping her breast and squeezing hard, almost as if he feared she'd vanish if he didn't hold her so fiercely.

"I heard what MacSporran said and I'll no' have you with me tonight." He slanted his mouth over hers, parting her lips with his tongue and thrusting deep.

Not even giving her a chance to catch her breath, he kissed her mercilessly. Nipping and licking, his tongue sliding furiously over and around hers, plunging and withdrawing again and again until she went limp in his arms and he broke the kiss.

He set her from him at once and stepped back, his breath coming in hard, fast pants. "I'm away to the moors to join Bran and the lads." He looked down at her, his eyes still dark with passion, almost blazing. "Now go back to the castle. I'll no' have you coming with me."

"Why not?" She lifted her chin. After such a kiss, and the odd feeling that he meant it as their last, she wasn't about to return to Dunroamin.

"Dinna trouble your head with why." He frowned at her. "You'll go because I said so."

"Oh yeah?" Cilla bristled. "That might have worked in the fourteenth century, but it won't with me." She folded her arms, stubborn. "Women do what they want these days."

"And what do you want?" His eyes blazed hotter and his burr went all buttery deep, its smoothness downright dangerous.

Cilla blinked. "I . . ." Her voice hitched, the damn tingles he always gave her making it impossible to think.

"Come, sweet." His eyes went hot and heavy-lidded, his gaze tracking slowly downward. "Perhaps if you tell me, I'll oblige you?"

"I . . ." Cilla bit her lip, sure the ground was tilting beneath her.

Smiling wickedly, he reached between them to inch up her skirt, sliding his hand up her thigh to cup and press the panty-covered heat between her thighs.

"Tell me, lass." He leaned close, licking, then nibbling her ear. "Your every desire fulfilled . . ."

"Stop trying to change the subject." Amazed she could even speak, Cilla jerked free. "I saw the way your expression changed when Wee Hughie started talking about Vikings, and . . . and your friend, Bran, was upset, too!"

His smile fading, he touched one finger to her clit and circled. Once, twice, and again before he pulled back his hand and stepped away from her.

"I would throw off my plaid and toss you down onto it and nibble on that tasty little sweet spot until there is no tomorrow," he vowed, his breath still harsh and his voice passion deepened. "But now isn't the time or place, and you need to leave."

"Hah!" Cilla tossed back her hair, hiding how limp-limbed he'd made her behind a flash of bravura. "I'm not going anywhere until I know what's going on."

" 'Tis a man's work." He crossed his arms. "I'll no' have you looking on if things get a bit wild."

"Wild doesn't scare me."

"This kind of wild should." He remained firm.

"Then at least tell me why you and Bran disappeared from the library." She could do firm, too. "I'm not budging until I get the truth."

He frowned and shoved a hand through his hair. "The truth, lass, is that thanks to Bran and the lads' keen eyesight and, this e'en, Wee Hughie's blethering, Bran and I have guessed what Mac's Viking ghosties are after."

Cilla stared at him.

Her heart started pounding, fast and furious.

In her mind, she again saw Gudrid and Sea-Strider standing in a corner, nodding and smiling when Wee Hughie started talking about Norse archaeological sites.

"Oh, my God!" She clapped a hand to her cheek. "There's Celtic treasure buried in Uncle Mac's peat fields!"

Hardwick nodded. "Aye, that would seem to be the way of it."

He glanced out over the moors, dark beneath drifting mist and low-hovering rain clouds.

"Some while ago Bran and the lads found a creel of tools hidden beneath an overhang in one of the peat bogs. They couldn't locate the basket a second time, or perhaps the ghosties moved it. But"—the corner of his mouth curved up triumphantly—"Bran used his ghostly power to conjure one of the tools to show me what they'd found."

"It was one of Wee Hughie's Marshalltown Archaeology trowels?" Cilla guessed.

"No' his own, mind." Hardwick's smile broadened. "But a tool just like his, aye. The word *Marshalltown* was inscribed on it, for sure."

Cilla blinked. "So you think the ghosties are using their Viking disguises and the trowels to search for buried treasure in Uncle Mac's peat fields?"

"I do."

"So that's why you don't want me with you on the moors." She understood now. "You're worried that if you catch them, they'll go wild?"

"Saints, but you're an innocent." His lips quirked. "Nae, that is no' my concern."

"Then what is?"

He leaned close, looking directly in her eye. "That you might swoon if you were present and looking on when Bran, the lads, and I went wild."

"How wild?"

"Think naked, screaming men and swinging steel."

"Oh." Cilla flushed.

"Indeed." He flashed his most wicked smile. "If you've ne'er seen a Highland charge, it isn't a sight for the faint of heart. Especially when we're after the kind of thieving scoundrels who're too lily-livered to show their own faces and creep about disguised as Viking ghosties."

Cilla's heart flipped. She'd read about the ferocity of Highland charges in history books. How bold and daring they were, the men indeed often throwing off their plaids as they raced to fight their foes.

She lifted her chin, her pulse racing. "I think I might like to see naked, sword-swinging Highlanders. . . ." She broke off, realizing she was talking to thin air.

He'd disappeared, leaving only his sexy sandalwood scent behind.

That, and the raging tingles causing her to press her thighs together.

Who would've believed the thought of naked, wild-eyed Highlanders with swords could be such a turn-on?

But, she had to admit, that wasn't quite true.

It was the thought of *Hardwick* naked that really excited her. The idea of his *sword* swinging free beneath his kilt that had her almost climaxing here, right in the middle of Dunroamin's broad front lawn!

So close, one touch of a finger would have her shattering.

She frowned.

Then she started tapping her chin, trying to decide what to do.

She needed exactly thirty seconds to make a decision.

And when she started walking, it wasn't in the direction of Dunroamin's front door.

If Hardwick got mad, so be it.

It'd be his fault for not letting them have real sex when they'd had the chance. She was madly in love with him, after all. So, of course, she had to have him.

By fair means or foul.

Chapter 16

"You're certain it was this overhang?"

Hardwick looked askance at the cutaway ridge of blackest peat. No more than a four-foot-tall gash in the rolling moorland, if it'd once held a creel of Marshalltown Archaeology trowels, there wasn't a sign of such a basket now. Looking equally innocent, a thick fringe of grass hung down over the cutaway area's top edge.

He shot a glance at Bran, not missing the stubborn set of his friend's jaw.

"There are hundreds of such overhangs on these moors. Natural ones and those cut by Mac's lads." He folded his arms. "I say we keep searching. Now that we know what we're after, there isn't time—"

"And I say it was this overhang!" Bran hooked his thumbs in his sword belt. "Could be I'm for seeing something you don't! Something I noticed last time but"—he rocked back on his heels, grinning—"slipped my mind till now."

Hardwick glowered at him. But he did turn back to the peat overhang to give it a better stare.

His jaw dropped at once. "By the Rood! There isn't any bog cotton."

"Just!" Bran thrust out an arm to indicate the delicate, white-topped heads of bog cotton dotting the moors as far as the eye could see. Tiny and shaped like candle flames, they dipped and bobbed in the wind, letting the peat fields look alive in a sea of dancing white.

Except above the overhang where they stood.

Hardwick's brows drew together. The longer he stared at the thick, bog cotton–less grass covering the peat cut-away, the odder the overhang looked.

He threw another glance at Bran, seeing at once that his friend thought so, too.

As did Bran's bonny fighting lads. Brawny, shaggy-maned Islesmen from Barra and few other Hebridean isles, they exchanged suspicious glances and drew closer, forming a tight ring around the black-glistening gash in the earth.

Swinging back toward the peat cut, Hardwick whipped out his sword and used its tip to probe the grassy lip of the overhang. The fringe of grass shifted at once, a large chunk of loose earth and grasses tumbling onto his feet.

"Hah!" Bran yanked out his own blade, eyes flashing. "I knew there was something funny about that cut-away."

Grinning broadly, he leapt onto the overhang, sinking to his knees in the soft, black earth. With gusto, he slid his blade along the rim of the overhang, easily lifting a good-sized clump of peaty grass.

"Have a care!" Hardwick warned as Bran's lads joined in, using dirk points to poke into the odd little mound. "If there's an ancient church or a kist of treasure buried here, it's Mac's and I'll no' see us doing damage to it."

"Ach! We're but flexing our muscles until the *ghosties* show their faces!" Bran laughed. " 'Tis those cravens what'll take a beating from our broadswords and axes! No' the good Mac's—"

Thump . . . screech . . . !

Bran froze as his sword blade shrilled along some-thing long and hard, its contours just visible beneath the now-thin layer of peat.

"A wall!" He jumped back, waving his sword in triumph. " 'Tis just like up Shetland way—an old Celtic church filled with treasure!"

" 'Tis a bag of sticks." Hardwick pulled the coarse linen sack out of the ground. "Nae, tools," he cor-rected, upturning the bag so that a rain of dirt-crusted shovels and spades tumbled out. "No' Marshalltown Archaeology trowels, but I'll wager the dastards have been using these to dig up Mac's peat."

"So say we all." One of the Barra men agreed, his words greeted with enthusiasm by his fellow Islesmen. "But where's the treasure?"

Hardwick set his hands on his hips and scanned the hills. Light as a northern night sky was in summer, wisps of earlier rain clouds and slow-drifting mist kept the contour of the moors soft and indistinct, the hills slashed with patches of deep, impenetrable shadow.

He stroked his chin, considering.

"Whate'er it is, it has to be hereabouts." Bran rammed his blade into the earth, leaning heavily on the sword's flashy jewel-topped hilt. "The fiends are like to be after keeping their tools close to hand!"

"Exactly." Hardwick couldn't agree more. "We just have to winkle it out."

He turned halfaway, then looked back, meeting the eager gazes of Bran's rough-looking Hebrideans.

"Somewhere out here there's some sort of ruin." He made a sweeping gesture with his arm. "An an-cient church, a longhouse, a Viking grave, whate'er. I say we split up and search all the land within a hun-dred paces, eyes peeled for any grass-grown lump, bump, or hollow that looks out of place."

He left out that he'd also be keeping an eye out for a tall and shapely, big-breasted beauty who could bewitch a man with one toss of her tawny-gold hair.

Just thinking of her brought hot stirrings beneath his kilt. Even now, he'd swear he still carried the musky taste of her on his tongue, could imagine the heady scent of her hot, wet arousal.

He frowned. Now wasn't the time for lust. Nor the damnable dizziness that swept him each time such tempting images rose to torment him. A nuisance visited on him by the Dark One, and a bleeding annoyance.

"Are we still for charging if the Viking *ghosties* put in an appearance?" The Barra man loomed before him, battle-ax in hand.

Hardwick blinked, focusing. The waves of lust-dizziness, when they came, seemed to be taking longer to fade.

He knuckled his eyes. "The stalwart who first spots our foes shall whistle like a curlew." He glanced round. "I trust all can?"

Bran snorted.

His Hebrideans looked offended.

Hardwick swept up his sword, knowing a show of bravura would fire their blood.

"Barra!" They shouted Bran's war cry, rattling swords or jabbing the air with long-bladed dirks.

"Then away with you!" Hardwick ran his own blade into its scabbard. "First curlew wheeple and we rally *to charge!*"

But hours later, after much tramping in circles and many more curses when an examined hump in the landscape proved to be just that—*a hump*—the men were still stamping about, their eyes yet keen but their spirits waning.

Ignoring his own worsening mood, Hardwick went down on one knee to inspect a suspicious-looking gap in a hillock. He found himself peering into a foxhole.

The wee creature hissed at him, teeth bared and hackles rising.

Hardwick pushed to his feet, swallowing his disappointment.

Who would've thought the night would unearth one small fox and not a trace of buried Celtic silver? No ravening Viking *ghosties*, either. Though he'd bet his kilt they were near. He could taste their thievery on the air as sure as he carried Cilla's sweet, hot scent on his tongue.

Pushing on, he looked out across the moors and past the dark bulk of Dunroamin to the rocky headlands of the coast and the wide sweep of the Kyle. The water glittered, glass smooth and still, the same deep blue of her eyes.

He stopped and sucked in a breath, certain something was tracking along in the mist beside him. A presence determined to parallel his long strides.

Affecting an air of casualness, he lifted a hand, meaning to flick his fingers and conjure a brimming cup of ale. This he'd toss back with pretended appreciation. Then he'd sleeve his lips and move on, seemingly unconcerned but with a ready hand resting on his sword hilt.

Unfortunately, the lingering effects of his lust-dizziness made the effort of conjure-flicking too great. He lowered his hand without trying.

He did think hard as to who might be following him.

The long-strided gait was too stealthy and masculine for it to be Cilla. And, praise the saints, too sure-footed for one of the Dark One's tottering gaggle of gap-toothed, flat-breasted hell hags.

He shuddered.

Then he threw his plaid back over his shoulder and struck off toward the spot where he judged his pursuant to be hiding. He'd gone but a few paces when the drifting mist parted and a tall, fair-haired Viking stepped from the gap to stare fixedly at him. No Viking *ghostie*, but a true ghost, the man wore mail and carried a huge, colorfully decorated shield and a nine-foot spear.

Hardwick stopped cold. Ghost he may be, but with the exception of Bran and his other ghostly friends, he'd ne'er grown wholly accustomed to running across others who dwelt in their mysterious, ethereal realm. Perhaps he'd need another seven hundred years, but for now, such encounters always startled him.

The Viking didn't share his reticence.

Striding closer, he raised his tall spear to point at a hillock to Hardwick's right. Half-hidden behind a copse of thick-growing birch and whin, it was an area Hardwick hadn't yet explored.

In that moment a sharp bird call pierced the air. Hardwick whipped around to see Bran and his lads racing toward him. He flashed a glance to where the Viking had stood, but the man was gone.

The bird call came again.

Not the long, sweet trilling of a curlew, but the harsh, agitated squawks of a bonxie.

Auk, auk.

"Gregor!" Hardwick grinned and grabbed Bran's arm when his friend drew to a panting halt in front of him. "He's found something—look!"

Thrusting his sword tip toward the sky, Hardwick indicated the fierce-looking bird. Gregor sailed past high above them, his great wings spread wide.

"Come!" Hardwick started running. "Gregor's the second soul who's called a warning. Our *ghosties* are beyond yon hill!"

"Barra!" Bran pounded after him, waving his sword.

Auk, auk!

Gregor's cries grew louder as the men burst into the birchwood. Some threw off their plaids as they stormed past trees and crashed through underbrush. All drew weapons and shouted their slogans. They glanced upward frequently, using the circling, swooping bird as their guide until other men's voices—shouts and curses—blended with their own.

Bloodlust high and hearts pounding, they ran on, swinging steel and eager for the fight. But the sight that greeted them when they charged out of the wood set them to laughing.

"By all the wonders!" Bran rammed his blade into the earth, gaping.

Hardwick stared, too, but held fast to his sword.

The Islesmen, now naked to a man, jigged, hooted, and jeered.

Their foes, guised indeed like store-bought Vikings, stood in the middle of an excavated longhouse, overflowing boxes and bulging sacks of silver artifacts littering the up-churned, peaty ground.

They huddled in a tight circle, clutching one arm over their heads and using the other to thrash the air above them.

The reason was plain to see.

"The bird is well trained, my friends." Hardwick strode forward, grinning broadly when Gregor made a particularly splendid pass. "One word and he'll be after more than just your heads."

"Call him off!" A quavering English voice rose from the huddle. "He's already drawn blood!"

"If you think a bird's talons are sharp"—Hardwick looked round at Bran's Islesmen—"wait till you taste the bite of our steel."

"Swords?" The man twisted to face Hardwick, taking care not to leave his head uncovered. "You can't be serious. We're unarmed. You can see our weapons there, in the pile by the trees. They're made of wood or plastic. Toys—no more! We aren't here for sword fights."

Hardwick folded his arms. "Why you're here is obvious. As for us"—the naked Islesmen drew near, forming a stern-faced circle around the ruined longhouse—"my friends and I relish a good and bloody round o' swording. Truth is, it's been too many years since we've enjoyed one!"

Beside him, Bran lifted his blade and ran his thumb lightly along the edge. When a bead of red appeared, he whooped and leapt forward, whipping the steel just beneath the nose of the nearest "Viking."

When he swaggered away, laughing, Gregor swooped down to perch on his shoulder.

"Be glad it was me what done that," he called to the trembling man. "Had it been one o' my lads here, your nose would now be kissing your toes!"

"What kind of crazy heathens are you?" Another man grew bolder now that Gregor no longer grazed their heads. Older than the others and with tatty, well-worn tweeds showing beneath his furred Viking vest, he aimed a superior stare at Hardwick. "I could have you arrested for threatening us."

Bran gave a contemptuous snort.

Hardwick sheathed his blade and went to stand toe-to-toe with the man, clearly the group's leader. "I've no time to discuss your first comment. Though"—he let his gaze sweep the little clutch of costumed Englishmen—"there's plenty hereabouts who'd wonder more at a Sassunach guised as a Norseman than a Highlander carrying a sword!"

The man glared at him, his mouth pursed tight.

"As for arrests, 'tis you who ought be fearful of the like." Hardwick bent to pick up a piece of black peat-stained wood that was clearly part of an ironbound oak chest. Holding it reverently, he turned back to the Viking "ghostie." "There are many witnesses to your nightly charades. Now that we also know the reason behind them, and where you burgled your guises, ach, well . . ."

"No' to mention that you're doing your foul deeds on Mac MacGhee's lands." Bran plucked his dirk from beneath his belt and used its tip to pick at his fingernails. "There's some would hang a body for what you've done."

That silenced the man.

But the first one seemed to have recovered his courage. "Oh, I say! There's no law in Scotland against trekking across free moorland, no matter who owns it. We—"

"There's always been laws against thieving." Hardwick spoke over him. "Especially in the Highlands."

"We weren't stealing." The man jerked his head, glancing at the other "ghosties" for confirmation.

When no one said anything, he blustered on, clearly improvising. "We . . . we're Viking scholars. Reenactors, if you will. We chose these moors for our training because they're so isolated and—"

"Filled with treasure?" Bran turned to one of the overflowing boxes of artifacts, scooping up a handful of silver amulets and necklaces made of brightly colored beads.

"In my . . . er . . . *travels*, I've heard of such men as you." He returned the Norse jewelry to the box. " 'Tis history thieves you are! Men who rape sites such as this and sell the plunder to the highest taker."

The tweedy man cleared his throat. "Now, see here. We've been researching this treasure for years." He whipped out a map board from beneath his Viking vest and waved it before him. "No one knew of it until we stumbled across a fleeting mention in the Icelandic Sagas. Only through painstaking study and searching did we find its location."

He continued in an authoritative voice. "We plan to turn over every last artifact to the proper archaeological authorities."

"As you surely mean to return Erlend Eggertson's red devil mask and the other Up-Helly-Aa costumes to the Galley Shed in Lerwick?"

Hardwick wasn't surprised when the man flinched

at his words. Avoiding Hardwick's gaze, he looked down at his map board, his expression mulish.

He said nothing.

Not that he had to. Guilt stood all over him.

Hardwick grasped the man's tweed-and-leather-patched elbows, gripping tight. "Be glad this is no' an earlier time, my friend. You'd have already breathed your last if it were."

The man spluttered, his color draining.

Hardwick released him, needing every shred of his strength to marshal his temper.

For two pins, he would have flicked his fingers and conjured a few lanterns and a cook fire, transforming the tumbled stones and churned earth of the ruined longhouse into the camp of a hard-riding party of wild and bloodthirsty clansmen. He'd make the air heavy with the tang of woodsmoke, onions, and rabbit stew, toss in the moist fug of spilled ale and damp evening mist. Above all, he'd summon a hanging tree with a rope slung round its stoutest branch.

Instead, he forced himself to remember where and *when* he was. He flashed a warning look at Bran's Islesmen, who looked more than eager to forget.

Even so, he drew his dirk. But unlike Bran, who was again using his to whittle his fingernails, he held the finely honed knife with just enough menace to jelly the knees of a man who didn't know him well enough to realize that if he'd meant true harm, he'd no longer be living.

"I'd hear the tale of this treasure," he said, his voice deceptively soft.

Tweedy glanced up, wetting his lips. "It's a great treasure. A Viking-age hoard to rival any found in Great Britain to date."

Hardwick frowned at the man. He didn't need to be told that. Just the goods visible at the top of the many brimming boxes and the overflow spilling out of the bulging sacks bespoke the find's worth.

Not to mention the treasure of the longhouse itself, which looked remarkably preserved, considering.

"Well?" He eyed the Englishman.

"Er . . . h'rr'mm . . . I told you. There was a brief notation in the Icelandic Sagas." The man clutched his map board to his chest. "Something about a Viking noblewoman named Gudrid who lived near Tongue and had fallen in love with a man her father considered beneath her."

He paused, shot a nervous glance at his companions.

"Go on." Hardwick's tone was stern.

"There isn't much else!" The man's face reddened. "Only that she determined to run away with her lover despite her father's disapproval. The sagas hinted that the young man, called Sea-Strider, was a great Viking raider and would bring plundered wealth to Tongue, which he and Gudrid hid at the longhouse of a trusted friend. It's believed they planned to use the treasure to finance a journey to Iceland to settle there, far from Gudrid's father's wrath."

"But they never made it." Hardwick frowned. It was an easy guess, the treasure still being here.

Tweedy shrugged. "The sagas fell silent on their fate. We supposed something happened and Sea-Strider was lost at sea. We did"—the man's eyes brightened for a moment—"find mention of a Gudrid at Castle Varrich in the time period in question. That clue is what led us here."

"I see." Hardwick slid a look at Bran.

But his mind was on the tall blond Viking who'd appeared to him. His heart clenched at the man's fate. He looked around, half expecting to see Cilla peeking at him from behind a whin bush, but she was nowhere to seen. His chest tightened at her absence. He felt a sudden need for her, thinking of the star-crossed Vikings.

Remembering the Vikings, he flashed another look at the motley little group.

"Why did you burgle the Galley Shed?"

Tweedy flushed. "That was . . . unfortunate, but—"

"Eh?" Bran edged closer, hand on his sword hilt.

"We didn't have the funds to purchase such costuming on our own." The man's chin lifted and his eyes glinted defiantly. "We only wanted to scare off any possible long noses until we recovered the treasure. We would have returned the costumes before Up-Helly-Aa."

"Indeed?" Hardwick exchanged a glance with Bran. "I'm thinking you ought to return them sooner."

"Aye." Bran nodded vigorously. "I'd say right now."

"Now?" The man's voice went squeaky.

The first man pushed forward, eyes bulging. "What do you mean now?"

Bran's Islesmen hooted and slapped naked thighs.

The "ghosties" blanched.

"You can't expect us to strip?" Tweedy's eyes rounded. "We're Englishmen, not Highland heathens!"

"Ach, you shouldn't have said that." Hardwick shook his head. "Now you've left us no choice. It's an honor thing, see you."

Stepping back, he spread his legs and crossed his arms. He made sure a wicked heathenlike glint lit his eye. "Truth is, we can't carry all this treasure back to Dunroamin. We'll have to leave it, and you, until I make it back to the castle and tell Mac we've found his ghosties. He and the local authorities can decide what to do with you."

"He won't be able to keep the treasure!" The first "ghostie" pushed forward. "Not all of it. We can make a deal with you, cut you in—"

"I *am* in." Hardwick glared him, not about to tell him that his treasure was Cilla. "My reward is catching you. And knowing that whate'er Mac gets out of it, he'll have enough to patch his roof and then some."

"We never meant the MacGhees any harm."
Tweedy tried to wheedle.

Hardwick ignored him. "My friends here"—he
jerked his head at Bran's Islesmen—"will keep you
company as you wait for Mac."

"You can't leave us here . . . naked!" Another English voice rose at the back of the ghostly cluster.
"We'll freeze."

Hardwick shrugged. "You should have thought of
that before you garbed yourselves in stolen clothes."

"If you're leaving these . . . er . . . men behind to
guard us, why do we have to strip?" Tweedy tried
again.

"Because"—Hardwick grinned—"it just might be
that when they see Mac and the local constabulary
heading this way, well . . . it could be they'll disappear."

"Run off?" Tweedy slid a look at the naked
Highlanders.

"Nae, disappear," Hardwick repeated, drawing
much mirth from the Islesmen.

"And wouldn't that be something?" Bran laughed.

Then he clapped a hand on Hardwick's shoulder,
pushing him away from the Viking "ghosties" and
toward the little wood of birch and whins.

"See you to it, then," he urged Hardwick. "Go fetch
Mac and see to your lady."

A short while later, Hardwick walked swiftly up to
Dunroamin's massive double oak doors, amazed by
two things. One, although he hadn't realized, it was
well into morning. The day's sun was already burning
the mist off Dunroamin's lawn, the bright, slanting
light almost hurting his eyes.

And that was his second revelation.

He was almost certain Mac was right.

That he'd indeed caught a fever or chill or some

such bane while out patrolling the peat fields each night.

Either that, or, as was likely the way of it, the damnable dizzy spells he'd had since visiting the Dark One were growing worse. In all his centuries, nary an illness had plagued him. Indeed, he'd thought one of the advantages of ghostdom was always feeling fit.

Yet his head ached and throbbed with greater frequency. The odd ringing in his ears had bettered, but wasn't completely gone. He also felt like sleep. A desire he hadn't really experienced since Seagrave days, when his life had been just that.

A life. A *human* life.

He reached for the door latch and paused, another thought stopping him in his tracks. He'd walked the entire way back from the Viking longhouse.

An unthinkable botheration for a ghost, unless the ghost chanced to be a ghost in love and bearing tidings that would surely please his lady.

He'd simply forgotten to act ghostly.

His news was too important for his mind to have noted the long trudge across the moors.

The instant he let himself into the castle, he did note Mac's booming voice coming from the conservatory. Heading in that direction, he followed the delicious aroma of fried bacon, eggs, and sausages, eager to impart his news.

His heart thumped with the glory of a victor.

He quickened his pace.

Already, he could see the admiration in Cilla's eyes.

But when he reached the little glass-walled conservatory and burst into its sunny, greenery-filled space, hers were the only eyes not to flash in his direction.

Everyone else eyed him hopefully.

Even wee Leo, who opened one eye to peer at him from where he sprawled in a patch of sunlight falling in through the tall windows.

Flora Duthie set down her teacup and angled her head, tipping her ear his way. Honoria paused in arranging packets of muesli on the sideboard near the door. Dusting her hands on her white starched apron, she turned his way. Like Flora, she tilted her head, her gaze expectant.

Others appeared equally keen.

It wasn't every day he strode in on their breakfast, after all.

Mac broke off a lively discourse with the colonel to jump to his feet. "I see the gleam in your eye!" He came forward, almost knocking over the potted coffee bean tree in his haste.

"Heigh-ho!" He grinned, grabbing Hardwick's arms. "Say me you caught my ghosties!"

"Aye—indeed!" Hardwick smiled back, distracted. Cilla always breakfasted with the residents. He knew her days better than his own.

Mac shook his arms. "Did you toast their feet on a wee bit o' dry sticks and bracken?"

"Nae." Hardwick brushed at his sleeve when Mac released him. "But swords and dirks were drawn."

"Were they in Viking costumes?" Violet Manyweathers slid a told-you-so look at the colonel. "Caught red-handed?"

"That and more, my lady. Not only—"

Hardwick caught a shadow shift outside and thought it might be Cilla walking on the terrace. But it was only the sun nipping behind a cloud.

He turned back to Violet. "Not only were the miscreants garbed in stolen Up-Helly-Aa trappings, they were looting a longhouse they've excavated in a hidden corner of Mac's peat fields."

Mac's eyes rounded. "Faugh! *A longhouse?*" He flashed a glance at his wife. "Why, my moors have enough strewn rubble from ruined longhouses to re-pave half o' Inverness! The stones are from the houses of the Clearances. 'Tis the same all o'er Sutherland—"

Hardwick cleared his throat. "This isn't a Clearance-era longhouse. It's a Viking longhouse, fairly well preserved, and"—he couldn't keep his lips from twitching—"filled with what just might be the richest hoard of Celtic- and Viking-age treasure to e'er be found in Britain."

Mac's jaw dropped. *"Treasure?"*

Birdie launched herself at him, nearly knocking him down in her excitement. "Mac! We're saved! Dunroamin is secure!"

Colonel Darling yanked a hankie from his pocket and loudly blew his nose. "I say! Who would have thought it?"

Violet began to cry.

Hardwick swallowed, his throat too tight for words. He stepped back, struggling against the ridiculous urge to throw his arms around every soul in the room and hug them tight, glorying in their triumph.

A victory that would be perfect if only Cilla shared it.

He glanced at the windows again, hoping he'd been mistaken about the sun shadow. But he hadn't erred. The terrace was empty.

"Looks like I won't have to cane my way past drip buckets much longer!" Flora Duthie's twittering voice rose from a corner table.

Hardwick turned back to the room.

The tiny woman sniffed. "Is it really a great treasure?"

Hardwick nodded. "The greatest I've ever seen."

Save the sapphire of my lady's eyes.

His heart squeezed, and he cleared his throat again. "You'll be wanting to call in your constabulary," he said to Mac, his chest tightening at the telltale glistening on the laird's face. "Perhaps contact Erlend Eggertson in Lerwick. He'll help make arrangements to get the Up-Helly-Aa costumes back to Shetland."

"And the ghosties?" Mac swiped his sleeve across

his cheeks. "Are they still out on the moor? They'll no' be getting away?"

"Ach, they'll be going nowhere." Hardwick grinned. "My friend Bran and his lads are guarding them. We stripped them naked as a bairn's bottom. If they run, they'll be doing so in all their shameful glory."

"Jumping haggis!" Mac hooted and punched Hardwick in the arm. "I knew I liked you! You really are a man after my own heart!"

Hardwick's own heart pinched. Unbidden came the image of the Dark One's inner sanctum and the root-dragons with their glittering black-scaled backs and swishing tails, their fiery red eyes and fetid, sulfurous breath. He imagined Cilla in their clutches, the gaggle of hell hags cackling with glee as the root-dragons pulled her into their lair.

He blinked and the vision faded, the bright morning light pouring into the conservatory making such a notion more than absurd.

Even though he knew it could happen.

A cold chill rushed up his spine. The conservatory seemed to fade around him, Mac's guffaws and the chatter of the residents dimming in his ears. He clenched his fists, fighting the dread building beneath his ribs.

Mac thrust his arms in the air and danced a little jig, laughing.

And *he* was being a loon.

Even so, he grabbed Mac's arm as soon as he stopped twirling. "Where's Cilla?"

"Eh?" Mac grinned and swatted at his kilt. "Ach, she's just for sleeping in," he panted. "She'll be down anon."

Hardwick started to feel foolish until he caught the guarded look on Birdie's face. When she slid a furtive glance at Honoria and that one promptly began rearranging her muesli packets, he knew something was wrong.

"What is it? Where is she?"

Mac slung an arm around his shoulders. "I told you, the lassie's abed."

"Nae." Hardwick shook himself free. "I dinna think she is."

The high color staining Birdie's and Honoria's faces said he'd guessed rightly.

He folded his arms. "Out with it, ladies. I know she isn't here."

He could feel her absence like a rip in his soul.

"She went sightseeing." Honoria broke first, chin high and lying out her ears.

"Where?" A muscle ticked in Hardwick's jaw.

Birdie said nothing.

"If you know something"—Mac went to stand by her—"you'd best speak up."

"Oh, posh!" Birdie waved a flustered hand. "She didn't want anyone to know."

"Know what?" Hardwick and Mac spoke together.

"She's gone to Seagrave." Birdie sounded defensive. "She went to Robbie and Roddie's cottage last night, asking them to drive her. They left hours ago."

"And why didn't she ask me?" Mac's brow crinkled.

"Perhaps she knew you'd tag along on her coattails?" Birdie smiled sweetly. "She has things to do there that she wishes to do alone."

"Humph." Mac frowned.

Hardwick's blood chilled. When Birdie opened her mouth again to argue with her husband, he used the opportunity to slip from the room.

He couldn't imagine why Cilla wanted to go to Seagrave, but whatever the reason, he didn't like it.

It was also dangerous.

There were other reasons beside his memories that had kept him from returning to his old home. The ruin's isolation, he'd been told, attracted unsavory souls.

Ghosts who used his home for revels and debauchery he didn't want Cilla to stumble into.

"Hellfire and damnation!" He stormed out of Dunroamin's heavy front door and scrunched his eyes against the blinding sunlight.

Where was soft Highland mist when a body needed it?

Scowling, he stomped down the broad stone steps, knowing there was only one thing he could do. He'd have to sift himself to Seagrave and fetch her.

He just hoped he wouldn't be too late.

Chapter 17

'Tis a man's work.

Cilla frowned remembering Hardwick's words. Much as she loved him, she struggled against blowing out a bitter breath. She did take a deep, back-straightening one. That was what she needed, about to tackle some serious *women's work*. Men didn't do what she was going to attempt. When it came down to it, only women were so daring, so utterly bold and determined in chasing their dreams.

Her throat swelled and an annoying sting of prickling heat jabbed the backs of her eyes at the thought of *her* dream. Forget the tingles he gave her and the to-die-for tongue swirls. His deep, hungry kisses that drove her to madness, and even his rich Scottish burr. Something she doubted she'd tire of even if she lived a thousand years.

His slow, sexy smiles and the way his dark eyes went all hot and simmering when he looked at her.

She didn't even need to think about his kilt.

All that was wonderful, but it was his heart and his soul that she really wanted, because her own would never be complete without him.

She suspected she'd known it the moment she'd seen him, and she wasn't going to let him go now.

So she blinked back her tears before they could fall and swallowed the lump in her throat. Strength and courage was what she needed. There would be time for soppiness later, if her plan worked.

Refusing to accept otherwise, she pushed her hair back off her forehead and took another few brisk and confident steps.

Confidence was the key.

Only if she truly believed would she have a chance of breaking through seven hundred years and reaching the bard-wizard who'd cursed Hardwick. Villains always returned to the scene of their crimes, after all. Aunt Birdie had assured her that even if he hadn't, enough residue of such a dramatic event would have seeped into Seagrave's walls for her to make contact with the minstrel.

As long as she kept faith that she could.

But doing so wasn't exactly easy. Already she'd covered half of the long grass-grown path that lead out to the imposing ruins of Hardwick's former home. Her determination and—oddly enough—the occasional tossed-aside soda can or water bottle and the bicycle tracks on the path were the only things keeping her from turning around and following the little coastal road right back to the tiny fishing village of Cruden Bay, where Robbie and Roddie had dropped her.

Her rock-iron will to make contact with the bard and urge him to undo the spell wouldn't let her turn back if her life depended on it.

And the litter and signs of cyclists assured her that the ruins weren't as dangerous as they looked.

Other people clearly came here.

Even so, she couldn't stop a shiver. Seagrave wasn't your archetypical Scottish cliff-top ruin, all tumbled walls and romance, wheeling seabirds and piles of mossy, indistinguishable rubble.

The ruins were in-your-face formidable. Bold, stark, and soaring, from this distance, anyway, they didn't look crumbled at all. Only bleak and derelict with the roof missing and large black rectangles of emptiness indicating the onetime placement of doors and windows.

Cilla took another deep breath and adjusted the shoulder straps of her rucksack. Filled with her lunch and, more importantly, Aunt Birdie's spirit-conjuring goods, the thing was starting to get heavy.

And something was watching her from Seagrave's hollow, blank-staring windows.

Hoping it might be the minstrel, in the way of spirits perhaps already aware of her mission, she quickened her step and plunged on. Chin high, she veered off the muddy, grassy track and pushed through into the heart of the ruin. A long, roofless corridor with many doors opening off both sides stretched before her. Eerie, damp, and earthy-smelling, it was anything but inviting, but she strode along until she came to a wide-open space that once could only have been a courtyard.

Though choked with weeds and brambles, there were enough clumps of fallen stone to sit on. Huge, empty windows facing the sea let in the light, and, best of all, here in the sheltered walls of the bailey, she'd be free from prying eyes.

Here, too, she'd be somewhat protected from the cold wind racing in off the gray, white-capped North Sea. Heavy waves pounded Seagrave's cliffs, the churning waters so different from the gentle, blue-swirling Kyle.

Passing by the fallen chunks of masonry—she'd learned all about stinging nettles at Castle Varrich— she went to one of the large, gaping windows and placed her rucksack on its broad stone ledge.

Another deep breath and a silent prayer, and she started setting up her minstrel-conjuring goods. Two white candles, each carefully set inside glass jars to block the wind. A genuine fourteenth-century oil lamp from the depths of Dunroamin's unused wing. Tiny and rusted, the lamp was just the thing to evoke a sense of the past century, or so Aunt Birdie had promised.

A little bottle of frankincense essential oil served the same purpose. Heart thumping, Cilla hoisted herself onto the window ledge and then unscrewed the bottle's cap, dribbling a few generous drops onto the stone.

For good measure, she touched a finger to the bottle's opening and then dabbed a tiny bit of the oil on the tip of her nose.

Then she closed her eyes and tried to concentrate, imagining the bard as a small bent man, grizzled and gray, and carrying a lute.

Unfortunately, she only felt silly.

Her eyes snapped open and she frowned. Despite the two glass jars, the wind had managed to blow out her candles. Worse, she'd not thought to return her matches to the rucksack, and the little packet was now gone.

The wind had surely claimed them. Sweeping the matches off the window ledge and sending them right down onto the crashing waves of the North Sea.

Damn.

Aunt Birdie had insisted the white candles were crucial.

And now she couldn't relight them.

Frustration tightened her chest. For a moment, her eyes stung again and her view of the tossing gray-and-white North Sea went blurry. But she blinked hard until the stinging heat receded and her vision cleared.

Crying never got anyone anywhere.

But fierce determination did, so she picked up the little medieval cruse lamp and held it so tight its rounded, bowl-like edge dug deep into her palm. Ignoring the discomfort, she concentrated again on her image of a wandering minstrel, willing the man to appear. Or, at least, to give her some kind of sign that he was present and willing to listen.

Nothing happened.

She breathed deep. Long, slow breaths designed to soak up the ancient scent of the frankincense. But all she inhaled was the tang of the sea and black, limpet-crusted boulders. Wet grass and a pungent waft of something she suspected was strongly related to the many lobster traps and fishing nets she'd seen at nearby Cruden Bay.

The frankincense couldn't compete.

Instead of feeling transported, she again began to feel ridiculous.

The minstrel wasn't here, wasn't reachable, or just plain didn't care.

Doomed before she'd even put her bard-conjuring tools into her bag. Knowing defeat when it stood before her, she sighed and opened her eyes.

"Oh, no!" She clapped a hand to her breast, mortified to discover that she *had* conjured someone.

A man.

Tall, clad in black, and handsome in a roguish sort of way, he stood across the bailey from her, leaning casually against the arch of one of the many empty door openings.

Arms folded and ankles crossed, he was looking right at her, clearly amused.

And she knew without asking that he was absolutely not a medieval minstrel.

She also couldn't shake the odd sensation that she'd seen him before. A notion that, although unsettling, was a lot better than if he struck her as some kind of Scottish ax murderer. Scotland was surely safer than certain parts of Philly, but even she had heard of the occasional weirdness.

Trying to look as if she encountered dark-clad mystery men in castle ruins all the time, she hopped down from the window and dusted her hands.

"Nice day for a walk, h'mmm?" She tried for casual.

The man said nothing.

But at least he hadn't moved.

She forced a friendly American smile, but let her mind race to what she could use as a weapon. Maybe the jagged edge of one of the candle jars if she smashed it quickly enough. *Does frankincense essential oil temporarily blind people if it's dashed in their face?* she wondered.

The man just kept studying her, an odd smile quirking across his lips.

Cilla dropped her own smile. It wasn't working, anyway.

She swallowed. "Are you from around here?"

"Scotland?" His deep burr said that he was. "Aye, so I was . . . once."

Cilla blinked. She didn't like the way he'd said that. "Once?"

He glanced aside, and she saw that he'd tied his sleek raven-black hair in a shoulder-skimming ponytail. He looked back at her as quickly and pushed away from the wall, taking a few steps toward her.

"Aye, once." His smile faded. " 'Twas long ago and a time best forgotten."

" *'Twas?*" Cilla slid a look at the two candle jars, wondering if she could spring for them.

It was one thing for Hardwick to use the occasional 'tisey and 'twasey. But this guy, though definitely a bit on the odd side, looked way too modern for such language.

She backed up against the wall, resting her elbow on the window ledge in a hopefully innocent-looking gesture. Even if she didn't have time to smash a candle jar, she could use one to bop him on the head if he tried anything funny.

She almost choked at the thought.

He looked powerfully muscled, certainly Hardwick's equal in strength or close to it. It was also a pretty good bet that he'd be fast on his feet. As for the damage his hands could do, she didn't even want to consider it.

In a word, he appeared lethal.

"I think I'll just be going . . ." She slid a look down the long door-and-window-filled corridor, not at all surprised that it now seemed even more sinister.

A dark passage filled with slanting shadows and the weird sense of strange little creatures darting and scampering here and there, flitting just out of sight before the eye could catch them.

Her fingers stretched for the candle jar.

His hand snapped around her wrist. He'd moved before she could blink.

"Hey!" She tried to yank free.

He smiled again, his grip like iron.

"The candles wouldn't have worked." He released her but crowded her space, looming tall before her, blocking her escape. "Not as you meant to use them. They would"—he rubbed his chin as he eyed her bard-conjuring goods—"have shielded you, though."

"Shielded me?" Was that high-pitched squeak her voice?

"Aye, they'd have protected you well. If they were still burning."

"I'm sure I don't know what you're talking about." She grabbed her candle jars and the frankincense bottle and stuffed everything in her rucksack.

It alone would serve as a weapon if swung deftly.

Mr. Ponytail met her eyes, challenging. "Ach, you ken well enough what I mean, Cilla."

His words jellied her knees.

He knew her name.

She caught her breath, heart thumping. "How do you know who I am?"

"How is it that you do not know who I am?" His lips twitched. "I thought you would have guessed by now."

"I think you're mad." Cilla tightened her grip on her rucksack, making ready to swing. "Maybe you heard Robbie and Roddie use my name when we stopped for tea in Collieston. There were other people in the tea shop. You could have been one of them."

"Ah, but you disappoint me." He clucked his tongue. "To think I troubled myself to come here."

"You needn't have bothered, but you can have the place to yourself." Cilla started away. "I'm leaving."

"Without hearing what I've done for you?"

Something in his tone stopped her. "I know you're not the minstrel."

He laughed softly. "I could be him if you wished. Nothing is impossible."

Cilla felt her pulse skip a beat.

Slowly, she turned.

He stood at the window, facing her, his tall, broad-shouldered form dark against the great expanse of the silvery twilit sea. Something about the way he angled his head and watched her made the fine hairs on the back of her neck stand on end.

She was *sure* she'd seen him before.

When he laughed again, his eye corners crinkling and his whole face broadening in a wide, self-satisfied grin, she knew where.

"Oh, my God!" Her eyes flew wide. "You're the devil! The red devil face at my window!"

She'd known the devil face had been real.

He clapped a hand to his heart and screwed up his face in a mock wince. "Recognized at last, though I must own that I am not himself, nae. Merely a favored keeper of a small corner of his boundless dominion."

She stared at him, trembling. "But the mask—"

"The *mask* and that wretched bird's meddling ruined what was meant as a warning to Seagrave." A look of remembered annoyance flickered across his face. "I wanted him to know how close I could come to you."

He glanced out at the sea, then back at her. "Had

I bothered to look deeper into the goings-on at Dun-roamin I would have foreseen Gregor's interference with the Up-Helly-Aa mask and chosen another guise for myself. As it was, some of my root-dragons were causing havoc at the time, misbehaving, and my mind was otherwise occupied."

"Root-dragons?" Cilla swallowed, fear constricting her chest.

He didn't seem to hear her, his gaze once more on the sea.

She moistened her lips, gauging how she could escape.

Up to now she'd believed he was just a loony. Now that he'd mentioned Gregor's name, she had little choice but to believe him.

She was talking to the devil!

And it didn't matter a whit whether he was the real one or, as he claimed, just some kind of hellish guardian. Either way was just a bit too much.

Ghosts, she could handle.

Vampires, werewolves, devils, and demons weren't her cuppa.

She was a paranormal-light kind of gal.

Unfortunately, she knew without asking that he wasn't going to let her go anywhere until he'd had his say. And—she must be really losing it—but for some oddball reason, seeing his flash of perturbation when he'd mentioned Gregor and the mask made him seem less scary.

Almost . . . human.

So she put back her shoulders and took a deep breath, trying to look braver than she felt. "Why did you want Hardwick to see how close you could get to me?"

"Because"—he leaned against the window ledge, crossing his legs at the ankles—"I meant to threaten him with your soul. He needed to see I could take it if I desired."

"You meant to take my soul?"

"It was a consideration, aye."

Cilla stared at him, pretended bravura forgotten. "And now?"

She had to know.

"I chose otherwise." He flicked a pebble off the window ledge, watching as it fell to the sea. "I decided to return Seagrave's soul instead. So to speak, of course, considering his soul never left him. Only his life—"

"What?" Cilla's eyes rounded.

Her heart slammed into her ribs and her blood roared in her ears. "Are you saying he's a real man again? You broke his curse?"

"You could put it that way, aye." He lifted a hand, examining his knuckles. "Though hearing the words makes me wonder what possessed me to do the like. I never did care for that cocky bastard."

"But—"

"Touch her and I'll kill you!" Hardwick burst into the courtyard, sword swinging. "A thousand times if that's what it takes!"

"Indeed?" The Dark One looked unconcerned.

"Hardwick!" Cilla ran between them, flinging her arms wide. "No fighting . . . please!"

He grabbed her, yanking her behind him. "Stay out of this, lass," he ordered, his voice terse. "You've no idea what he can do. I have to fight him."

If he had the strength.

He'd spent the best part of the day trying to sift himself to Seagrave. Again and again, he'd failed, each attempt either not working at all or only getting him to the outermost reaches of Mac's lands.

Until he'd summoned all his will for one last effort that landed him facedown in the mud of the path leading to his former home.

He'd needed forever to push to his knees.

Then he'd staggered about like a drink-taken fool, picking his way through weeds and fallen masonry and only gaining some semblance of his strength when he heard Cilla's voice coming from the depths of the ruin.

Her voice and a laugh he recognized at once.

He shuddered, determined to keep her from the fiend's clutches if it was the last thing he did.

"Conjure a blade, Dark One." He narrowed his eyes on his foe, fury pounding through him. "We both know you can. Fight me like a man. . . . If you dare!"

The Dark One remained where he was, leaning arrogantly against the ledge of a window that had once been one of Hardwick's favorites.

"I can summon a thousand swords," he taunted, recrossing his legs casually. "One for each death you've threatened me with. But alas"—he sounded bored—"I'm here for another reason."

Hardwick balanced his blade, readying to lunge. "Name one good enough to keep me from running you through."

"It would be foolhardy." The Dark One's gaze dipped to his mud-splattered kilt and the dirt smudges on his knees. "Not wise at all in your condition."

"My condition?" Hardwick glared at him.

The Dark One shrugged. "If you do not know—"

"I know that my blade craves blood." Hardwick flung his left arm behind him, seizing Cilla's wrist when she tried to clutch at him. "It's been too long since its thirst's been quenched!"

"And how long has it been since you've been a man?"

"That's a fool question if e'er there was one." Hardwick refused to answer it.

A Highlander was *always* a man.

And on a more practical note, the Dark One knew to the hour how long Hardwick hadn't been a flesh-and-blood man.

He wouldn't be baited.

Especially not in front of Cilla and, with surety, not when she was crying.

He blinked, catching the bright glitter in her eyes out of the corner of his own. The funny way her lower lip quivered and her breathing seemed to have gone all shallow and *gulpy*.

"O-o-oh, don't you see?" She twisted free of his grip and tossed back her hair. "He's lifted the curse. You're whole again, just as before! That's why he's here. He came to tell me."

She flashed a look at the Dark One as if they were old friends.

Hardwick frowned.

The Dark One may once have been a man, but Hardwick doubted he'd ever been anyone's friend.

Sheathing his sword, he folded his arms. "That canna be." He dismissed the notion at once. "You forget I sifted myself here. Were I *others* again, I would no' have been able to do that."

"And you'll ne'er be able to do it again." The Dark One drawled the words. "Transporting yourself here used the last reserves of such powers left to you. They've been dwindling ever since you hurtled back to life through the redemption tunnel."

Hardwick snorted. "Redemption tunnel! I've ne'er heard the like in all my centuries."

The Dark One arched a superior brow. "Perhaps because you were cursed and forbidden entry?"

"And you sent me into such a miracle-spending place?" Hardwick put his hand back on his sword hilt. "I dinna believe it. I ken your trickery."

Annoyance flashed in the Dark One's eyes. "You wouldn't comprehend a thimbleful of my capabilities. Though I'll ask if you haven't felt weakened of late? Easily wearied and desiring mortal needs, such as sleep and other pesky habits?"

Hardwick set his jaw, not about to admit the like. True as the queries were.

As unobtrusively as he could, he slipped his sword hand behind his back and flicked his fingers to summon his shield.

Nothing happened.

He tried again, this time using more vigorous wriggles. But he failed anew. His shield didn't appear in his hand as was its usual wont.

In the window, the Dark One's lips curved in a knowing smile.

A smile without warmth.

"It's quite true, I assure you." His voice was smooth, sovereign. "But if you persist in doubting me, I'll regret my largesse so much that I'll reverse your good fortune!"

At his words, Cilla stifled a sob.

Hardwick shot a glance at her, not missing that she'd blanched. The hand she'd pressed to her mouth trembled. She really did believe the whoreson. And seeing that she did gave his heart an unexpected lurch. His stomach clenched and churned, disbelief making it impossible to hope.

A pain, sharp and stinging, squeezed his heart.

He drew a deep breath, considering the Dark One with distrustful eyes. "If this be true . . . to what do I owe the honor?"

His foe threw back his head and laughed. "Not yourself, be sure of it!"

"What, then?"

His face sobering, the Dark One glanced aside, his gaze skimming out over the dark waters of the North Sea to the distant horizon beyond. When he turned back, he wore a grieved expression so surprisingly sincere Hardwick almost felt sympathy for him.

Knowing better, he folded his arms instead, waiting. The Dark One pushed off the window ledge, a whiff of sulfur swirling around him. "It was your lady, Seagrave. I . . ." He made a gesture, looking annoyed again. "I should not have gone to Dunroamin—"

"You what?" The ground dipped beneath Hardwick's feet. His sword hand began to itch again. "Dinna tell me you—"

"Your lady can explain later." Impatience edged the Dark One's voice. "Press me and I shall leave you without an explanation. As is"—he glanced once more at the sea—"suffice it to say that it was not wise for me to see her. She reminded me of someone I knew long ago. Someone—"

"Someone you loved and lost." Cilla finished for him.

Hardwick scowled at her.

The Dark One nodded. "It was many years past." He looked at Hardwick, his obsidian gaze going deep. "Longer centuries than even you could count. But I never forgot. Her loss pains me to this day."

He drew a long breath and released it slowly. "I nearly undid your curse that day I appeared to your lass at Dunroamin. Even"—he gave a bitter-sounding laugh—"felt bad for having frightened her. Imagine! But once I returned to my temple, I caught myself. . . . Until you strode into my inner sanctum, offering your all for one night in her arms. When you refused my offer of her soul for the pleasure—a test, no more— I remembered how I'd held my own woman's cold and limp body, begging gods who wouldn't listen to restore her to me. And I . . ."

He looked aside again, his expression hardening.

"You were moved to give us a chance." Cilla's voice broke on the words.

She reached for Hardwick's hand, twining their fingers.

He frowned, not believing a word. "There's more. Even if you were *moved* by my lady's resemblance to someone you knew thousands of years ago, I'll ne'er accept you'd release a soul so easily."

The almost imperceptible tightening of the Dark One's lips proved it.

Wanting the truth, Hardwick yanked his hand from Cilla's and whipped out his sword again. Raising it with lightning speed, he pressed its tip beneath the Dark One's chin.

"Tell me now how it really was, or I'll do my best to prove you can be killed."

"Do you wish to spoil a romantic tale in front of your lady?" The Dark One cocked a brow, a look of mock surprise on his handsome face. "A pity . . ."

"Speak." Hardwick pressed his sword tip harder against the Dark One's neck.

As if swatting at a fly, the Dark One flicked a hand and the blade vanished, reappearing in its sheath at Hardwick's side.

Smiling coldly at his little victory, the Dark One took a step forward. "The truth, Seagrave, is that I had no choice. There are powers in the Otherworld even greater than myself and my master. You evoked them yourself when you refused Cilla's soul to be taken in exchange for your boon."

"I broke my own curse?" Hardwick still couldn't believe it.

"Call it what you like." The Dark One shrugged. "Your selflessness unleashed the only power I cannot battle. The eternal strength of a pure and loving heart. In the moment you roared '*Nae!*' at me, your love for your lady ripped open the entrance to the redemption tunnel and, much as I would have wished otherwise, I could not have prevented you from hurtling into it."

Hardwick stared at him, too stunned for words.

Somewhere deep inside him, something coiled tight and then sprang free, releasing his doubt. His heart thundered wildly and his throat worked, the emotion clogging it making it difficult for him to deny his foe's words.

Now he knew why he'd been plagued by such weari-

ness of late. The all-too-mortal maladies he'd brushed
aside as lust-dizziness.

"By all the saints!" He grabbed Cilla and pulled
her against him.

She sobbed, flinging her arms around him and holding tight. "I told you it was true! I also believe he
loved a woman who looked like me."

She threw a glance at the Dark One. "You did,
didn't you?"

For a moment, his eyes darkened and a shadow
crossed his face. But rather than answer her, he turned
to Hardwick.

"Your journey from here, Seagrave, is your own."
Looking his formidable self again, he gripped Hardwick's shoulder, squeezing hard. "Use it wisely. You
know I'll be watching."

And then he was gone.

Only a stir in the wind and a faint whiff of sulfur
indicating he'd even been there at all.

Chapter 18

"Wow." Cilla began to shake all over.

The Dark One, or whoever he'd really been, might have vanished, but he'd upturned her world in his passing. Tiny whirlwinds still eddied across the court-yard's grass-and-weed-clogged expanse, little twirling gusts of dried leaves and whatnot settling onto the ancient, muddied ground.

Her pulse leapt and skittered, showing no sign of slowing down.

She could still feel his presence.

The portent of his revelations hung heavy in the air. So thick, she almost choked on the hope he'd left with them. A tight, hot-throbbing knot grew in her throat, and her eyes began to burn.

She squeezed them shut and took several long, deep breaths, trying to ground herself.

But it didn't do any good.

The wild, giddy exhilaration coursing through her wasn't going anywhere.

So she did the unthinkable.

She started to cry, this time not bothering to check her tears.

"Cease your crying, sweetness." Hardwick grasped her by the arms, holding tight. He was scowling again, the distrust back in his eyes. "There may no' be a reason to rejoice, and if there isn't, I canna stand the sight of your pain."

"But it *is* true!" She blinked up at him, her heart thundering wildly. "All of it. I know it here," she cried, pounding a fist against her breast. "I see it on you, too. There's something different!"

And there was.

A sliver of doubt where only confidence had been before.

"You must believe!" She leaned into him, winding her arms around his neck, willing him to have faith. "If you don't, maybe the undoing of the spell won't work. It could be reversed, or the redemption tunnel might pull you back up into it."

"I'm no' sure anything has happened to *be* reversed. And I'm more than skeptical about the so-called redemption tunnel." He shook his head, denial all over him. "There's only one way to know for sure, and I'll no' risk that."

"I say we do . . . try!" Swallowing against her tears, Cilla lifted up on her toes, kissing him hard and fierce before he had a chance to pull away.

She wound her arms around his neck, clinging to him in case he tried. "Please . . ." She let her tongue glide deep and pressed herself against him, well aware that the feel of her breasts rubbing across his chest might sway him.

He did groan, the hot slide of his own tongue tangling with hers. His sexy sandalwood scent drifted around her, flooding her senses and making her swoon. "Lass . . ." He pulled back to nip and lick her lips, then splayed his fingers across the back of her head, angling her face to kiss her more deeply.

"See." She breathed the word against his mouth. "We're kissing and nothing is happening." Breaking away, she let her tongue glide along his jaw and then swirled its tip across the bottom of his ear. "No bogeymen jumping out of the shadows, no red devils, no—"

She jerked back, her eyes widening at the sudden rock-hard swell lifting his kilt. Hot, heavy, and demanding, it thrust urgently against her, making her burn even through the thick woolen folds of his plaid.

"Oh, my . . ." Her breath caught and her heart galloped. Leaning in for another kiss, she rubbed herself against him, already melting.

"O-o-oh, nae." He set her from him forcefully, scowling darker than she'd ever seen. "As you've noticed, something *is* happening, and we must end it here and now."

He stepped back, breathing hard. "I shouldn't have forgotten myself, and I'll no' be endangering you—"

"Does that mean you won't trust me, either?" Cilla stepped back, too. But she shrugged off her jacket as she did so, tossing it onto the grassy, rubble-strewn ground. "I thought we'd moved past all that. Have you forgotten the bliss you've given me? How I've lain open before you, begging, then quivering beneath your kisses?"

She lifted her chin, knew her eyes were blazing. "Yes, I mean *those* kisses."

She wouldn't have believed it, but he flushed. "Lass . . . dinna do this."

"Or"—she glared at him, on a roll—"how you gave me those looks during my broken-china class, making me feel your fingers playing with me, even slipping beneath my panties to dip in and out of me and then rub my clit until I could hardly see straight, much less hold a workshop!"

"Cilla . . ." He shoved a hand through his hair. "You've seen the dangers. The Dark One's word canna be trusted. I'll no' risk—"

"I believe him!" Grinning now, she reached for the buttons of her blouse, undoing them with a speed and deftness that surprised her. "As for trust, there are some who'd say I'm the one who's needed the most trust in this twosome!"

Her blouse landed near her jacket.

The tilt in his kilt jerked.

She tossed back her hair, sent her bra flying. "Well?"

He turned away, his hands clenched at his sides.

Cilla bit down on her lip, drawing blood. Then she bent to tug off her shoes and socks. Straightening, she grabbed her belt buckle, undoing it so swiftly she broke a nail. Heart pounding, she ripped open her waist snap and yanked down the zipper. It took her less than a wink to rid herself of her pants and panties and kick both aside.

The moment she did, Hardwick tensed. As she looked, a great shudder ripped through him and his fisted hands tightened visibly, his knuckles now white.

She drew a deep breath and straightened her back.

It was now or never.

"Turn around." Her voice brooked no refusal. "I'm naked."

"Damnation!" He whirled to face her, closing the distance between them in two great strides. "I'd sworn no' to touch you again. You shouldn't have done this," he growled, reaching for her, pulling her so hard against him she gasped. " 'Tis too late now. . . . I canna help myself."

He snaked an iron-strong arm around her waist, crushing her even more. "Ach, sweetness, did no one e'er tell you what a naked woman does to a Highlander?" Gripping her face with his free hand, he slanted his mouth over hers, claiming her lips in a rough, hungry kiss.

The swift, hard, devouring kind that showed no mercy.

She cried out, spreading her hands across the broad width of his plaid-draped chest. Her entire body trembled, her legs almost giving out when he broke the kiss to look down her. Holding her gaze, he reached for the large Celtic brooch at his shoulder, ripping open its clasp.

The instant it sprang free, he tossed it aside and whipped off his plaid, tossing it across the cold stone of the window ledge.

"Are you doing that for the reason I think?" Her gaze flitted to the plaid, then back to him.

Hope leapt inside her.

Her heart raced and a blaze of tingles caught fire between her legs. Every hot, curling tongue flick he'd given her swirled across her again, making her belly clench and her knees weaken. She wanted those long, slow licks now. The sweet, shattering releases he gave her.

She wanted *him*, the long, hard length of him gliding hotly in and out of her.

"You've pushed me too far, lass." His gaze heated, sweeping the length of her. It was bold, possessive, and almost predatory; the sliver of doubt she'd glimpsed earlier was nowhere to be seen. "You know fine what I'm after. I told you"—he reached for her breasts, first palming, then squeezing and plumping them—"a Highlander once tempted will stop at nothing to get what he wants."

He swept one hand down her side and around behind her, digging his fingers into the rounds of her buttocks. "And if you didn't know, it's no' just any bare-bottomed lassie that fires our blood."

Taking his other hand from her breasts, he caught her chin and lifted her face so she couldn't look away. " 'Tis the smooth, shapely warmth of a big-bosomed, round-hipped lass that stirs us. If such a well-made woman is also eager and hot-blooded for a tumble and"—he leaned close to brush his lips lightly over hers—"just happens to be the lass a man loves more than life itself, well, then, you can be assured there's no stopping him."

Cilla's heart latched on to one word.

She pulled back, blinking. The wretched tears were jabbing into her eyes again. "Are you saying you love me?"

He arched one brow. "If you have to ask, sweet, I've been doing something wrong."

"Oh, my . . ." She gulped. Her lower lip quivered before she could stop it.

"I'll no' be asking you the same fool question." His hands went to his kilt belt and before she could blink again, he'd undone it, sending both the belt and his kilt sailing.

Nothing remained to clothe him except the wide gold armband winking at her from just below his right shoulder.

Her eyes rounded.

So the rumors were true.

That one time she'd caught a fleeting glimpse of him hadn't been a fluke. And he was more than just naked beneath his kilt. He was flat-out magnificent.

Even more so than she remembered.

She swallowed hard, flushing.

He stood back, letting her admire him. "Nae, I'll no' make you declare yourself," he said, a note of pride thrumming on the words. "I've known for long that you love me."

His declaration made, he gathered her in his arms and plunked her down onto the plaid-covered window ledge. Spreading her knees, he stepped in between her thighs, his arms sweeping round behind her, holding her secure.

"I have but one regret." He looked down at her, his expression clouding. "I—"

"You're still worried that the Dark One lied." She reached to curl a hand around his neck, not liking the crease marring his brow. "I swear he was on the level. I'm sure—"

"Sweeting, I no longer care what happens . . . after."

He slid a hand beneath her, lifting her so that her slick, wet heat slid against him. "Only that I have you now. But if you'd know what bothers me, 'tis only that . . ."

He made a broad sweeping gesture. "I'd have rather loved you in this chamber when it was at its finest. My greeting room"—he fought back the memories, the images searing him—"this was where I welcomed guests arriving by sea. Far below, where you now see only black rocks and angry, swirling waves was once a landing platform e'er watched and kept at the ready. This room awaited such visitors, filled with all the comforts of my day. Furred rugs covering the floors and richly colored tapestries on the walls; this very window ledge, cushioned and private, protected from curious eyes by heavily embroidered hangings of—"

"And you think that matters to me?" She reached down between them, gripping him firmly. "I'd have you take me there"—she jerked her head at the stony, nettled floor—"if that was the only way I could have you! Here, on your plaid in the window, seems more than fitting!"

Hardwick's heart fell wide, his soul tumbling. "Lass." He bit out the word, sucking in his breath through tight-clenched teeth as she moved over him, sliding down onto his need like a burning, honey-damped sheath.

The world as he knew it split.

Seven hundred years of agony spinning away as if it'd ne'er been.

She wrapped her legs around him, her eyes glittering as she locked gazes with him, the deep flush of her passion sweeping across her breasts.

"Hardwick . . ." She held fast to his shoulders, her nails scouring his flesh.

He smoothed a hand along her lush curves and down across the soft skin of her belly, and lower to the damp curls he knew so well. Need lancing him, he toyed with them now, teasing and plucking before he slid his fingers deeper to the one spot he knew would shatter her.

Scarce able to breathe, he circled the delicate bud with his thumb, flicking and teasing until she arched her back, her hips bucking and her pulse throbbing beneath his fingers.

His own need wound tight around him, the sleek, slippery heat of her almost more than he could bear.

He threw back his head, meaning to roar with the wonder of her, but bliss as he'd never believed possible stole his cry. Unending pleasure crashed over him and he swept his arms around her, seeking her lips. He plunged his tongue in and out of her sweet, silky-wet mouth using the same hot rhythm of the long, smooth glides of his body joining with hers.

And then she jerked her head away, the whole of her tensing as she sucked in a great, shuddering breath and clamped her legs even tighter around his hips. She gave herself over to her release in a way he'd never seen a woman do, her cry of pleasure breaking at last to merge with his own.

"O-o-oh, Hardwick . . ." She gasped his name again, a soft breath against a world set on fire.

A world—now that it was settling—he feared to see.

Not that he felt anything threatening.

But with the heat of his lust ebbing, good sense prevailed and he knew without cracking an eye that there was a very good chance he'd open them to see a gaggle of eager, hand-rubbing hell hags waiting to claim him.

With surety, the Dark One wouldn't harm Cilla.

That much he'd seen to be true.

The trouble was, now that he'd claimed her fully, he couldn't bear to let her go. As if she knew, she shifted in his arms, winding her own loosely around his neck, her head resting lightly on his shoulder.

The trust in her cuddling almost broke him.

"That was . . . beautiful," she breathed, making it worse. "If only . . ."

"I'm sorry, lass." He smoothed his hands up and down her back, hoping to soothe her. "I shouldn't have risked—"

"You should have long ago." She squirmed to lean close, kissing him. "I've been waiting all this time, and now . . ."

He opened his eyes, not liking her tone.

Sure enough, her brow was furrowed and she'd taken her kiss-swollen lower lip hard between her teeth. But he saw, too, that the pitiful ruins of his onetime greeting room were empty. The Dark One wasn't lounging against the wall in a corner, leering at them.

And, best of all, there wasn't a root-dragon or hell hag in sight. Relief swept him, the unexpected shock of it almost stealing his breath. His heart started thumping, hard, fast, and triumphant.

He could scarce believe it to be true.

Needing proof, he stepped back, glancing round. Long evening shadows filled corners and stretched across rough, uneven ground that had once been smooth stone and rich, furred coverings. But nothing stirred save the night breeze pouring in through his erstwhile windows, a scatter of dried and loose leaves blown across fallen stone.

His fists clenched on the truth, the joy of it dampened only by the stinging heat spoiling his vision and the hot, swelling lump thickening his throat.

Still, he couldn't be sure.

Quickly, because the worry on his lady's face plagued him, he slid a hand behind his back and wriggled his fingers in the direction of his discarded sword.

The blade remained where it was, cast aside in the heat of his passion.

Heart thundering, he flicked a forefinger at a crumbled wall niche, trying to conjure the basin and ewer that had once stood there.

But the basin and ewer didn't appear, the ancient niche remaining as it was now, filled with nothing more interesting than a few tiny bits of fallen mortar and the smelly leavings of perching seabirds.

Hardwick's heart almost leapt from his breast.

He stared at the niche, well aware his jaw had slipped.

Not that he cared.

Truth was, he'd ne'er seen anything more beautiful, except, of course, his lady.

"Dear God, Cilla, you were right all along!" Ignoring the crack in his voice—and hoping she hadn't noticed—he plucked her off the window ledge and caught her up in his arms, swinging her round and round until dizziness left him no choice but to release her. "I do believe the spell is broken. . . ."

He set her down, the still-there furrow in her brow damping his triumph.

"What is it, sweet?" He slid his arms around her, drawing her close. Gently this time. "Are you no' pleased that we have time now?"

She glanced aside, worrying her lip again. "It's just that, well, I've fallen in love with you."

He tightened his grip on her, squeezing. "Ach, but that's a cause for celebration. No' for long faces and creased brows."

"It isn't just that." She looked up at him, pink tingeing her cheeks. "I've come to love Scotland, too. At least"—she glanced down again, nudging a clump of grass with her toe—"Dunroamin and the residents. I can't imagine not seeing any of them anymore. I'll even miss little Leo and Gregor. Colonel Darling and his bluster. As for you . . ."

She pressed a hand to her lips, tears spilling down her cheeks.

"Ach, lass, you needn't say good-bye to anyone. No' now." He wrapped his arms around her, hugging her near. "I was going to let Mac and your aunt tell you, but we caught the Viking ghosties and, you'll ne'er believe it, a great treasure with them!"

"A treasure?" She blinked at that. "In Uncle Mac's peat fields?"

Hardwick nodded, grinning. "Sure as I'm standing here. You can ask Robbie and Roddie on the drive back."

An ordeal he wasn't looking forward to, having ne'er ridden in an automobile.

Not that he'd let on that he was inexperienced, of course.

Feeling brave already, he remembered his gallantry and snatched his plaid off the window ledge, whirling it around her shoulders before she took a chill.

Truth was, she looked almost feverish.

"Then Uncle Mac and Aunt Birdie's troubles are over." She clutched his plaid around her, the color in her cheeks deepening. "I'm so glad they'll be okay. With the end of summer inching nearer, that'll make it easier when the time comes for me to leave. Knowing they're—"

"*Leave?*" Hardwick stared at her, stunned.

Only now realizing what a dolt he'd been.

Women needed words.

'Twas the first lesson his father had taught him about the fairer sex all those many years ago. Men lived by deeds and the good steel of their swords. Lasses wanted wooing, required a man's heart laid bare before them.

His lass was plucking at his plaid, avoiding his gaze.

"Of course I have to leave." Her words pierced him. "Americans can't just stay in Scotland. Not unless—"

"By all the living saints!" He grabbed her again, kissing her hard. "Do you think I'll be letting you go? Now that I've my life back to share with you?"

"But—"

He kissed her again, silencing her.

"Did I no' tell you I dinna like that word?" He pulled back to look at her, shaking his head. "There's no place for it our future unless"—he glanced aside, pretending to consider—"you have something against me asking your uncle if we can build out the unused wing of Dunroamin. In exchange for helping round the place, of course. I can assist him with his peat businesses, and—"

"You want me to stay?" She launched herself at him, nearly knocking him to the ground. "With you, at Dunroamin?"

"No' just that." He caught his balance, then pulled her close. "I want you to be my wife."

"O-o-oh, yes!" she cried, her smile almost blinding him.

Or maybe it was the damnable stinging heat pricking his eyes.

Either way, he knew one thing.

Life didn't get any better.

Epilogue

Up-Helly-Aa
Fire Festival of the North

"Is it everything you expected, sweetness?"

Sir Hardwick de Studley, for some while now proud and effective manager of Dunroamin Peat Enterprises, slung an arm around his wife Cilla's shoulders as they stood in the boisterous crowd swelling Lerwick's cobbled High Street.

"O-o-oh, yes." She leaned into him, toasty warm despite the icy, racing wind. "I do think you broke our record."

His brows arched. "Our record . . . ?" But then he threw back his head and laughed, squeezing her. "A man is always good of a morn."

"The word"—she lifted on her toes to nip his ear—"is *incredible*."

Looking pleased, he dropped a kiss on her brow. "You haven't seen anything yet."

"Oh?" She trailed gloved fingers down the front of his plaid. "I'm tingling already."

"Next time I may no' even let you have breakfast." His dark eyes glinted wickedly. "I, after all, will have had my own."

"You're so bad!"

"Only in ways meant to please you." He winked.

"And do I please you?" She edged closer, sliding a discreet hand beneath his sporran to splay her fingers across the impressive bulge there.

She pressed and squeezed, smiling innocently.

He ran hard.

"You ask?" He sucked in a breath, releasing it in a puff of white. "For truth, if you *pleased* me anymore, 'tis we who'll be the night's entertainment and no' the marching guizers parading down the street!"

"I'm delighted to see you so happy." Cilla removed her hand, pleased indeed.

She was happy, too.

Deliriously so.

Never would she have believed life could be so rich and full, every breathing moment a joy. Beaming up at him, she knew that joy sparkled in her eyes. Her good fortune amazed her, and there hadn't been a day she wasn't grateful.

There was just one little thing that niggled her.

A worry she wasn't sure how to address.

"To be sure, I'm happy, sweeting." He reached to brush her cheek with the back of his knuckles. "There isn't a single thing I want except you."

Cilla bit her lip. "What if—"

In that moment, a great cheer rose from the torchlit procession, and the Viking-clad guizers thrust their arms in the air, waving their fiery, spark-spewing brands high above their heads.

A rain of ashes showered across the spectators.

Around them people laughed and ducked. Others brushed good-naturedly at their shoulders. His face ruddy with the January cold, Hardwick turned to flick away several red-glowing sparks that glimmered on her sleeve.

"See, lass? There's the reason I told you no' to dress in your finest." He held up sooty, ash-stained fingers. "By the time the ceremonial galley torching is

by with and we arrive at the first fest hall, your clothes
will be covered with burn holes—"

"I don't mind." Cilla glanced at the tiny scorch
marks, the tense moment passing. She laughed when
the wind sent another cascade of sparks into the
crowd. "It's fun and . . . oh, look!" She pointed. "Here
comes Erlend Eggertson in his red devil mask."

Hardwick glanced in the direction she indicated.
The large, grinning mask dipped and bobbed toward
them, prominent against the hundreds of furry-vested,
horn-helmed "Vikings" filling the street.

The blazing procession lit the sky as the merry
guizer squads passed by, some shouting to family and
friends waving frantically from the curb. Others raising
deep voices in rousing Nordic song.

Erlend Eggertson swung his mask their way, slowing
his pace as the others pressed on to the burning site,
each guizer pitching a flaming torch onto the doomed
longship's deck until its decorated timbers leapt to
blaze.

Thunderous applause and shouts came from near
the burning galley as the Guizer Jarl jumped free.

Erlend Eggertson bobbed closer.

Behind him, flames shot heavenward, the crackle
and roar almost deafening. The crowd surged forward,
hastening toward the fated ship.

Then, just as Eggertson was within a few yards, he
was caught up in the mob, too, his red devil mask
swept away before he could reach them.

He turned back once, seeming to thrust his burning,
tar-soaked brand toward one of the dark, emptied al-
leyways leading off the High Street.

Live well.

His greeting hung in the air and then, like his costume mask, was swallowed up by the din.

Cilla shivered.

The Shetlander's voice hadn't sounded anything like

she remembered. But before she could open her mouth to say so, another Shetlander rushed up to them, elbowing his way through the crowd.

"The de Studleys, right?" He drew to a panting halt, sleeved his damp brow. "I've been looking all over for you. Eggertson sent me—"

"Aye?" Hardwick slid a glance at his wife. "We just saw him go past."

The man's eyes widened. "Ach, but you couldn't have." He pulled a handkerchief from a jacket pocket and dabbed at his forehead. "That's why I'm here. To let you know he's abed and couldn't make the festivities. Food poisoning, he thinks. A shame it is, too, coming now, of all nights."

Cilla frowned. "But—"

Hardwick squeezed her elbow, silencing her. "Did someone else wear his costume, then?"

The man laughed and shook his head. "Eggertson's? Not a chance. He's so proud of that devil face he wouldn't even let his sons wear the thing."

Hardwick and Cilla exchanged glances.

The Shetlander smiled. "He swears he'll be fit as a fiddle by tomorrow's eve. He'd like you to join him— join us—at one of the private fest halls for a party he's arranged in your honor. Our thanks for helping to get our costumes back to us."

"We'll look forward to it." Hardwick nodded.

The man touched his brow and turned, disappearing the way he'd come.

"I knew there was something funny about the way the mask bobbed over to us." Cilla grabbed Hardwick's arm. "It was him! The Dark One. He came to say good-bye and wish us well."

Hardwick snorted. "That one ne'er does anything so mundane. He'll have had a reason."

Cilla considered. "Well, he did—"

She broke off at the look on her husband's face. Half-turned away from her, he was staring in the

direction the Dark One had pointed, a look of amazement on his handsome face.

She saw why at once.

Two Vikings stood in the darkness of a narrow al-
leyway. Tall, proud, and festively dressed, the woman's long blond braid identified her at once, as did
Sea-Strider's colorfully painted shield and nine-foot
spear.

If there'd been any doubt, the strange, otherworldly
glow that shimmered about them was more than
telling.

Their smiles, however, were a surprise.

Almost beneficent, there was something about them
that pricked the backs of Cilla's eyes. She swallowed
hard, willing the hot lump in her throat to recede.

She really was too emotional lately.

"What's she carrying?"

Cilla blinked, Hardwick's words making her start.

"H'mmm?" She squinted, trying to see better
through the crowd.

Not that she needed to.

The woman had left the alley opening and was coming toward them. The blazing light of the Up-Helly-
Aa flames clearly showed the tiny wooden sword and
the little Viking-painted shield in her hands.

"Oh, my God!" Cilla stared as Gudrid approached,
her smile saying everything. "She knows."

"Knows what?" Hardwick looked at her.

But then the Norsewoman was there in front of
them. Silent, she handed Cilla the miniature sword
and shield, nodding solemnly when she took them.

"Our thanks." The woman's voice was soft, melodic.
"And our blessings."

On the words, she vanished.

And at the edge of the crowd, Sea-Strider no longer
stood in the entrance to the alley.

What remained was a strange but jubilant welling
in Hardwick's chest. It was a feeling that increased

the longer he observed how tightly his wife clutched
the tiny wooden sword and shield.

When she started blinking rapidly and a tear rolled
down her cheek, he grabbed her and slanted his mouth
over hers, kissing her fiercely.

"Odin's balls, woman!" He released her to swipe a
tear off his own cheek. "Whye'er didn't you tell me?"

She looked up at him, the uncertainty in her eyes
splitting him. "I . . . I was afraid you wouldn't be
pleased. That you'd rather things would have stayed
as—"

He reached for her again, squeezing her as hard as
he dared. "No' pleased?" he roared the words, causing
heads to swivel. "Our first child, and you think I'm
no' pleased?"

The swivel-heads slapped shoulders and cheered.

Hardwick ignored them.

Ne'er a man of words, he thrust his hands in her
hair and kissed her again. Rough, fast, and furiously,
showing her beyond doubt how very happy she'd
made him.

Around them the night burned brightly. And beneath his lady's heart a flame of a very different nature flickered and grew, the thought filling him with
more joy than he would've believed possible.

As if she knew, Cilla tightened her arms around
him, sighing.

He pulled back only long enough to flash her a grin.
"By the saints, but I love you."

Then he resumed kissing her, this time slow and
sweet.

After inheriting a medieval Scottish castle, all Mindy wants to do is sell it and escape to Hawaii's sunny beaches. Bran of Barra, the irresistible Highland ghost, has other plans for the bonnie lass he's seen walking the halls of his home. Soon the former flight attendant is once again crisscrossing oceans—and dimensions—to be with her sexy kilted ghost.

Turn the page for a sneak preview of
Allie Mackay's next fun and fresh
paranormal romance.
In stores February 2010.

MacNeil's Folly
New Hope, Pennsylvania

Mindy Menlove lived in a mausoleum.

A thick-walled medieval castle full of gloom and shadows with just the right dash of Tudor and Gothic to curdle the blood of anyone bold enough to pass through its massive iron-studded door.

Within, the adventure continued with a maze of dark passageways and rooms crammed to bursting with rich tapestries and heavy, age-blackened furniture. Dust motes thrived, often spinning eerily in the light that spilled through tall stone-mullioned windows. Some doors squeaked delightfully, and certain floorboards were known for giving the most delicious creaks. Huge stone-carved fireplaces still held lingering traces of the atmosphere-charged scent of peat-and-heather-tinged smoke. Or so it was claimed by visitors with noses sensitive to such things.

Few were the modern disfigurements.

Yet the castle did boast hot water, heating, and electricity. Not to mention cable TV and high-speed Internet. MacNeil's Folly was also within easy driving range of the nearest pizza delivery service. And the daily paper arrived without fail on the steps each morning.

Luxuries made possible because the ancient pile no longer stood in its original location somewhere on a bleak and windswept Hebridean isle, but on the crest of a thickly wooded hill not far from the quaint and pleasant antiquing mecca of New Hope, Pennsylvania.

Even so, the castle was a haven for hermits.

A recluse's dream.

The only trouble was that Mindy had an entirely different idea of paradise.

White sand, palm trees, and sunshine came to mind. Soft, fragrant breezes and—joy of joys—no need to ever dress warmly again. A trace of cocoa-butter tanning lotion and mai tais sipped at sunset.

A tropical sunset.

Almost there—in her head, anyway—Mindy imagined the castle's drafty drawing room falling away from her. Bit by bit, everything receded. The plaid carpet and each piece of clunky, carved oak furniture, and even the heavy dark blue curtains.

She took a step closer to the window and drew a deep breath. Closing her eyes, she inhaled not the damp scent of cold Bucks County rain and wet, dripping pine woods but the heady perfume of frangipani and orchids.

And, because it was her dream, a whiff of freshly ground Kona coffee.

"You should never have dated a passenger."

"Agggh!" Mindy jumped, almost dropping the mint chocolate wafer she'd been about to pop into her mouth.

All thoughts of Hawaii vanished like a pricked balloon.

Whirling around, she returned the wafer to a delicate bone-china plate on a tea tray and sent a pointed look across the room at her sister, Margo, her elder by all of one year.

"What of your water-cooler romance with Mr. Computer Geek last year?" Mindy wiped her fingers on a napkin and then frowned when she only smeared the melted chocolate, making an even greater mess. "If I recall, he left you after less than six weeks."

"We parted amicably." Margo peered at her from a high wing-backed chair near the hearth. "Nor was it a 'water-cooler affair.' He only came by when the computers at Ye Olde Pagan Times went on the blink. And"—she leaned forward, her eyes narrowing in a way Mindy knew to dread—"neither did I move in with him. I didn't even love him."

Mindy bit the inside of her cheek to keep from snorting.

It wouldn't do to remind her sister that she'd sung a different tune last summer. As she did with every new Romeo that crossed her path, whether they chanced into the New Age shop where Margo worked or she just stumbled into them on the street.

Margo Menlove was walking flypaper, and men were the flies.

They just couldn't resist her.

Not that Mindy minded.

Especially not when she was supposed to be mourning an unfaithful fiancé who'd choked to death on a fishbone during an intimate dinner with a Las Vegas showgirl.

A fiancé she now knew had had no intention of marrying her, had used her, and—much to her amazement—had left her his family's displaced Scottish castle and a tidy sum of money to go along with it.

Generosity born of guilt, she was sure.

The naked pole dancer from Vegas hadn't been Hunter's only mistress. She'd spotted at least three other possibles at the funeral.

They rose before her mind's eye, each one sleazier than the other. Frowning, Mindy tried to banish them by scrubbing harder at the chocolate smears on her fingers. But even though their faces faded, her every indrawn breath suddenly felt like jagged ice shards cutting into tender places she should never have exposed.

She shuddered.

Margo noticed. "Don't tell me you still care about the bastard?" She leaned forward, bristling. "He used you as a farce! His lawyers all but told us he only needed you to meet the terms of his late parents' will. That they'd worried about his excesses and made arrangements for him to lose everything unless he became a bulwark of the community, supporting their charities and marrying a good, decent girl!"

"Margo—"

"Don't 'Margo' me. I was there and heard it all." Margo gripped the armrests of her chair until her knuckles whitened. "What I can't believe is that you didn't see through him in the first place."

Mindy gave up trying to get rid of the chocolate. "You'd have fallen for him, too," she snapped, scrunching the napkin in her hand. "If he'd—"

"What?" Margo shot to her feet. "If I were a flight attendant working first class and he'd sat in the last row—wearing a wink and a smile—and with his kilt oh-so-conveniently snagged in his seatbelt?"

"It wasn't like that. . . ." Mindy let the words tail off.

It *had* been like that, and she was the greatest fool in the world for not seeing through his ploy.

But his dimpled smile had charmed her, and he'd blushed, actually *blushed*, when she'd bent down to help him with the seatbelt buckle and her fingers accidentally brushed a very naked part of him.

When the buckle sprang free and his kilt flipped up, revealing that nakedness, he'd appeared so embarrassed that accepting his dinner invitation seemed the least she could do to make him feel better.

He'd also been incredibly good-looking and had a way with words, even if he hadn't had a Scottish burr. He could look at a woman and make her feel as if no other female in the world existed, and, topping it all, he'd had a great sense of humor. And, besides, what girl with red blood in her veins could resist a man in a kilt?

What wasn't to love?

Everything, she knew now.

Furious at herself, Mindy slid a glance at the hearth fire. A portrait of one of his ancestors hung there, claiming pride of place above the black marble mantel. An early MacNeil chieftain, or so Hunter had claimed, calling the man Bran of Barra. His was the only ancestral portrait in the castle that didn't give Mindy the willies.

A big, brawny man in full Highland regalia and with a shock of wild auburn hair and a gorgeous red beard, he didn't have the fierce-eyed glower worn by the other clan chieftains whose portraits lined the castle's long gallery. His portrait—the very same one—hung there, too. It was his mirth-filled face that she always sought when she was convinced that the gazes of the other chieftains followed her every move.

Bran of Barra's twinkling blue gaze looked elsewhere, somewhere inside his portrait that she couldn't see.

Only by keeping her eyes on him could she flit through the endless, dark-paneled gallery without breaking out in goose bumps.

Sadly, his roguish smile now reminded her of Hunter's.

Scowling again, she turned away from the portrait and curled her hands into tight fists. How fitting that Hunter had also dashed her only means of reaching the upper floors of the castle without having a heebie-jeebies attack.

"You can get back at him, you know." Margo stepped in front of her, a conspiratorial glint in her eye. "Have you thought about turning the castle into an esoteric center? I know the customers at Ye Olde Pagan Times would love to hold sessions here. Fussy as Hunter always was about image, he'd turn in his grave."

Mindy stared at her. "Didn't you hear what I said earlier? I'm selling the castle. I want nothing more than to get as far away from here as—"

"But you can't!" Margo grabbed her arm, squeezing tight. "The castle's haunted. I told you, I got an orb on a photo I took in the long gallery yesterday. Three orbs if we count the two faint ones."

"Orbs are specks of dust." Mindy tried not to roll her eyes. "Everyone knows that."

Margo sniffed. "There are orbs and *orbs*. What I got on film was spirit energy. I'm telling you"—she let go of Mindy's arm and tossed back her chin-length blond hair, a style and color both sisters shared—"you can put this place on the paranormal map. People will come from all around the country to ghost-hunt and—"

"Oh, no, they won't." Mindy flopped down on a chair, her head beginning to pound. "There aren't any ghosts here. Hunter was sure of that, and so am I. And"—she aimed her best my-decision-is-final look at her sister—"the only place I'm putting this miserable old pile is on the market."

"But that's crazy." Margo sounded scandalized. "Owning a haunted castle is the chance of a lifetime."

"Yes, it is." Mindy sat back and folded her arms. "It's my chance to go back to the airlines and move to Hawaii. I can invest the money from the sale of the castle and what Hunter left me, and live off my flight-attendant salary. It'd be no trouble at all to commute from Oahu or even Maui. And best of all"—she felt wonderfully free at the thought—"I doubt there are many Scotsmen in Hawaii. They can't take the heat."

"You're not thinking clearly." Margo picked up her purse and moved to the door. "I'll come back in the morning after you've had a good night's sleep. We'll talk then."

"Only if you're ready to help me find the right real estate agent," Mindy called after her sister's retreating back. "I've already spoken with a few."

And each one had sounded more than eager to list MacNeil's Folly.

Mindy smiled and reached for the mint chocolate wafer she'd almost eaten earlier. Then she helped herself to another and another until the little bone-china plate was empty. Chocolate was good for the soul.

And there weren't any ghostly souls spooking about the castle.

Not disguised as orbs or otherwise.

Her sister was crazy.

And *she* was going to Hawaii.

But first she needed some sleep. Margo was right about that. Regrettably, when she left the drawing room, she found the rest of the castle filled with a thin, drifting haze. Cold and silvery, thready wisps of it gathered in the corridors and snaked past the tall Gothic window arches. An illusion that surely had everything to do with the night's full moon just breaking through the fast-moving rain clouds and nothing at all to do with the orbs that her sister claimed were darting around the long gallery.

Or so she thought until she neared that dreaded room and caught the unmistakable strains of a bagpipe. A haunting old Gaelic air that stopped the instant she neared the gallery's open door.

A door she always took care to keep closed.

Mindy's stomach dropped and her knees started to tremble. But when she heard footsteps on the long gallery's polished wood floorboards and the low murmur of many men's voices, she got mad and strode forward.

It wouldn't surprise her if Margo and her crazy New Age friends were playing a trick on her.

A notion she had to discard the minute she reached the threshold and looked into the angry faces of Hunter's Highland chieftain ancestors. There could be no doubt that it was them, because with the exception of Bran of Barra's portrait at the far end of the long, narrow room, the ferocious-looking clansmen's large gold-gilt portrait frames were empty.

She also recognized them.

And this time they weren't just following her with their oil-on-canvas eyes.

They were in the room. And they were glaring at her.

Glaring and floating her way.

Some even brandished swords.

"Oh my God!" Mindy's eyes rounded and she clapped a hand to her cheek.

Heart thundering, she tried to slam the door and run, but a handful of the scowling clansmen were quicker. Before she could blink, they surrounded her, their huge kilted bodies blocking her escape.

Kilted, plaid-draped bodies she could see through!

Mindy felt the floor dip beneath her feet as they swept closer, their frowns black as night and their eyes glinting furiously in the moonlight. Soon, she feared, she might be sick. She wished she could faint.

Her sister wasn't the crazy one.

She was.

Or else she was about to meet a gaggle of real-life ghosts.

And since the latter seemed more likely than that she'd just lost her marbles, she took a deep breath and lifted her chin, peering back at them as if they weren't a pack of wild-eyed see-through Highlanders.

Then she folded her arms and waited calmly. It was a trick she'd learned in airline training.

How to keep cool at all times.

She just hoped they couldn't tell she was faking.

She was sure she didn't want to know what would happen if they guessed.

ABOUT THE AUTHOR

Allie Mackay is the alter ego of *USA Today* bestselling author Sue-Ellen Welfonder, who writes Scottish medieval romances. A former flight attendant, she spent fifteen years living in Europe and still makes annual visits to Scotland. Proud of her own Hebridean ancestry, she belongs to two clan societies: the MacFie Clan Society and the Clan MacAlpine Society. Her greatest passions are Scotland, medieval history, the paranormal, and dogs. She is married and lives with her husband and Jack Russell terrier in her home state of Florida. Visit her on the Web at www.alliemackay.com.

**Did you know
Allie Mackay also writes
as Sue-Ellen Welfonder,
penning passionate
historical romances set in
medieval Scotland?**

Look for her latest sensual Scottish
historical romance in March 2009:

Seducing a Scottish Bride

And be sure to discover these other recent Scottish
historical romances by Sue-Ellen Welfonder:

HIGHLANDER IN HER DREAMS

Allie Mackay

After stepping through a magical gateway,
Kira Bedwell finds herself face-to-face with
Aidan MacDonald, the irresistible Scottish
highlander who has visited her in dreams. Now
that their romance transcends dreams to reality,
they find themselves under attack by Aidan's
enemies. And it will take all of their courage and
will for their love to survive beyond time itself...